SCARED OF LOVE

"I know just how much control the Sabers have, Damion. And I know that if you and your family decide to leave us alone and let us live here no one is going to bother us."

He watched the defiant anger sparkle in her eyes, and in her voice he heard the fear of a woman who faced a battle she could not afford to lose. What startled him more than anything else, however, was the blaze of raw desire that suddenly seemed to fill him.

They were standing inches apart, and her voice faltered as she finally saw through her own rage. Words died on her lips, then deserted her mind as he reached to touch her cheek.

"Don't," she whispered.

"Scared now, Kairee—scared enough to run?"

"You'll never make me run, Damion Saber," she said frigidly.

He bent his head and their lips barely touched. The contest began with the gentlest caress as he lifted his head and their eyes met. His arms tightened about her and this time his mouth sought hers in a kiss so heated she felt as if her lips were aflame.

"This is insanity," he grated in a harsh, panting whisper. "I know that, but damn your beautiful soul, I can't wipe you out of my mind." Before she could utter any more protests, his lips silenced hers and passion caught them in a grip that obliterated their surroundings, their barriers, and their control . . .

WILD WYOMING HEART

SYLVIE F. SOMMERFIELD

ZEBRA BOOKS
KENSINGTON PUBLISHING CORP.

ZEBRA BOOKS

are published by

Kensington Publishing Corp.
475 Park Avenue South
New York, NY 10016

First printing: July 1988

Printed in the United States of America

To Shannon, Andy, T.J., Gary Jr.,
Michael, and Anthony,
the sunshine of my life,
who continually show me the things
that make it all worthwhile.

I do hope you enjoy reading this historical adventure as much as I have enjoyed writing it. I would like to send you my newsletter to share our current news with you. If you would like to request one just send an S.A.S.E. and print your name and address clearly. If you enjoy this book, tell a friend.

Sylvie

Sommerfield Enterprises
2080 West State Street
Suite 9
New Castle, PA 16101

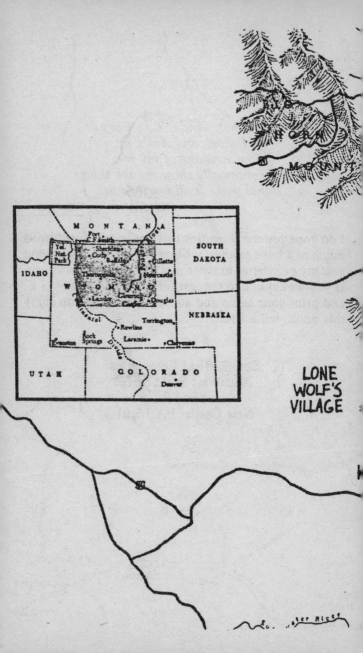

BIG HORN MT.

MONTANA

Fort
C.F. Smith

Sheridan
Cody
B. Kalo

Tensleep

SOUTH
DAKOTA

Gillette

YEL.
Nat.
Park

IDAHO

Thermopolis

W Y O M I N G

Newcastle

Lander

Glenrock
Casper

Douglas

Continental

NEBRASKA

Torrington

Rawlins

Divide

EVANSTON

Rock Springs

Laramie

Cheyenne

UTAH

C O L O R A D O

Denver

LONE
WOLF'S
VILLAGE

Sw. water River

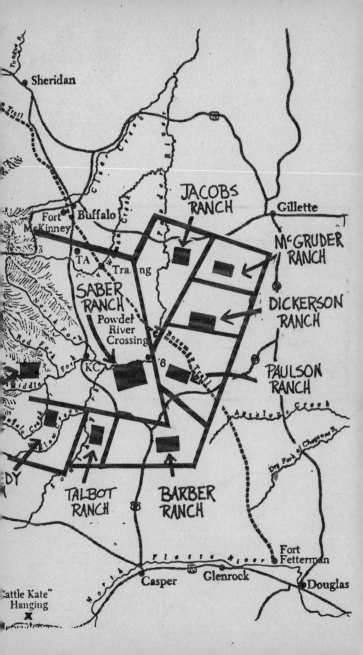

Prologue

The wagon train moved in a slow, undulating line across the flat plain heading toward a rapidly setting sun. Soon it would stop for the night, and this excited the girl who sat next to the driver of the third wagon in the column.

She was a beautiful blonde and the flush on her cheeks and the bright glow in her misty gray eyes reflected her interest in the man who rode near the head of the wagons. She could not seem to keep her eyes from him.

"Now, girl," the man who sat next to her chided teasingly, "we'll soon be settlin' for the night and that man you got your eyes on will be hoverin' around you like a moth around a candle."

"I know," she replied, laughing softly. She ignored Jeremy Byler's teasing, aware that he approved completely of Elliot Saber. "I just wish . . ."

"Sure. You wish he was goin' on with us instead of headin' off on his own to build that ranch he's been talkin' about for so long. Well, gal, it'll only be a few months separatin' you. Come next spring he'll have the house up and he'll be comin' for you."

"I know that, too, Jeremy," she said with a wistful

smile. Then her face sobered. "It's just that . . . I can't fight this feeling."

"What's that? You been dreamin' again? Those nightmares keep hurtin' you. You got to forget the past, Em. You can't let it reach out to drag you down."

"I wish he would take me with him now," she said softly. "I . . . I just get the feeling I might never see him again."

"Now that's foolish, girl. The man's crazy about you. He just wants to get the house up before he drags you out into the wilderness. I can't fault him for that. He just don't want to make it any harder on you than it has to be."

"But Jeremy . . ."

"Don't argue with me, girl," he said with a chuckle. "He's the stubborn one. You're goin' to have your hands full when you marry that one."

"He's stubborn," she agreed, "but he's strong. He wants to build the biggest and best ranch in the Wyoming territory. And he'll do it, with my help. I'll bear his sons and we'll have a grand life together."

"I believe that. I really do."

Emma Martin grew quiet again, but her gaze remained on the broad-shouldered man who rode ahead and her eyes were dark with old memories that still haunted her.

Elliot Saber rode easy, well used to the saddle. It had been that way from the time he had become old enough to mount a horse.

He was a man who exuded an aura of tremendous strength, his body hard and heavily muscled from hours of strenuous work. His face was tan and looked as if it had been roughly hewn from a slab of mahogany. His eyes were nearly as black as his hair and

10

his mouth was firm and straight.

"Well," the man riding next to him began, "you gonna be leavin' us come tomorrow?"

"Sure am. I got that ranch all staked out."

"And a pretty woman to build it for."

"You're right again." Elliot chuckled. "Emma's the most beautiful woman this side of the Mississippi—or the other, for that matter. I'm a lucky man. Emma and I are going to build something big and permanent, something to hand down to our sons."

"Sons. You expecting to have a bunch of them?"

"As many as Emma cares to give me."

"Well, from the way she looks at you, I expect you'll be havin' a whole passel of them."

They laughed, but Elliot could not help turning in the saddle and waving at the girl about whom they spoke.

Just before the sun set, the wagons were turned to form a circle to make camp for the night.

When the moon was high, Emma slipped away from the firelight and ran toward the dark shadows beneath a stand of nearby trees. She knew that there Elliot waited for her.

She heard his deep laugh as he caught her up in strong arms and crushed her to him, kissing her until she was breathless.

"Oh Elliot . . . Elliot," she whispered with a sigh.

"God, Emma. It's going to be hard to leave you."

"Don't leave me."

"Now Emma, we—"

"I know, we talked about this before. But I'm strong. I can work hard. I can work with you. We can build the ranch together. Elliot, please . . . you must let me go with you."

11

"Don't make this any harder on me than it already is. I have to leave in the morning. I . . . I don't want to fight with you, not tonight."

"Elliot, please . . . please let me go with you."

"No, Em . . . no." He caught her face between his hands and kissed her hungrily, silencing her protests.

They made love, knowing it would be long days and nights before they would see each other again.

The next morning Emma watched Elliot ride away in the company of his friend, Jim, who would, one day, be the foreman of the ranch Elliot planned to build.

By nightfall the two men had put many miles between themselves and the wagon train and were tired enough to begin making camp.

James Sinclair had been Elliot's friend for many years and they had always had the ability to talk and to understand each other. It was no different now as Elliot turned to his companion.

"You've been damn quiet, Jim."

"Don't want no disagreements with you."

"So you think I'm making a mistake?"

"About the ranch?" Jim asked innocently.

"Don't play dumb. I mean about Emma."

"If you want to know the truth, yes. There's a lot can happen between now and the time you get that house up. If it was me, I'd have brought her along. What if she runs across someone a little more . . . convenient and you end up without her?"

"Without her? How the hell could I build all that if I didn't have Em to build it for? I can't even think of doing it without her."

"Then why the hell don't you go back and get her? Now. Tonight."

Elliot sat for a long time in silent thought. Then he rose.

"Want to come with me?"

Jim laughed delightedly as he jumped quickly to his feet. "You bet your life I do. I wouldn't miss seeing Em's face when you tell her."

"We should pick up the train by mid-morning tomorrow."

"Then let's ride."

They could not push their horses too fast because the animals had not rested long, yet it was only an hour before midday when they reined in their mounts and sat staring at the ominous spirals of smoke that rose in gray tendrils in the distance.

"No," Elliot whispered. "No . . . Emma."

They urged their horses to a run and crested the hill. The sight they beheld brought a groan of blind agony from Elliot.

The remnants of the wagon train lay before them, burnt almost beyond recognition. Bodies were strewn haphazardly in the dust. There was no sign of life.

The ranch rose from bitterness and pain across hundreds of acres of Wyoming's lush range. During the first year Jim and Elliot worked alone in a desperate struggle to wrench from the reluctant elements the life they wanted to build. Elliot never again spoke of Emma or her loss, though he had carried her body from the smoldering camp to bury it on the land they would have shared.

The following year Elliot brought Elenor Pritchert to the ranch as his bride. She gave him a son, but her frailty and the secret knowledge that Elliot had never loved her drained her spirit and she died.

Two years later Elliot again took a bride, a bride who took Jim completely by surprise until he discovered that the purpose behind the marriage was land. Elliot had found a way to acquire several hundred more acres of land by marrying the daughter of the sub-chief of a nearby tribe.

"They might have been the ones who killed Emma," Jim protested.

"We don't know that," Elliot argued stubbornly. "I want that land, Jim."

"What about Southwind? She thinks she has a husband. Are you ever going to tell her the truth, that she's a price you paid for more land?"

"Keep your mouth shut!" Elliot said angrily. "My ranch is going to grow for my sons, no matter what I have to do!"

"Or who you have to hurt?" Jim added quietly.

"Who's hurting anyone?"

"God, you've changed, Elliot. Before Emma died—"

"Jim, I don't want you to talk about the past. Southwind is going to have a child. I'll have two sons. I'm building an empire, Jim . . . an empire."

Southwind did bear Elliot a second son, but only a year later she returned to her people.

Elliot had his two sons, he had his empire as the ranch brought vast wealth, and somewhere along the way the doors to his heart closed. Even his sons lost the power to reach within and touch the place that had always belonged to Emma.

Chapter 1

Twenty-seven years later . . .

Damion Saber replaced his rifle in the boot of his saddle and nudged his horse forward until he found the carcass of the beast he had shot with deadly accuracy.

The two men who rode with him were silent until they viewed the remains of the animal that had preyed on their cattle for several weeks.

"Damn big mountain lion," one remarked.

"You're sure as hell some shot, Damion. Caught him clean—one shot. By God, some shootin'."

"Well, it looks like he won't be bringing down any more of our calves," Damion said coldly. "Let's get back to work." He wheeled his horse about and rode away, and for a moment the two men exchanged glances.

"That boy's just like his old man. He's got a stone where his heart oughta be."

"You'd best not let him hear you slighting the old man or you might be in the same shape as that carcass over there."

"Well, you gotta admit the only one comes near bein' as hard as the old man is this one."

15

"What about the young one?"

"Britt? Well, maybe he's hard, but the boy can smile once in a while and he don't believe in all work and no play."

"Speakin' of play, where is he anyway? I ain't seen him around the ranch for a couple of days."

"Boy's gone off to see his ma. He does it now and again. The old man just pretends he don't know he's goin'."

"I tell ya, Hank, when the old man's gone there's gonna be trouble 'round here. I think that's the time I'll push on."

"You mean trouble between his sons?"

"Yeah."

"They're a couple of tough little roosters, but they're both smart."

"They're both the old man's boys, and they both think of this place as theirs. Yessir. When the old man goes, so do I."

"He's too blamed tough to die before he's a hundred anyway. He's too ornery to want to go and miss the fight."

"Ain't ornery. Took him a hell of a lot of sweat and blood to put this together. He'd like nothing better than to see the boys share it—equal."

"They're like oil and water. They just don't mix—I don't suppose they ever will—but I'd sure like to see it. I sure would."

Their exchange ended, they followed in the direction Damion had gone.

Damion was still in a cold, black mood. He always felt the same mind-throbbing hatred toward anything that cast any kind of threat on the Circle *S*. His killing of the mountain lion was not eliminating a nuisance to his herd; it was destroying a predator that threatened something of his . . . his. He laughed to himself. If his father heard him referring to the Circle S as his, he'd find himself in another verbal tangle with the older man, with whom he always seemed to come out second best. It was "ours," he thought, "ours." His father's, his, . . . and his brother's.

Britt. Every time he thought of Britt he came up just as confused. As boys they had played together, but as men they couldn't seem to understand each other. The gap was growing wider every day, yet the more he reached for answers, the more elusive they became.

Damion rode with the inherited easy grace of a man born to the saddle. He was tall and broad of shoulder and the gloved hands that held the reins were large with long, slender fingers. The deep tan of his skin came from days in the hot sun, where the strength of his hard-muscled body was continually being tested by physical labor that kept his form lithe and supple.

His eyes were narrowed beneath the wide brim of his hat as he rode into the sun, but their deep blue coloring was still startling against his dark skin and the midnight black of his hair.

The short stubble of a black beard and the dust on his clothes gave evidence of long, hard hours without benefit of a bath or clean clothes, which, at the moment, he desired more than anything else. But Damion had walked in his father's footsteps too long to go home for a much-needed rest before the day's work was finished to his satisfaction.

He sighed deeply and let his gaze wander as he rode. He loved the Circle S with a passion that was surpassed, maybe surpassed, he thought—only by his father's.

Once again he mused with bittersweet feeling that he would never understand his father, either. Oh, he knew

17

what his father wanted—what he expected—but he would never hear the answers to questions he did not know how to ask.

He could remember a boyhood spent trying to please his father, trying to pull from him one word of praise or gratitude, or even a word that recognized he had tried.

Sometimes he had thought he had seen a gentle look, a touch of love. But it had been gone before Damion could grasp it. Still he tried, and now he was not even sure why he did.

Anyway, he thought, there was a lot to do before he would see the main house, clean clothes, and hot food tonight.

Before he could channel his thoughts to his next move, his attention was caught by an approaching rider. He needed no one to tell him who it was. He could recognize his brother at any distance. He reined up and waited, taking a thin cigar from his pocket and putting it between strong, white teeth. He struck a lucifer against his saddle horn, lit the cigar, and waited.

If Damion rode like an expert, Britt rode like the breath of the wind. He was as much a part of the environment about him as the eagle that soared in the blue, cloudless sky.

The horse skittered to a stop just inches from Damion's.

Britt grinned amiably, his smile white against his bronzed skin. His ebony hair was shaggy, touching the collar of his shirt. He looked as wild and untamed as the mountain lion Damion had just killed.

Damion had never been able to read what lay behind his half-brother's habitually laughing obsidian eyes and would have been more than surprised to know that Britt was just as uncertain about him. It had been hidden well beneath what always appeared as a wild, devil-may-care attitude. Damion would have been

18

catapulted into a state of total shock if the deep respect and admiration Britt felt for him had ever been put into words. But all his life Britt had been incapable of doing just that. He realized there was a wide chasm growing between him and his brother and felt helpless as he watched it grow, not knowing how to cross it. To Britt it seemed that Damion stood like a rock against everything he did or thought. He could understand even less the sense of frustrated rebellion this roused in him, while, to Damion, Britt's attitude toward the Circle S seemed frivolous and uncaring. This the older brother found very difficult to tolerate.

"Been visiting, Britt?" Damion asked quietly. It was meant to be just a polite question, but to ears that purposefully sought inflections in the voice that were non-existent, it was a mild condemnation of his lack of devotion to the ranch.

"Not that it's your affair," Britt retorted with a smile devoid of any warmth, "but my mother's people were having a celebration and she sent for me. I imagine I owe her that much, since everything else is supposed to be devoted to the Circle S."

Britt would have liked to have retracted the words the moment he said them, but the chilly narrowing of Damion's eyes built a new resistance.

"No one says you have to devote anything to the Circle S. Spend as much time with your mother's people as you like—all your time, if you choose."

"You'd like that, wouldn't you, Damion? Then you could be pretty damn sure the Circle S—your beloved Circle S—would be all yours someday."

"You know damn well he'd never do that. It's meant for both of us. He wouldn't cheat you out of what's yours."

"I wonder if that's more his conscience than his love for me. Too bad, Damion. Father's fair play is going to

19

cheat you yet."

"Why the hell do you have to twist up everything I say? It's always been true that the Circle S will be as much yours as it is mine. I'd think you'd take a little pride in it."

"Maybe there's already too much pride involved," Britt said softly. "Maybe there's been just too much take from the Circle S and not enough give."

"You've been talking to your uncle Lone Wolf again," Damion prodded. "Could be you're spending too much time listening to the wrong people, Britt."

Anger flashed in dark eyes, but the white smile remained intact.

"There's two sides to everything, Damion."

"Who says there isn't?"

"Have you ever listened to any other one than Father's?"

"We're his sons, Britt," Damion reminded him. "We owe him a lot, at least some respect for what he's built for us."

Britt chuckled. "As you like it, Damion. I've been gone three days. I'll get back to work in the morning. Does that satisfy you?"

"You don't have to satisfy me."

Now Britt laughed softly. "I know that. I just wanted to make sure you did."

He kicked his horse into motion before Damion's angry answer could be put into words.

Damion watched him ride away. Britt could always manage to irritate him, no matter what humor he was in. It was the arrogant smile, the untamed aura, the sense that there was a part of Britt that wanted to share with him and another, warring part that wanted to strike out.

By the time Damion felt his day's work was satisfactory, the sun was already touching the horizon.

20

He headed toward the main house to prepare for an occasion that was always a tedious affair for him, the evening meal, during which he must face his father's intensive questioning and the taunting humor of his brother, who seemed to find a great deal of amusement in Damion's position of having to answer for the day's activities.

The ranch house sat long and low against the horizon and he approached it slowly. In the stable he saw to the care of his horse personally, then he moved across the wide, clear area between the bunkhouse and stable that brought him to the main house.

The porch was long, running the whole length of the house, nearly a hundred and thirty feet. He strode up the four steps, crossed the porch, and opened the front door to enter the always cool interior.

He stood in a large, square entrance hall, from which doorways on either side gave access to two spacious front rooms. The hall extended to two more short halls, one of which led on one side of the house to the three bedrooms, and the other to the dining room and kitchen. The house appeared like a box with an end open that embraced a patio. Only one bedroom on the left and the kitchen on the right had entrances onto the patio, which could also be reached by walking down the length of the entrance hall and through the wide double doors leading outside.

The bedroom off the patio was Damion's, and he always chose to reach it by going down the hall and across the patio. He found that by doing so he could gain access to his room without disturbing anyone else in the house.

He entered his room with a sigh of relief, but it was short-lived, for before he could begin to remove his dirty clothes, a light rap on his door brought a wry grin and a disbelieving shake of his head. He opened the

21

door and smiled at the girl who stood on the other side of it.

"Damn, Maria," he said with a chuckle, "do you ever miss anything? I didn't think anyone would know I was home yet."

Maria was a pretty girl of just over nineteen years. Her parents had come to serve the Saber family shortly after Elliot had begun building the ranch and Maria had been born on the Circle *S* several years later.

She was slim and dark, her thick black hair hanging in one long braid. Her almond eyes were a golden brown and usually filled with gentle humor.

"It is for me to know when you come and go and what you desire. My mother would be angry with me should you want something and no one was here to get it for you."

If there was a double meaning in her words, Damion tried not to read it in her eyes. He did not need the problems such an acknowledgment would bring.

"I shall see to your bath at once, and I have already placed your clean clothes on the bed."

"Fine. I need a bath. Are my father and brother here?"

"Your father enjoys a glass of his special drink while he waits for you and your brother to come to dinner."

"And Britt?"

"He is not home yet."

"But he . . . never mind. Thanks, Maria."

He closed the door and meditatively walked back into the room. He had seen Britt just a few hours before, presumably on his way home. "Now I wonder where he went," he asked himself aloud.

His hands stroked her quivering flesh while their lips hungrily blended in seething passion. Their panting

22

struggle was not overheard in the empty house.

Her soft moan of deep pleasure was muffled against his lips as the strong heat of his body possessed hers. Her hands slid down the hard muscle of his back to urge him deeper within her and her slender legs clutched him frantically as they moved together in their mutual need for fulfillment.

Soft words, spoken in a language she did not understand, and the demands of his powerful young body were all that filled Anna's mind. They moved together with no restraint to their passion until they soared and only the soft moans of completion touched the air.

He rolled to his back and drew her against him, holding her for a time in silence.

"I have missed you," he announced, chuckling softly. She sat up and as he looked up at her his eyes filled with the sheer enjoyment of the sight she presented.

Anna McGruder was extremely pretty, and she knew quite well how to enjoy her beauty. She had married Samuel McGruder five years before and realized her mistake after he had brought her to his ranch and then had changed his nature to the extent that he would beat and abuse her. She could not escape, so she had learned to take her revenge in the only way she could.

The McGruder ranch was so small it could hardly be called one at all. It was a strip of land that lay between the Saber ranch and the small town of Buffalo, and it was this proximity to the Saber ranch that gave Anna the opportunity she sought. Anna took pleasure in life with an abandon that had startled Britt Saber when at first she had approached him. Then, adaptable as he was, he quickly learned to enjoy her. Anna asked nothing of him. It was the only way Britt could live, and Anna knew him as very few others did. The knowledge came not from him, but because of what others said, and what he refused to say.

"You have missed rolling in the hay with me," she responded with a laugh.

He reached up to lightly run his fingers down the creamy softness of her skin.

"You're a pleasure to come home to, Anna, and I like you more than you believe."

"You like me and I like you," she replied quickly. "We are very satisfactory for each other."

He chuckled and pulled her back down into his arms.

"Britt?"

"What?"

"You were gone three days this time. Maybe one day you will go and not come back."

He was silent as his fingers moved over her flesh.

"No . . . I don't think I'll go and stay. I don't suppose I belong there any more than I do here."

"But you belong in both places," she protested.

"Anna," he said bitterly, "trying to have two lives is like trying to make love to two women at the same time. Somewhere along the line someone gets cheated."

"What do you fear being cheated of?"

"Fear?" he repeated in momentary anger. In a swift move he was on his feet and beginning to dress. The look in his eyes was one she had always hated, for it turned everyone away. It was cold and forbidding.

"Britt, don't go yet."

"I have to be back at the ranch for dinner. It's the gathering of the Saber 'eagles.'" He laughed harshly. "I'd never be forgiven for missing it. Would you want to have my father or Damion angry at you?"

"Not me. They're both enough to scare anyone."

"Then come up here and give me a kiss. I'll see you sometime next week."

Anna gazed up at him. How beautiful he is, she thought. How wild and beautiful. He had always reminded her of a sleek, clean-limbed panther, with his dark, graceful body and his dangerous eyes. Yet she wished . . .

Letting the thought trail off, she rose and went to him and he caught her close and kissed her until she clung to him dizzily.

"I'll see you soon?" he questioned softly, but she was sure they both knew the answer to that. She nodded without speaking and heard his soft laugh as he kissed her lightly again. Then he was gone, quietly, like a surefooted predator.

Britt rode slowly toward the Circle *S*. He knew, deep within, that one of the reasons he had gone to see Anna was to prove something to himself, and she had perceptively voiced his concern. What was he afraid of? He just wished he knew.

He wondered if his life, or his thoughts and fears, would have been different if his mother had not been Indian. Somewhere deep inside was the frustrated feeling that he always fell short of what his family expected of him, yet he truly did not know what it was they wanted.

If only Damion was not so strong, so sure. If he just said he needed Britt, needed help. If just once . . .

If only his father, whom he felt sure knew where he disappeared to occasionally, would ask about his mother, would let him know that the blood that flowed in his veins did not matter to him, that he loved him. But Britt knew well the words would never be said, had never been said for as far back as he could remember.

Britt remembered childhood days when he had first realized he would always be competing with Damion. It had come out in games, as children, and in rougher competition as they grew. Yet he did not know what they were competing for.

It didn't matter, he thought. Damion always came

out the winner one way or the other. Maybe that was why he showed Damion such defiance. Maybe it was Damion he was afraid of.

When he arrived home he bathed and changed quickly, and as he walked down the hall to the large front door where drinks were habitually shared, he heard the voices and knew his father and Damion were already discussing the day's work. He stepped into the room and both men turned to look at him.

"Evening." He smiled. "Looks like I'm just in time for a drink."

"Pour one, boy, and sit down. Dinner will be ready in a while."

Elliot would not question where Britt had been, no matter how badly Britt might want him to do so.

He poured a drink and took a healthy swallow before he turned and saw Damion looking at him. He raised his drink in a silent toast, winked with a wicked smile, and drank the rest of it.

"Damion, I want you to ride over to the Barber ranch tomorrow. He's got a couple of horses I want you to look at. If they're as good as he says, you buy 'em. We have to strengthen up our string."

"I'll do that first thing tomorrow," Damion replied.

"I hear the Barbers are going to have a big barbecue," Britt said.

"Oh?" Elliot furrowed his brow questioningly. "What for? They celebrating something?"

"Yes, the party's for Joan."

"Joan," Damion interrupted. "I haven't seen her for . . . what . . . five years?"

"A little over five. She must have been about fifteen or sixteen when she went off to school."

"Her father is a foolish man," Elliot said. "Wasting money on an education for a girl who's only going to get married and raise kids anyhow."

"From what I hear, he doesn't have too much money to waste," Damion remarked with a laugh.

His father's attitude and Damion's arrogant laughter irritated Britt.

"Maybe," he said quietly, "she might not want to get married and raise kids. Maybe she wants to use her mind. Maybe she wants to be able to protect her land when her father isn't there to do it."

Elliot's face grew red with what Britt thought was the obvious penetration of his guilty thoughts.

"Just who the hell do you think she has to protect herself from?" he demanded.

"Anyone who might want to go about cheating her out of her land . . . for any reason," Britt answered. His words were for his father, but his eyes held Damion's.

"You under the impression we're reaching for more land?" Damion questioned in a dangerously soft voice.

"Aren't we?" Britt replied quietly.

"You got something against us growing?" Elliot inserted.

"Depends"—he looked straight into Elliot's eyes—"on how we go about growing. If it's taking something we've got no right to, then no, I'm not for it. It's been done before and look at the result."

There was no doubt both Elliot and Damion knew what Britt was talking about. The reference to his mother and his birth were a blow meant to be vicious. What they did not know was that Britt immediately regretted personalizing the issue and had no idea why he had done so.

Damion recovered quickly. "Let's go tackle that food that smells so good. I'm so hungry I could eat burnt buffalo."

They walked into the dining room where Margurite and Maria were already placing steaming dishes on the table.

Britt took the opportunity to flirt outrageously with Maria, bringing a blush and soft laughter from her.

"Britt," Damion whispered as he passed his chair, "don't you ever get tired or do you think it's your job to keep every woman in the territory happy?"

Britt chuckled. "I'm doing my best, brother, I'm doing my best."

The meal passed uneventfully, which was a rare occurrence that pleased everybody. Later Elliot went to his study to work on accounts. Damion, nearly exhausted from a day of hard work, decided to go to bed early. He heard Britt ride away and knew he was headed either for a woman or a card game and some drinking. He had to admit to himself that the intangible problem between the three of them was steadily growing. He just prayed that nothing would come along to cause a violent eruption before time could heal it.

His last thoughts that night were the same as those of so many nights before. He wanted to maintain the control he thought his father expected from the man who would one day run the ranch, but could he do so if he knew his father was trying to take over the Barber land? Just what would his father expect Damion to do about it?

Chapter 2

Kairee Kennedy sat atop the wagon seat and looked with well-camouflaged dismay at the small house before her. To say that it was in extremely poor condition would have been somewhat of a compliment, she thought miserably.

The house was made of great squared pine logs well fitted together. It was weathered but still sturdy. There were two winglike protrusions from a tent-shaped center that were bedrooms, and the center room, which formed the balance of the house.

Kairee liked the idea of the long porch that ran the length of the house. It faced west and she imagined evenings there with her family enjoying the pleasure of the setting sun. In time . . . she thought, in time they would make it a home.

Her father stood before the weather-beaten cabin and gazed at it with a calculating eye while Kairee and her brother exchanged looks. As far as they were concerned, the small ranch they had been willed by their uncle Rob, a man they had not seen since they were babies, was more than a total disaster. Gregg Kennedy felt the same emotions Kairee felt. He, too, had come out of necessity rather than desire.

When Kairee and Gregg's mother had died, their father had lost track of the small business that had supported them. By the time his children had fought to help him regain his former stability, the business was beyond redemption. The death of a long-lost brother and the property he had left in his will, a small ranch in far-off Wyoming, had given them a new lease on life and they had sold what was left and had packed up, traveling slowly the immense distance from Ohio to Wyoming.

Now, as brother and sister stared at the dilapidated house and the neglected land, neither of them was quite sure the move had been a very good idea. It was only their father's excitement about beginning again, away from memories of the past, that buoyed their spirits at all.

"The house is repairable with a little work," Stephen Kennedy said optimistically. "Gregg and I can make it livable in a short while."

"That barn looks like it's seen better days, Pa." Gregg laughed. "If we're going to use it, we'd better get on repairing it pretty quick."

"Well, we'll be here for some time before the wagons with the furniture come, and the men with the herd."

"Herd?" Gregg laughed again. "You make sixty head of cattle sound like a million."

"It's a beginning, my boy." Stephen smiled in response. "It's just the beginning. This range looks excellent to grow a large herd on. In a few years we'll build the sixty into six thousand, maybe more."

Gregg and Kairee exchanged worried looks again. This enthusiasm they had faced before. Their father's continual optimism sometimes frightened them, yet they knew a new start was necessary, even if just to hold their small family together. They were relieved that at least their wagon carried enough essentials for survival until the balance of their equipment arrived.

Gregg helped Kairee down from the wagon and they came to stand beside their father.

Kairee was tall and slender and walked with a dancer's grace. Her hair, the color of corn silk, was drawn into a coil at the nape of her neck. Cloud gray eyes were wide and intelligent and under usual circumstances were ready to smile. Yet they were a chameleon's eyes, darkening to a steel gray in anger and softening to a pale, hazy blue-gray when she was happy or excited. Her eyes darkened now with determination as she turned to her father.

"Is there a well, Pa?" Kairee questioned. "I'd like to get some water and try to make it clean enough to sleep in tonight."

"The well's out back. I was told there was some good water here for grazin' cattle and for drinkin'. Gregg and I will help you." He walked into the house and Gregg followed. Kairee stood alone, looking at the new home she was to keep. For a moment reluctant tears filled her eyes and she felt a stab of loneliness and longing for her mother. Then she angrily brushed the tears away. It did no good to weep over things that could not be changed.

She was pleased about one thing. Gregg's wife, Lucy, and his daughter, Cassie, would be coming with the wagons of furniture. She knew they would lend her some support. She could never have borne being a woman alone with all the responsibility to face. She shrugged these thoughts aside and moved toward the house.

If the outside of their new home was worn and shabby, the inside was worse. There was a kitchen, a square front room, and a bedroom on either side of the front room.

The windows were so dirty only a vague light shone through to dance among the cobwebs. There was no sign that any furniture had ever existed in the house except for a large, formidable stove and a rickety table in the kitchen.

"Gregg and I are going out to check the barn," Stephen said.

"Or what's left of the barn," Gregg added with a laugh.

"Kairee, just do what you have to. When Lucy comes, we'll all pitch in. The house can be fixed up," her father assured her.

"Get me some water, Gregg, and we'll light up that monster of a stove. I suppose you'll have to chop some wood first." Kairee began to roll up her sleeves. "If we want to eat any supper, we'd better get busy."

"Well, I'm hungry," Gregg said. "I'll get some wood and start up your stove, if it works. Then I'll unload some things from the wagon and we can see about fixin' some supper."

"Bring my broom so I can knock down these cobwebs and give us enough space to eat in."

"Right."

With grim determination Kairee covered her hair with a large bandana and the three set about doing what they could for the balance of the day.

There was a fireplace in the largest of the rooms and they found, to their surprise and pleasure, that it was in reasonably good working condition. After Kairee had scrubbed the floor, she spread blankets before it, thankful they would have a warm place to spend the night.

There was little conversation at the evening meal, and afterward Gregg and Stephen sat on the blankets in front of the now low-burning fire and began talking in subdued tones.

Outside the sun was just beginning to set and Kairee walked out on the porch to watch the beautiful display by Mother Nature. It was the end of their first day in Wyoming territory and Kairee was not sure it should not be their last. She folded her arms and rubbed briskly. Though it was getting cold, she was held motionless by the beauty about her. Such conflicting emotions battled for supremacy within her. She felt a child's urgency to run back to the familiar, and a woman's curious need to see and taste whatever the future might bring.

It was going to take a tremendous amount of work by all of them to make the house livable and the land profitable enough to allow them to survive.

Her only security was that Gregg and she were both fighters. She knew Gregg and Lucy needed this new start for their own sakes as well as for little Cassie's. Slowly she forced all reluctance from her mind and set her thoughts on making as much success of this move as she could.

The glow of the one lamp they had brought with them cut through the coming darkness, drawing her attention to the fact that the immense land being shrouded in night could still overpower her. With renewed determination she turned and reentered the house, closing the door firmly on whatever doubts she had brought.

The small house was cheerful in the soft lamp glow and its warmth filled her with peace.

Britt sat his horse in total surprise. It was the wee hours of the morning and he was making his way home after a long, profitable card game and a few drinks too many. Because of the drinks, he was not sure he was actually seeing what was before him.

As far back as he could remember, the old Kennedy ranch had been deserted. The Sabers had used the land

and its abundant water supply to graze their herds since Britt had been a boy. Now, it looked to him as if someone intended to occupy the ranch on a permanent basis. There was a wagon sitting near the barn that would only come with people meaning to stay.

He hoped not, for he was more than certain his father would not be pleased to have to surrender an ounce of land or water he was using.

If it had not been near morning, he would have ridden down to see who was there. It would wait until tomorrow. He spurred his horse into motion and rode the rest of the long miles home, finding his bed near dawn.

Despite his late hours, Britt was up early enough to join his father and brother for breakfast, though they had already accomplished several chores before coming in for the morning meal.

"What time did you get home last night, Britt?" Damion asked with some amusement. "You'll be dead on your horse today."

"I'll be fine." Britt grinned amiably. "Don't worry about me. I'll get my work done, but I've got something to do this morning first."

"Something else to do?" Elliot questioned. "Just what something is more important than this ranch?"

"Just something to satisfy my curiosity."

"About what?" Elliot pressed.

Britt had not meant to say much about what might be some transient travelers, but now he had no choice. He knew his father would be prepared to attack anyone who harbored a thought of taking his land.

"I thought the old Kennedy ranch was deserted a lot of years ago," he said.

"It's been empty since I was a kid," Damion replied. "You know we've been using that land. Why?"

"Went past there last night. Somebody's makin' themselves at home there."

"Who is it?" Elliot demanded.

"How would I know? It was the middle of the night, I told you. Maybe just somebody passin' through and stayin' for the night."

"We need that land and that water. It's too late to move the herd now," Elliot insisted. "Damion, I want you over there today. If it's someone just using the place, haze 'em along."

"I said I'd go over today," Britt protested.

"I need you for something else," Elliot said gruffly.

"Something else . . . like what?"

"Like a lot of work you've been neglecting lately," Elliot said in blunt semi-anger. Britt wanted to resist, but he could see too clearly that resistance was exactly what Elliot wanted. It would be an opportunity for Elliot to enforce his own law, the law he expected his sons to live by. The law that continually put Damion first.

Britt clamped his lips in a firm line, and his eyes sparked fire, but he refused to answer.

"I'll ride out just before noon," Damion said. "I have to go over a couple of things with Jim. He's a good foreman, always looking for ways to improve things around here."

"Noon then," Elliot replied. "By supper I want to hear you tell me those squatters are on their way."

"I'll do my best, but what if—"

"No what ifs," Elliot said firmly. "Get 'em off my land."

He left the room and both Damion and Britt watched the closing door in silence, then they looked at each other.

"His land," Britt said softly. "Is there any place around here that isn't his land?"

"It's just an expression," Damion protested. "He's

had our cattle on that land for so long he just thinks of it as his. Besides, whoever it is was probably just spending the night. All this is nothing."

"You'd better be right about that"—Britt chuckled irritatingly as he started out of the kitchen—"or you might just have to shoot somebody."

Damion glared at the vacant doorway and heard Britt's derisive laughter fade.

Damion was not in the best of moods when he walked across the clearing to the bunkhouse where Jim Sinclair and several hands waited.

Once he had discussed with Jim several special projects for the day, he went to the stable and saddled his horse.

He rode slowly, unsure himself why he felt such reluctance to do what needed to be done. It was only a matter of making sure a trespasser left quickly.

It was a long ride and he approached the house just before noon. As he drew closer, he was surprised to see two riders just leaving.

"Well, whoever it is, they must be coming back. They left the wagon. Guess I'd better check on it."

Damion came closer and saw a spiral of gray-white smoke rising from the chimney. He rode up to the front porch and was about to dismount when the door opened.

It would have been difficult to decide who was more surprised, Damion or Kairee.

Damion was well used to the advantages of being one of the wealthy Sabers. He was also well used to women being drawn to his striking good looks. It had been his key to the arms of many lovely women, and it was obvious that he absorbed Kairee's loveliness in one glance. He dismounted slowly.

Kairee had made breakfast, then had urged Gregg and Stephen to hurry, for they had decided to ride back along the trail to see about the progress of the wagons

36

bringing the balance of the family as well as two men who would be working for them. With this group would come the rest of their worldly possessions. A second two men were driving the sixty head of cattle to the ranch.

Kairee had fought the night's misgivings and had tried to build her excitement to match her father's. If she had been less than successful, she had kept it well hidden.

She had decided that before she began her work she would look over the land that belonged to them. Maybe it would make staying easier. She opened the door and stepped out on the porch and was taken completely by surprise when she looked up into the bluest eyes she had ever seen.

Each regarded the other in a moment of silence, then, suddenly, both seemed to come awake at the same time.

"Hello," Damion said. He smiled as openly as he could, trying to control both his curiosity and his interest.

"Hello," Kairee answered. She found it quite difficult to believe her own reaction. She was actually shaking. It was more from a premonition of danger than from any physical attraction, yet she missed nothing, admitting in some secret part of her mind that he was the handsomest man she had ever seen.

He walked up the two steps to the porch and crossed to stand close to her, making matters worse by towering over her. His overpowering size added to her sense of alarm. She wanted to fight back against some intangible threat that she could not even name.

Things might have been resolved through polite conversation if he had not decided to begin in the worst possible way.

"I'm Damion Saber, and this is Saber land you're trespassing on. I'm afraid we can't let you stay here.

37

Where did you come from, and where are you going?"

"Saber land," she protested in a controlled voice. "I'm afraid it's you who have made a drastic mistake. We are not trespassing. This is our land."

"Our?"

"My father, my brother and his family, and myself. And I haven't the faintest idea just who the . . . Sabers happen to be. At this moment it's you who are trespassing, Mr. Saber."

"It's pretty difficult to trespass on your own land. Our herds have been grazing this land for years. You'd better push on and find some free land. They're homesteading west of the mountain pass. You should be able to find a nice piece of land there."

"Really, Mr. Saber"—her voice revealed her growing anger—"you've made a mistake if you're trying to threaten us or push us off our land. We're here to stay."

"Well, first off," he said, his irritation growing, "nobody threatened you and nobody's pushing. But you're the one who made a mistake. You are not here to stay."

"And just what do you intend to do about it?" she demanded belligerently.

This defiance was something so totally new to Damion that for a moment he was left speechless. The Sabers walked tall and had faced no opposition to their will, especially from a woman. Few in the territory had ever challenged the Sabers.

Damion's arrogance and pride got between his anger and his self-control. If Kairee had been a man, Damion's anger could well have forced him to violence, but she was a very beautiful woman, so the anger was frustrated.

"Look," he said as coolly as he could manage, "I didn't come out here to argue with you, just to warn you. Get off Saber land, or we'll just have to put you off. Tell that to your father and your brother. If they think it's worth the trouble you're going to stir up for yourselves, then stay. But don't say you haven't been warned."

He turned and walked away, going down the steps to his horse and mounting before he looked at her again.

If he was angry, Kairee was furious, and it glowed in her storm gray eyes and challenged him in the defiant lift of her chin.

"Get off my property," she snarled, "before I shoot you!"

"Just remember what I said," he replied firmly. "I wouldn't want to have to toss that pretty behind off this land personally, but I'd do it. So be a good little girl and move along." He gave a half salute as he spurred his horse and rode away, leaving Kairee so mad she could well have shot him.

She walked back into the house and slammed the door behind her. Her family would not return until late that night and she had no one with whom to share her anger and no one on whom to vent it, so she took it out on the house. She attacked her work with a vengeance, silently cursing the blue-eyed stranger who called himself Damion Saber.

She refused to acknowledge the more subtle effect he had had on her. Despite their battle, she had been aware of everything about him from the breadth of his shoulders and the aura of power he exuded to the clean scent of soap, leather, and maleness. She was aware also of a reaction that was more than unwelcome.

By the time the sun was ready to set, the house was absolutely clean, Kairee was very tired, and most of her anger had drained away, leaving her more worried than anything else.

She was not a child. She recognized the strength in Damion and the assurance. He would have to have a powerful force behind him to be so demanding. Yet she knew her family did not have the luxury of choosing to

39

move on. They had no money and this was the only thing they owned. She was certain they would not run.

She prepared some food, assuming her father and brother would return soon, then relaxed before a low-burning fire to wait.

The sound of a solitary horse approaching alarmed her. Was he returning to press his argument further? Or had he realized she might be alone tonight, and defenseless.

She rose and went quickly to pick up the rifle her father had left. She had been taught to shoot as a child and had used the gun often, though never against a man. She was frightened, but she had no intention of letting him know it.

Footsteps crossed the porch and there seemed no effort to silence the sound. Then a brisk knock on the door surprised her. Her anger flared again. Was he so self-assured, so arrogant, that he thought she might be cowering in fear? Did he think to frighten her away?

The knock sounded again and she walked to the door and jerked it open as she pointed the gun with grim determination.

"Oh!" she gasped in total surprise. Backing up a step, she kept the gun leveled at the smiling man who stood before her.

At first she thought he was an Indian, and she was not quite sure what to expect. He grinned, his smile white against his bronzed face, his eyes glowing warmly.

"I'm sorry. I didn't mean to frighten you. This is just a neighborly visit."

"I'm not the least bit frightened," she responded, "but I've met one neighbor today and it wasn't the friendliest of meetings."

"I take it"—he chuckled softly—"you have locked horns with Damion."

"Damion Saber, and you might say we did more

than lock horns. What connection does that have with you and your . . . neighborly visit? Just who are you anyway?"

Now he laughed openly and she smiled, strangely liking the sound of it.

"Well, I'm not sure I want to put a name to myself. From that look in your eye and the way you handle that gun, it just might prove dangerous."

"It will prove more dangerous if you don't."

"All right," he said quietly, "my name's Saber too, Britt Saber."

"You're his brother?"

"'Fraid so." He crossed his arms over his chest and leaned against the door frame. "That doesn't mean I'm going to get shot, does it?"

"Of course not."

"Then it's safe to come in?"

"Depends."

"On what?"

"On why you want to come in."

"I don't understand."

"If you've come to warn me away from here too, you might just as well leave the same way your brother did. With no success."

"So," he said softly, "old Damion got his feathers singed, did he? My my, that is interesting. Doesn't usually happen, you know. He usually gets whatever he goes after."

"Not this time. This ranch is mine and no one is going to push me off it."

"The last I heard, the man who owned this piece of land was old Rob Kennedy. He's been gone, left the place deserted, ever since I can remember. What right do you have to it?"

Kairee smiled. "My name is Kennedy, Kairee Kennedy, and I have every right."

Chapter 3

Now Britt stood erect and his smile faded. The situation had taken a most unexpected turn. The last thing he had imagined was that these people would lay claim to the Kennedy name and be the genuine proprietors of the ranch whose land and water he knew were needed by the ever-growing herd of the Circle *S*.

"Kennedy," he repeated.

"That seems to surprise you. Did you think my family and I were just trying to steal someone else's land? Rob Kennedy, the last man who owned this land, was my father's older brother. He died and left it to us."

"We didn't even know old Rob had any living relatives. He left here when I was just a kid. We've been using this land for a long time."

"Well, you had best get used to not using it. We're going to run our own stock here. Pa intends to build up this ranch to what it should have been years ago. This"—she swept her hand to encompass everything—"is a terrible waste."

"Maybe your father and mine should have a little talk before you settle in. I'm sure an offer could be made that might satisfy everybody."

"Offer? We're not interested in any offers."

"You haven't heard it yet. Maybe you ought to let your father decide. Maybe you're being a bit hasty."

Kairee was stung by his male arrogance. It was as if she had little or nothing to say about anything. She smiled sweetly, and if Britt had known her better, he would have recognized it as a sure sign that her claws were coming unsheathed.

"Mr. Saber, I'll tell you like I told your brother: Get off our land. We don't need your interference and we don't want any offers. We just want what belongs to us and to be left alone. I hope I'm making this clear enough so we needn't have any more 'neighborly visits' by your family. I assume there are several others?"

Britt laughed softly again, mentally changing his impression of Kairee. She was no simple rancher's daughter but a woman of spirit and intelligence.

"Nope. There's only Damion and me. And this was a neighborly visit, at least for me. You didn't even invite me in for a cup of that good-smelling coffee."

It was against her better judgment and he knew it as he watched the decision being made.

Finally she agreed. "Come in. I'll get you some coffee."

He stepped inside, closed the door behind him, and walked slowly across the room, his eyes following her slim figure as she moved toward the stove. With deep appreciation, he watched her pour the coffee. Britt had an eye for beautiful women and he decided very quickly that Kairee Kennedy was one of the prettiest he had seen in a long time.

He also decided he would not mind spending a great deal of time with her, at least until his father forced them from the valley. That was one thing about which he was sure. Elliot knew that grazing cattle in this valley was a very difficult task. Fighting the battle of winter, raising enough to keep them fed during the cold

43

days, took all the Sabers' combined energy. Even Britt was sure the Kennedys would not stand much of a chance against nature, and even less of a chance against Elliot Saber.

He took the cup from her hand and she motioned him to a seat before the fire, then she sat opposite him.

She wanted to question him about life here in Taggert Valley—he could read it in her eyes. But she did not want to hear any more warnings to leave the place they had chosen to make their home. He decided at least to lower the barriers of battle long enough to tell her how he felt about the valley, and his home.

"You've only been here for a day?" he inquired.

"Yes."

"Then you have a lot to see. Taggert Valley is beautiful. Why don't you go riding with me tomorrow and I'll show you a bit of it."

"Tomorrow . . . I can't. Everyone will be here and there's a lot of work to do. I can't just leave it all up to Lucy."

"Lucy?"

"My brother's wife."

"How many of you are there?"

"Pa, my brother, Gregg, me, Lucy, their daughter, Cassie, and four hands Pa coaxed to come along. I hope they stay."

"Not many working hands to run a ranch."

"We'll get by," she replied stubbornly.

"So come riding with me a couple of days from now," he coaxed with a boyish smile. "How can you run a ranch if you don't know anything about it? There's not an inch of this whole valley I don't know. I'd like to show it to you," he added quietly.

"You're so different from your brother," Kairee said, then she flushed at the way she had put unintended words to the thoughts in her mind. "I'm sorry. I didn't mean to say that," she admitted, her cheeks pink with embarrassment.

"Don't be sorry." He laughed wryly. "You couldn't be more right. There's no one in the territory of Wyoming who doesn't agree with that. Damion and I are half brothers."

"I see."

"No, you don't see, not yet. But I suppose you will one day, if you're still bent on stayin'."

She could hear a subtle touch of bitterness in his voice and a shadow of pain momentarily danced in his eyes. She had the strangest feeling, a combination of sympathy and pity. He read it well and rose before the sharp anger that pricked him could surface in words. It was a look he had seen too often before, and a look he did not want to see in her eyes.

"We're bent on staying," she answered quickly.

"Then," he said with a casual grin, "you'd better go riding with the best guide in the territory."

"All right. This is Friday. Next Friday should give us enough time to get fairly well organized. I'll see you next Friday."

"You'll most likely see me before next Friday." He chuckled, knowing full well his father would be fit to be tied when he found out who had taken over the ranch and that they had no intention of going away. "But anyway, we'll make it Friday morning. You ride?"

She looked at him with a teasing half smile. "Probably as well as you do."

"We'll see." He laughed. "But I guess from the way you handled that gun, if you can ride as well, you're a darn good rider."

"My father taught me both. One never knows when a woman will have to defend herself . . . in case someone tries to take something she hasn't a mind to give."

"Well, Kairee Kennedy," Britt said quietly, "you

45

don't need to defend yourself from me. This is one Saber you don't have to fight. I'll see you Friday."

She nodded and watched Britt turn to leave. Kairee followed him as far as the door and watched him mount and ride away. She gazed after him with a puzzled frown. In a day she had met two Sabers, as different from each other as night from day. She was not sure just which one of them she should fear: Damion, with his angry defiance and forceful pressure, or Britt, with his smile and his carefree attitude. Which one of them was the real threat? she wondered.

Britt rode toward home. This was, he thought with a devilish grin of pleasure, the first time he would enjoy the evening meal. It would be the first time he would enjoy the perpetual battle that raged between the three of them, and the first time he would be able to watch Damion face his father with something less than success.

He returned to the ranch and found it fairly empty except for Margurite, who ran the kitchen, and Maria, her daughter, who took care of the rest of the household.

The two women saw to the needs of the three men, which were slight. Elliot demanded little except that his meals be well cooked, his clothes clean, and his house presentable. Britt was gone more often than not and Damion was a dark, quiet force that kept everyone doing his best simply because it was expected.

Walking through the dim, cool house toward his room, Britt was again aware of the strange feeling of alienation that always pricked him when he was in the house of his father. What annoyed him more was that he carried the same feeling when he walked through the village of his mother.

46

He could ignore it for now, for he knew it would not go away. He had lived with it too long to worry about it. Besides—he smiled to himself—tonight would be a different situation.

Thinking of it made him think also of Kairee Kennedy, a very surprising addition to the Saber problems. She was damn pretty, he thought, with her wide eyes and her air of self-control that roused the sudden desire in him to see just how far that control would go.

Just as he reached for the handle on his door, he heard a soft voice from the end of the hallway, several feet from him.

"Mr. Britt?"

He turned, then smiled. "Maria?"

"You are home so early. Is something wrong?"

"No, nothing wrong." He walked toward her and watched her eyes widen as he came closer. It was the only outward sign of the tensing of her nerves and the breathless effect he always had on her.

He walks like the lion, she thought, every move graceful and slow, as if he were stalking prey. She was frightened of something she sensed in Britt but was never able to put a name to.

He stopped very close to her and she gazed up into his dark, smiling eyes.

"What could possibly be wrong on the Circle *S?*" He chuckled. "I've just come home early to see your pretty face." He let his voice soften to a suggestive whisper that brought a bright flush to her cheeks and a frustrated look to her eyes.

She could feel her heart begin to pound. He was too close and she was almost physically overcome with a sense of danger. Yet he had not touched her, was just standing close, between her and the path she must take to find safety in the kitchen.

47

"Do not tease me," she whispered.

"Saying you're pretty is not teasing, Maria. It's the gospel truth." He reached out and took hold of one thick braid and slowly, without pressure, he drew her closer to him.

She seemed to be caught in a strange, warm, mesmerizing flow that made her legs too weak to run and her body warm with the tingling expectancy of something new and untasted.

"You are very beautiful, little Maria," he whispered. One hand still held the braid of her hair and the other slid about her waist to draw her close to him.

Britt had watched Maria many times, and her seduction had been planned for whenever the opportunity arose. Now seemed as good a time as any. They were alone and he was tense with the same uncontrollable fury that always possessed him when he thought of the forces that seemed to bend his life against his will. He could not fight them, but he could find temporary relief in the arms of a beautiful woman.

At that moment Maria's obvious innocence and lack of defenses seemed to excite him. He moved closer, molding her young, supple body to his lean frame, and bent his head to kiss her.

"Britt!" The voice was hard and very familiar. Maria leapt as if she had been burned, but Britt only chuckled with taunting amusement as he turned to face Damion's angry glare.

"What's the matter, brother?" Britt smiled and his voice was an open challenge. "Was what I was doing infringing on something you've staked out as private property?"

"Maria, go to the kitchen." Damion's voice was firm but gentle. He knew Maria had no defense against Britt's expertise.

With a soft, inarticulate sound Maria slipped past Britt and ran. For several minutes there was utter silence thick with thoughts that had nothing to do with Maria.

"There's a limit to everything, Britt."

"Who sets the limits, Damion, you?"

"Leave Maria alone."

Britt grinned and shrugged. "If she belongs to you, you should have told me."

"She doesn't belong to me."

"Then why don't you mind your own damn business?"

"If you want to hurt someone, Britt, don't make it someone who's too innocent to understand what the hell is brewing in you."

"You so sure someone was going to be hurt? Besides, what are you doing here so early? I thought you gave the Circle *S* your all. What are you doing, Damion, slipping?"

"I might ask you the same thing—not only why you're here so early, but where you were most of the afternoon. Every time you go off to take care of your own 'business,' someone else has to pick up the load."

"I do my share around here." Britt's anger was finally stung and the challenging smile grew tight and forced. "Besides, you're the boss. If the load needs picking up, as you say, why don't you do it . . . brother?"

"I'm sick and tired of protecting you, Britt. You know damn well it takes the three of us to keep this ranch running right."

Again Britt chuckled softly. "Are you suggesting that if I don't, as you say, do my share, I should leave? Do you think it would be that easy, Damion?"

Damion sighed. "It isn't that way, Britt, and you know it. The Circle *S* is as much yours as it is mine."

"Oh, I know it," Britt replied coolly. "I just wanted to make sure you did."

"Damnit, Britt," Damion said quietly, "what is it that's pushing you?"

49

There was a breathlessly still moment, a moment when the brothers attempted to reach each other as they had when they were children.

Britt wanted to cry out the intangible fears, the uncertainty that tore him apart. Damion wanted to bridge the chasm that had grown between them. The moment was pregnant with these combined forces as the brothers mentally searched for the words to heal past wounds.

"Britt! Damion! Where the hell are you?"

The harsh, ever-commanding voice of Elliot Saber fractured the poignant moment to irretrievable fragments and Damion noted the bitter smile that touched Britt's lips just before he pushed past Damion and strode to his room.

Damion turned to walk back into the huge parlor, aware that something had been lost that might never again be found. He felt immensely tired.

"You're home early," Elliot said as soon as Damion walked into the room. "Where's Britt, out enjoying some filly in the hay again?"

"He's in his room. Why are you sitting on Britt so hard, Pa? He does his share of work and then some."

"With you ridin' him," Elliot remarked, laughing harshly.

"I don't need to ride him. If anything, he's better with the men and the cattle than I am. He's nearly a wonder with the horses. In case you haven't noticed it, he's doubled the size of our horse stock."

"And when he feels like workin', he does, and when he doesn't, he just gets lost. He doesn't pay enough attention to what we're tryin' to build here."

"Just what are we trying to build?" Damion questioned thoughtfully.

"What's eatin' you?" Elliot demanded. "I thought you felt the same way about the Circle *S* as I do. Is it so damn much to ask my sons' care about what I've

50

worked so hard to give them?"

"We do appreciate it, Pa, both of us. But you keep driving yourself. There's no need to anymore. We're big enough. Why can't you just sit back and enjoy what you've done. The ranch is in good shape."

"We're big enough," Elliot repeated softly. He had removed his leather gloves and now he struck them against his thigh as he walked toward Damion. "I didn't come here and fight the land and the weather just to be another small rancher. I didn't have sons to see them grubbing for a little piece of it. I didn't sacrifice to build this place to see it drain because my sons don't want to grow. We're not big enough. You've never been without, Damion, and I don't ever want to see you be. You give everything to this ranch and it will pay you back. You short it and you'll see the day when some other smart rancher comes rolling into this valley and eats you up just because he knows he has to keep growing, keep getting bigger, or go under to some man who has more guts than he does."

"Why does everything have to be a war? We don't have to prove anything."

"It is a war!" Elliot said angrily. "First you fight the land, then the weather and the Indians. Then you fight any who would stop you from keeping what you've gotten."

Damion gazed at his father with a deep frown drawing his dark brows together. He was surprised to find his mind had jumped to a defiant gray-eyed girl who had told him she meant to fight him. He wondered if he would be able to get her off the old Kennedy land before his father took a hand in the matter, and what frightened him most was that he just wasn't sure his father couldn't, or wouldn't, resort to violence.

He found it startling that he remembered everything about her, from the soft look of her skin to the anger in her eyes.

He would at least have a day or so, he thought. After all, they were just squatters on land that didn't belong to them. Maybe enough pressure, or a substantial offer of money and help in moving, would be enough to solve the problem.

What took him by surprise was that he had to control the small but very irritating thought that he wanted to see her again. All she could possibly be to him was trouble.

Before Damion could voice any thoughts about the intruder, Britt entered the room. He walked to a small cabinet and took a bottle of whiskey from it and three glasses.

Elliot and Damion were silent, somehow knowing Britt had something to say that neither of them were going to be happy about.

Britt poured three drinks. Taking two in one hand and one in the other, he walked toward Elliot and Damion and handed one to each.

"Surprising," Elliot stated quietly.

"What?" Britt questioned, the same half-amused glow in his dark eyes.

"Not only to find you here, but to find you in a drink-sharing mood."

"It's been a very eventful day." Britt laughed. He raised his glass in a silent toast, then tossed the drink down in one fiery gulp.

Both Elliot and Damion drank, but their eyes were filled with suspicion.

"Eventful?" Damion prodded.

"For me, anyway. By the way, Damion, did you go over to see who was trespassing on . . . *our* land?"

Damion's eyes grew stormy and his mouth tightened. Without looking, he could feel his father's eyes on him. He glared at Britt, who smiled evilly in return.

"Yes," Damion grated, "I talked to them."

"Them?" Britt asked softly.

Britt watched his brother with grim satisfaction and noted more reaction from Damion than he had expected. A glow of sudden knowledge touched him. Damion had crossed paths with Kairee Kennedy, and she had breached defenses in Damion no other woman had ever come close to breaching.

"I rode over and warned them off," Damion growled. "I doubt very much if they're going to be any kind of threat to the Circle *S*."

"Well, I have to disagree with you . . ."

"You've got something on your mind, Britt. Why don't you just spit it out?"

"Don't get excited, Damion. It's probably only information you've already gotten," Britt said innocently.

"What information, Britt?" Elliot demanded.

"Why, the names of our squatters."

"What difference do their names make? They're not going to be here long enough for us to get friendly," Damion retorted. But his eyes never left Britt's and somewhere deep inside he knew there was a lot more Britt intended to say.

"All right," Elliot said, "stop the horsing around, Britt. What're their names and why should it make a difference to us? They're leaving one way or the other."

Damion stiffened at the threat in his father's voice, but Britt laughed softly and rose to pour himself another drink. He held it close to his lips and smiled across the glass rim at Damion.

"I don't think so, Pa. I think these people plan on staying a long time. You see, their name is Kennedy. They're old Rob Kennedy's relatives . . . and the land belongs to them."

Chapter 4

"I don't believe it," Elliot thundered. "Rob Kennedy had no kin. These people are lying."

"In time we could prove it," Damion said quickly.

"Time! Don't you realize what these people will do with enough time? They probably have men all set to work the range. By the time we prove who they are, or aren't, they'll have stolen enough of our cattle to strip us."

"Rustlers," Britt whispered.

"Very clever rustlers. Being cattlemen, they could rob us blind."

"There's the law, Pa." Damion said. "All we would have to do would be catch them with one head. The law could take care of it."

"The law is miles away," Elliot replied, "and it's a law that doesn't care much for the Sabers. You remember that Marshal Thomas isn't too fond of us to begin with. He won't put out much effort to help us. In this country, Damion, a man has to defend what belongs to him in the only way that people like this can understand—with a gun."

"I hope you're not suggesting that I go over there and chase them out with a gun, for God's sake," Damion exploded. "I'll go and talk to them again tomorrow. I'll convince them we're not about to be robbed. At least I'll give them a chance to move out before I go shooting anybody."

"You keep saying 'them,' Damion," Britt remarked casually. "I was over there late this afternoon. The only 'them' I saw was a beauty, about twenty or so, with big gray eyes and a figure like—"

"For Christ's sake, Britt, are women all you can think about?" Damion snapped.

"Well, that one is worth giving a second thought to . . . or a third . . . fourth." Britt shrugged.

Elliot was watching Britt and Damion and realized that something had leapt between them he had not seen before.

"A woman?" he questioned.

"Britt's right, Pa. She's just a girl, really. Her father brought her with him," Damion explained.

"Her father says he's Rob Kennedy's brother, and he's brought more of his family than just her. There's her brother, his wife and little girl, and four hands. Looks like they came to stay," Britt supplied.

"You know a hell of a lot about them for such a short visit," Damion replied. "Just how long was that visit?"

"Why, Damion." Britt laughed. "Just because I had sense enough to come with a friendly smile instead of a clumsy threat, you don't have anything to get upset about."

"Damnit, you two, quit snappin' at each other's heels. We got a bigger problem on our hands than your personal likes. We have a threat here you two don't seem to understand." Elliot looked directly at Damion. "Get out there tomorrow, and by next week I want those land grabbers to be on their way back where they came from. And you"—he turned to Britt, whose smile faded—"I want you to stay away from them. 'Pears to me you only need to string a little bait to get your brother snappin'. You stay out of this. Let Damion handle it."

Britt stood stiffly erect, his face a mask that hid the emotions that tore at him.

Damion sensed his brother's pain and at that moment he could have struck his own father.

"Sure, Pa," Britt said, retreating to his cool, casual, half-amused attitude. "You sure as hell don't want your half-breed son speaking for the Circle S. Don't worry, I have a lot of other . . . jobs to do." Britt set his glass down and strode from the room. In a minute the front door closed with a resounding crack, and silence filled the room.

"That kid." Elliot said in disgust. "He gets more and more like his ma every day. Maybe I ought to think twice about giving him half this place. Maybe that Indian blood has made him wilder than I thought."

"Pa," Damion said with a cold anger in his voice that Elliot had never heard before, "that is the hardest and most vicious thing I've ever heard you say. Whatever his mother was, she was good enough to be your wife and she gave you a son. The day Britt walks away from this ranch—if it's because of your pigheaded prejudice—I go too, because I don't think I could work beside a man who's so damn blind."

Damion left the room, trying to rationalize his wild anger at both his brother and his father. He had been a buffer so long he was beginning to feel bruised by the contact. He knew quite well where Britt had gone but was not prepared to face any further confrontation.

Tomorrow, he thought, he would ride over and rid them of the problem that was creating the wedge. Then he would hope time would heal the raw wounds and give them all some peace.

Lucy Kennedy looked about the small house. Kairee had done well in such a short time, but a tremendous amount of work was still necessary.

"Well, I must say, Kairee, you've done wonders with this place. You must be exhausted. Why don't you relax? After the meal, I'll do the dishes and Cassie can help me. Tomorrow we can tackle this place together. Of course, it's going to take a little short of a miracle to make something out of this place. My gracious, it looks to me like it's been years and years since a human hand has touched it."

Lucy Kennedy was a pretty woman with a personality, as Gregg said, bubbling like a pot of continually boiling water. Her hair was warm brown and her hazel eyes were the first to find humor in mundane things. She was small of build but softly rounded. Her heart-shaped face glowed with a golden tan and her wide-mouthed smile was always present. She and Gregg had been childhood sweethearts and Kairee doubted if Gregg had ever given a thought to looking at another woman.

Gregg was lean and hard muscled. His eyes were the same gray-blue as his sister's, his hair a thick sandy blond. He was only a year older than Kairee, yet at twenty he seemed much older. His face was rugged, and the harshness of it was softened only by his eyes, which were warm and gentle, surprisingly so for a man.

"We have all those supplies to unload from the wagons," Kairee said.

"They've been sitting all this time," Lucy said with a laugh. "They can surely sit until tomorrow. After all that food Gregg and Pa and the two drivers put away, neither one of them will be of any use to us, so we may as well get a good night's sleep."

"I agree with that," Gregg said from a comfortable seat by the fire.

"Did you have any problems while we were gone, Kairee?" her father questioned. "I had some reservations about leavin' you here alone."

57

"Good heavens, Pa, it was only a day," Kairee replied. "Nothing special happened."

Kairee was not sure why she did not tell them of the Sabers' visits. Maybe, she thought, it was because they all seemed so content in this new home that she found it hard to reveal that any kind of trouble lingered so near. Besides, she had made it more than clear to the Sabers that they were here to stay. Maybe their visits had simply been a threat to see if they could be scared away. Well, she thought determinedly, they were now firmly entrenched, and no one would be able to push them. She turned to gaze upon her father.

Stephen Kennedy was a man whose face was lined with the stories of his life. The trials as well as the times of happiness had left their marks. His eyes were a warm and intelligent gray, and his body still retained its strength, though he had labored from childhood. His hands were hard and callused, yet they too could be gentle.

He seemed satisfied with Kairee's response and let the conversation drift to the coming of their small herd of cattle. He was filled with enthusiasm about their future and Kairee allowed herself to drift into the comforting pleasure of contentment.

Lucy and Gregg drifted off to bed only a short time after they had finally coaxed an exhausted but still reluctant Cassie to her bed, leaving Kairee and her father alone. It was a peaceful silence in which the two sat.

"Kairee girl, you don't regret comin'?"

"No, Pa. The place is so beautiful I can hardly believe it, and I've only seen it from the porch. Tomorrow I'm going to take a nice long ride before I begin work. I'd like to see our new promised land."

"The promised land," Stephen repeated. "That it is, Kairee. We can build this place, you'll see. It's got a lot of promise. I'd sure like to see you and Gregg fixed up with something good before I'm gone."

"Don't worry, Pa, you've got a lot of years left. We'll all work together and make this one of the finest ranches in Wyoming."

Stephen reached out to lay a gnarled hand against her hair.

"You're pretty, girl, so pretty. Like your ma. I want you to be happy, Kairee. I want you to marry some fine man and have some good, strong kids."

"Pa, I wish you'd stop believing that marriage to some . . . fine man is all it will take to make me happy. I like kids, but that doesn't mean they're all I need to fill my life. I . . . I want a man who understands me . . . who cares what I think and feel. I don't think I could marry a man who just wanted a comfortable brood mare. Right now I just want to work with you and Gregg and Lucy to make a good home for us. Let's let tomorrow, and my future, take care of itself."

He watched her, knowing he had never truly seen within Kairee's heart.

She bent forward to kiss his cheek. "Go to bed, Pa. I'd like to sit by the fire a while longer if you don't mind."

He nodded, rose stiffly, and left her alone.

Kairee thought back over the very eventful day, and about the two men who had made it so.

She had liked Britt, sensing that a woman would be able to laugh with him and enjoy even the smallest pleasures of life. There was a little-boy quality about him, wanting to seek out the fun and the sweet treats of life. And yet there was a bitterness, a hurt he was having a very difficult time facing and would, under no circumstances, share with another. She had felt toward him as she would have toward Gregg, if he had been hurt or unhappy.

She thought of Damion, a man who would allow no one, especially a woman, to find the place he had protected so long against intrusion. She had sensed the steel core within him, had heard the sharp edge of the blade in his voice. But his eyes had been as blue as the bright Wyoming sky, and they had pierced deeply to touch a well of uncertain emotions that had been flowing like a slow rivulet ever since. He was solid and powerful and she would have compared the feelings he had evoked in her to the high Big Horn Mountains that rose against the horizon of the valley—breathlessly beautiful, but deadly dangerous. She could still feel the power of his presence, and it both excited and frightened her.

She sighed deeply and rose to extinguish the fire. Walking across the room, she pushed open the window to let in the cool night air. Then she returned to her blankets and after a short while she slept.

The dream was a warm mist that enveloped her. He came to her from the mist and drew her into his arms. His kiss was gentle and searching, and she responded with the complete giving of a woman.

It was ethereal and she could not retain the substance of it. She only knew his touch was magic . . . and his eyes were as blue as the Wyoming sky.

Kairee rose before the sun, when the first streaks of early dawn had awakened only the birds, whose soft melodies began to fill the air.

She dressed quickly, for she wanted to ride today, and she wanted to ride alone. She knew her family would be concerned about her going out alone, so she tiptoed quietly from the house.

She saddled her own horse and mounted. Then she walked the horse for awhile so the sound of their activity would not reach those still asleep. Once she felt sure she was out of earshot, she coaxed her horse into a trot, then she bent low in the saddle and urged him faster and faster until he was in a full, long-strided run.

She was exhilarated and only drew the horse in when she sensed he had begun to tire. Now, as they moved slowly, she allowed herself to fully enjoy the beauty that surrounded her. She was awed by the force of nature about her.

It was here, she thought, that the creator must have intended to bring man, in humility, to his knees. It would be an unforgettable experience for anyone.

She let her horse pick his way delicately along the pebbled shore of a shallow stream, the banks of which were lined with aspens. Behind these rows of graceful trees lay fields of buttercups and splashes of purple harebell and white yarrow. The huge peaks of the snow-tipped mountains were reflected in the small lake from which the stream ran.

This rare moment vanquished all the regrets she had had about coming. She had never seen a place as beautiful.

She dismounted and tethered her horse so it could crop some sweet grass. Then she walked slowly down the bank of the river.

The early morning breeze was still cool from the night and the sun was just half up on the brink of the mountain's crest. The stream by which she walked was crystal clear and she slowed her steps when she saw several nice-sized fish dart about.

She knelt by the stream and cupped some of the water in her hand and tasted it. She sighed in pleasure and laughed at herself. There did not seem much to be dissatisfied about in this valley.

She made a quick decision, which was not uncharacteristic, and sat on a flat stone to remove her boots and draw her riding skirt into a bunch so she could wade into the water.

*   *   *

Damion had found the night's sleep disrupted by the unwanted presence of a slim, gray-eyed woman he would just as soon have forgotten.

He had risen early because of this and had decided obstinately that he would ride to the Kennedy ranch at once to see if the reasons for their imminent departure were understood.

As he rode slowly, his mind was on the words Britt had spoken the night before. Obviously Britt had had the same appeal for her as he had for most women. That it irritated him much more than usual was something he purposely ignored.

He rode through the aspen trees with little sound. The brush and wildflowers were so thick they muffled the sound of his horse's approach. That was why he saw Kairee long before she had any idea another human was present. He reined in his horse and remained motionless, absorbing the sight before him.

She knelt by the stream and drank a little water, then his attention was totally absorbed as he watched her remove her boots, bunch her dress about her hips, and wade into the water.

Her legs were long and slender and the sun danced in her shiny blond hair. He could hear her soft laugh and at that moment was startled by the tightening in his loins.

How easy it would be to tumble her to the ground, to strip off the interfering clothes and take her. The thought angered him as much as his body's demanding reaction.

Damn, he thought, I'm like a wild-headed boy. She's beautiful beyond any doubt, but she's dangerous. She could bring me more trouble than it would be worth. She could well be the final wedge between me and Britt and Pa, the wedge that could break what little threads there are left to tie me and Britt together.

He felt his pulses begin to race as she reached up to

unpin her hair, then shook her head, letting the golden mass tumble about her. The sunlight caught it in ripples of light and Damion could almost feel its softness in his fingers.

He swallowed thickly and his hands clenched the reins. Desire leapt through him like a raging wildfire and he had to grit his teeth to keep from calling out to her.

Instead he nudged his horse forward slowly.

She was totally unaware of his presence as he grew closer. In minutes he was within a few feet of her and it was only then that she sensed his presence and spun about. Fear of the unknown lit her face momentarily, then faded quickly when she recognized him.

Kairee was startled but strangely unafraid. She half smiled, first from embarrassment at being caught in such a disheveled state, and second because his eyes seemed to warm the blood that flowed in her veins. The glow in the depths of his sky blue eyes left her without defense. He had put no words to what she could read and she had no way to fight what had only been felt and left unsaid.

He dismounted slowly and walked to the edge of the stream.

She shivered a little, surprised to find that her heart was pounding, and only the rippling sound of the water lapping about her calves reminded her of where she was and what was happening.

He was so handsome, she thought. She took note of the finely chiseled mouth and the startling blue of his eyes against his bronzed face.

She knew a sudden and astonishing urge to go to him, to reach out and touch him, to feel the warmth of his skin beneath her hand. Her gaze drifted down his body, lingering on the breadth of his chest and the lean waist and hips. She found herself caught in some remarkably unmaidenly thoughts. She frowned at her

63

own reaction and pulled her eyes from him.

She could not allow this wild and very difficult-to-control emotion take her mind from the obvious danger he represented. Slowly she walked from the water to stand beside him. She loosened the hem of her dress and let it drop about her, then she raised her hand to capture her hair and try to bring it under control.

He reached out a hand to stop her, not even knowing the reason himself. She looked up at him blankly for a moment, then his hand slid into the soft folds of her hair and he drew her to him.

It was only then that she read the fire in the depths of his eyes accurately. She stepped back so suddenly he was surprised into realizing what he had fully intended to do.

"Damn," he said softly as he dropped his hand. "I'm sorry. I didn't mean to do that."

"You didn't do anything," she returned, absolving him.

"But I meant to. You know it and so do I, only I can't," he added more to himself than to her.

"I don't understand what you're talking about."

"I was on my way to talk to you and your family. I was on my way," he said firmly, "to find out what you intend to do about leaving."

She flushed but quickly turned her back on him and walked to the rock she had sat on to remove her boots. She sat down now and pulled them on. She was trying to gather her thoughts. The firmness of her voice matched his when she spoke again.

"We are not leaving the valley. I thought I had made that clear to you the first time." She stood. "So you can save yourself the trip. My father and my brother will tell you the same."

His gaze was so intense she could not meet his eyes without experiencing the strange, raw emotion he could stir in her.

"Do you know," he said softly, "I don't even know your name."

"Kairee," she replied quietly.

"Let me tell you something . . . Kairee. This land will break you. If it doesn't, my father will. He has over thirty-five men close enough to fight now, and more he can call at any time. He has gunfighters. You stand no chance of building anything in this valley. Go somewhere else, Kairee, before you pay a price greater than you know. Go find another valley, one that doesn't have any grief to go with it."

"My family and I have fought battles before. This land is all we have, and we have run far enough. We'll stand and fight here, we'll live . . . or die here, but," she said quietly, "we'll stay here."

He needed to reach her, to make her understand. He needed to make her taste some kind of fear so she would know it.

He reached out before she understood what he was doing and grabbed her wrist. With a strength she could never hope to combat, he pulled her against him and his other arm went about her to hold her more firmly.

He took the softness of her mouth in a kiss meant to destroy her strength and reserve.

Neither were prepared for the overwhelming force that struck without warning.

Kairee felt a flow of sudden heat that seared her will and left her without breath and without control of a body that seemed to be dissolving.

Damion too was shaken to the core when the current of desire ripped through him like a piercing sword.

Lips meant to be brutal softened, and bodies meant to do battle blended for one blinding perfect moment.

Then with a cry that was nearly despair, Kairee pushed herself away from him. They stood, inches apart, breathing in rapid gasps and staring at each other.

Chapter 5

"You're a damn fool if you think you can survive out here. What are you, some little farm girl from back East whom the land has been good to? Well, this land isn't good to anybody. You have to fight like hell to get and hold what you want."

"And you tell me this because you're one of the powerful Sabers and you want to keep me and my family from being hurt." She laughed bitterly. "It's your greed that makes you yell so loud. You want our place. Well, you can watch every cow you've got die before you see us get driven off our land!"

"Don't you understand the difference between someone trying to help you and greed?"

"I understand very well," she said in a voice quieted now in the aftermath of almost uncontrolled anger. "We don't want to interfere with you," she added, "and you can just stay away from us. If you can't treat us like the neighbors we want to be, then just stay away altogether."

His face was rigid with anger, but somewhere deep within he fought a battle against himself. He needed her rage, he thought wildly, because it was the only defense he had against the desire to take her into his arms again, the desire to feel the soul-filling emotion that had overflowed within him when their mouths had merged.

"It's not that easy to do," he said calmly now.

"Try it," she snapped.

"Kairee, I want to talk to your father, or to your brother. One of them must have enough common sense to face the truth."

"I don't want you to talk to them. You . . . you don't understand what this means to my family, and . . . and I don't think you'd understand if you talked to them forever. From the lofty mountain top, the bottom looks a long way off," she added softly.

She turned and walked away from him and it took every ounce of self-control he possessed to keep from following her.

Damn her pride, he thought miserably, and damn his father's pride as well.

She mounted her horse and rode away without looking back.

He walked to his horse slowly and started back to his house. He fought the thoughts in his mind, but slowly they swelled into one all-consuming plan. He meant to make sure Kairee wanted to leave the valley, and he knew only one sure way.

Kairee had tears in her eyes and she brushed them away angrily. What was worse, the anger was directed at herself.

She could still taste his hungry mouth on hers and feel the searing heat that had erupted within her and had made her feel as if she had been melting against the strength of his rock-hard body. She had wanted him! Damnit, she had wanted him! She had wanted to feel his hands hot against her flesh. She had wanted to feel

67

him deep inside her, touching the roiling need and easing it until she could cry in his arms.

She hated him. She hated this strange power that could make his touch turn her into a seething cauldron of passion.

There would be no more confrontations with Damion Saber. They were too dangerous. But there would be no backing away either. If the Kennedys wanted the chance to build something permanent—if she wanted to keep her family whole and self-sufficient—they had to hold to this land. It was all they had. With determination she went to find her horse.

When she rode up to the ranch and dismounted, she led her horse to the corral and saw to his care before she walked back to the house. By the time she reached the top step of the porch she could smell breakfast cooking.

Inside she was greeted with questions about where she had been.

"Kairee girl," Stephen questioned, "where've you been?"

"Out riding, Pa." She sat down at the table. "I'm sorry to have left you with breakfast, Lucy."

"No bother." Lucy laughed. "Cassie and I made breakfast." She ruffled her daughter's hair as she passed her to carry more food from the stove to the table.

Cassie was a bubbling replica of her mother and her eyes were continually filled with enthusiasm.

"Mama let me turn the flapjacks over and I only spilled one," she said proudly.

"That's not bad Cassie." Kairee laughed. "I still can't turn them without messing them up."

"There isn't much to do today until the boys get here with the herd and the horses," Gregg announced. "I think I'll just ride out and see what this place has to offer."

"You might scout out some trees," Lucy said. "We need a room added onto this house. Kairee can't sleep on the floor come winter. She'll freeze. It's already getting nippy outside. And besides, where are Smokey and Rusty going to sleep when they get here with the cattle? The drivers are sleeping outside, but it'll soon be too cold for that. You'd better get something up for the four of them."

"I'll do that. Pa and I will have Kairee's room up in no time. We'll start on a bunkhouse and Smokey and Rusty can help us finish it when they get here."

"Well, I guess Lucy and I can finish cleaning up the house and getting the furniture in," Kairee replied.

"Pa and I will unload the wagons before I go anywhere."

The day began to ease into routine work and Kairee threw herself into it with enthusiasm, an enthusiasm meant to involve her mind and body so she could keep her thoughts from roaming to a steel-eyed man and the unwelcome feelings he aroused in her.

Work had always been a balm for Kairee when she was confused or faced with a problem. But this was the first time it failed her. Despite all her efforts she could not shake the feeling of a shadow hanging over her, as if some unexpected threat hovered near and she did not know from which direction to expect it.

The evening meal was filled with the same laughing confusion and soon afterward the family began to settle. It was Cassie who drifted off to sleep first in Gregg's arms. He lifted her and carried her to bed and Lucy followed.

Stephen, too, stood, stretched, and yawned. "Night, Kairee girl. Sleep well."

"Night, Pa."

She watched him walk to his room. Her father was such a strong man, she thought. He suffered his losses and still kept the group together. She knew he would never run from the threat of the Sabers and she felt a deep, warm pride. No one, least of all an arrogant man, would make her run either.

She spread her blankets on the rough plank floor before a fire that still burned crisply, but she was strangely sleepless. She just did not want to lie there and let her mind drift. It drifted in directions from which she preferred to stay away.

She walked to the door, took a heavy wool shawl from a hook behind it and threw it about her shoulders. Then she went out on the porch.

The wind rustled softly through the tall gold-tipped aspens and the stars against the black velvet of the sky seemed almost close enough to reach up and touch.

She deeply inhaled the fragrant night air. It was not as chilly as she had thought it would be, so she draped the shawl across the banister of the porch.

Her horse nickered softly and with a smile she walked from the porch toward the corral. When she reached the rail fence, she stretched out her hand and called to him softly. "Cinnamon . . . come on, boy . . . Cinnamon."

The horse ran to her at once and nuzzled her outstretched palm affectionately with his velvet nose.

She caressed his long, arched neck and for one moment she felt a surge of loneliness. In the breadth of this immense country she felt so small, so insignificant, so alone. The battle they had chosen to fight seemed, at this vulnerable juncture, more than she could handle. She had to be strong and independent, but she longed for the strength of a shoulder to lean on and someone to calm the fears that tore at her. Tears lingered on the edge of her lashes and for this one moment her courage was at it lowest ebb.

Damion kept himself busy, driving his body with physical labor and deliberately closing his mind to all thoughts of Kairee and the unbelievable feelings she had set to motion within him.

With grim determination he made his plans. Later that night he would ride to the Kennedy ranch. One way or the other he must convince them their untenable position was dangerous.

He meant to enforce the words with whatever threats proved necessary to get her father and brother to seek safer ground. If nothing else worked, he would be blunt about what his father was capable of doing, although he was more than certain he would be forced to make choices and he was torn between his need for his father's acceptance, his love for the Circle *S*, and his knowledge that the guilt he would share by helping drive the Kennedys from their land would keep him from enjoying sleep again.

Britt was absent from the dinner table that night and Damion was relieved. He knew Britt saw between all his words much more efficiently than his father and he did not want Britt suspicious about his methods or motives. Besides, he was not too sure Britt did not harbor plans of his own concerning the Kennedys.

Damion would be the last to acknowledge the mist of jealousy that filled him. He only knew he did not want Britt and Kairee together—for her welfare, of course.

He sat at the dinner table in silence, his mind momentarily caught in the spell of wide gray eyes and a mouth as soft as satin. Elliot had to speak twice before

71

Damion heard him. He looked up suddenly when Elliot's voice grew impatient.

"Damion!"

"What?"

"Where were you? You seemed to be miles away. Is there some kind of problem?"

"No . . . no problems. Things are running pretty well."

"You don't sound convinced," Elliot charged astutely. "Are those squatters on the Kennedy place giving you trouble?"

"They're not squatters."

"They're squatters," Elliot said firmly. "I thought you were goin' to handle gettin' em off our land."

"I am handling it. They've got just a little better than nothing. They look about as poor as church mice. I don't see what harm they can do."

"They probably got a long rope and running irons. It'd be easy to change the Circle *S* brand. Before we start losin' beeves, you'd better do something. You know damn well they're an example to others. One set of squatters can be enough fuel to start a range war."

Damion sighed and rose from his half-eaten meal. "Don't worry. I guarantee you they won't be here long enough to cause any big problems."

"See that they're not," Elliot replied. He was used to having the last word and Damion did not have the inclination to argue. "Where are you going?" Elliot asked as Damion turned to walk away.

"I've got some unfinished business to see to," he said flatly.

"Damion," Elliot called, but the door had already closed behind Damion, who had heard his father's call but had not wanted to elaborate on his intended mission.

As he mounted his horse and prepared to ride the

distance to the Kennedy ranch, he thought of his father's words and realized there was a lot of basic truth to them. He knew the laws his father lived by, laws he had lived by all his life.

On the open range, ownership of a calf was determined by the brand on the cow. But if the calf escaped the roundup and grew big enough to leave its mother without being branded, or if it was orphaned by causes natural or unnatural, there was no way of proving who owned it. That simple, natural fact led to trouble and strife between ranchers, especially if one was devious enough to believe in the old axiom that anything he found on the open range was his.

Wyoming law defined such a maverick as "all neat cattle, regardless of age, found running at large in this territory without a mother, and upon which there is no brand." It belonged to any man who could drop his loop on it. "A wide loop" or "a long rope"—the two terms meant the same thing. They meant trouble and loss for the owners of large herds.

There were rustlers and rustlers. Their methods varied and so did their community status. The distinctions among the various kinds of rustling were like the differences between professional prostitution and an occasional fling. It was one thing to slap your iron on a maverick when you happened on him in the course of a day's riding. But it was another to scour the country deep into another man's range. Experts would be able to pen calves in some lonely corral in the foothills, then brand them in spring roundup. Damion knew quite well a small rancher living in the valley would have adequate opportunity to do just that.

He had no idea what the Kennedy brand might be, but brands could be burned over, blotching them so badly they could not be read.

He approached the Kennedy ranch from the south so

73

the barn stood between him and the house. He circled the barn but drew his horse to a halt when he saw a flutter of movement near the corral.

After a few minutes he realized what he was seeing. It was Kairee standing by the rail of the corral while a large stallion nuzzled her hand.

He watched for a minute as she flung her arm about the horse's neck and rested her head against him. It was a poignant scene of sadness and he was caught by a feeling of sympathy.

His peripheral vision told him the house was already dark and he assumed the family must all be asleep. He entered the yard between the house and the barn and dismounted. He let the reins of his horse drop to the ground. Well trained, it obediently stood while Damion walked slowly toward Kairee. He did not want to frighten her, so he spoke her name softly while he was still several feet from her.

"Kairee."

She gave a startled gasp as she spun about. "You . . . Damion . . . what are you doing here?"

She measured the distance between where she stood and the house and he sensed she was shaken enough to be preparing to run. The last thing he wanted was for her to dash into the house in panic.

"Kairee, we have some unfinished business to talk about."

"It's rather a strange time for a neighbor to come calling. I suggest you go home and come over tomorrow, when my whole family is awake."

He moved closer slowly. He was close enough that he could have reached to touch her. In the light of a pale, low-hanging moon she looked like a shimmering vision. In a moment of complete self-honesty he knew this was why he had come . . .

Kairee could feel his presence like a force. It wove

74

itself about her like silken cobwebs, and she could not seem to tear her eyes from his as he moved even closer.

Her hair had been twisted in a thick coil atop her head and pinned. In a quick move, before she could raise her hands to protest, he reached for the pin and let her hair slip free.

It tumbled about her shoulders, and touched by the pale light of a white moon, it took on a glaze of silver-gold.

He knew he should speak, do something to deny the fierce need that exploded through him, but he could not find words, could not say a thing that would create logic for her out of an emotion he could not understand himself.

He had convinced himself that he would merely try to frighten her, to turn her against any attempt her family might make to stay. In his self-assurance, the last thing he had reckoned with was that he could be caught in the web in which he had meant to trap her.

He reached out a hand to gently touch her cheek and watched fascinated as her eyes widened until they seemed to dominate her face, until he was drowning in them.

He had not realized that he had stepped closer and raised his other hand.

"Don't," she protested feebly, but his hands had already framed her face, his fingers lacing into her hair. He knew he had wanted to touch her like this from the moment they had first met.

Kairee's mind struggled in a turmoil. There was no voice to answer her queries, to explain the turbulent depths into which she seemed to be tumbling without control.

The night was musical with the calls of nocturnal animals. The breeze was soft, but the quiet expectancy within her was so thick with heavy silence she could have cut it with a knife.

She struggled valiantly for a way to resist but found herself enmeshed in a need to feel his arms about her. Her eyes held his and there was an odd look to them as he lowered his head.

Her lips trembled, inches below his, and he bent to touch, to taste, gently at first, with a feather-light touch that brought a soft murmur from deep in her throat.

Then suddenly his arms were about her and her feet were lifted from the ground until she almost lay against his iron-hard body. His mouth found hers with unbearable intensity. It was hard, insistent, as it moved, slowly seeking and finding, stirring fires that smoldered, then burst into flame. It was the sweetness of awakening spring, the thunder of passion, and the blending was explosive.

Kairee was suffused by a warmth and she lost what control she had had over her thoughts, letting them spiral downward into oblivion.

She knew only that his open, hungering mouth was upon hers, devouring the sweetness within. She knew her arms were about his neck but cared not how they had come to be there. Her head now rested against the breadth of his chest as he effortlessly lifted her against him and moved the few steps to the open barn door. Inside its dim interior he let her feet slide to the floor, but his arms did not want to relinquish her to reason. They bound her against him until her breath was lost and she clung dizzily.

Again he cupped her face in his hands and in the soft light their eyes met and held. Then his mouth was upon hers again, and his tongue was insistent until she met it with her own, first with hesitancy, then with welcome, and finally with passion.

Slowly her mind began to argue. It was insanity! This crazy new feeling was beyond anything she had ever known.

"Damion, don't," she moaned against his mouth as her hands slid between them, trying to force them apart. Against his size and strength, her attempt was ineffectual.

"I can't let you go, Kairee," he groaned softly against her hair. "I want you and I know you feel the same. I want you, Kairee." His voice died to a whisper and the warmth of his mouth sought hers again until she was swept beyond knowing anything but the sweet heat of their passion.

He released her only long enough to draw her with him to a bed of hay left long ago. It was dry and useless but would be soft beneath them.

He drew her down with him and she found the warm security of his arms again. Only this time the effect was different. Through her clothes she could feel the heat of his body and she gasped audibly when she felt his hand cup her breast for a heart-stopping moment.

Buttons were expertly undone and his mouth sought softness with a fiery intensity. She was lost, wanting him as much as he wanted her.

A warmth spread through her as she surrendered to his touch, a magical touch, which wove a spell that left her nearly mindless.

His mouth was heat against her flesh as he caught one passion-hardened peak and tasted deeply. She felt the rigid, manly boldness of him pressed against her and she knew a wanting, a desire for an end to this searing flame that tore at her.

He came into her then and she felt a first, sharp, piercing pain that made her gasp followed by a warmth deep within her that caused her to sob with pleasure.

He began to move, slowly, kissing her, caressing her, loving her until her body began to answer his.

His joy in her enthralled him as they began to move

77

together and he had the intense pleasure of knowing she had slipped beyond all reality but him and was giving from the depths of her being.

Their senses rose together on the crest of a passion wild beyond anything they could have imagined.

Caught in wave after wave of gloriously exultant pleasure, Kairee could only cling to the solidness of his huge frame as their bodies, their passions, and their completion, molded them into one.

His hard body filled her and she felt a stunning, beautiful, expanding bloom of ravaging rapture that made her arch against his deep, full strokes until a wild, soaring ecstasy burst upon them and he clasped her to him as if he could draw her within himself and hold her forever.

Kairee felt the thunderous beat of his heart against her naked breasts and heard their ragged breathing, and time seemed to be poised on the brink of eternity as they clung together.

He lifted his head and their eyes met again. Then his lips touched hers gently, tenderly, and he drew her close. She felt a strange sense of rightness in his arms and for this moment all enmities were lost in the perfection.

Chapter 6

It seemed an eternity before Kairee could control her breathing and struggle for words. Even then she could not summon the words that would come near to expressing what she was feeling. Her body had betrayed her, had totally destroyed her will, and she found it beyond belief that she could have experienced such a traumatic emotional upheaval.

Damion was no less entranced than she was. He had prepared himself only to shake her will, only to make her realize her own vulnerability. But instead he had exposed his own vulnerability. He had found himself lost in the sweet taste and touch of her, lost in a tangled cobweb of thunderous emotions that he knew he hadn't the strength to break. In emotional retreat he fell back on her distrust and anger to protect him from saying things he could not mean, could never mean.

He moved to lie beside her. After a few minutes he felt secure in the fact that he could summon some control over his will, control enough to find the words that would stop the strange, almost uncontrollable urge to say what he was truly feeling instead of what he knew must be said. But before he could speak, Kairee sat up and began to gather her dress about her.

The silence that hung about her was one that he had never experienced before. It was a silence that seemed to forbid words. She had withdrawn from him so completely that he could feel the wall between them grow.

"Kairee?" He spoke her name quietly, but she gave no answer. To Kairee it seemed as if she had to concentrate on forcing her hands to move, as if, if she allowed him within her thoughts, she would be totally unable to battle the force of his hold.

He sat up beside her and reached to grip her shoulders to turn her face to him. Then he said the two words that were the last thing Kairee needed to hear.

"I'm sorry," he said softly. He had not meant that he was sorry about what had happened, only that he was sorry that he might have hurt her in any way. But Kairee seemed only to hear what her mind told her must be true. Damion Saber had come to battle her in the only way he had thought she might be vulnerable. And, she thought painfully, he had been more than successful. From the heights of pleasure she plummeted to the depths of self-recrimination. She had been easy. Lonely and frightened, she had allowed him within defenses she should have reinforced the moment he had first touched her.

He had bent her will once, but she vowed silently that he would never be able to do it again. She would not freely hand him the weapon he could use against both her and her family.

"Why be sorry, Damion?" She laughed harshly. "You did what you came to do, didn't you? To see if you could prove your point? Well, if you think this will change our determination to stay here, you've made a mistake."

"You're wrong on more than one count, Kairee. I came here intending to prove how impossible it is for

80

you and your family to stay here. What happened was . . . as much beyond my control as it was yours."

"I should have known."

"Known what?"

"You'd like it if we left now, wouldn't you? The laugh would be yours, wouldn't it, Damion? You drive us off, but not before you have your fun and prove you are the strong Damion Saber, master of all he touches."

"That isn't true, Kairee."

"Then you and your family won't mind if we stay here," she challenged. But she could feel the answer in the sharp tensing of his muscles.

"Staying here will be a disaster for you," he replied quickly.

She pushed his hands away and rose. She was a darker shadow in the semi-darkness. "I think what you are afraid of, Damion," she whispered, "is that if I stay it might prove a disaster for you. Well, put your mind at ease. I've no claim on you. I want nothing from the Sabers except to be left alone."

Damion reached to grab his shirt and scramble to his feet, but Kairee was already running toward the door. By the time he reached it, she was already moving up the steps to the house. He shrugged into his shirt, thinking about what she had said.

He knew she felt he had planned this carefully and had meant to reduce her to pleading with him. He knew it was not the truth, just as he knew she would never accept the truth, especially since he still found it hard to accept himself.

He sighed deeply, wishing there were some way he could get his father to accept the Kennedys, but he knew it would be like stopping a summer flash flood.

Maybe it would be better if he tried to forget what had happened here tonight, he reflected. Yet a small voice in the back of his mind, which he tried in vain to smother, laughed out the exultant taunt that he would not be able to forget quite that easily.

He and Kairee had no solid ground on which to build anything, and he knew deep down that the battles had just begun. With slow and reluctant movements, he dressed and rode away from the ranch.

It was a long and very thoughtful ride, and he was filled with regret for what had happened, yet he sensed he had touched some incomparable thing that he might never touch again. He wondered, if the opportunity came, if he would reach again to find the intangible thing that seemed to have pierced some part of him.

It was in the small hours of the morning that he left the barn after stabling his horse and walked toward the main house. He crossed the patio and went inside, closing the door softly behind him.

In the corner of the patio, in the depths of the shadows, the sound of a match scratched, then the golden glow of the flame touched the cigar held between strong white teeth and sparked an amber reflection in Britt Saber's eyes. They were narrowed against the haze of smoke, yet filled with curiosity.

"So the tomcat prowls tonight, brother," he whispered. "I wonder just where you've been prowling."

Kairee moved across the room still dimly lit by the red coals of the dying fire. She sagged to her blanket. After a moment, she buried her face in her hands and wept silent tears.

She hated Damion Saber, but more than that she hated herself. He had only had to reach for her. She had come to his arms willingly and that left the most bitter taste of all.

He had not tried to camouflage his open lust behind sweet words. She remembered clearly, too clearly. He had said he wanted her—wanted her, and that was all. "Oh, damn you," she whispered, unsure yet if she were damning Damion Saber or herself.

Then another thought made her catch her breath and a numbing fear coursed through her. At this moment she could be carrying his child! The thought made her heart pound and perspiration bead on her forehead. It would be harsh punishment for one mistake, but she knew she would have to live with the possibility until nature could prove the fact one way or the other.

She understood the tragedy that might occur should her fears become reality. She could never marry a Saber, even if he wanted to marry her, she thought miserably. To have a man forced into marrying her, a man whose entire family were enemies of hers, would be a situation she could not bear.

It took long hours of bitter recrimination and helpless anger before Kairee could find sleep and even that sleep led to vague and unwelcome dreams.

Damion felt as tired the next morning as he had been the night before. He knew it was because his sleep had been intermittent and filled with troublesome dreams.

When he came to the breakfast table, his father was already there, and, to his surprise, so was Britt.

That Britt was uncommonly quiet went unobserved by Damion for some time and he slowly became aware that Britt was also watching him with a puzzled look in his eyes.

"Something on your mind, Britt?" he questioned.

"No . . . not really," Britt replied with a slight shrug and a half smile. "I just found it hard to sleep last night."

He watched with pleasure as Damion's hand froze with his coffee cup midway to his lips.

"Oh?" he said.

"Yeah . . . kept thinking I was hearing things."

"Hearing things?" Damion laughed. "You been drinkin'?"

"Not last night," Britt answered with a grin. "Last night I was home early. In fact I was surprised that I couldn't find you. Were you out?" he added innocently.

"Were you looking for me for some special reason?" Damion inquired, deliberately ignoring Britt's questions.

"Just wondered," Britt said shrewdly, "if you wanted any help driving those squatters out of the valley."

He knew his thrust had been accurate as soon as he saw Damion's eyes grow cold and the muscle in his cheek jump as he clenched his teeth. Yet Damion's reply was cool and unaffected.

"You needn't worry about it, Britt. When I need your help, I'll ask for it."

So, Britt thought, it had been the Kennedys'. He had watched Damion ride in from that direction but had not been sure. Kairee Kennedy had drawn Damion with the same magnetic beauty with which she had drawn Britt. He also wondered just how Damion's nocturnal visit had been received, and by whom. He was about to insert several more pointed questions when Elliot interrupted.

"What progress are you making with those people, Damion? I want them out of this valley before the snow sets in. I would have thought you'd have had them out by now."

"Maybe Damion's manners are so nice that our new neighbors have decided to stay," Britt chided. "Maybe I ought to take a ride over myself and see what I can do."

Damion's voice was like chips of ice and his eyes were even colder. This time Britt was more than surprised. Damion was much more sensitive about the situation than he had thought.

"I told you, Britt, if I need help I'll ask for it."

"You sure you want them out of the valley?" Britt asked softly.

"Now what the hell do you mean by that?" Elliot interjected gruffly. "If you're making a point, Britt, I wish you'd get to it."

"Not making a point, Pa," Britt answered. "I was just wondering if Damion hadn't gone soft all of a sudden. That Kennedy girl is damn pretty."

Elliot chuckled as he leaned back in his chair. "So that's what you two roosters have been peckin' at each other about. Get this straight, both of you. I don't want some pretty filly causin' trouble around here. There's lots of pretty girls in this territory. 'Course I think you both know that. If she's pretty, she's just another one. Maybe I ought to ride over and explain to our 'neighbors' that this valley just isn't safe. Maybe this is a job I'll have to do myself."

He rose and left the table, and Britt's smile faded as he realized with a start that he had never seen Damion as furious as he was right now. He had expected his father to chastise Damion or maybe move Damion aside for the first time in his life and ask Britt to finish a job Damion had started. He had not expected his father to take on the job himself, and he had not expected the kind of wild anger he saw reflected in Damion's eyes now.

What he had really hoped for was that Elliot would have taken the situation from Damion's hands and given it to him. What he had wanted was for Damion to know how it felt to be relegated to second place, to be pushed aside, to feel the helpless sense of frustration Britt had lived with for so long.

But Britt could feel no sense of satisfaction, for

Elliot had not reacted as Britt had expected, and neither had Damion.

He felt a sudden flush of anger at himself, anger at the pang of jealousy that struck like a lightning blow. Damion had been with Kairee Kennedy last night. He was sure of it. Yet Damion looked less than happy about it. He would gladly have prodded Damion into an explanation if he had thought it would work, but he had never been able to push Damion over the edge of his anger and he was sure he would not succeed now.

"One of these days, Britt," Damion said as he rose, "your sense of humor is going to bounce back into your lap and I don't think you're going to find it so funny."

"Why so angry, Damion? Somebody step on your toes today . . . or last night?"

But Damion was already regaining control of his anger. It had quivered through him like a white hot bolt when he had realized what Britt must know, and what he would be adding to it in his own thoughts.

"Don't worry about me getting my toes stepped on, little brother." He grinned. "It hasn't happened yet . . . and I don't intend to let it."

He left the room and Britt watched the empty doorway for several minutes, trying to sort out what Damion had actually said. Had he been with Kairee or not? He rose slowly. It was something he would find out for himself.

Elliot Saber approached the Kennedy ranch with grim determination. It had been through his efforts that old Rob Kennedy had never succeeded with the place. He had effectively driven Rob away and he would do the same to these intruders who were trying to grab what was his.

He had nearly worked himself to death to build the

Circle *S*. It was, he thought, only the beginning of a dynasty. There would be Sabers to rule and control this valley for generations. That was why he had bred sons and he'd be damned if these squatters were going to drive a wedge between his sons any bigger than the one already there.

Nothing had been allowed to stand in Elliot's way, not even the women in his life. He thought of Damion's mother, Elenor. She had been weak. He had pushed Damion hard to grind out any of the gentle sensitivity Elenor might have given him. Sensitivity had no place in the building of an empire. This situation with the squatters—and he would never think of them as anything more—had brought the first sign of Elenor's gentle nature he had seen in Damion, and he meant to squelch it now before it bred ideas, ideas that someone could share this valley with the Sabers. It was his kingdom, and he'd share it with no one.

He thought of Southwind, Britt's mother. She had been of use to him, for with her had come more land and more water. But she too had flawed her son. He was as wild as the prairie and did not give the Circle *S* the serious devotion Elliot demanded. He laughed, drank, and womanized too much, and the sharp barbs of his humor often pricked both Elliot and Damion until they drew blood. And he wasn't yet sure that wasn't what Britt wanted.

When had his sons become so distant, so different? He had raised them both with the same iron hand and had tried to instill his will and desires in them. Yet lately they seemed to be turning on each other.

Damion was the logical one to head the Circle *S* when he was gone. Britt, no matter what else he felt, still carried his mother's blood. Britt would have to be second, to work under Damion, for the good of the Circle *S*.

His mind dwelt on everything, everything except the ghostly shadow that was always on the periphery of his mind. Emma . . . Emma. After all these years she could still bring the pain, still bring the tears and the loneliness. He had never given himself to another as he had to his beloved Emma. He had built for Emma, had done all he had done with the memory of Emma . . . and the guilt he still carried.

He could still see the misty gray of her eyes and the gold of her hair in the sunlight as she had begged to go with him. She had died, but she had still gone with him, for he had never loved again, not anyone.

He approached the Kennedy ranch now with the sun behind him so that it framed the two men who stood on the porch in its brightness.

He rode up to the porch but did not dismount.

"Mornin'," he said casually.

"Morning," Stephen replied. He waited, sure of whom he was greeting, but well aware the visit by the legendary Elliot Saber was not a neighborly one.

"I'm Elliot Saber."

"I kind of figured you were," Stephen replied. Gregg stood by silently, sensing the unseen and unspoken threat and prepared to defend his father if necessary. He drew confidence from the fact that his gun stood just inside the door.

"Would you like to step down and come in, Mr. Saber?" Stephen inquired.

"No, I don't think so. What I've got to say will be short and sweet. This isn't a social visit. I've been using this range for nigh onto twenty years. You're on property that doesn't rightly belong to you."

"It takes more than using property to claim ownership, Mr. Saber."

"Not out here. Man who settles it, clears it, and works it, owns it."

"Whose law is that?"

"Law of the land or"—Elliot shrugged—"law of the strongest, you might say. A man who wants to keep what he works for has to be ready to fight for it."

"That may be your law," Stephen said stiffly. "But the law of this territory says this land is mine. I have a deed for it all signed and sealed. My family is here with me, and"—his voice grew firmer—"we're going to fight for it if we have to."

"Mr. Kennedy," Elliot asked with a laugh, "how many hands you got beside your family? Wouldn't it save a whole lot of trouble if you just moved on? Besides, I knew old Rob Kennedy, who worked this place before you, and he never said anything about having kin. How does anybody know you're kin at all. Maybe you're just squatters trying to take over what belongs to someone else."

Kairee had stood just within the doorway, close enough to hear but not to be seen. She heard the threat and her anger began to grow. First Damion, then Britt, and now their father. Did they really think her family was going to desert everything and run at their command?

She reached behind the door and took her brother's rifle. With it held firmly in her hand, she stepped out onto the porch.

There was no fear in the glint of her gray eyes, only anger. But still all three were totally amazed at the effect her appearance had on Elliot Saber.

He sucked in his breath with a harsh gasp, as if someone had struck him a fierce blow, and his face went gray.

To Elliot it seemed as if a hand from his past had reached beyond the grave to touch him. Emma! he thought in one desperate, uncontrolled moment—the same slim body, the same golden hair, and, worse, the same misty gray eyes.

A tremor shook Elliot's body until he felt he might disintegrate from the force of it. His hands trembled to the extent that he had to grasp the pommel of his saddle to keep himself from jerking the reins.

"Who the hell are you?" he choked out.

"I'm Kairee Kennedy," she said coldly. "Your sons have already had our answer. We're not leaving. I'll thank you, Mr. Saber, to get off our land as quickly as possible."

Elliot wanted to say a million things, but he was unable to cope with a vision that had walked from the inner recesses of his mind to stand before him. He repeated her name in a whisper of disbelief.

"Mr. Saber," Stephen said, "are you all right?"

They had seen the ghostly white of his face and the sheen of light perspiration that lay on it.

He struggled for a few minutes against the cry of almost sheer agony that wanted to bubble to his lips.

"I'm all right . . . I'm all right," he said, but his eyes never left Kairee. It was a long moment before he seemed to forcefully tear his eyes from her.

"I came by to give you a warning. If you don't pay any heed to it, you've got your own selves to blame if anything happens. There's a high penalty for branding any mavericks on Circle *S* land. Remember that. I wouldn't want a range war to break out around here. If it does, we'll have to do whatever is necessary to put a stop to it."

He wheeled his horse and raked it with his spurs until it leapt ahead. In only seconds he was a dim form riding away.

Elliot rode far enough that the house was out of sight, then he reined his horse to a halt.

He could not believe it. She looked almost exactly like Emma. It was as if Emma had walked from the past to the present to stand before him. It was such a painful thing that he had to use every ounce of his will to bring himself under control, then he forced himself to nudge his horse forward and ride on.

Kairee had watched in amazement the transformation in Elliot. In a matter of minutes she had read conflicting emotions: anger, arrogance, and pride. Then they had crumbled before another, and if she hadn't known better, she would have labeled it fear. But there was no reason for any of the Sabers to fear them.

Kairee understood one blatant truth, however. She and Damion Saber were a world apart and too many things stood in the way of their ever being able to reach each other. It was an impossibility and the less she thought of Damion, the better it would be for everyone concerned.

During the balance of the day it was not hard to force Damion to the back of her mind. But the day waned. The white moon rose and the stars twinkled in a brilliant profusion in the night sky.

She prayed quietly before she sought sleep, prayed that those few moments with Damion Saber had not resulted in the planting of his seed within her.

She could almost taste the tragedy that might follow if it were true. It could set fire to a volatile situation and cause a disaster that would consume them all.

She ruled her heart with an iron will while she was awake. But sleep became the master of that will and the dreams of gentle hands and a hard, seeking mouth brought soft moans of pleasure that were swallowed by the night.

Chapter 7

They moved like a slow, undulating mass, with the two riders moving from side to side, hazing the cattle forward.

Gregg had gone out day after day to watch for the coming herd, and four days later was rewarded first by a cloud of dust in the distance and then by the lowing of the cows as they moved slowly toward him.

He approached the coming herd with a happy shout and received a reaction from the two men that indicated their gratitude in reaching their destination. They spurred their horses ahead to meet Gregg.

"'Bout time you boys got here," Gregg said with a laugh.

"What do you mean, about time?" one retorted. "We been makin' near fifteen miles a day. For this scroungy bunch"—he waved toward the herd—"that was as fast as we could push 'em without havin' any of 'em droppin' on us."

"I'm sure you did, Rusty," Gregg said quickly. "I was only kidding. You made damn good time. Did you lose any?"

"'Bout six head and a couple of calves."

"Not too bad. What's your count now?"

"Forty-eight head. But there's bound to be some

weak ones yet. Might lose a couple more."

"Let's get them onto the ranch," Gregg said. "There's a hell of a lot of work to do before cold weather sets in."

"This the land of milk and honey you talked about?"

"Well, as far as I can see, you're bringing all the milk with you. I haven't found any sign of honey yet."

They laughed. Gregg turned to the second man. "Smokey, glad to see you."

"Not half as glad as I am to get here. I been stuck in this saddle so long I feel like I'm growin' on it."

"Well, you'll be out of it for awhile," Gregg said.

"Why?" Smokey laughed. "You think we're goin' to herd these cows on foot?"

"Nope. We got a lot of building to do," Gregg replied.

"Building?" Rusty questioned. "Building what?"

"Well, let's see," Gregg chuckled. "A room for Kairee—the house only has two bedrooms—a bunkhouse for you two, and, if it hasn't fallen down by the time we get there, we have to do a hell of a lot of repairs on what's left of the barn."

"Anything else?" Smokey questioned wryly. "Seems to me we're startin' from scratch."

"Pretty near," Gregg answered quickly. "Let's get these cows home. Then we can have some supper and Pa can explain everything."

"Why is it," Smokey began suspiciously, "I get the feeling there's a hell of a lot more you oughta be tellin' us."

"There is, but Pa wants to talk it over with you. Let's get going. We can be at the ranch come suppertime and I think Kairee and Lucy are cookin' something special."

"Let's go. I'm so hungry I could eat a blanket," Smokey declared.

They took charge of the herd again and with sharp calls and slaps against their thighs with their hats they urged the cattle toward home.

Smokey Burrows and Rusty Williams had been with the Kennedy family for several years. No one knew where they had come from nor anything about their past. They only knew that both were content to work for a minimum of money and a place to live. And if some believed the two had shady pasts they were keeping to themselves, the Kennedys were more than willing to let such secrets stay buried.

Smokey Burrows had ridden onto the Kennedy property one early dawn. He was as exhausted as his horse and they soon found he had a wound in his left shoulder only half healed. He offered no explanations for this. When he had been given shelter and food and had had his wound cared for, he solemnly offered his help.

He was a sturdy, squarely built man of twenty-six or so. His smokey blue eyes were where he had gotten his name and that was the only thing known about him. His hair was sandy and shaggy and he sported a full mustache of a darker brown of which he seemed extremely proud.

Generally soft-spoken and thoughtful, Smokey kept his own counsel, and the gun slung low on his hip reminded likely transgressors that he intended to keep it that way.

Rusty Williams was just as mysterious as Smokey. He had appeared suddenly, asked for work, and had remained loyal long after the money to pay him was gone.

He and Gregg had become close friends, yet Gregg knew better than to question his past, for the gun he wore looked as if it had seen a great deal of use. The holster was worn and looked as if it were a part of his apparel, like a shirt or shoes.

Yet Rusty was the more humorous and lighthearted of the two. His pale blond hair, despite what efforts he made to control it, continually remained unruly, and his hazel eyes laughed easily. He was tall and reed slim, yet his lean body was wiry muscle, which gave him a strength that was deceptive.

Both men had ridden almost from the time they could walk. Punching cattle was something they knew well and if they had been asked, they would have been the first to claim it was all they wanted to do.

They pushed the cattle as hard as possible and by the time the sun was nearing the horizon they could see the house in the distance.

Lucy gazed pensively from the open doorway, then walked back into the house and closed the door behind her.

"Is Daddy coming, Mommy?" Cassie asked Lucy.

"No, Cassie, I don't see any sign of them yet."

"They should be here for supper," Kairee offered. "You know Gregg doesn't miss many meals."

Lucy laughed. "I expect if he runs across Rusty and Smokey we're going to have three very hungry men on our hands. I think I'd better get cooking."

"I'll help you," Kairee said quickly. But before Lucy could answer, the sound of an approaching horse brought silence to the room.

Kairee's heart leapt and she felt a quiver rustle through her, strumming her nerves. Every day for the past three days she had jumped at every sound, trembled at every unwelcome thought that a Saber might ride over the hill at any moment.

Since Elliot's visit, there had been no sound, no action, from the Circle S. But she knew nothing had been resolved.

She had thought constantly about her contact with the Saber men. Each had been devastating in its own way. She wanted no contact with them again, but especially not with Damion Saber. She was more than angry at herself that she had been unable to erase him from her thoughts, or from her dreams. But she was grimly determined that one way or another she would.

Now, just the sound of a horse approaching made her mouth go dry and her heart pound.

It was only a few minutes before heavy footfalls crossed the porch and a knock on the door, though anticipated, still made her jump.

Lucy watched Kairee's face go pale. She had no idea what might have occurred between Kairee and the Sabers, but it was the first time she had ever seen Kairee frightened.

"I'll see who it is," Lucy said softly.

"No . . . no, I will," Kairee declared. She pressed her lips together firmly and walked to the door. There was no way she would let any Saber frighten her into hiding in her own home.

She walked to the door and opened it. Britt Saber leaned against the wide frame of the door, his thumbs hooked on his holster belt, his broad-brimmed hat tipped to the back of his head, and a grin of pleasure on his face that it had been Kairee who had answered the door.

"Well, Kairee. I'm glad to see you didn't forget." He motioned toward her, taking in the fact that she was dressed for riding. He did not know that she had ridden out earlier in the day to carry food to her father, who was felling a nearby stand of trees.

"Forget?" she questioned once she had regained her composure. No one must know, she thought, that the idea of seeing Damion before me when I opened the door brushed every other thought from my mind.

"You did forget, didn't you?" Britt laughed in disbelief. He pressed one hand against his chest and molded his face into a mask of tragic sorrow. "I am most thoroughly crushed. How can you forget that we were to go riding today. You did promise," he added.

"I . . . I really hadn't expected you to come."

"Not expected me? Why?"

"I just thought . . . well . . ." She sucked in her breath and expelled it rapidly. "I didn't think I'd see a Saber around here."

"Well, Kairee"—his smile faded—"there are Sabers . . . and then there are Sabers. We're not all cut from the same cloth, as you'll find out. I have an engagement to go riding with a lovely lady. I'd really like to take you to see some of my part of the country. Kairee, don't judge me by anybody else. I'm Britt Saber . . . nobody's shadow . . . nobody's man but my own."

Kairee held his eyes for a long time. Despite his almost little-boy quality, she sensed a current within him that might very well drown anybody caught in it. She wanted to refuse, and she was more than surprised when she spoke.

"All right." She smiled for the first time. "Let's go."

Now Britt's smile reappeared as Kairee turned to Lucy.

"I'll be back in an hour or so, Lucy. In plenty of time to help with supper."

"Don't worry about supper. Those men will be so hungry they'll eat anything I throw at them. You haven't been out of this house for almost three days. You deserve some time for yourself."

"Thank you, lady." Britt laughed. "I owe you a debt."

"This is my sister-in-law, Lucy," Kairee said, "and that quiet little girl in the corner, whose heart you've just captured, is her daughter, Cassie. I must say it's the first time I've seen Cassie so silent."

"Hello, Lucy. I'm pleased to meet you."

"Hello, Mr. Saber."

"Britt," he corrected.

"Britt." She smiled, charmed beyond what she would

ever admit.

If Britt had charmed Lucy, he had Cassie in a state of worshipful awe. "Hello, pretty one," he said gently.

"Hello . . . can I call you Britt too?"

"I'd be unhappy if you didn't."

"Okay." Cassie laughed.

"Maybe," Britt said, "next time you might want to go with us."

Cassie was about to leap at the offer when Lucy intervened. "Next time, Cassie. Not now."

Britt winked at Cassie. "Don't worry, little one. Ask your aunt . . . I don't forget appointments with pretty ladies. Especially one as pretty as you."

Her eyes sparkled and Kairee began to wonder about the differences in the Saber men.

They left the house and Kairee insisted, against all Britt's protests, that she would saddle her own horse.

"You're a stubborn lady, aren't you?" he questioned as he watched her saddle the horse expertly.

"Independent, maybe. I don't want any favors."

"Especially from a Saber," he added.

"From anyone."

"I like you, Kairee Kennedy," Britt said softly.

Kairee turned to look up at him. For a moment their eyes held and Britt could feel the deep penetration of her gaze. He felt as if she had reached within him and had found the black, empty center, tearing aside a curtain to let in a beam of sunlight.

Then she took the reins and walked with him to his horse. They mounted and rode away.

He liked to hear her laugh; in fact, as the afternoon wore on, he found he liked just about everything about Kairee Kennedy.

They had ridden for awhile as he pointed out some of the most breathtaking views. He had chosen them carefully and now he knew why. No matter what his father or Damion felt, he wanted Kairee to want to stay.

Now they were holding their horses' reins and leading them behind them as they walked along the edge of the stream.

"The stream is beautiful," she said.

"It's called Willow Creek," he replied. "It's a branch of the South Fork. Those mountains in the distance are the Big Horns."

"They're breathtaking. This land is so . . . so—"

"Big," he supplied with a chuckle.

"Almost overwhelming."

"It is, or seems, almost endless."

"Then I don't understand."

"Don't understand what?"

"Why the Sabers feel no one else has a right to any part of it."

"There you go again."

"What?"

"Lumping all the Sabers."

"So how are you all different, Britt Saber?"

"Oh, Kairee," he said with a laugh, "there are more differences than similarities. We're . . . we're three men on whom nature played an immense joke by making us blood relatives."

"So tell me about this joke, Britt," she said gently, sensing something fragile that must not be broken. "Let me see if it's really funny."

He stopped walking and looked down into the smokey, elusive blue-gray of her eyes. He searched for a long time.

"You really want to know, don't you?"

"Yes . . . I really do."

"Suppose we give these horses a rest and go sit under those trees. It's a long, long story."

"All right."

When they found a spot for the horses to drink, they loosened the girths of the saddles and tethered them so they would not wander. Then they walked to a small stand of aspens and found a seat beneath one.

They remained in comfortable silence for several minutes, Kairee still caught by the vast beauty of the country and Britt caught by the picture she made with the mountains behind her and the sun kissing her hair into gold fire. Then she turned to look at him again and smiled. "I'm sorry. I was drifting."

"That's all right. I was enjoying the scenery too."

"You were going to tell me a story about nature's devious ways, weren't you?"

"I said it's a long story, but I guess it's really not. My father came out here about twenty-eight or -nine years ago. To tell you the truth, I don't know why . . . or even from where. Something happened. I don't have the answer to that either, but I thought I was close a time or two when I had his friend Jim drunk enough to talk. Either Jim was careful, or scared to talk, but anyway Pa married and had Damion." His eyes grew introspective and Kairee suddenly felt that Britt was somewhere else.

"Damion," he said softly. "He must have loved Damion's mother . . . anyway, she died. After awhile he decided he needed more land and more water, so he married my mother. I'm not sure he'll ever forgive her for having me. You see, it was only the land and water he bargained for, not a half-breed son to share the empire he planned on building for his white son.

"My Indian mother should have known better. Maybe she did, maybe she finally understood, because she left him and went back to her people. My father decided I should stay with him and the law said he was right. So now I stand with one foot in one world and one foot in the other."

"But you're both your father's sons. One day you'll

share the Circle S, won't you?"

Britt's mouth twitched in a lopsided grin. "I have a feeling that's what Damion believes too. But no matter what he lets Damion think, I have a feeling I know my father . . . maybe better than Damion does."

"Is it that you know and understand him, Britt," Kairee asked softly, "or has your mother twisted your mind?"

Now Britt laughed, but the laugh was uncertain. "Would you believe that my mother has never said a word against my father? I think she still loves him. I don't understand how she could have been betrayed like that and still love him, but she does."

Damion seemed to leap into Kairee's thoughts. How could a woman love a man who did not want her? The thought frightened her and she forced it from her mind. She did not care a whit for Damion Saber. He was a dangerous man, a man who could capture a woman's heart, then crush it as casually as he took a breath. He would be like mercury, elusive and unable to be tamed. Despite her efforts, she was surprised at her next words.

"And Damion, does he understand your father?"

"Damion and Pa . . . well, they're different, and yet they're a lot alike. Damion's as hard and strong as Pa, maybe in some ways even stronger. He'll hold the Circle S, all right, and probably build it into the empire Pa seems to want. I just wonder sometimes if it's what Damion wants or—"

"Or if he loves his father as much as you do and is trying in the only way he knows how to be what he wants," Kairee added quietly.

For a minute Britt remained silent, then he laughed again. "I didn't bring you out here to talk about my brother or my problems. You're easy to talk to, Kairee, but I'd rather talk about something more interesting, like you."

"Me?" She smiled. "There's nothing much to talk about. There's me, Gregg, Pa, and Gregg's family. We had some difficulties and now we're starting over again. When Uncle Rob left us the ranch, it was like a godsend."

"I'd say for all of us. You're the prettiest thing to come to this territory in a long time."

"And you have a smooth tongue." She laughed.

"I speak only the truth, Kairee." His voice was warm and his eyes caressing. "I'd like to get to know you better . . . to be friends."

"Is that possible, Britt? What about Damion and your father?"

"Back to Damion again," he replied. He was smiling, but she sensed again the deep current just below the surface.

"I'm just curious about his . . . their reaction."

"I think you know what it will be."

"And I think they should know by now what ours is."

"By now . . . obviously you and Damion have locked horns again."

He watched her cheeks pinken and her eyes drop from his, and he knew the confrontation had been a lot more than she meant to admit. The sharp taste of jealousy surprised him and annoyed him. He was Britt Saber, well used to having any woman he set his mind on.

The jealousy was accompanied by an emotion he did not want to recognize. It grated along his nerves and he could taste the bitterness on his tongue.

Damion! Always Damion! And always the Circle S, as if there were nothing in the world that came before it.

His curiosity about what had truly happened between his half brother and Kairee was something he had great difficulty containing. To condemn Damion was not the way to battle whatever effect their meeting might have had on her, but the words of anger and

102

frustration were there and he could barely suppress them.

"Your brother . . . Damion—the Circle *S* is the most important thing in his life, isn't it?"

Her question was both cautious and quiet, but he knew she was listening intently for his answer.

"I told you, Kairee, Damion is a lot like Pa, and the Circle *S* is one thing about which they feel the same." What Britt said next would touch Kairee in a way he could not understand. "Pa bred sons for the purpose of starting something, and that something is supposed to mean more to us than anything else. For Damion . . . well, Pa has the son he wants. For me"—he shrugged—"filling his shoes is more than . . . well, maybe more than I care to do. If I marry, if I have children, I don't want them to think they have to fit into my mold. I'd rather see them happy."

"And Damion," she whispered, "will expect his children to . . ."

"To fit into the Saber mold. I feel sorry for any of them. It's too big a mold, too much to give."

He looked at Kairee again, intently studying her face. Then to keep the conversation from growing into something he could not handle, he laughed. "No more talk about Damion. I'd rather concentrate on you. In a couple of weeks there's a big cattleman's meeting up in Buffalo. I'm sure every rancher in the territory will be there. There's a lot of celebrating. It'll be fun, Kairee, and I'd like to share it with you."

"Pa doesn't know about it . . . and I'm not too sure he could afford to go."

"I could—" He stopped speaking the moment her eyes snapped up to meet his. "Ah . . . sorry." He chuckled as he raised his hands as if to ward off an attack. "I didn't mean to say that."

She laughed with him and he felt a surge of desire so strong he could no longer control it. He bent and kissed

103

her. It was a sensitive yet uncomplicated kiss.

Kairee was at first taken by surprise, then a darker thought held her. Could she wipe Damion's memory away with another's touch? She allowed the kiss to deepen and felt his arms come about her and pull her close to him.

Suddenly she realized the unfairness of her actions. She was not reaching for Britt; she was reaching for Damion.

She put both hands against his chest to move them apart. She could read clearly in his eyes that Britt had been shaken by the swift encounter. His gaze was warm and he held himself in deliberate control.

"Please . . . Britt, I think I had best go back."

"Kairee . . ."

"No Britt, we . . . we can't say anything. Not now. You don't know me, and I don't know if I could . . . please, Britt, just take me back."

"Not angry, Kairee. I wouldn't want you upset. I want to see a lot more of you, Kairee Kennedy. I want to get to know you."

"I don't want to be the cause of trouble."

"The trouble was here long before you came."

"I need to think, Britt."

"I'm not pushing you, Kairee." He smiled quickly. "But I'll be around. You can count on it."

They rode home, doing their best to keep the conversation on a more comfortable plane. But Kairee was filled with a tumultuous storm. Despite Britt's gentle touch and her own wild need to wipe Damion from her mind, she could still feel the brand of Damion's hungry mouth on her and the touch of his hands that had brought her body to life.

She drew her determination before her like a shield. One way or another she would cut the Sabers from her life.

Chapter 8

Kairee had been home less than an hour when her father came into the house. He was tired from the heavy labor of cutting trees, but he was smiling.

"Kairee! Lucy! Cassie! Gregg and the boys are heading in with the herd. I just spotted them from the hill."

Excitement ruled the Kennedy ranch for the balance of the day and through a long evening filled with stories of the trip told by Smokey and Rusty. It was only afterward, as the long shadows of evening closed about them, that Stephen explained to Smokey and Rusty the situation they found themselves in.

"I'd understand if you boys rode on. I don't want any trouble here. But"—he put his arm about Kairee who sat nearby—"we have reached a point where we will not run again. Our backs are to the wall and we intend to stand here."

Both Smokey and Rusty were silent for awhile and the looks they exchanged indicated an understanding beyond what any of the others could fathom.

"Range war," Rusty said quietly.

"I hope not," Stephen said. "It will take a lot to force me into a fight. I want to live in peace."

"How big is this Circle S outfit?" Smokey questioned.

"Big," Gregg answered.

"How big?" Smokey forced the question.

"Smokey," Stephen said, "their ranch is more than six times ours, and they have a small army of men."

"Jesus!" Smokey grated. "Sorry, ma'am." He nodded toward Lucy. "What do you expect to do against a crowd like that?"

"Live in peace," Stephen replied. "It takes two to make a fight. The law is on my side and I have no intention of drawing a gun against them and giving them an excuse to do battle. We just won't fight."

"Mr. Kennedy," Rusty said gently, "I was down on the Pecos in the middle of the River City range war. It ain't pretty, and outfits like the Circle S, they don't seem to mind if you draw a gun or not. If they've set their mind to pushing us to a fight, then they'll push 'til you have to pick up a gun or crawl. I don't crawl for no man."

"Rusty, I don't expect you to crawl, but if you don't use your gun, then they can't. I ask you boys to give it a try. But you don't owe us anything. You're free to go if you want to."

Smokey laughed softly and in a second or two his laugh was joined by Rusty's.

"We don't owe him anything!" Smokey declared.

"No . . . nothin' at all," Rusty echoed, "unless, of course, you'd say our lives were worth something."

"Not much," Smokey choked out, "but it's the only one I've got and I'm fond of it."

"Me too," Rusty answered. "Reckon we ought to run, Smokey?"

"Reckon I don't. Reckon I'll stand here."

"Then I guess I stand too." Rusty looked at Stephen and his smile grew ever broader. "It looks, Mr. Kennedy, as if you still got us on your hands for a while longer."

"I'm grateful," Stephen said softly.

"No more grateful than the rest of us, Pa," Kairee said as she reached across the table to put her hand on Smokey's. "You're part of this family, and none of us will ever forget what you're doing for us."

Smokey suddenly seemed flustered. He searched for words to explain the way he felt, but found none. His sentiments were echoed in Rusty, who felt as if he had come home from a long journey.

Kairee found her blankets more comfortable that night with the security of two supporters near. Yet when she sought sleep, her mind began to reach. In the darkness she tried to fight the battle of forgetfulness and lost.

They stood near, the Saber men, each in his own way a force that tormented her: Elliot Saber, with the strange reaction she had read in his eyes when he saw her; Britt Saber, with his subtle furies and his gentle touch; Damion Saber—Damion, who had touched her with a blinding force and had left her forever changed.

She had to keep them from her mind. She had to force them from her life. But at this moment she had no idea how.

Britt whistled lightly through his teeth as he finished dressing. He felt exuberant, and the reason was Kairee Kennedy.

He had been thinking of her from the moment he had left her, and he hurried now to dress, hoping to leave the house before his father or Damion found something for him to do.

But his timing was bad and he cursed to himself when he left his room and walked down the hall only to come face to face with both Elliot and Damion on their way to breakfast.

"Mornin', Britt," Elliot said sharply. "Come on into breakfast. There's a problem and we have to talk about it."

Britt felt his heart thud harshly. The last thing he wanted was to be tied to his father or his brother today. He had plans to ask Kairee to ride to the village with him and meet his mother.

"Pa, I've got—"

"Got what? More plans to disappear for a day or two? Well, change them. This is something important."

He walked away, expecting Britt to follow. Britt exchanged a cold glance with a very curious Damion. "I suppose you've cooked up something special for me today, Damion," he spat.

"Britt, this is a real problem."

"What is it?"

"Twenty head were run off last night."

"Rustlers?"

"Sure."

"Pa has suspicions?" Britt asked, but he knew the answer before it came.

"He thinks the Kennedys have started something. He's fired up today like I've never seen him. From all I can get out of him, he rode over there the other day. I don't know what happened, but . . ."

"But what?"

"He's been drinking."

"Pa?"

"Last night I went to his room to talk to him. He was drunk—passed out on the bed dead drunk. He was mumbling a name, sounded like Emily or Emma. I don't know. But he sure as hell is tied up in knots. I warn you that it's best not to push him today."

"Damn," Britt muttered.

108

"You were going someplace special?"

"Special . . . ah . . . no, not really. Come on, let's go talk to Pa."

Damion gazed after Britt's retreating figure. He was completely certain Britt was lying and this took him totally by surprise. Britt might taunt and torment, but he never lied. He wondered why he had the uncomfortable feeling he wouldn't like the reason if he knew it.

Slowly he followed Britt to the table to join their father.

Nestled against the low range at the foot of the Big Horn Mountains, the weather-beaten house looked at first glance as if it might be deserted. But several horses moving about in the corrals and a fine wisp of smoke gave evidence of human presence.

Within the house four men sat around a table. They were playing cards, but the atmosphere was one of expectation, as if they were waiting for something.

They all seemed to react with new alertness as the sound of an approaching horse was heard. In a few minutes the door opened and a man walked in.

"Boys," the man said with a pleased grin, "how's it going?"

"Fine, boss," one man answered. "We hazed off about twenty head or so. Got the iron to 'em and we're holdin' 'em up in a box canyon."

"Circle *S* steers?"

"Yep."

"You branded 'em down on the Kennedy range?"

"Just like you said, boss. Anybody nosing around is gonna get real suspicious of the Kennedys and the Jacobses. They won't be able to prove nothin', but it will sure keep their minds off us."

The four men who sat at the table had obvious respect for the man who had just come in. But it was grudging respect tinged with distrust and fear. He sensed he held them by a force they could not fight, and he was more than a little sure the force was profit.

The newcomer was a tall man, his six-foot body heavily muscled. His eyes in his tanned face were almost a colorless blue, and as frigid as the mountain peaks behind them. They were eyes that could freeze a man with the mesmerizing effect of a deadly snake.

His hair was almost silver-white and it too seemed an almost unacceptable interruption of nature. It was as if Mother Nature had begun to color him and then had forgotten somewhere along the line to finish her work.

"Good job," he said. "I want you to ride down to Stone's camp and tell them to run the bunch they've got up to Fort McKinney. Keep them under close watch and tell one of them to ride into the fort and talk to Richard Docherty. He'll buy all they've got. Then come back here and lay low for awhile. I'll send you word when I want you to move again."

As if to prove the effect he had on them, all four men rose, disregarding the card game in which they had been involved, and began to make preparations to leave.

"I'll be in contact with you boys soon. Don't get into any trouble with anyone and keep those guns in your holsters. I don't want any attention on you, especially from Elliot's two boys."

"Okay, boss. By the way, I crossed paths with the Saber boy. You know, the half-breed one."

"Yeah?"

"That boy's got a burr under his blanket. He always looks like he's ready to explode. Anyway, I was listenin' to him talk. He was drinkin' some and he was talkin' to old man Jacobs and Samuel McGruder.

Askin' if they was losin' heads too. He ain't one to mess with."

"What's your point, Magee?"

"We got a couple of renegades ridin' with the other bunch. You think they might spill something to him when he's visiting that Indian ma of his."

"Better talk to them, McGee. Caution them that I don't stand for mistakes and I don't pay for them. If we keep the Sabers' attention on some of the other ranchers, I don't think they'll be looking for you."

"I rode out to look over those Kennedys the other day."

"And?"

"Puny bunch. Ain't got much. But the gal, Kairee's her name, she's a looker."

"Stay away from there, Magee."

"I ain't botherin' them . . . just lookin' is all."

"Keep that in mind. I don't want your yen for some girl bringing them down on us."

"Okay boss, okay."

"You boys ride out now. Make sure you travel without being spotted. I'll meet you here again in about three weeks. We got a lot to do before the snow flies and you lay up for the winter."

They moved quickly, and in less than an hour they were four retreating specks in the distance.

He stood and watched, then he smiled in grim satisfaction, strode to his horse, mounted, and rode away.

For the first time in a long while Britt and Damion were riding together. But they rode in a silence that would have clearly told anyone that they had been forced into it by a situation beyond their control. They rode slowly, bent slightly forward in the saddle to examine the ground.

It was the second day they had ridden so, but the telltale signs they sought continued to elude them.

Finally it was Britt who drew his horse to a stop, then Damion did the same.

"Twenty head and no sign of them," Britt grumbled. "Might be a good idea if we were to split up. We could circle around by the river and meet back here."

"That will take us along the line between the Talbot place, the Barber place . . . and the Kennedys," Damion said thoughtfully.

"Well, we can count out the Talbot place. Talbot doesn't even own any cattle. He's a smart man just sticking to raising horses. That way he's got no quarrel out here."

"Yeah," Damion said, "he's smart. But he might have seen something, or they might be crossing his land. Better check on Talbot, Britt, then cross over to Barber's ranch. I'll go down the creek and check on the Kennedy place."

"Why don't we just do what Pa ordered," Britt said casually. "We'll check them out . . . together."

Damion pressed his lips together firmly but did not argue. His attempt to control Britt's movement had been obvious and he had no intention of fighting about it while there was still some semblance of peace between them. He nodded. "Let's go."

The long, hot day did not bring answers. Whoever had run off the cattle had made a good job of it.

Mitchell Talbot, as far as the Sabers knew, was interested in his horses as deeply as Elliot was in his cattle. He was proud of his stock and bragged often that he raised the best horses in the territory. And they were. The Sabers had bought horses from Talbot for several years and had never been disappointed.

His ranch was very small in comparison to the Circle *S*, but it was enough to keep his horses.

The Sabers bordered the Kennedy ranch on the north and Mitchell Talbot's ranch formed the eastern border. As Britt and Damion rode across the boundaries, neither had their minds totally on the search they were making. Both were too well aware of the short distance to the Kennedy ranch.

As they crested a hill, they looked down at a rolling meadow in which grazed a small herd of horses.

"Damn nice-looking stock Talbot runs," Britt remarked. "Look at that chestnut. I wouldn't mind having that beauty."

"Too damn beautiful to have no one around to protect them," Damion offered. "He's taking quite a chance ranging them this far out, especially if we have someone who doesn't look too closely at people's brands."

"Rider coming," Britt announced.

"Where?"

Britt pointed some distance away to a rider moving slowly toward the Talbot ranch.

"Who is it?" Britt asked. He squinted into the sun, seeking the rider's identity.

Damion knew who it was. There was not a doubt in his mind. It was as if he could feel her. The rider was Kairee. But why was she going to see Mitchell Talbot, a man who lived alone? It stirred questions in his mind that he had no intention of verbalizing for Britt.

Damion shrugged, declaring, "I don't see any trails around here to follow. We're wasting valuable time we could be spending doing the work we left to go on this wild goose chase."

"Yeah, maybe you're right. If someone deliberately hazed those cows away, they sure didn't come along here."

"Maybe the boys have had better luck than we had. Come on, let's go back."

They turned their horses about, but Damion could not resist another look. He turned to watch the figure in the meadow disappear into a stand of tall aspens. He would have given anything to have been free to ride down to talk to her, but as it had all his life, the Circle *S* and his father called him back.

"But we need at least half a dozen more horses, Kairee," Smokey said firmly. "We can't just run these into the ground."

"Where are we supposed to get them, Smokey?" Kairee asked. They were walking from the half-finished bunkhouse toward the main house. "And where are we supposed to get the money to buy them if we find someone who wants to sell them?"

"Rider came by yesterday was tellin' me there's a ranch borders ours to the east. Name's Talbot. Anyway, he's not a cattleman. He raises horses. Prime stock, I'm told."

"Well, Smokey what are we supposed to do, ride over and ask him to give us a few? Maybe we'll just promise to pay him someday, when we're as big as the Sabers."

"No, Miss Kairee." He laughed. "I don't expect he'd take to that too easy. What I was thinkin', though, is you might pay him a sort of neighborly visit. Maybe see if he needs any help with anything, help he might be willing to trade something for. And that something might be a pony or two."

"You are a very clever man, Smokey. I might just take that little ride, if you wouldn't mind saddling my horse and pointing me in the right direction."

"That will surely be my pleasure. Yessir, it surely

will," Smokey answered.

Gregg, his father, and the balance of the men were engrossed in the repairs on the barn and a small bunkhouse for the four men. Wyoming winters, according to Smokey, who had traversed Wyoming before, were more than severe and the houses had to be made as winterproof as possible. Kairee's room would be the last addition.

Kairee felt it would be much simpler if she spoke to Talbot first and then told her father. That way if she was unable to get any horses, Stephen would not have to receive another disappointment.

Kairee had fallen in love with the land about them almost from the first day. It would be a struggle, but she believed that if they could endure through the first winter, they would survive. She refused to allow the thought in her mind that winter might be easier to overcome than the Sabers.

She rode slowly, knowing such rare and beautiful days were slipping by fast, and she concentrated only on the pleasure she found. She had no idea that she was being observed.

It was quite a distance between the Talbot ranch and hers and she had to rest her horse several times, but she knew she was close when she ran across small, clustered herds of horses.

She realized immediately that they were of excellent quality. If there was a way to exchange something in return for at least two of these prime animals, she intended to find it.

The ranch house was small and seemed to be deserted when she rode up. To her eye, the square house could not have contained more than four rooms, and her curiosity was stirred by thoughts of the family who lived in such close quarters.

She dismounted and walked to the front door and

knocked. There was no answer. She knocked again. It seemed there was no one home.

She walked down the three front steps and crossed the wide yard to the barn. As she came closer, she noticed that the door stood open.

It was impossible to see when she stepped from the bright sunlight into the dimly lit barn. She hardly had time to adjust her eyes when a voice came from its recesses.

"Well, you're a new face around here."

He seemed to step out of a pool of blackness. The effect was startling, for his hair caught a ray of light through a crack in the wall and it was a white glow in the darkness. As he walked toward her, she was touched by a surprising urge to turn and run.

"I'm Kairee Kennedy. We have the land that borders on yours."

He smiled, and she realized he was handsome. But still something resistant echoed within her.

"Good afternoon, Kairee Kennedy. I'm Mitchell Talbot. I know you and your family just moved in a short while ago. I've been meaning to ride over and be a bit more neighborly, but my best mare is having a problem."

"Oh, can I help?"

"Well, I think I've done all I can for now."

"What happened?"

"A bear got her foal, and she was trying to protect it and got herself clawed. I lost the foal. I'd sure hate to lose her too, but she's been torn up pretty bad. What can I do for you?"

"Oh, I was just paying a neighborly visit. But I'm going to send Smokey over. He's one of my hands and he's got a magic touch with horses."

"Well, that's kind of you, Kairee. It looks like I'm going to have a friendly neighbor."

"That's what neighbors are for."

His eyes were assessing her shrewdly. "Welcome to the valley, neighbor. I have a feeling we're going to get along just fine, though I'd bet you haven't been welcomed too well around here."

"What makes you say that?"

He laughed. "I've lived here for five years or so. I think I know all the ranchers hereabouts."

"We don't want to infringe on anybody's life or land, but we're going to stay here and build our ranch too."

"And the Sabers aren't giving you any trouble? I think they've been using your range for a long time."

"Well, they'll have to get used to the fact that they won't be using it any longer. If we have to, we'll fence it."

"That's never been done out here. You'd make a lot of enemies."

"Where do you stand, Mr. Talbot?"

"Mitchell."

She smiled and nodded her acceptance of this.

"I chose, when I first came here, not to run any cattle. I'm a horse breeder by affection, and a man who hates trouble. I'm no threat to any of the ranchers and I supply the horses they need. We get along well, but even I wouldn't attempt to fence my range."

"We don't want to give anyone any trouble. We just want to be left alone."

"Have you met the other ranchers yet?"

"No . . . just a couple of the Sabers," she said dryly.

"The old man is like a she bear with cubs when it comes to his place. I wouldn't string a fence around him and his boys if you don't want trouble."

"How does anybody fight the Sabers?"

"Nobody does. The Sabers cast a long shadow. A smart rancher would just do his best to stay out of it."

"Well, thanks for your advice and the warning." She

117

smiled. "Come over and meet my family."

"I will, thank you."

"And I'll send Smokey over to see if he can help with your mare."

"Thank you again." He laughed. "I will be in your debt. She's one of my best breeders. What can I do to repay you?"

"Don't worry about it. Someday we might need something."

"Well, it's yours."

"Good-bye Mr. . . . Mitchell. Thank you again."

"It's been my pleasure to meet you."

He watched her walk to her horse and ride away. There was a glow in his crystal eyes that might have shaken Kairee a great deal had she seen it.

When Kairee disappeared over the horizon, Mitchell Talbot walked back in the barn. He continued ministering to the injured mare, but his mind was on the smiling gray eyes of Kairee Kennedy, and how he could make use of the situation between her and the Sabers. Such speculation and a small touch of desire began to grow in the fertile ground of his thoughts.

Chapter 9

Damion heard very little of Britt's conversation as they started back to the ranch. He could not wipe away the single thought that plagued him, an inane, inconsequential thought that made absolutely no sense at all.

Kairee had looked so small and defenseless riding across the breadth of the valley alone. What was worse was that he had had to restrain himself with a great deal of effort to keep from riding down and warning her again of how vulnerable she was. He would have laughed if he hadn't felt so damn defenseless himself.

They were nearly a helpless group against his father's force. He knew it, and he knew they knew it too.

He had been an instrument of his father's will for a long time. He had always thought, all this time, that he wanted what his father wanted—to see the Circle *S* be the biggest and the best. But now he suddenly felt uncertain. How far could it go? How far would he allow it to go?

Why did she have to be so damn stubborn? he asked himself. How easy it would be. There was plenty of land beyond the Big Horns. They could live in peace there . . . only, damnit, he didn't want her to leave

119

either. He wanted . . . a way out of the dilemma.

". . . and so we ought to hit the river where they might cross and . . . Damion?"

"Huh . . . what?"

"It isn't much of an idea, but if you can come up with something better, I'd be grateful. If we run back to Pa and tell him we didn't cover every inch of this land, he'll be hoppin' mad."

"Maybe you've got a good idea, Britt, but I still think we ought to split up. You go down by the river and I'll swing around and try the edge of the bluffs. We can put things together later to see if we come up with anything."

"Sounds good. I'll meet you later."

Britt swung his horse away from the path they were on, but for several minutes Damion sat on his horse and watched Britt disappear.

With slow and deliberate movements, he swung his horse around and headed back in the direction he had come.

Kairee had crossed the valley on the way to Mitchell Talbot's. She would cross it again on the way home and he would be there. He tried to convince himself that it was to try to convince her to change her plans, but he could not blind himself to the fact that he wanted to see her again.

Kairee was pleased with the idea that she had made at least one friend in the valley. She smiled to herself as she thought of Smokey's idea—deliberately charming a neighbor so that one day they might be able to strike a deal about horses. At least it seemed to be working so far. Now, she thought gleefully, if Smokey would agree to ride over and help with the injured horse, they might just be able to—how had Smokey put it?—

120

swing a deal.

The horse picked its way delicately across the valley and Kairee rode without concentrating on where she was. Deep in thought, she let the horse go his own way, knowing he knew well where food and water lay.

She passed through a stand of aspens and started across the sloping meadow to the valley floor. Then her attention was drawn to a circular area in the midst of the grass that was darkened as if it had been burned. Her curiosity was aroused and she rode toward it.

When she drew her horse to a halt, she was looking down on what had once been a rather large fire. In fact, spirals of grey-white smoke still rose from it.

What Kairee did not know was that a lookout for the rustlers, having spotted her approach, had warned the men who were branding mavericks that belonged to the Circle *S*. They had left quickly, throwing some dirt on the fire to extinguish it.

She dismounted and walked to the smoldering remains. It was only then that she noticed the object projecting from the midst of the blackened wood. It was a branding iron.

Kairee bent to grasp the iron and withdrew it from the embers. It was still hot, and she thought at first it had been broken. Then on closer examination the truth struck her.

It was only a straight length of iron with a curved tip, a tip that could be used for only one purpose—to alter another brand.

The quick realization came that she had interrupted rustlers at work. But whose cattle were they branding? They were on her property and she knew what this would look like to the Sabers should they be searching for such evidence. The Kennedys would look guilty.

She wanted to cool the iron enough to carry it home and show it to her father. If they took this evidence to the Sabers, it might just be the step that would help heal the breach between them.

She layed the iron in the grass and ran to her saddle to get her canteen of water. Opening it while she walked back to the iron, she knelt beside it. Slowly she poured the water over it. It hissed and steam rose, but slowly the iron became cool enough to touch.

She took the scarf from around her neck and wrapped the iron carefully.

It was only then that a soft, insinuating voice from behind her made her breath catch.

"Hello, Kairee."

She spun around and came face to face with Damion Saber. His sardonic smile and the look in his eyes told her exactly what he was thinking.

Damion had waited beneath the aspen trees in a spot that was carefully chosen so she would not see him in time to change directions.

His mind was set. He would try his best to make some kind of peace with Kairee. Doing so might be the only way to reach beyond her barriers and convince her to think logically. She must understand that this affair could end in disaster.

He watched as she rode through the edge of the stand of aspens and he was about to mount his horse and follow when he saw her rein to a halt. Had she seen him? No, she was looking at something else. It seemed to be something she was purposely looking for, because she dismounted and walked toward it as if she had known exactly what she would find.

He watched closely and saw her bend to pick something up. In a moment of utter shock he recognized it—a running iron.

Now he watched her, hoping to understand what

part she had in what must have occurred here in the past few hours.

He saw her go to her horse for the canteen and deliberately cool the iron. Of course, he thought. Someone she knew had been foolish enough to leave evidence behind and she was going to remove it.

He walked from the shadow of the trees and she was so engrossed in what she was doing she did not hear his approach until he spoke.

"Hello, Kairee."

She whirled about, shock written clearly in her eyes.

"Damion!" she gasped.

"Did I interrupt some serious business? What happened Kairee, some of your men forget and leave the evidence behind? It's a good thing you came along to clean up after them."

Kairee looked at what seemed to be incriminating evidence in her hand, then back at Damion and her gray eyes sparked with defensive anger.

"You don't honestly believe this belongs to me!"

"Why else would you be taking such good care of it? I'm pretty sure it wasn't meant to be left behind."

He walked closer to her and Kairee tipped her head to hold his gaze. She would be damned if she would allow him to back her down, even if the overpowering maleness of him tingled along her nerves and made her senses begin to swim.

"How do I know it wasn't your own men who left this for the purpose of trapping someone so you could make everyone believe it was us?"

"Don't be stupid, Kairee." He laughed. "The Sabers don't have to resort to tricks. We can catch a rustler without anybody's help."

"And a Saber accusation is enough, isn't it?" she asked coldly. "Once the Sabers point the finger, it's obvious whoever they point it at is guilty. Is that the way you keep all the other ranchers around here on their knees? Are they all afraid of the Sabers?"

"We don't want anybody afraid of us. We just want them to respect what belongs to us."

"Like you respect what belongs to someone else."

She watched his eyes narrow and he moved even closer. Still she stood her ground.

"Listen to me, Kairee," he said urgently, "I'll bury this damn running iron. I'll forget I ever saw it. Only try to understand that there could be an explosion around here that could hurt a lot of people."

"Not if the Sabers don't want one."

"What's that supposed to mean?"

"It means that I know just how much control the Sabers have. I know that it's you and your family who do the pushing, and I know that if you and your family decide to leave us alone and let us live here no one is going to bother us. I know that it would be very easy for you to make this look like we did something wrong—in fact, I think you've done just that, only I'm not going to let you get away with it."

He watched the defiant anger sparkle in her eyes, saw the rise and fall of her breasts against the fabric of her blouse, and in her voice he heard the fear of a woman who faced a battle she could not afford to lose.

What startled him more than anything else was the blaze of raw desire that suddenly seemed to fill him, and he knew with a fatal certainty that he had carried the taste of her with him from the first time they had been together, carried it like a searing wound deep inside him—wanting her, wanting to erase her from his mind and knowing somehow deep inside that he couldn't.

They were standing inches apart, and her voice died as she finally saw through her own rage. She saw the flame dance in the depths of his eyes and it was like watching the approach of a ravenous predator. She felt her breath suddenly catch. Words died on her lips, then deserted her mind as he reached to touch her cheek.

She raised her hand to brush him away. "Don't."

"Scared now, Kairee . . . scared enough to run?"

"You'll never make me run, Damion Saber," she said frigidly. "This time I'm not afraid of you."

"You're wrong, Kairee. This is something I don't understand, but you should be afraid."

His voice was soft and she could feel the warmth of his body close to hers. An alarm echoed deep inside her, a warning that they were caught in something that was beyond their understanding—beyond all reserves of resistance either might have.

He reached out and put his hands on her waist, drawing her body against his. He bent his head and their lips barely touched. The contest began with the gentlest look as he lifted his head and their eyes met again. Each searched for something that the other could not afford to reveal.

His arms tightened about her and this time his mouth sought hers in a kiss so heated she felt as if her lips were aflame.

"This is insanity," he grated in a harsh, panting whisper. "I know that, but damn your beautiful soul, I can't wipe you out of my mind. I tried to be rid of you. I tried . . . God . . ."

Before she could utter a protest, his lips silenced hers.

Slowly, slowly, like the lightly falling leaves in their colorful splendor, they fell to the soft grass.

Passion caught them in a grip that obliterated their surroundings, their barriers, and their control.

They kissed wildly, feverishly, his open mouth hot and hard against hers, parting the softness of her lips to thrust boldly with his tongue, to taste deeply, searchingly.

The search was answered by her soft moan and the intensity of her mouth as it returned the seeking avidly.

Pride, resolve, anger, all were being destroyed by the waves of uncontrolled passion that washed over them. They crumbled like dunes of sand against the onslaught of the ocean.

She felt his hands as they moved over her. The magic of his touch seemed to send shards of sensation through her as he pushed aside the fabric of her blouse and his lips tasted the warmth of her flesh.

The scent of her, the softness of her, drove him wild with a need he had never experienced before, a need to possess completely, to find the depths of her, the very center.

His mouth fit so perfectly to hers, and with slow, gentle movements of his tongue he melted her lips until they flowed apart beneath his.

The tremor that went through her was echoed in him, heating his blood to a demanding level. She shivered and drank in his presence, wordlessly telling him of the sensual pleasure growing within her.

His hands slid upward, brushing the firm swell of her breasts, lingering, learning the satin curves, seducing her nipples into a tightness that inflamed him as much as her ragged moan.

His lips moved with slow heat across the taut skin of her throat. Her head tipped back and her eyes closed as she abandoned herself to these marvelous sensations.

His lips found the soft curve of her breast and drifted over it, then closed with melting gentleness over her nipple. She shivered and arched into the caress, knowing nothing now but the pleasure he gave her. A blind hunger made her want to cry out in anguish and fierce delight. The world fell away, leaving only Kairee and Damion and her soft cries of ecstasy filling the empty blue sky.

She rubbed her hands across his chest to curve them over his shoulders, savoring the hard heat of his flesh, massaging his strength with rhythms of passion.

His fingertips grazed the smoothness of her inner thighs and gently stroked the liquid heat beneath the burnished blond curls.

Eyes closed, Kairee could only feel the fluid pulsations uncoiling deep inside her body.

For long moments he savored this exploration of her sensitive recesses, drinking in each soft cry, each hot shivering of her tender flesh.

His fingers traced each hollow and curve of her until she was twisting, her hips blindly seeking. She cried out and he drank the cries with hungry lips and found he was lost in the intense sweetness and excitement his touch summoned from her.

Kairee moaned as muscles deep inside her body tensed and relaxed, the wildness gathering and melting through her in shimmering waves. She could feel the waiting strength coiled in his muscular body. His hips moved against hers, telling her how deep was his need.

They met, seared, joined in a long, inflaming caress. He moved with aching care, lifting her beyond reason. He fit her perfectly. Hot and moist, her body arched to meet each demanding thrust until she was blinded to all but the sensual pleasure that blossomed like an opening flower. It grew and grew until it coursed its way to her very core, sending passionate convulsions rippling through her, and the shock waves of completion shattered her, leaving her clinging to the only solid thing in a world filled with an explosion of a million stars.

Her breathing was a ragged gasp that matched the harshness of his as they tumbled without control back into the world of cold reality.

Slowly Kairee became aware. The soft sound of a bird's call, the scent of wildflowers and soft grass, drew her back to a realization that stung her eyes with the heat of tears.

Damion lifted his head to hold her eyes with his. He saw the tears glistening on her lashes, the softness of her skin, the tangled mass of her hair.

Kairee saw the sheen of perspiration on the bronze of his skin and the shadows of near disbelief in the sky blue of his eyes.

Against the breadth of the blue Wyoming sky he suddenly seemed a deity of nature, strong and virile.

Slowly he withdrew and turned to lie beside her. It was one moment that bridged the gap between fantasy and reality, for both knew this explosive thing that existed between them was something they could not control, something as dangerous as it was magnificently beautiful.

There were so many things he wanted to say, but the futility of words was underscored by a new awareness in her eyes.

All her promises to herself lay broken at her feet, smashed to minute splinters along with her will and her pride. She had succumbed to the wild, mysterious hold his touch seemed to have over her, and self-recrimination flayed her nerves raw.

He heard the dry sob she tried to control and drew in his breath, searching for words. He turned on his side and reached an arm about her to turn her to face him.

Kairee's mind struggled in turmoil. No answers came to the surface. She was afraid to plunge into the turbulent depths because of what she might find there.

For this long moment she was still somewhat awed by her total awareness and her knowledge that this was an impossible situation.

"Kairee, you have to believe that when I came here I never intended this to happen. I don't want to hurt you . . . I never meant to hurt you."

"But, of course," she concluded bitterly for him, "I must understand that the Sabers always take what they want, even if it's just a moment's fling."

"I don't exactly recall your fighting me very hard," he snapped, stung that she considered what had happened a part of a game she had lost, as if he had taken something and rendered it valueless.

Her cheeks grew heated. "Would it have done me any good to have tried? I cannot see Damion Saber allowing such resistance without calling it a challenge."

"You're lying to yourself."

"And you're lying to both of us if you think this will solve anything. I won't say that I understand any of the Sabers. You're all dark, hard men who demand everything of others. Are you and your brother cut from the same cloth as your land-hungry father?"

It whipped through him like a bolt of lightning, a jealousy that tasted bitter on his tongue. Britt!

"Why do you ask?" he ground out with the angry desire to hurt. "Have you tried any other Sabers? Did I start something that you found you wanted more of? How is my half brother, by the way, as good as I've heard the other . . . ladies say he is?"

Kairee gasped at the sudden blow of his words, then her eyes filled with rage. She twisted from his arms and he let her go, controlling the urge to keep her close to him and kiss her into submission, to ravage her until she could not think of Britt anymore. He refused to recognize his own emotions by submerging them in a black cauldron of jealousy.

"You're on my land now, Damion," she cried as she gathered her blouse about her, and he was certain he would never be able to wipe the vision of her face from his mind. She stood with the sun turning her to burnished gold, her eyes like the dark clouds of a summer storm. "So I'm warning you. Get off it. Don't come near me again. It's long past the time to teach you and your illustrious family a lesson. We wouldn't leave this land now no matter what you offer or what you threaten."

"Nobody has threatened you. Can't you see I'm just trying to do what's best for you too? If you start a range war, I can tell you that the Circle *S* can end it. You can't win, Kairee. Why not convince your family to go before someone gets hurt?"

"I won't honor your foul thoughts with a denial you won't believe. I will only tell you for the last time, we won't run. And I will give orders, and carry them out myself if I have to. If you trespass on our land again, you're to be driven off. If you won't go, they can shoot you and you can rot in hell!"

Damion rose in one lithe movement and grabbed her wrist to pull her against him.

"I don't want the situation to continue any more than you do. There's only one answer, Kairee, and that doesn't include playing one of us against the other."

"Your conceit is amazing. Do you think I would play the trollop for both you and your brother while I begged you to let us stay on our land? You may be a Saber, master of your own kingdom, but you will never be master over us. Go and play king with some other wide-eyed girl who might believe in you."

She tore her wrist from his grasp and ran to her horse. He watched her ride away, knowing full well a part of him wanted to ride after her.

But he battled his wayward thoughts into submission and bound them with ties of suspicion and jealousy. Kairee Kennedy was a beautiful trap into which he never intended to fall again. It was not enough that her family was most likely guilty of robbing them already, but her soft lips and warm body were a threat to his own peace. It seemed that whenever he was near her some part of his will ceased to function. It left him shaken to know one slim, gray-eyed girl had the power to make him forget obligations, honor, and everything else he had lived his life by. One soft taste of her lips and he could become a mindless fool, caught in a force that would reduce him and all he loved to ashes.

His anger had circled and circled the idea of Kairee in Britt's arms, but now the thought stormed him. Had they been together? Had he been right in thinking she had shown Britt the same wild passion they had shared, that she would be willing to use that passion to divide and conquer?

What he chose to ignore, to lock silently away, was the soft, nagging thought that he could not forget her touch and did not want to forget it, that he had tasted something beyond anything he had known and the taste was addictive.

Somehow he would wash her touch away. But at that moment the question he could not answer was how.

Chapter 10

Kairee rode home, stopping just a short distance from the ranch to make sure her clothes were straightened and her disheveled hair was brought as much under control as possible. Just touching her hair inspired the recollection of Damion's hands sliding into it, caressing it. She shook the memory and continued home.

Once her horse was cared for, she started toward the house from the barn. Halfway there, Cassie sprang from the porch and ran to her. They continued back toward the house together.

"Where'd you go, Aunt Kairee?"

"To visit a neighbor, Cassie. One who's going to sell us some horses . . . cheap, I hope."

"What's cheap?"

"It doesn't cost much," Kairee answered with a laugh.

"Aunt Kairee?"

"What?"

"Horses cost a lot of money, don't they?"

"Sure do, Cassie."

"Maybe," Cassie said shrewdly, "you ought to just buy ponies. They're only half a horse and maybe they would only cost half as much."

"I don't think it works that way, Cassie." Kairee laughed. "I think ponies cost as much as horses. You see, they grow up."

"Oh." The disappointment was obvious.

"You'd like a pony of your own, wouldn't you?"

"Yes . . . I guess so . . . only I guess I'll never have one."

"Maybe someday."

"Aunt Kairee, while you were gone Mr. Saber came here to see you."

"Which Mr. Saber?" Kairee had been with Damion, so it could only be Britt or Elliot Saber.

"Not the one you went riding with."

"Elliot Saber . . . Damion's father. Why, Cassie?"

"Well, he came over to talk to Grandpa, but Grandpa and Daddy were out with the cattle so he talked to Mama."

"What did they talk about?"

"I don't know. I don't understand what they were talking about. I only know Mama was mad."

"Your mother?" Kairee said in surprise. It was a very difficult thing to incur Lucy's anger.

"Uh huh, she was mad."

"What did he do to make her mad?"

"I told you, Aunt Kairee, I don't know. Mama said I had to go out and play. She always does that when she doesn't want me to listen."

Kairee chuckled, but she went up the porch steps rapidly and opened the door.

Lucy was in the midst of assorted jobs. She had bread rising near the fireplace and she was scrubbing the wood table in preparation for rolling out the dough. Kairee knew at once that Lucy was still angry. Her way of letting off the pressure of anger was always to throw herself into physical activity.

133

"Lucy, I heard we had a visitor today."

"Oh, Kairee, that man is the most . . . impossible person I've ever met. He acts like he's a king! Like God created this whole territory just for him."

"Calm down, Lucy, and tell me what he said."

"He came here looking for you at first."

"You told him where I was?"

"I just told him you weren't here."

"Good. The less he knows, the better. I've got a strange feeling he might do something to make sure I don't get any horses."

"I don't understand all this, Kairee. He acts like he owns this land."

"He's used it for his cattle since Uncle Rob left. I think that was nearly twenty years ago. I guess he thinks he has a right to it."

"Well, he doesn't!" Tears sprung to Lucy's eyes, and Kairee realized suddenly that she was not mad, she was frightened.

"Cassie, why don't you go and see if Smokey is in the barn. Tell him to come up to the house if he is."

"Okay," Cassie replied. She left quickly and Kairee turned back to Lucy.

"All right, Lucy, what did Elliot Saber have to say?"

Elliot had watched Britt and Damion ride away. He had faced all sorts of problems with the differences between his sons. But he had a feeling if he did not put a stop to this one quickly it was going to sever what fragile relationship there still was.

He had gone to saddle his horse and had ridden alone to the Kennedy ranch. He had hoped to find Kairee gone. To look into the reflection of Emma's calm gray eyes would be disconcerting. But even if she were there, frightening two women would not be that difficult. Frightened enough, he hoped they would put pressure on the men to leave.

He rode the distance with his mind not on the Kennedys, but on his sons. He was an observant man, and it had not taken him long to see that both his sons faced some inner turmoil when it came to the Kennedys. He was more than certain the reason was Kairee. It never occurred to him the fault was partially his.

Reluctantly, his mind settled on Kairee. Elliot Saber was a man nearing fifty. But he was still a powerful, virile, and handsome man. His sons could be seen in the rugged planes of his face and in the breadth of his shoulders. Would they be drawn to Kairee as he had been drawn to Emma?

He thought now of the effect Kairee could have on the dynasty he intended to build. He knew instinctively, like any born conqueror, that divided they could fall. And Kairee Kennedy, with the beautiful gray eyes, could be the wedge that split them forever.

He rode up to the ranch house and sensed with accuracy that there were very few, if any, inhabitants around. Striding to the front door, he knocked. When the door swung open, he looked into Lucy's startled eyes.

"Mr. Saber." Her voice registered her shock.

"Mrs. Kennedy, may I come in?"

Lucy felt a shiver of fear and did not understand it. Surely he would do her no physical harm. Yet she felt an overpowering threat.

"I . . . I'm afraid my father-in-law isn't home. I imagine it's he you'd like to speak to."

"Is your husband home?"

"No, he isn't. Perhaps if you come back later, Mr. Saber, or Gregg could come over and talk to you tonight."

135

"That's not necessary, Mrs. Kennedy." Elliot smiled and the smile frightened her even more. "I can talk to you. I'm sure you'll relay my message."

"Come in." Lucy stepped aside and let him pass her and enter.

He looked around and his look told Lucy without words that he saw how terribly little they had.

Her chin jutted out defiantly. They had little in the way of possessions, that was true, but Lucy and Kairee kept the house neat and clean and she refused to let this man make her feel ashamed.

"If you will sit down, Mr. Saber," she said with much more confidence in her voice than she felt. "I'll get you some coffee if you like, and I made some gingerbread yesterday if you'd like some."

"I'll take the coffee, thank you," he replied and walked across the room to the table. It was only then that he noticed Cassie seated on a low bench near the fire watching him with wide eyes.

"Cassie," Lucy said in a firm voice that Cassie knew was not to be argued with, "I think you should go outside and play for awhile."

"Yes, Mama," she replied reluctantly. She left with the firm feeling that her mother needed protection.

Near the creek she made a castle of sand and pebbles, and kept one eye on the house.

Elliot sat at the table, overpowering the small room with his presence. Lucy placed the steaming cup of coffee before him and he noticed with satisfaction that her hands were shaking.

Then she sat down opposite him and when their eyes met, some of his certainty slipped.

"What is it you want to say, Mr. Saber?"

"I'd like to think I'm talking to a reasonable and understanding woman, Mrs. Kennedy," he said in a deep, resonant voice. "Are you?"

"I would like to think so, Mr. Saber," she replied in a chill voice.

"Then you must understand the foolishness of this situation."

"Foolishness?"

"Surely you don't think you and your family can succeed here. You have less than nothing and this range can break bigger outfits."

"We don't have less than nothing, Mr. Saber," Lucy replied coldly. "We have each other. We're a family. Surely you, with your two sons, understand that."

She had struck the first blow and for a moment Elliot was shocked. Then he smiled. At least she wouldn't cry.

"I understand that, family or no family, you don't belong here. Don't you think it would be . . . wiser to talk your husband and his father into going back where you came from?"

"I don't talk my husband into anything. Gregg does what he thinks is best for this family. I would not dishonor him by suggesting he had done otherwise. This is our home now, and we will make it a warm, productive, and profitable one."

"That's fairly impossible."

"Why?"

"I could tell you a hundred reasons. But the best one is that this range belongs to me and I intend to graze my herds on it. There just isn't any way you're big enough to stop me." He stood up. "Tell your men that and tell them that I have the strength to back up what I say."

"The law says that this range is ours," Lucy answered stubbornly. "We've a legal deed."

Elliot laughed. "The law is in Buffalo, my dear Mrs. Kennedy, and I'm the law around here. You tell your men. Move out before some serious . . . accidents occur."

Her face went pale at the almost open threat, but he

was already at the door before she had gathered her thoughts together enough to react.

"He actually threatened us!" Kairee said in disbelief after Lucy had finished recounting her story.

"Not really. He just referred to 'accidents.' Oh, Kairee for the first time I'm frightened. Gregg—"

"No! Lucy, don't tell Gregg about this. Not yet. He might do something foolish. That's most likely what Saber wants Gregg to do."

Kairee rose and started for the door.

"Where are you going?"

"This has been my day to pay neighborly visits," Kairee replied. "I think it's about time one of the Kennedys called on the Sabers."

"Kairee, that's crazy. Gregg and your father will be furious."

"You're not going to tell them. Lucy, listen to me. This man is powerful. Against men he'll use a gun. But against a woman he might not. At least I can try to make him bend a little. Gregg might just get himself shot. Then where would we be?"

"Oh . . . I wish we'd never come here."

"Don't say that, Lucy. We'll get through this. And when the Sabers find out we won't leave, they'll leave us alone. We'll make this ranch one of the best in Wyoming, and we'll be happy here."

"You really believe that?"

"Yes, I do. You had enough courage to come out here and face all this. Don't lose it now, Lucy. Not when Gregg might need you the most."

She had struck the right note with Lucy, for she knew Lucy's love for Gregg was much bigger than the entire Wyoming territory.

Cassie watched Kairee ride away again and shook

138

her head, wondering why, since they had come to this valley, everybody seemed to be so tense. Oh well, she thought as she went back to her play. Everything would be all right. Her family would see to that. They always did.

Britt and Damion arrived home almost at the same time and nearly half an hour before Elliot returned from the Kennedys'.

It was nearing dinner time and both men were puzzled by Elliot's absence. He was a habitual man, and he usually had two drinks before he ate his dinner.

"You suppose a problem came up somewhere?" Britt asked thoughtfully.

"What kind of problem could come up that Jim and the other men couldn't handle? He's just out checking over a few things, probably making sure we're doing our job," Damion replied, but some nagging warning pricked his mind. When his father did something out of the ordinary, there was always a damn good reason for it. He wondered what his father might be up to, just as Britt did, though neither would suggest they do anything about it yet.

Damion had poured himself a rather large drink and sipped it while he watched Britt through narrowed eyes.

Britt lounged lazily in a chair near the fireplace and Damion, in honesty, had to admit that he would be nearly devastating to women with his sleek panther's body, his dark good looks, and his easy, laughing manner.

Had Kairee succumbed to it? he wondered bitterly, pushing aside the strange new feeling he had never experienced before. It was a possibility he refused to envision, for to do it would be to unleash the monster

139

that was tearing at him—jealousy.

"Run across anything today?" Damion inquired casually as he sat in a chair opposite Britt.

"No sign of anything wrong. Whoever it is, they're clever as hell. You'd think there'd be some sign of them."

"I ran across a dead fire coming down from the top of Slater's Ridge. Found a running iron in it still warm," Damion supplied, purposely leaving out his confrontation with Kairee.

"That's over pretty close to the Kennedy place."

"That doesn't mean they're guilty. Someone could be making it look that way."

Britt laughed harshly. "You going to feed that thought to the old man? You know damn well he isn't going to swallow it."

"No, I suppose he isn't," Damion said thoughtfully. "Britt . . . maybe I'll just hold that information for a time. Just until I look into it a little more. I wouldn't want him to go off half-cocked and do something we'll all regret."

"Suit yourself. Maybe it's a good idea." Britt eyed Damion. "You going to go over to the Kennedys'?"

"Might. If I can trace anything back to there."

"You think they're guilty?"

"To tell the truth, no."

"We missed a few head every so often before they got here," Britt offered.

"Britt, Pa wants the range. He's not going to care if they're guilty or not as long as it gets them out."

"You're awfully anxious for them to stay. Is it truth you see . . . or is it Kairee?"

Damion could not seem to be able to help uttering the next question. "What's between you and Kairee?" he asked softly.

Britt's eyes held his and he smiled. "That, my dear

140

orother, is none of your damn business."

"She's trouble."

"Don't worry about me. I've handled trouble before."

"Maybe this one will bring more than you expect."

"Why so worried about me, Damion . . . or is it yourself you're worried about? A little competition is good for the soul . . . and your soul sure as hell needs some."

Britt chuckled before he noticed that Damion was less than amused. He realized at once that Kairee Kennedy meant more to Damion than he would admit. He was about to prod further to see just how deep Damion's feelings lay when his father returned.

Elliot immediately poured himself a drink and carried it with him as he walked back across the room to stand in front of the fire between his two sons.

"Well, what did you two run across today?" he questioned bluntly.

Britt was the first to answer. "I didn't scare up a thing. If there's somebody systematically running off our stock, he's doing a damn good job of vanishing. There isn't a track or a sign of anything. I ran across a lot of our boys and they say the same. Nothing's moving."

"And you, Damion?"

"The same. I scouted as far as the Kennedys'. Crossed the border to their property . . . but I didn't find anything. It doesn't look like anybody from their place is up to anything. Besides, I don't think there's enough of them to do anything serious. You're talking about a job that'd take four, maybe six, men."

Damion was uncomfortable under his father's intent gaze. Despite what Elliot Saber had done, or even what he might be thinking of doing, Damion still respected his strength and his accomplishments, and he was not

141

used to lying to him. All Damion had ever done had been for the love of his father and the good of the Circle S. It was hard now to change that.

As he studied his father more closely, he was shocked to see telltale signs of loss of sleep and too much drinking. There were dark shadows beneath Elliot's eyes and the hand that held his glass clenched it until the knuckles were white. Damion suddenly realized there was something wrong with his father that had nothing to do with rustling Circle S cattle.

Damion watched Elliot, and Britt watched Damion just as closely. Something hovered near the Saber eagles, and none of the three knew exactly what it was or what to do about it.

Before any of them could try to put words to the tension that hung in the air, Maria came to announce that dinner was ready.

Both Damion and his father poured themselves another drink to carry to the table with them.

The conversation during the meal was desultory and consisted of questions from Elliot and brief answers from Britt and Damion.

It was near the close of the meal when Elliot offered more.

"I rode over to the Kennedys' today too," he said almost as if it had been an afterthought. But both brothers knew well that Elliot Saber planned out and thought over carefully everything he said or did.

Damion's hand clenched around his glass of whiskey and Britt was surprised to see his face pale slightly.

"Oh," Damion said. His voice seemed calm and unaffected, but that was the way Damion handled emotional situations, and Britt knew it. "What did you expect to find over there?"

"I sent you and Britt looking. I wasn't expecting to find them branding my mavericks. I was just repeating my warnings. I don't think the Kennedys intend to take me seriously," he added with a smile that was less than amused.

"You talked to old man Kennedy?" Damion questioned.

"No, he and his boy were both gone. So was his daughter. The only ones home were his daughter-in-law and his granddaughter. Weak links, I'd say, in the Kennedy chain."

"For Christ's sake, Pa!" Damion exclaimed angrily. "You didn't threaten a woman and child, did you?"

"Not in so many words." Elliot shrugged. "But a chain is only as strong as its weakest link. In this case, I think I've found it. If we can shake up and scare his daughter . . . well, a scared woman can put a lot of pressure on a man. Enough pressure and he'll pull up stakes and get out."

Damion rose from his chair and turned his back on his father. Filled with disgust at what he felt the Sabers were sinking to, he poured himself another drink.

Britt, for the first time, felt the same as Damion. He gazed at his father, his dark brows furrowed in a deep frown.

"I don't make war on women and kids, Pa," he said softly, "and I have no intention of scaring Kairee Kennedy. She's a nice girl and she's no weakling. You might find she's one of the stronger links in the chain of Kennedys."

Damion heard his brother's words, but he heard them with connotations that came from his own black, tangled thoughts. It seemed Britt knew a whole lot more about what kind of person Kairee Kennedy was than he did. He kept his back to both men, for he was shaken by the thought that if he turned to face either of them—if he read the truth he didn't want to see in Britt's eyes—he might lose his fragile grip on his emotions.

"You can say what you want," Britt continued, "and I'll do anything else you ask me, but I don't go around scaring women and kids."

"Britt," Elliot sneered, "don't be the weak link in my chain. I won't stand for it."

"Pa!" Damion was angry now. He spun around to face his father, unable to recognize the emotion that made him rise against a father he could have given his life for to defend a half brother he was jealous of and had never understood. "Why don't you give this a little time? Let us see if we can find who's been rustling. I agree with Britt. I don't push women and kids. It seems to me you're hot on getting rid of these people for some other reason than just range land. What could they have done to fire you up so bad? They've only been here a short while. How can you judge so quick? How the hell much land and power is it going to take to make you happy, and how much are you willing to pay for it? Your life? . . . Britt's? . . . mine?"

Elliot's face had paled. Damion had struck too close to home. Kairee Kennedy had to be gotten out of the valley. He could never look into Emma's gray eyes again or see her face in Kairee's. Yet he couldn't tell either of his sons about the mountains of guilt he bore and the battles he fought. He believed neither of them would understand. Therefore, he resorted to anger and force, as he had done when they had been boys and had crossed his will.

"And how the hell much of our range—my life—are you willing to give up to the latecomers who want to squat here and eat up the range I carved out of this wilderness? She's got to get out of this valley! You understand?" he raged. "She's got to get out of this valley! And one way or another I'll protect what's mine. With or without my ungrateful sons!"

Damion had heard the "she" in Elliot's demand and he slowly began to wonder if his father was frightened of something much more devastating than the loss of land.

But before Damion could speak, the front door opened. Both men turned in surprise at the sound of footsteps down the short entranceway. Then Kairee appeared in the doorway.

Her face was pale with rage, but Damion could only see how vulnerable and beautiful she looked. He took a step toward her at the same time that Britt stood up, obviously with the same intention, for he said her name softly, so softly Damion was the only one who heard it.

"Kairee."

"Stay where you are please, gentlemen," Kairee said coldly. "I have come to say something and then I'll leave and I hope never to see any of you again."

They were surprised into motionlessness and Kairee took a deep breath. Then her cold voice broke the silence.

Chapter 11

Gregg removed his hat and wiped the sweat from his brow with the crook of his arm. He and Rusty had branded several mavericks that had been added to the herd on its way to the ranch.

Rusty and Gregg had taken turns with the iron. One rode out, roped the maverick, and literally dragged it back to the fire.

A well-trained horse held the rope taut while Rusty dismounted and the two men expertly wrestled the calf to its side. Then came the stench of burned hair and an angry bellow from the calf and the branding was done.

"Damn hot work," Rusty grunted as he loosened his rope from the last belligerent calf and let it return to its mother for comforting nursing. "I could use some cold beer."

Gregg laughed. "Cold beer," he replied, "is like asking for rain in the middle of a desert. But I could sure enjoy one too."

"We gotta take a rest," Rusty said. "My back is broke and I gotta have somethin' to drink, even if it is warm water."

He walked to his horse, gathering his rope into a large circle as he did so. Then he hooked the circle of rope over the saddle horn and reached for his horse's reins to lead it back toward the fire.

Gregg replaced his hat atop his head and was about to say something more to Rusty, when he noticed Rusty's attention had been drawn elsewhere.

He turned his head to let his eyes follow Rusty's and saw riders approaching.

"Somebody comin' hell bent for leather," Rusty said.

"You know them?"

"Too far. Can't tell yet."

They waited while the riders grew closer, and despite the fact that they did not know the riders by name, both men instinctively felt the rippling sensation of danger.

The three men stopped within eight feet of Gregg and Rusty.

The man in the center of the three drew their quick attention. He was nearing fifty but had the clear gaze of a man much younger. His body was whipcord lean and he was as relaxed in the saddle as a man would have been in a rocking chair.

His eyes were gold-brown and his hair black, with the exception of the white patches at each temple. His smile was just on the border of friendly, but not quite.

"Hello boys," he said quietly. "Branding?"

Neither Gregg nor Rusty appreciated the obvious innuendo in his voice. They stiffened but could hardly take offense at a question. Yet both knew instinctively what was possible in a confrontation like this.

"Yeah," Gregg answered shortly.

"What brand?"

"That your business . . . friend?" Gregg questioned.

"I'm Jim Sinclair, foreman for the Circle S."

"I thought that might be who you were," Rusty said. "I've heard a lot about you . . . and your boss."

Jim flashed a wintry smile. "Askin' your brand is just a neighborly question . . . friend."

147

"We're the Bar *K*," Gregg said quickly, trying to put an end to the force that seemed to be building, "and we're branding some of our own mavericks we got on the trail out. There's no cattle here that belongs to the Circle *S*."

"Didn't say there was," Jim replied. "I just saw your smoke and thought I'd drop by and talk. You're real close to Saber land and that's my job."

"We know where the boundaries are," Rusty said, his anger rising.

"Do you now?" Jim seemed amused. "Well then, you won't have any problem in making sure you don't . . . accidentally cross over."

At this point, Rusty was about to lose his temper. It was only Gregg's restraining words, softly spoken, that held him immobile.

"We know"—Gregg's eyes held Jim's—"and we'd appreciate the same in return. You're on Kennedy land."

The atmosphere seemed vibrant with an electrical charge as the men mentally seemed to stand toe to toe.

"Well, I been riding Kennedy land for near twenty years. There's a lot of our cattle still on your land. We want to weed them out."

Gregg was silent for some time, knowing he was being pushed, being tested, and he was calculating just how hard he should push back without starting a full-fledged war.

"Seems more logical to weed 'em out come spring roundup. Otherwise you'd be riding all over our range and weeding out any mavericks you run across."

"We're only looking for cattle carrying our brand," Jim said coolly.

"Then me and the boys will weed 'em out and haze 'em back onto your land."

"Wouldn't want to put you to that much trouble,"

148

Jim said agreeably.

Gregg grinned amiably. "We don't mind being neighborly and doing that little job for you. In fact, we'll see to it real soon." His smile was cool. "Keep you from having to ride our range too. We can handle any that might be here."

There was a mild touch of respect in Jim's eyes as he realized Gregg had dug in his heels and intended to stand where he was. He also knew the next move was his and if any trouble came of it the fault would be his as well. He made his decision quickly. There would be other days, other confrontations. Besides, he wanted to talk to Elliot first to see just how far he was supposed to go.

It would not be the first time he and Elliot had fought together, had raised their guns in defense of Saber land. Most likely it wouldn't be the last. Jim made his decision.

"Fair enough. You haze 'em over. We'll be looking for 'em."

"I'll do that," Gregg answered, but he breathed a sigh of relief. He realized how tense he had been when he felt his body shake with the release of taut nerves.

Jim nodded and the three turned their horses to ride away.

"God," breathed Rusty, "I thought we had had it this time. I was sure we were going to have to slap leather. Three to two isn't exactly equal."

"I think we were just being tested."

"Damn scary test, if you ask me. I was in town the other day and I heard this Jim Sinclair was a hard man. He's been with the Saber ranch since it was started. From what I can tell, they came out here together."

"Well, I can see he's hard, but I think he's fair, and I think he thinks first before he does anything."

"If he's an example, I can pretty well imagine what

149

Saber is like."

"Yeah," Gregg said thoughtfully. "Let's get back to work."

They returned to their work, but Rusty noted that Gregg remained deep in thought for the rest of the day and spoke very little on the ride back to the ranch.

When Gregg and Rusty arrived home, they found everyone present but Kairee. When Lucy was questioned about Kairee's absence, her nervousness was apparent.

"She's just gone out for a ride."

"A ride? This late?" Gregg said with concern. "It'll be dark by the time she gets back. Maybe I ought to go out and look for her."

"No, Gregg," Lucy said quickly. "She'll be back soon. By the way, she went over to visit the Talbot ranch today." Lucy was doing her best to change the subject, and Gregg knew it. He only kept his silence until he and Lucy could be alone. He did not want to open up a cask of worry for his father and he did not want to frighten Cassie.

"Mitchell Talbot?" Gregg questioned.

"Yes. She wanted to see his horses. I guess he has a reputation for the best around."

"I hear he doesn't run any cattle at all," Stephen said thoughtfully. He was seated before the fire and Gregg watched the firelight dance across his face. He saw the lines of years of worry. Somehow this sight seemed to freeze the determination within Gregg to a solid core.

He sat down opposite Stephen to talk, and to keep his father's mind off Kairee's absence as well. He had a feeling Kairee was out for more than a ride.

*   *   *

150

Kairee's face was white with fury, and her eyes were storm-cloud gray and wide with the effort it took to control her rage. Her body seemed to quiver with tension.

When Damion momentarily regained the power to draw his eyes from her, he glanced at his father. If he was surprised at Kairee's obvious emotion, he was totally shocked at his father's.

Elliot's mouth was pinched into a harsh line and his face had grayed. He seemed to be holding himself under control only by immense effort. Whatever there was about Kairee Kennedy, it was something that could strike his father a nearly mortal blow. He knew for certain Kairee was the "she" Elliot had been so unnerved about.

"I've come here to look at the three men who are so scared they might have to share their kingdom with the common people that they resort to frightening women and children. Well, we're not frightened. You can't scare us off."

"Kairee, what are you talking about?" Damion demanded.

"Ask your father. Ask the mighty Elliot Saber who came to our ranch today and scared my sister-in-law to death."

Both Damion and Britt looked at their father, whose face was frozen into a mask that revealed nothing about his emotions. He spoke firmly and with cool control. "I frightened no one."

"That's not true," Kairee retorted.

"I merely pointed out to her the foolishness of your family's staying here. There is no way you'll survive."

"You mean there's no way you'll let us survive. Well, do whatever you want, Elliot Saber. We'll stay here. We'll stay if we have to pour our blood into this ground, and nothing you can do will change that. We

151

wanted to live in peace with you, but you're too arrogant to accept that."

"This was my land before you were born, girl," Elliot declared. "I'm the one who carved it out of nothing. Now you come-latelies think you can come along and just take it. Well, you can't. You're right. I'm not going to give it up, and my sons will help me protect it."

Damion and Britt were being forced to the wall, forced to choose sides, forced to decide whether to stand with people who seemed to be ready to strike out at them, or stand with their father.

"Of course." Kairee said softly, aware deep within that she would not be able to make such a choice. Her eyes moved from Elliot to Britt, and then to Damion. Their gazes met and held. "Of course they will," she said. "What does justice have to do with it? The Sabers just take what they want and to hell with anything else."

It seemed to Damion and Kairee that they stood alone in a world tossed by a cataclysmic turbulence.

"You're wrong, Kairee," Damion said quietly. "My father is defending what he built. Isn't there any justice in that?"

"You defend what he does, no matter what. How can you do that when you know he is wrong?"

"He's my father, Kairee," Damion reminded gently. "What do you expect me to do? What would you do?"

Kairee knew there was some truth in his words. Some part of her respected his defense, his support of his father, his resistance to deserting him.

"You're alike, all you Sabers." Her voice cracked in choked misery. "Well, we'll have to prove to you that you can't have your way—you can't own the world. I'm giving you all a warning." Her voice lowered. "Stay off our land, for the next Saber seen on it will be shot for trespassing. Remember my warning."

She wheeled about and was gone, and Britt, who had been watching the confrontation, moved swiftly to follow her.

Damion meant to do the same, but seeing Britt follow, he was stung into immobility by a black cloud of jealousy.

He turned to face Elliot in time to see a fleeting look of pain and longing cross his face, a look so full of anguish that he found it difficult to believe.

As soon as Elliot felt Damion's eyes on him, he brought his features under iron control.

"There is going to be some trouble, Damion. I'm glad you were smart enough to stay on the winning side."

Damion gazed at his father and a look of sadness touched his eyes. "I didn't stay because you're going to win, Pa," he said softly. "I suppose you just wouldn't understand my motives. But it doesn't matter now. The damage has been done."

"No damage. We'll run them off," Elliot said confidently. "They'll never last out the winter because nobody is going to sell them supplies. By spring they'll be ready to leave."

Damion shook his head. "You really have to make a war out of this, don't you? I have a feeling, Pa, it might just be a war that costs you more than you bargained for."

"You're not going squeamish on me, are you?"

"If you mean am I going to see anybody die by my own hand, no, I'm not. If they lose their battle with the land, it's one thing. I'll only use my gun in defense of you and the Circle *S*. But I won't start it." Damion's tone was final. He turned and left through a different door so he would not have to see Britt, or worse, Britt and Kairee.

He walked through the dark shadows to the barn

153

and was saddling his horse before he realized not only what he was doing, but why. Fight as he might, he could not remove Kairee's face from his mind, nor her angry and frightened words. He wanted one opportunity to explain before the real war began.

Kairee was down off the porch and beside her horse, gripping the pommel of her saddle and preparing to mount by the time Britt caught up with her.

He gripped her shoulder to turn her to face him. "Kairee, wait."

She struck his hand away and for the first time he saw the tears in her eyes.

"Leave me alone, Britt. I don't think I can stand much more of the Sabers tonight, none of them." She turned back to her horse.

"Kairee, if you want to stay on this range, you had better stand here and talk to me."

"What is there left to talk about?" she asked bitterly.

"Survival," he stated quietly.

Now she turned to look at him. "Survival," she repeated. "Whose, the Sabers', or ours?"

"Yours, if you'll listen to reason."

"I don't understand you."

"Maybe I don't understand myself. I hate him . . . but I love him too. I hate what he's trying to do to your family, but I've been by his side and watched his struggle to get what he has. He's hard, Kairee, but he's had to be hard."

"And Damion?" she said.

"Damion . . . he's Pa's son too. Did you come here, Kairee, because you expected either of us to desert our father and our land to stand with you? Aren't you asking a lot more than you'd be able to give? Would you desert your family?"

Kairee sighed deeply. "I suppose you're right."

"Kairee, you're going to find it hard to survive a winter. If I know Pa, the first thing he'll do is cut off your supplies. Without them, by spring you'll be more than anxious to leave."

"What can we do?"

"My mother's people. I think they'd help you. If you want to go there with me, we'll find out. They can supply all you need. They've been surviving here for a long, long time."

"Britt, why are you doing this?"

"I just think the battle ought to be fair. Besides"—he grinned—"a pretty girl's gratitude wouldn't upset me either."

"I am grateful, Britt. I . . . I just wish it could be different. Britt, your father seems to hate me."

"It's not you, Kairee. It's some imagined threat to his ranch. He values it pretty highly. Sometimes higher than . . . anyway, I think it's something that could change."

"I think you're wrong about that, Britt. I saw it in his eyes when he first came to our house, and I saw it in his face tonight. There's something about me that seems to make him angry or . . ." She didn't want to say "afraid," but Britt knew it.

"I'll see if I can talk to him. I'll mention it."

"No, Britt, please. It might just be my imagination. I don't need him any more upset than he is."

"All right. Do you want to go see my mother's people?"

"Yes, we'll need all the help we can get."

"When, tomorrow?"

"No, not tomorrow. In a couple of days. I'll have to break it to my father. He'll most likely be furious that I came here tonight."

"I'll ride home with you."

"No! Please no, Britt. I want to ride alone. I have to think. Besides, all I need to do is ride up with a Saber at my side, even if he is a semi-friendly one. I'll be fine. It's a beautiful night and a short ride."

"But Kairee—"

"No, really, Britt, for now I'd rather ride by myself."

"All right," he agreed reluctantly.

She smiled and mounted, then she looked down at him. "Don't worry about me. I'll get home just fine. Thank you, Britt."

"For what?"

"For at least giving us a chance."

"I can't guarantee my mother's people will help you. It's just . . . well, they haven't got too much affection for my father. They can't fight him, but"—he smiled—"it might give them a way to irritate him a little."

"We don't mean you any harm. We don't want to take anything that belongs to you. We just want to be left alone to live our lives in peace on our own land. It's not a great deal to ask."

"Depends on who you're asking, Kairee. I'll wait two days, then I'll ride over."

"It would be better if I met you. I don't want to start anything, especially with the only Saber who's shown any kindness. I'll be down by the Powder River early in the morning two days from now."

"I'll be there."

"Good night, Britt."

"You sure you don't want me to ride at least part of the way with you?"

"No, really, it's an easy ride, and I want to think."

"Good night then, Kairee."

She turned her horse and he watched her ride away.

It was a confusing thing to love his father as much as he did, want his approval as much as he did, and still do something like he had just done to undermine his

156

father's plans. Hate warred with love. Jealousy warred with understanding. Britt felt himself desperately in need of a strong drink, a soft woman, and a way to escape his father's eyes back at the house.

He went to the barn and saddled his horse without noticing the fact that Damion's was already gone. With one fluid movement he mounted and rode away.

Kairee was regaining her equilibrium. She found it hard to believe she had taken the bull by the horns and had done what she had done—face the lion in his own den.

She was more than certain her entire family would be furious with her if they discovered what she had done. She just wished it had had some effect on their situation, but it hadn't.

All she had managed to do was put another barrier between her and . . . God! She had been thinking about Damion. What a useless thing. He had stood with his father, hadn't he? He had chosen sides.

Damion's face lingered before her and, despite all mental battles, the warmth of the night, the glow of the moonlight, and her own vulnerability overcame her.

She could feel the strength of him, the roughness of the stubble of his beard against her skin. She could taste the deeply masculine taste of his mouth as it had plundered hers with wild recklessness. Yet now she was left with a dark void she had no way to fill. It could never be. He was a Saber and she was a Kennedy. It was like oil and water. They could never mix.

Her control slowly returned. She would not drop her pride in the dust for him, and that must truly be what he expected. Their confrontation had already proven it. He would use her and discard her, possibly with some amusement that a Saber had proven to a Kennedy who

157

was the stronger.

Tonight, as far as she was concerned, they had fought their final battle. If it took every ounce of strength she could gather, she would wipe Damion Saber from her mind . . . from her senses . . . from—

The darker shadow that sat beneath the trees moved and she reined her horse to a halt. For a minute fear touched her. But from the breadth of his shoulders, the ease with which he sat relaxed in the saddle, she knew it could only be one person. She could feel his almost animal-like magnetism before she could even see his face.

She wanted to kick her horse into motion and run. But she did not. She waited in almost breathless expectation as he rode to her side.

"Kairee"—his voice was deep and vibrant—"it's time we talked."

Chapter 12

"I really don't see that we have too much to talk about now, Damion. I know where you stand. You made that very clear."

"You don't try to understand anybody's position but your own, do you?"

"Mine is not the most enviable position. And yours . . . it seems to me that the Sabers simply want the whole Wyoming territory as their own."

"My father has a right to protect what he built, and as his son I have a responsibility too. What do you want me to do, Kairee, spit on my father, throw what he has given me back in his face, dishonor both him and myself by standing against him?"

Again Kairee sensed something beneath Damion's words, as if what he was trying to tell her was only a shadow of the powerful thing he held leashed within him, a thing to which even he could not put a name.

He brought his horse close to hers and bent forward to rest his hand on the pommel of her saddle. It brought him within inches of her. She remained immobile, her chin firm and her eyes defiant. She was not going to let him see one ounce of fear in her, even though her heart pounded so loudly she was sure he could hear it.

Why did her defenses seem to be made of sand every time he was close to her. She groaned inwardly. All her good intentions and determination seemed to melt into an emotion she did not understand, or did not want to understand.

"No one's denying that right, Damion. Why do you deny ours?"

"Kairee, we can't talk like this. Get down. Come and walk with me . . . talk to me, and listen to me."

"No, I can't do that."

"Why?" he asked softly. "What are you afraid of?"

"I would be a fool not to be afraid of you."

"I didn't say you were afraid of me. I don't want you afraid of me. But maybe you're just a little bit afraid of yourself. Just a little afraid that you might really understand."

She stared at his leonine face. The tightness about his mouth should have alerted her to the fact that he was containing a raw emotion that was eating at his control.

The dying sun was behind him, casting his face half in shadow, and she could not read his eyes.

Feeling the situation was beyond repair, she turned her face away from the heat of his gaze. She had felt it sear her skin, seeking something. Seeking what? her willful mind demanded.

"Look at me, Kairee," he said. When she failed to respond, he reached to take her face between his fingers and turn it toward him. "Look at me, damnit."

"Make sense and I will!" she snapped, angered now more at the effect his touch had had on her than anything else. She was prepared to deny anything, to battle anything he could fling at her. What she was unprepared to battle was the electric excitement he had the power to stir in her.

There was an enormous silence in which she could

160

hear the rapid beating of her heart. The world that contained them seemed devoid of any other life. She gazed up at the painted sky, shuddered at its breathtaking nearness, and was awed by the magnificence of the setting sun.

Damion studied her face in the sunset and thought, How lovely she is . . . yet how unreachable.

The protective shield she had built as an invisible barrier stood in his way, retarding any and all advances he wanted to make toward her. Perhaps it was this very thing, this elusiveness, that made him desire her more.

"Kairee, don't shut all the doors between us. If some of us don't reach, don't talk, this whole thing is going to explode beyond any hope. We've got to stop it."

Suddenly vulnerable to his tenderness, she felt tears brimming in her eyes. Angry at herself for evincing such weakness, she became momentarily disoriented.

"I am making sense. You just refuse to acknowledge what is true," he added.

Before she could answer, he reached to jerk her reins from her hand. Unable to stop him, she could only sit on her horse, grip the pommel of her saddle with trembling hands, and try to summon the courage it would take to withstand him.

He dismounted, then tied both horses' reins to a tree branch. Then he walked silently to her side and raised his arms to help her down.

She refused his help, not wanting him to think she was succumbing to his heady masculinity, though that fact was obvious in the trembling of her hands.

She dismounted herself, turned, and stood very close to him.

"You're insistent," she said as coolly as she could. "A Saber trait." Her laugh was soft and almost bitter. "You wanted to talk to me, so talk."

"What a consummate actress you are."

"Stop the nonsense and tell me what it is you have to say to me that you forcibly have to stop me out here. Is it because you think I won't fight you, Damion? That I'm really afraid?"

He raised his arms into the air and let them fall heavily to his sides, shaking his head negatively. Then he turned and walked a short distance from her.

Slowly he began to speak. "Kairee, you have to understand the things that have helped create this situation. My father is not how you see him."

"I can only understand what I see and hear. Elliot Saber's shadow falls over everyone in this territory."

"Why not, Kairee?" Damion demanded. "Where was everyone else when this place was a godforsaken wilderness, when he had to grub and scrape to pull the Circle S out of the dirt? He's a strong man who's always had to fight for what he wanted. But he fought! Do you think he built all this just for himself? No! He built it for Britt and me. He built it to last through a lot of generations."

"He has no right to everything! He has no right to what belongs to someone else!"

"Even someone who's not strong enough to hold it?"

"How can anyone try when he drives them away? How can anyone survive when not only Elliot Saber but his sons as well use the Saber name like a weapon?"

"That's not exactly true. Surely you would understand that a man of my father's stature has a right to expect his sons to be strong, to be the kind of men worth what he's built."

"Is that how he judges you and Britt—by whether or not you're willing to fight, or even to die, to protect what he owns?"

"How can he know that the Circle S will stand, unless he sees he can depend on us to care for it as much as he does."

Kairee's voice lowered. "And what if you can't fill your father's shoes? What if you fail to be another Elliot Saber? What then, Damion?"

"I'm not Elliot Saber! I'm my own man! But I'll tell you why I'll continue to fight to keep my father's dream alive."

For a long moment Damion was silent. Then he began to speak again. His voice was filled with an unloved child's awe over the creation of a miracle. He told of Elliot Saber's arrival in the territory when there had been no other but he. Kairee heard what must have been Damion's day-to-day diet, stories of his father's glory, which must have lowered the child's self-esteem until he surrendered the idea that he could ever be the man his father was. It seemed that Elliot had carved with bare hands the beginnings of an empire.

Damion talked on, unaware that Kairee was moving closer behind him. Caught up in his memories, he spoke of his mother and of a small boy's attempt to measure up to what was expected of him. He was trying to explain his father, but Kairee heard the son. She heard rejection and a need for love. She heard loneliness and frustration. She heard all that Damion had no idea he was saying.

"Can you understand it, Kairee, if I tell you that I cannot desert him. I am his son!"

The cry was one of need, and at that moment Kairee hated Elliot Saber with a passion she found difficult to believe.

He turned to face her now. The sun touching the horizon and beginning to disappear bathed the world around them in a flaming haze. He looked into eyes filled with warm topaz flecks in the dying sunlight.

Unable to help herself, she stretched out a hand to touch him and he stared at her intently, as if he could never finish devouring her with his eyes. Only inches from each other, their eyes locked compulsively. He sighed, reached to take her outstretched hand, pulled her close to him, and closed his eyes briefly. He could feel her warm, trembling form shudder against his. She felt his lean body grow rigid and tense as it was influenced with passion and desire.

"You must know the truth, Kairee," he said softly. "You must know you cannot win. You must go." The last words were a groan, but he clung to her and would not let her pull away from him. A wave of fear swept through her and she shivered, for she knew if this touch were all of him she would have, if they fought to the death, she could not go.

Then he moved her away, caught her face in his hands and lifted it to him. They kissed, again, and again, and again, until the strength that made Damion Saber drained from him and he could only be what he was—a man who wanted, needed, this woman in his arms.

Then he stood before her, looking into her eyes until Kairee had no strength to resist. She, too, was caught in a whirlwind of emotions that tore at her, stripping her of all but the flame of passion that was raging, like a forest fire, beyond all her efforts to control it.

They stood beneath the tree, each breathing in the scent of the other, each aware only of the other's presence.

She sensed hurt in him she wanted to heal, and they clung to each other for several moments, unmoving and silent, each feeling the beat of his heart against the other's body.

He gripped her more tightly and his desire overrode all else. With deliberation he pushed the future from his mind.

With hands infinitely gentle they undressed each other, wanting to touch, to absorb, to learn. Touching

Damion's warm skin became an erotic sensation for Kairee that aroused her to tingling excitement. He exuded a body heat so warm that contact with him set her on fire.

His emotions were raw nerve ends and he gasped audibly as he knelt before her and gathered her to him to bury his face into her full, firm breasts.

She abandoned herself to him and he to her, and both forgot everything except the moment. Their desire mounted, but the need to hold it, to linger over it, was profound.

The grass was cool beneath them and he lay beside her, devouring her slim nakedness with both the eyes of passion and the gentle hands of possession. He wanted to take all, and he wanted to give all.

His lips tasted the sweetness of her mouth, then moved across her body slowly, slowly, lifting her senses with each kiss. He licked his tongue lightly across roused nipples, then caught them, one, then the other, bringing a soft cry of sweet pain as she felt him tease with his teeth, then suck fiercely.

Her hands caressed the sinewy muscle, tangled in his hair as he moved down her body. Gentle fingers forced her legs apart. His mouth teased the flesh of her thighs, moving slowly to seek out the tender bud, which brought a cry of near anguish to her lips.

Her body arched toward this searing invasion and he tasted deeply of the nectar buried within until he heard her sob and sensed she sought a peak too soon.

He rose to take her hot, open mouth with his, then his body surged as he felt her move against him and her mouth begin an exploration that sent a lightning streak of power shooting through him.

Her hot, velvety tongue caressed his swollen manhood and a feeling tore through him, stimulating him, elevating him, sending him into the weightlessness of ecstasy. Their senses pyramided higher and higher until neither could bear more.

Only then did he rise up to slide within her body. Overcome, they made love feverishly, frantically, as if they could never get enough of this loving. They moved together as one, lifting, rising, surging, until their cries mingled and they endured a rapture that drove them to the peak of madness.

As Damion descended that exquisite plateau of sexual euphoria, he wondered how a man could feel such happiness, and such fear, at the same time.

In that final, exquisite moment he grabbed the fragrant, thick strands of her blond hair and brought her eyes level with his.

They sank into the depths of each other in every way and he watched the fire rage behind her eyes, felt her hands, her body, urging him more deeply within her. He reveled in the intoxicating pleasure of knowing he could send her spinning into soft, tumbling clouds of ecstasy.

They lay in an embrace of spent passion, legs entwined, his face buried in the curve of her throat, his arms bending her to him fiercely, as if he would never let her go.

She kept her eyes closed, refusing for a time to return to a world that held nothing for them. She sensed that now he would assume she understood what he felt, and that he would expect her to convince her family of his point of view.

But she knew she could not, she would not, despite the enormous sexual appeal he possessed, the erotic passion she could not resist.

She stirred and he knew the rare, magical encounter was over.

He rose on his elbow and looked at her, brushing a strand of hair from her face. He read her resolve in her eyes and the anguish of it tore him in two. No matter what they had shared, Kairee had found the strength and the resolve to continue the battle.

He rose and stood above her, his nude body firm and muscular, the epitome of athletic perfection as the last rays of the sun gave it a glowing bronze hue.

She rose to stand beside him and the tears that touched her cheeks answered his unspoken question.

She knew if she did not become strong she would bend before his will like a willow before a storm. Whatever her body's call, or her heart's call, she would not submit, and in the finality of her stare he knew it.

"Don't be a fool, Kairee. Don't try to fight something you cannot win."

"What is it you want from me?"

"You could marry me, Kairee . . . and your family could find land somewhere else. I don't want to hurt you, Kairee. But you've got to let go." She was crushingly aware that he had said nothing about loving her. Love did not enter into the picture when the Sabers wanted something. She would be a means by which they could acquire what they wanted. She ached for one tender word, for a denial of what she knew. But words of love never came. She was suddenly caught between wanting to be with him and refusing to allow him to bend her to his will, as if she would be content to surrender only because he felt his demands took precedence over her own.

"Do you honestly believe I should be the one to sacrifice everything so you can retain your honor?" she cried bitterly. "What of mine? Is there to be no will in the world but Damion Saber's? You ask too much, Damion. You ask more than I am capable of giving."

"You could be happy with us, Kairee . . . with me."

"You ask me to do what you can't do. No, Damion! No, I could never marry you. Not unless you were

167

willing to come halfway. Not unless you were able to give as much as you ask me to give." She wanted to cry out, not until you can say you love me and tell me I'm not a pawn in a contest that has no meaning.

"I can't do that. Kairee, for Christ's sake, be reasonable. I thought you understood. I thought . . . What about this? Will you throw it away?"

"Will you?" she challenged. "Tell your father to forget the land he wants. Tell him to forget his empire and be just another rancher."

"I can't buy the woman I want at the expense of my father."

"What makes you think you can buy me at all. I'm not for sale. Neither is the Bar *K*."

His anger was replacing his control. He had been so certain. He knew he had possessed the woman in Kairee. For a short, breathless time he had owned her heart and her body. But now he realized there was a part of Kairee he had not touched, a strong core that demanded something that seemed to be beyond his grasp.

It was a kind of defeat he had never tasted before. They stood at an impasse. Both wanted to reach across it but were too stubborn to discard the problems that weighted them down.

"Why am I asking so much, Kairee?" Damion questioned. "You could be part of the biggest ranch in the whole territory. I could give you—"

"I told you, Damion, for what you want to give, you ask too great a price."

She bent to gather her discarded clothes and he did the same. They dressed in silence. Despite the magic they had shared, the gulf between them was wider than it had ever been.

"Do you understand that either way you and your family will not be on this range come spring?"

"Don't count on that." She started toward her horse, but he intercepted her, and paying no attention to her efforts to remain out of his reach, he pulled her into his arms.

"This can't end between us, Kairee."

"It ended before it began. I was a fool to believe what we shared meant something to you. I should have known that if you wanted something as much as you wanted us out of this valley you wouldn't hesitate to use whatever means were necessary." She wanted to hurt him as much as she was being hurt. "But you can console yourself," she said brutally. "You are Elliot Saber's son. Go home and tell him what you have done. Maybe for the first time in your life he will say, 'Well done, son. You are finally the son I wanted.' Maybe now he will be convinced you have become the man he's obviously been trying to mold you into."

The shock of her deliberate brutality rocked him and she twisted from his arms and mounted before he regained the ability to stop her. Her harsh words had struck the most vulnerable part of him, a part he had unwittingly given her to destroy.

He watched her ride away and felt a sudden hollowness, as if someone had torn the center from him and had left him empty.

He sank down beneath a tree and surrendered to self-examination that was more intense than any he had dared before. It was well into the night when he finally rose, mounted, and rode toward the Circle *S*.

The next morning there was a thick, heavy silence at the breakfast table on the Circle *S* ranch.

Damion seemed lost in his own thoughts, dark thoughts, for his brow was furrowed and his mouth tugged downward at the corners.

Britt, usually effervescent, was just as caught up in his own ruminations.

Elliot watched his two sons, knowing instinctively the concerns that preyed on their minds. He thought of Kairee Kennedy, and the old misery burst within him, aided by the guilt of deeds carried out over many years.

He felt pressed into a corner, into a battle, though he absolved himself of the consequences by telling himself that the fault lay with the Kennedys.

Elliot had reigned unopposed for nearly thirty years. He would not abdicate his throne because one gray-eyed girl tore at his memories and resurrected an emotion he thought he had buried long ago.

He was involved in his own dark thoughts for quite some time before he realized that Britt and Damion were engaged in quiet conversation. He listened, observing his two eagles closely. He had played them this way all their lives, watching their struggle to stand tall in his eyes, to receive the promised rewards: their father's approval, and the Circle S.

With these two extensions of himself, he had ruled and would continue to rule. He thought with pleasure of the two ranchers who had finally given up their battles with him and with the elements in the rough and rugged land in which they lived.

Roger Paulson and Jasper Dickerson had finally signed the papers that would extend Elliot's land several thousand acres. It would not be long before the majority of the others fell into line and gave him what he wanted—all except the Kennedys, the damn, infernal, intruding Kennedys.

Fortified by the promises of the past and his overpowering desire to become nearly an omnipotent king in his territory, Elliot Saber refused to admit that a pair of wide gray eyes might have the ability to shatter those promises, and, in doing so, shake the walls of his kingdom, his fortress, his sanctuary.

In time, he thought, his sons would need to bring new blood to the Circle *S,* women of his choice, strong, wealthy women. For a long time Elliot sat in silence, imagining himself a Caesar with an empire at his hand, so long, in fact, that he missed much of the conversation between Damion and Britt.

When he did return to it, it was because of the grim, closed look on Damion's face. It was at this point that Britt's last words came to him.

". . . so I'm taking Kairee to my mother's people. She wants to meet them, and since I've told them about her, they're anxious too."

"That's out of the question," Elliot inserted domineeringly and both pairs of eyes turned to him in surprise.

"Out of the question?" Britt repeated. "What do you mean?"

"I mean I don't want the Kennedys cozying up to your mother's people and gettin' the idea they can stay. What do you expect to get out of it? And what do they expect to get?"

"I don't expect to get anything out of it. Hell, Pa, what harm can it do you if Kairee and her family make a few friends?" Britt asked, but his eyes dropped from Elliot's quickly and Elliot was certain his wild son's plans went deeper. He searched for the answer and found it.

He smiled a cold smile that never touched his eyes. "If you're thinking of getting them any help from your mother's people, forget it. They don't have any choice but to stand with me. Lone Wolf and I are blood brothers, and"—he chuckled softly—"whatever else you might have in mind won't work. In the eyes of her people, your mother and I are still married. They will honor that union and you can't do much about it."

For one instant he saw raw hatred in Britt's eyes. It was covered immediately, but it had been so hard and sudden that Elliot felt a tingle of premonitory fear.

He had not been to see Southwind since she had left him, but now he planned to make a point of visiting in the next few days to renew their commitment.

No matter what the situation between himself and Britt, Britt's mother's people were honorable and they would stand behind words spoken a long time before.

"If you're still married, why don't you bring her back here . . . where she belongs?"

Elliot shrugged. "It was her choice to go. She wasn't happy here. No one forced her to return to her people." His voice softened. "I'm sure she explained it to Lone Wolf the same way."

"Yes," Britt replied, "I'm sure she did." He turned his gaze to Damion, who had remained silent during the exchange.

Damion's thoughts were on Kairee. Had Britt assured her of help from his people? Is that why Kairee had been so confident they could survive the winter? If that were the case, he would have to make Kairee understand the truth. This time he knew his father was right. Southwind's people would not go against a man they considered a blood brother, a husband of one of their own.

If Kairee was depending on Britt for help, Damion was going to stop it. And he could give himself all the reasons in the world to do so, except the truth: he would not tolerate the thought of Britt and Kairee together.

Chapter 13

Gregg told his family about the confrontation at supper. Surprisingly, he seemed to Kairee to be much too calm.

"You don't understand, Kairee, they could have caused Rusty and me a hell of a lot more trouble than they did."

"Gregg is right, Kairee," Stephen said. "We don't want to be involved in a fight. We'll stand without drawing guns. I want no blood spilled on my land."

"Neither of you understands," Kairee protested. "These men don't respect that kind of thinking. They're . . . they're bandits! They're men who don't know the meaning of sharing."

"What do you expect us to do, Kairee?" Gregg asked gently, not fathoming her fierce protests. "There are six men here, two women, and one little girl. Do you think we ought to raise guns against them?"

"Oh Gregg," she said quietly, "I don't know what to do. I'm afraid. I'm afraid they're going to be able to force us out of here."

"Kairee, how can they?" Stephen asked. "We'll stay on our land, and we won't raise a gun to them. Anything else they do would have to be breaking

173

the law."

"The Sabers are the law."

"Pa, I've been thinking about something," Gregg interjected, changing the subject. He could sense a strange kind of panic in Kairee and he was worried about the source.

"What, Gregg? I'm interested in any ideas that might help."

"We could fence our land."

"Fence it? It would take years to cut and skin enough trees to make fences."

"We don't have to use trees."

"What the hell else do you make a fence out of?"

"I've been hearing about a new thing they're using. It's called barbed wire."

"Barbed wire. What's that?"

"I don't know much about it, but I'd like to go on up to Buffalo and look into it."

"We got nothing to lose," Stephen said. "Why don't you go ahead and see about it."

"Gregg," Lucy said quickly, "would you mind if Cassie and I went with you? There are some things we need and Cassie hasn't seen a town the size of Buffalo."

"I don't see any reason why not. It will do us all some good."

Kairee stood and watched their pleasure at the idea of a trip to Buffalo, saw their excitement over the idea of fencing their land, while deep within her intense fear crawled through her veins.

It seemed as if her whole world had suddenly gotten beyond her control, and there was no one with whom she could confide her fears or share her tears.

She fully intended to meet Britt and journey to his mother's home. In fact now she found it difficult to have to wait until the appointed time.

If the Indians could show them how to survive the

long hard winter—if they would help them in any way—she would be grateful. What worried her was the problem their promise of help might create, both for her and for Britt.

She knew how Elliot Saber thought and, to her distress, she knew how Damion thought as well. She wondered how Britt would react to the fence. Would he turn from them also?

Gregg, Lucy, and Cassie left for Buffalo with the wagon the next day. It would be at least two weeks before they returned. The following day Kairee rode to the river to meet Britt.

Britt arrived almost an hour before she did. He had laughed at the fact that he was excited about meeting her. "Like a schoolboy," he had muttered, but still he had left for the meeting early.

He dismounted and tied his horse to a bush, then he sat on a flat rock near the water and rolled a cigarette. He struck the match against the rocks and cupped it in his hands to prevent the breeze from extinguishing it.

He looked out over the plains, realizing he was looking over land that belonged to the Sabers for as far as he could see.

What did he feel? he thought. The question seemed unanswerable. He had always felt a part of the land, a part of the elements, but never quite a part of the Saber empire.

What tore at him was that he wanted all of him to belong to something or someone and he felt as if pieces of him were irretrievably scattered to the four winds and he would never be able to gather them.

He thought about Kairee. Kairee . . . she was so different from any woman he had known. And he thought about being a Saber. He wanted to be a Saber, to be part of the tremendous accomplishment that was the Circle *S*. Yet he wanted to belong to his mother's people too, free to roam the wilds, not answering to any man but himself. And now . . . now he wanted to share all of it with someone else. And that someone else was the one he should not love, should not want, the one who was the greatest danger to him ever being a whole Saber, or a whole man.

He was confused, knowing what he was doing would be construed by his father as deliberate treachery, not to mention what his remarkable brother would think.

"What an opportunity for you, Damion," he said softly to the wind. "The Circle *S* would be all yours for damn sure. All the old man has to find out is what I'm up to and good-bye Britt. Well, maybe then the choice would be made for me. Sure as hell seems I can't make one for myself."

The sound of Kairee's horse coming made him rise and he tossed the cigarette on the rock and ground it out with his boot.

She drew her horse to a halt and he walked toward her. "Hello. I thought you might have changed your mind," he said.

"Why?"

"I don't know." He grinned. "I just had the thought in the back of my mind that the Saber name might have scared you away."

"Britt," she said softly, "for today can't we dispense with the battle? I'm not afraid of any Saber, and . . . and I'd like to enjoy the day rather than fight."

"Sounds good to me. For today it's just Britt and Kairee."

"Yes . . . Britt and Kairee. How far do we have to go, Britt?"

"It's quite a ride. I hope you told your family you won't be back until late tonight."

"My brother and his family are in Buffalo buying . . . supplies. They won't be back for awhile. There's just Dad and me for now, and the boys."

"Boys?"

"I mean"—she flushed—"the men who work with Dad and Gregg. Dad calls them 'the boys.' I guess it's a habit."

"How many of them?" he asked. Then he laughed. "And that's not a Saber question. It's just Britt's curiosity."

She laughed with him and he found he liked the sound of it.

They rode slowly, talking and laughing together, then stopped to eat some food Britt had brought along.

After a pleasant hour of relaxation, they began the journey again with Britt assuring her that it was not much further.

By early afternoon the dwellings of Britt's mother's family could be seen in the distance and a cloud of dust told them riders were coming toward them.

Britt was greeted with wild enthusiasm by several young men of the village, who kept appreciative eyes on Kairee while she smiled into their open, pleased faces.

"Your mother awaits your arrival," one young man said. "She received the message you sent that you bring a friend to speak to her."

"Is my uncle, Lone Wolf, here?"

"He is."

"I want to speak to him too."

"He knows?"

"Yes." Britt smiled. "I imagine he does. He seems to know what I'm going to think, do, and say before I do it."

"He waits in his lodge."

"Good." Britt allowed the conversation to be filled

177

with amusing and witty remarks as he enjoyed their acceptance of Kairee. They approached the village as a group.

When they dismounted, Britt led Kairee in the direction of his mother's lodge. Kairee entered behind Britt and stood looking across the room at a woman who was certainly not what Kairee had expected.

It took only seconds for Kairee to see who had given Britt his wild, untamed, and nearly beautiful looks. Southwind was exquisite.

She seemed too young to be Britt's mother until Kairee looked into her eyes. There lay her age and her pain, and the memories she kept for herself.

She was taller than Kairee had expected her to be, and very slender. Her almond eyes were nearly black and her hair, the color of a raven's wing, hung to her waist, long and straight.

"Mother," Britt said as he crossed to her and bent to kiss her cheek. Kairee saw the way Southwind's hands clutched her son, as if she were afraid he would suddenly disappear.

"My son," she said in a deep, melodious voice.

"Mother, this is Kairee Kennedy. She has wanted to meet you."

"Kairee," Southwind said quietly, "you are welcome here."

"Thank you."

Southwind turned to Britt again. "Your uncle would speak to you."

"I'll go see him for a few minutes. You make Kairee comfortable. Kairee, if you don't mind, I must talk to my uncle about what help you might need."

"Shouldn't I come too?"

"No," Britt cautioned, then he smiled. "It has to be . . . ah . . . man to man."

"You mean no women." Kairee smiled to show she understood.

"That's right, no women. I'll be back soon."

He left and for a moment Kairee felt uncertain and slightly uncomfortable. Southwind's keen eyes were assessing her and she knew it.

"Come, sit down. We will talk," Southwind offered graciously. It suddenly struck Kairee that she was getting a more civilized reception here than she had from her white neighbors, the Sabers.

"I have wanted to meet you for a long time," Kairee began. "Ever since . . ." Kairee stopped and her cheeks flushed with embarrassment.

"Ever since you found my son was half Indian," Southwind replied, a smile tugging at her lips. Her voice was well modulated and educated, a fact that further surprised Kairee.

"I'm sorry, I—"

"You needn't be sorry. You've recently come from back East. I'm sure you heard stories of the wild savages out here. It is not your fault that it is your expectation to see such people."

Southwind sat opposite Kairee, and again Kairee perceived that Southwind missed nothing about her and could almost read her thoughts.

"My son has discovered some wisdom at last." She laughed softly.

"What?"

"His interest in women has been, to say the least, healthy. I had worried about him. Now I see he has finally developed a discriminating eye."

"Thank you." Kairee suddenly relaxed, sensing she could open herself to this woman and be understood.

"I will tell you a bit about the 'savage' side of Britt's life. Lone Wolf and I are brother and sister. Both of us

179

were first educated at the missionary school that used to be down on the Powder river . . . on Saber land. It is no longer there. Father Martin chose to send Lone Wolf and me to a school in the East. He felt Lone Wolf would need the education to keep his people whole and I . . . I would need it more as a defense. Anyway I enjoyed my brief sojourn east." She laughed again. "But I enjoyed my homecoming far more, at least for awhile."

"Then," Kairee said quietly, "you met Elliot Saber."

Southwind's eyes darkened with memories, then she bent slightly toward Kairee. "You cannot condemn a man for what he is; you must know and understand what he was. Elliot Saber was not always the man you see now."

"I find it difficult to believe."

"So does my son," Southwind said. "I speak to him and sometimes I believe I confuse him more than he already is. Being part of two such different people has brought my son much unhappiness. He has tried to remain loyal to both, but this is difficult when he finds it hard to understand either one."

"Southwind, could I ask you a . . . very personal question?"

"Why I no longer live with Elliot Saber? Why I left him while Britt was still a boy? Why I did not take Britt with me when I came home?"

"I don't mean to pry into such personal things, but . . . if I knew Elliot Saber better, maybe we could understand . . . find a way to deal with him. And at least I could try to understand Britt better."

"There are . . . so many things that I have not even told my brother, or my son."

"Southwind," Kairee questioned impulsively, "do you still love him?"

"Of course," Southwind answered quickly and with

surprise in her tone. "Does one turn off love like it was a small thing? The problem was never that I did not love him, but that I saw he could not love me. There were too many things that stood between us. Love was not one of them."

"And these same things are a barrier between a father and his sons," Kairee said thoughtfully.

"His sons," Southwind repeated. "I worry about my son so often that at times I forget that Elliot has another son."

"Britt doesn't talk of his brother?"

"Very rarely."

"The brothers are not close?"

"You are used to a close family," Southwind stated.

"Yes, I am."

"The brothers," Southwind said meditatively, "could have been close. As small children they sometimes were. But they were allowed to grow apart. Now there is . . . a barrier."

"Their father?"

"Not so much him as the Circle S and their own need for the one thing they still can't understand. Their father has not found the ability to give."

"His love."

"And respect. For some reason they both have been blinded by the need for this."

Seeing Britt through his mother's eyes gave Kairee insight not only into him but into Damion as well. She felt saddened by the knowledge of what truly drove Damion, and why Elliot stood between her and Damion as he had stood between the brothers and even between Britt and his mother.

"There is so much I wish to learn," Kairee said softly, feeling the sting of tears in her eyes.

Southwind bent toward her and laid a hand over one of Kairee's. "We will talk again. We will find a way.

181

There is much to say and now is not the time."

"But—"

"Don't worry." Southwind smiled. "We will speak again."

Kairee was more than certain that Southwind meant what she said, and that she was more than capable of finding a way to do it.

Lone Wolf and Britt sat across a small fire similar to the one in Southwind's lodge.

"It is the truth, Britt," Lone Wolf said. "Your father and I are blood brothers. My sister is still his wife, despite the many hundreds of times I have urged her to break the tie. She lives alone and that worries me. But she insists she will walk her own path."

"Why does that limit what you can do for Kairee and her family?"

"It is a matter of honor, Britt," Lone Wolf explained quietly. "You, of all people, know that even better than I. Your father has changed so much over the years. But there was a time when we rode together, hunted together."

"That time has passed."

"Yes, but the promises made in honor never pass. If that were true, my sister, your mother, would have freed herself from him."

"She won't explain that," Britt admitted. But he knew deep within that the explanation was just as elusive as the answer to his own questions. What prevented him from leaving his father and coming to live here where he would be accepted as a man?

"The woman you brought with you . . ."

"Kairee."

"Kairee. Have you told her all there is to tell? Do you truly believe they will survive?"

"With our help I believe they could."

"Britt," Lone Wolf questioned, "how much does this woman mean to you? Are you not blinding yourself? Your father is a force that will be almost impossible to combat."

"What they need most is help and protection."

"Your father would not harm her."

"I wish I could be as sure of that as you are."

Lone Wolf thought deeply for some time and Britt did not make a sound to interrupt. Then Lone Wolf spoke as if a decision had been made.

"All that I can promise you is that if they are in danger of being hurt I will extend the hospitality of my village. In the meantime, I will teach them some ways to battle nature. I cannot do more than that now."

"It's a step in the right direction and I'm pleased at your offer. I will return when I have taken Kairee back. I want to spend a few days with my mother." Britt chuckled. "I will ask questions as I did when I was a boy and probably get the same results."

Lone Wolf laughed with him. "Your mother is a formidable woman. Even when we were children she was as much a warrior as I was. When we were sent to the white school, she did better than I . . . but don't tell her I said so. I must live in the same village as she."

"I know. When I came crying to her as a child, she had the most remarkable way of adding logic to everything. She taught me much."

"I'm pleased you will return and stay for awhile. We could go hunting and talk."

"Good. Well, I'd best get back. It's a long ride and I'd like to have Kairee home before it gets too late. I'll be back soon."

Britt walked across the wide area between his uncle's lodge and his mother's. When he started to enter, he could hear soft laughter from inside.

He was pleased with the sound and more pleased when he saw the two women seated close together, laughing over something.

"What's so funny?"

"Your first attempt at riding a horse without a saddle," Kairee explained with a giggle.

"You told her about that?" he accused his mother in mock anger. Her smile grew broader.

"Better that than some other stories I could tell her, my dear son."

Knowing quite well that this was more than true, Britt wisely kept silent.

"Kairee, I'm afraid we have to get started back. It's still going to be pretty late by the time we get there."

"Lone Wolf agreed to help?" Southwind questioned.

"Within limits. It's about as much as I expected. At least it's some protection."

Kairee rose and turned to face Southwind. "I'm very grateful for your hospitality. I would like very much to visit you again and to have you come meet my family."

"I would like that. One day I will come," Southwind agreed. "Have a safe ride home. And Kairee?"

"Yes?"

"Do not lose heart. All will be that is meant to be."

"Yes," Kairee said softly, "I'll remember that. Good night."

"Good night."

Britt and Kairee rode in silence for some time. It was Britt who spoke first. He explained the extent to which his mother's people would help her.

"Your mother is a very special woman, Britt."

"No one knows that better than I."

"And she loves you so much. She is very proud of you."

Britt's eyes darkened and Kairee did not want to question what to her looked like disbelief. Finally he spoke softly. "Yes, I suppose she would be."

"Britt, I'd like to return sometime. I would truly like to talk with her again. It's been so long since I lost my mother, and I would sincerely like to get to know yours better."

"That's wonderful, Kairee. She'll be pleased, and I'd like to bring you back, sometime when you can spend a few days. I would like to show you what was once my childhood playground."

It was very dark. The moon, hazed by grey-white clouds, shed very little light. Kairee could see the mellow glow of golden light from the house as they rode up. It was a warm and comforting sight.

In the front yard Britt said good night and left. She tied her horse to the rail, planning to let her father know she was safely home before caring for the animal.

She walked up the steps, across the porch, and opened the front door.

The tall form that untangled his legs and rose to stand before the low-burning fire brought an unexpected gasp of shock from her.

"Damion! What are you doing here?"

His face was grim, but he extended a hand to her as he walked toward her. Suddenly a feeling of terror clutched her.

"My father!" she cried. "Where is he?"

"He's in the bedroom, Kairee. Don't worry and don't be frightened. He's going to be all right."

"What do you mean, he's going to be all right?" she demanded. "What happened?"

"He's been shot."

Damion watched in dismay as Kairee's eyes grew cold and her face bitter.

"Why, Damion? He was the one who wanted no blood. Why did you have to shoot him?"

185

Chapter 14

Damion had pushed Kairee from his mind or at least he thought he had been successful for the part of the day when he could take out his frustration in physical labor. But the prolonged silence at supper proved to be so difficult he left the table early, only to find the confines of his room unbearable. He felt as if he were being pulled in two directions at the same time.

He raged at himself. Until Kairee had come into his life it had been difficult, but at least he had known his goals and where his life would be leading him.

He had only to work, to build the Circle *S* into the best ranch in the territory.

It would have been best if she had agreed to marry him. It would have been much better if she hadn't been so stubborn and had understood that the whole situation could only end one way. Would Elliot Saber have made war against the woman who one day could have given him heirs who would guarantee the continuity of the Circle *S*? No. He would not have done so. But Kairee's stubborn attitude had ended any hope for peace.

When Damion realized that the long evening and an even longer night were both going to be unbearable, he left the house and rode to town, where he got very thoroughly drunk. The next day he was rewarded for his effort by a headache to end all headaches.

The dust and dirt of the day's work was enough to irritate him and the headache made his nerves taut. This in combination with Britt's absence was all the salt his wounds could bear.

"Jim," Damion called out to the Circle *S* foreman.

"Yeah?"

"Where the hell is Britt?"

Jim's eyes avoided Damion's. "I ain't the boy's keeper, Damion. He's gone off again. I expect, to see his kin."

Any other time Damion would have accepted this with a grumble, but some instinctive sense told him there was much more to it this time. In all the years of his growing up, Damion had known Jim to be a demanding taskmaster, a hard worker, but never a man to lie or to bend the truth.

"Jim?"

"Yeah?"

"Britt has really gone to Lone Wolf again?"

"Most likely."

"There is a little more to it, Jim?"

"Well," Jim said hesitantly, "when he rode off, he said where he was going, but he rode in the direction of the Kennedy ranch. I guess he had him an idea to go there first."

"Why?" Damion's dark brows drew together in a frown. "Why would he go there first unless . . . Is that all you know about it, Jim?"

"I swear, Damion, that's all he said and that's all I know."

Damion watched Jim ride away. He sat his horse in frozen immobility as pictures chased themselves around in his mind, pictures he found unwelcome.

187

Britt and Kairee . . . Britt and Kairee.

His jaw clenched as he forced his teeth together and the muscle in his cheek twitched. His eyes darkened and a flame touched them. For a long time he sat as though he were chiseled from rock, then suddenly making a decision, he wheeled his horse about so sharply that it reared and the front hooves pawed the air. Then he spurred it lightly and rode away.

Jim watched through saddened eyes. Again, as he had many times before, he wished he could say all the things tied up within him.

"That man," he muttered, "is gonna see real trouble brew between those two boys while he's setting back tryin' to see which one is worth what he's got. I sure as hell wish something would come along to wake those boys up."

Damion rode slowly but with cold determination. When the Kennedy ranch came into view he stopped to examine it and the area around it, but there was no sign of life.

He nudged his horse forward and rode down to the house. Still there was no sign of anyone about.

Dismounting, he walked up on the porch and knocked. He waited, knocked again, and waited. Was his knock unanswered because no one was home or because those inside chose not to answer? He reached out for the latch and the door swung open. When he stepped inside, he called out.

"Kairee! Anybody home?"

He walked across the room to stand near the fireplace. The Circle S was larger, furnished better, and by far more beautiful. But he could feel the comfort and hominess in this house, something sadly lacking at the Circle S since . . . He could not remember when he had felt such serenity in his home.

He was surprised when his eye caught a small music

box sitting on the roughly cut mantel. It seemed almost frivolous in the austere atmosphere. He picked it up and opened it and was rewarded by a tinkling version of Brahms's Lullaby.

No matter how barren and empty the house seemed to be, as he held the music box in his hand he could feel Kairee's presence.

He sighed, closed the box, and set it back on the mantel. He would have looked further, but suddenly he realized he was intruding. He started toward the door, when all at once Stephen filled it, a rifle in his hand pointed at Damion. Stephen's eyes were wary and untrusting. He knew quite well who Damion was. He was only curious about what his purpose was in being in the house.

"You're trespassing, Mr. Saber," Stephen said quietly.

"Mr. Kennedy, I'm sorry. I knocked, but I thought maybe you didn't hear me."

"Doesn't give you the right to come in. I was in the barn. I take it this is another friendly neighbor visit, Mr. Saber." Stephen smiled.

"I'm looking for Britt."

"He's not here."

"Have you seen him?"

"Can't say as I have."

"Where's Kairee, Mr. Kennedy?" Damion asked softly.

The two men looked at each other with calm speculation that belied the emotions coursing through them both.

"What does one of the Sabers want with my girl?" Stephen's eyes glittered dangerously. "Don't get any ideas about sniffin' around here. You Sabers might own the majority of the range, but I own this ranch and there's nothing you can do about that. I just don't want

189

you thinking you can get any ideas about Kairee. She's a good girl and I won't let her mess with a family that only wants to cause us trouble."

"I didn't come here to cause Kairee, or you and her family, any trouble."

"You won't be too surprised if I find that rather hard to believe."

"Believe it or not, it's true," Damion declared, his irritation beginning to show. "Why don't you put that rifle away, unless you intend to shoot me. If you do, you'd better get on with it because loaded guns pointed at me get me angry, and I just might wrap it around the porch pole out there."

Stephen had to smile in the face of Damion's growing anger, but he lowered the barrel of the rifle.

"Now you tell me, Mr. Saber, just what you are doing in my house and looking for my daughter. It should be pretty obvious that the Sabers and Kennedys haven't got much in common."

"Have you given real thought to what your determination to hold this land is going to cost you and your family? There's so much land on the other side of the Big Horns. Why don't you go?"

"And why should we—so the Sabers can have more? My God, what is enough for you people? We're staying put."

"Then," Damion said in a steel-bladed voice, "you should help me convince Kairee that marrying me would be the wisest thing she could do. And it would sure as hell save a lot of bloodshed, which I can almost guarantee would occur."

"Marry! Mother of God! Whatever gave you the idea Kairee would consider such a thing?"

There was a silence pregnant with truth, a truth Stephen could not miss. But his love for and loyalty to his daughter had been too strong too long. It would certainly stand before anything this arrogant man could throw at him.

"Mr. Saber," Stephen said in a deceptively low, controlled voice, "my daughter is a sweet and giving girl. If she thought she could save her family by coming to you, she would. But I'll see you dead before I let her."

"Why? For Christ's sake, can't you see what could be prevented?"

"Yes. I can also see a cold and demanding man who expects to walk over people and have everything he wants. I see heartbreak and tears for Kairee. No. She'll not be part of the Sabers. She'll never be part of the Sabers."

He raised the rifle again and this time he meant the threat. "I suggest it's time you get off Kennedy land."

He watched with an alert gaze, prepared for anything.

"I want to stay until Kairee comes back. I want to talk to her . . . let her make her own choices."

Damion could not say the words that burned into his mind. I think she's with my brother! I think they are together and I won't tolerate it. Kairee belongs to me.

"I don't think so." Stephen jerked the rifle in the direction of the door. "I said it's time to go."

Damion sighed. It was no use arguing with a loaded rifle. He passed Stephen slowly and walked out the door, with Stephen right behind him.

As Damion moved down the steps, he could feel sweat pop out on his brow and an itch began in the center of his back. It would be easy, he realized, for the Kennedys to rid themselves of one Saber. After all, he was trespassing.

He mounted and looked at Stephen, who stood on the top step of the porch.

"I'd suggest you don't come back here, Mr. Saber, at least not without planning on using your gun."

"There will be no guns if I can help it, Mr. Kennedy,"

Damion said grimly. "And I'll find a way to talk to Kairee. That I promise you. I'll find a way."

Before Stephen could answer, there was a sharp crack of a rifle and Damion's horse reared in fear. He tried to control it while he watched with horrified eyes as Stephen folded slowly, a bright red stain growing on the front of his shirt.

The wounded man dropped the rifle and it clattered down the stairs. Stephen looked at Damion in absolute shock, then his body fell forward and in a minute lay in the dust at the foot of the steps.

Damion muttered a curse and slid from the saddle to run to Stephen's side. He knelt beside him and rolled him to his back. Bending forward, he pressed his hand against Stephen's chest and breathed a ragged sigh of relief when he felt a steady heartbeat.

Damion knew it was quite possible that the men who worked for Stephen could be gone for a day or for several. It was not uncommon for men tending cattle to be gone for as long as a week at a time. In winter they slept in strategically placed cabins called line shacks. In summer they bedded down on the open range.

If Kairee had gone with Britt to his people, it was possible they would not be back soon either.

Damion knew the danger of trying to carry Stephen all the way to Buffalo, where the only doctor could be found. It was up to him to see that Stephen remained alive. It was nightmarish to imagine what would happen if Stephen died. Who would believe he had not died at the hands of a Saber, even if Damion deserted him now, which he knew he could not do.

He lifted Stephen easily and carried him back into the cabin. He had no idea whose room he carried him to, but it did not matter. All he needed was a bed.

He layed Stephen on the bed and removed his shirt to examine the wound. He began to wonder then if the would-be assassin had meant to hit Stephen, or had meant to kill him. He had been nearly in a direct line with Stephen and he knew beyond doubt what would have happened if he had been found dead on Kennedy land. There would have been a bloodbath.

The wound had bled freely and he was grateful for that, for despite the loss of blood, it had washed the wound clean. It had hit high in the fleshy part of his chest and had exited just below the shoulder blade, which led Damion to believe the assassin had shot from a height. Now he was even more certain the bullet had been meant for him.

He rose and left the room in search of something he could use as a bandage. In a chest in another small bedroom he found some white cotton petticoats. These he tore quickly, wondering with a smile if Kairee would be more angry over their destruction or over his rummaging through her things.

He took a bucket and went to the well for water. It took very little time to heat it, then he washed the wound carefully and padded it, grateful once more that the bullet had gone through and did not have to be dug out. Once he had Stephen bound securely, there was little else he could do except wait for someone to come home. He could not just leave Stephen, even though he knew his life was no longer in danger. He did not want the blame for this and he meant to stay to defend himself.

He left Stephen breathing shallowly but safely and went out to make some coffee, thinking it could prove to be a long wait.

He took the coffee and went to look in on Stephen again. Satisfied, he sat before the fire and stretched his legs out. Sipping the coffee, he began to consider why whoever had shot had not shot again. Both he and Stephen had been open targets. He ravaged his mind for ideas but could come up with only one. Someone wanted the attention of the Kennedys and the Sabers to be on each other, and not on something else. But what, and who?

Damion returned to the bedroom often, but there was very little change in Stephen. He remained unconscious, though Damion knew he was out of danger. But if the bullet had been just a bit lower. . . .

The day lengthened into evening and he found he was hungry. He was surprised to realize he had not eaten all day. He rummaged around in the kitchen and was again reminded that these people did indeed have very little. He thought of the elaborate meals at the Circle *S* and felt a tightening in his chest.

He found bread and freshly churned butter and ate several slices of this with more coffee. It was substantial enough to hold him.

Allowing his mind the release of fantasy, he imagined a small place like this, occupied only by him and Kairee. But he eventually had to temper this dream with reality. He was part of the Circle *S* and Kairee would be part of it too, even if only to keep the battle from going any further.

Thoughts of Kairee brought his mind unwillingly to Britt. They were together, and that fact ate at him like a malignancy. He chewed on the idea until the turbulence of his emotions brought him to his feet.

Again he went to check on Stephen, hoping he would awaken before anyone came so there would be no doubt as to who had shot him. But Stephen remained unconscious.

His nerves were stretched taut over his untenable position. If the attackers came back before any of the family, he would be hard-pressed to keep from getting shot before he had a chance to explain.

The idea that he could have just left Stephen where

he was without explanation occurred to him, but he had no intention of running back and hiding behind the Circle S for something he had not done. Besides, he was not going to have his father defending him.

The sun set and the shadows in the house lengthened until he moved to light a lamp and throw another log on the fire.

He dragged the uncomfortable rocking chair close to the fire and propped his feet against the hearth. He may have looked totally relaxed, but every nerve was tuned to hear movement from Stephen's room or sounds of someone coming.

It was late, and Damion was beginning to believe that Kairee and Britt were either spending the night with Britt's mother or spending the night elsewhere. The possibility of that did not make the waiting any easier.

Contemplating the entire situation involved him so deeply that he did not hear the horses. He stretched, yawned, and squirmed into a more comfortable position. It was only then that he heard the door open and close.

For a minute he was shocked at his own resistance to turning around. It did not have to be Kairee. It could be any number of others.

Then it struck him. If Kairee were here, then she most certainly could not be spending the night with Britt. This revelation brought him slowly to his feet.

She stood before him, her face still filled with the shock of his presence. And for that few minutes he absorbed her beauty like a balm for his frayed nerves.

She was more than just beautiful. She was a vibrant force he could feel with every sense he possessed.

He wanted to go to her and take her in his arms, but he could not. He had to tell her what had happened, make her understand that the attempt on her father's life had not been any of his doing.

He started toward her and watched the emotions that played across her face as she began to realize the significance of his presence. It could only mean that something was drastically wrong.

He extended a hand toward her, but she made no move. Her eyes were wide with panic now.

"My father! Where is he?"

"He's in the bedroom, Kairee. Don't worry and don't be frightened. He's going to be all right."

"What do you mean, he's going to be all right? What happened?"

"He's been shot."

He read her thoughts and he hated the accusing bitterness as her eyes grew cold.

"Why, Damion? He was the one who wanted no blood. Why did you have to shoot him?"

"Don't be a damn fool, Kairee. Would I shoot a man, drag him back in his own house, bandage him, and then wait to be called a killer?"

"A clever man might do just that," Kairee said as she started past him toward the bedroom. Damion made no move to interfere but followed behind her as she pushed the door open and moved swiftly to her father's side. She knelt by the bed and took one of his hands in hers.

"Pa?" she whispered.

To Kairee, Stephen looked close to death. His face was gray and his breathing seemed shallow.

Damion had come to stand close behind her, wanting to comfort her but knowing she would be less than receptive to any overtures he might make. No one could have prayed harder for Stephen to open his eyes than Damion did.

Then suddenly Kairee gave a soft sob as Stephen's hand tightened in hers and his eyes fluttered. "Pa," she choked out.

Stephen was disoriented. His eyes flickered from Kairee's tear-streaked face to Damion's. The last thing he remembered was watching Damion mount his horse.

It took him some time to fit the pieces of the puzzle together.

"Who did this, Pa? What happened?" Kairee begged.

"I don't know, girl. Last I remember I was chasing this one off our land." Stephen's voice was raspy and weak as he struggled with his memory.

"Did he shoot you, Pa?" Kairee asked in an angry whisper.

"Damn it, Kairee," Damion said, "I told you what happened."

"I'd rather have my father's version than yours," Kairee said coldly without turning to look into Damion's angry face. "Pa, please tell me what happened."

"I need . . . I need a minute to get it all together, girl. Could you get me some water?"

Kairee started to rise, but Damion put a restraining hand on her shoulder. "I'll go," he said softly.

He turned and left the room, closing the door behind him.

"Pa, try to tell me before he gets back. Did he try to kill you? You don't need to be afraid for me," she lied purposely. "Smokey and Rusty are back and they're outside. I have all the protection I need. I have to know if he tried to kill you."

"From what I can piece together out of my memory, I don't think so. The shot was from a rifle. He didn't have any kind of gun in his hand at all. Besides, the shot seemed to come from a long way off."

Kairee was stunned by the feeling of relief that flooded her and left her weakly clinging to her father's hand while hot tears touched her cheeks.

The truth of Damion's words struck her. It would have been much more clever for him to have gone home and left her father to die. No one would ever have known he had been there.

Of course suspicions would have arisen, but who in the territory would have believed a Kennedy's word over a Saber's?

Damion returned with a tin cup half full of water. Kairee took it from his hand without meeting his eyes and bent again over her father to let him drink.

Stephen sagged back wearily on the pillow.

"Kairee, he needs to rest," Damion said gently.

Stephen's eyes had already closed and Kairee had no arguments to make against Damion's words. She turned away from the bed and walked out of the room.

Damion followed, pulling the bedroom door closed behind him.

He and Kairee faced each other over a greater distance than the width of the room.

"Your father told you it wasn't me." He stated the fact instead of asking the question.

"Yes," Kairee said softly, "he did."

"I've been giving what happened a whole lot of thought, Kairee." Damion went on to explain what had happened. "I don't think the bullet was meant for your father."

"I . . . I don't understand."

"I think that bullet was meant for me."

Chapter 15

Kairee's face was filled with disbelief. But her mind twisted his words until it harbored similar suspicions.

"You think one of our men thought my father was in danger and tried to shoot you to protect him."

"And shot your father by mistake."

"That's impossible."

"No more impossible than me shooting him and hanging around so you could find me with him. Don't you at least wonder why I didn't just finish him off and ride away?"

"If one of our men had seen my father fall, he wouldn't have just left him."

"You can trust them?"

"All four of them," she said definitely.

"Then none of this makes any damn sense at all."

"Yes," Kairee agreed wryly, "the Sabers and the Kennedys are the only ones at each other's throats now. The rest of the people in this entire valley are all at the feet of the great Saber clan."

"Kairee. . . ."

"Damion, I'm exhausted and I'm hungry. I'm also grateful for what you've done for my father. I'll fix us both something to eat and some hot coffee, if you'd like

199

to stay."

"I'd like that. I'd also like to stay until someone gets here to help you. You can't care for him alone."

"That's not necessary," Kairee said quickly. "My family will be back soon," she lied, "and I certainly expect Smokey and Rusty before long."

At any other time her naïveté in thinking Damion was going to believe what he knew was not true would have been laughable, but now he did not want to upset her. She was nervous enough in his presence. He knew it because he could feel it, just as he found it difficult to keep his own feelings under control.

Damion carried in some wood for the stove while Kairee began to prepare a meal.

As she cooked some eggs and made some coffee, Damion returned to the bedroom to check on Stephen. He was sleeping deeply, a healing sleep that Damion believed would last through the night.

Returning to the central room, he found Kairee placing the plates on the table. He sat opposite her and they ate with little conversation.

While Kairee cleared the table, Damion busied himself building a fire in the fireplace. Kairee would be expecting him to leave soon, but he did not plan to do so.

After considering lie after lie about his motives, he finally had to admit the truth to himself. He did not want to leave her. She called to every sense he had and he had no will to resist.

He knelt before the slowly growing fire, feeding several small logs into it, unaware that Kairee's eyes were on him.

Without his attention on her, Kairee was able to admire the virile man who knelt by the fire. Free to enjoy his nearness, Kairee found she could not ignore the aura of tremendous energy that emanated from him.

His body, as he stretched to position the logs, was outlined by the glow of the fire. It was powerful with its taut muscles and graceful lines. His face was carved mahogany, handsome and strong. The hand that held the log was large, with long, sensitive fingers, and had been tanned gold by the sun.

She was caught in a memory, a memory of his touch, of the feel of his hard hand gentle against her flesh. She held her breath as a tingle of awareness rushed through her, a sensation so exhilarating that she almost called out his name.

She made no sound, but still he seemed to hear the call of her mind, for he turned at the peak of that magical moment and their eyes met and held for an instant of endless time.

He saw her look of total awareness and recognized it . . . recognized it because it was only an echo of the fire that licked through him. Slowly he rose.

There was no doubt in Damion's mind. Despite any reason he could give, Kairee and Kairee alone was the reason he was here, the reason he had stayed, and the reason he could not leave.

Her features seemed to him a work of art and the glow in her gray eyes made his respiration quicken.

He leaned toward her, and if it had meant the saving of her life she could not have moved. He reached out a hand and very gently caressed her cheek, surprised to see her eyes suddenly glaze with tears.

Then he slowly put his arms about her, and with a strangled sob she moved into them. His embrace tightened and he bent his head to let his mouth fuse with hers and his tongue slipped between her parted lips to taste and savor the caverns of her mouth.

He was a man accustomed to controlling himself and it bewildered him that with her there was no control. It was as if he had no power at all except the magnificent emotion that surged through him at her touch.

Kairee felt the warmth rush through her and she was filled with calm assurance, as if the world and its troubles were far away. He was an undeniable force and his kiss made her weak and dizzy. She wanted the touch of his hands and the feel of his hard body. Her heart began to pound and her breathing became labored.

His mouth ceased its tormentingly sweet possession and he held her a little way from him.

Each knew this night was meant to be. Everything but the need to touch was forced from their minds and hearts as gentle hands reached to remove the clothes that stood between them.

He wanted her now for more than just a moment's pleasure. He wanted her leisurely, sensuously, tenderly, and thoroughly. It was no less for Kairee, who wanted him with every sense she possessed, to see, feel, taste, hear, smell, and enjoy the complete and beautiful experience.

He kissed her forehead, her cheeks, and then her mouth again as his hands began to move over her, making her body quiver with sensuous pleasure. He stroked her back and arms, then captured her breasts, savoring the texture of her skin beneath his fingertips. He inhaled the sweet scent of her hair and felt the pulse of desire grow to a throbbing demand.

She moved against him, wanting—no, needing—more of the fiery rapture his touch elicited.

Her hands slid up over his shoulders and she gave the whisper of a sigh and closed her eyes to let her senses soar. She absorbed everything about him, the heady masculine smell of his body that mingled the scents of pine trees and sun, leather and the musky scent of man.

He took her hands in his, kissing each finger, her wrists, the curve of her elbow, then drawing her arms about him again, he molded her body to his.

She could feel the hardening of his manhood against

her and the iron sinew of his body as he cupped her buttocks with one hand to press her even closer.

His mouth trailed kisses from her hot, parted lips, down her throat, to gently caress a nipple hardened by the flow of heated desire.

He vowed this night would be one of ultimate perfection, for it could be the last they would ever be able to share.

He drew her down with him to the rug before the fire and studied her face in its glow, a face lit with passion.

He continued, with hands warmed by the heat of her body and lips seared by the touch of her skin, to lift her toward a pinnacle such as she had never known.

They lay together, entwined about each other, hands searching, caressing mouths heated by a flame growing higher and higher.

He tangled his hands in her hair and his mouth attacked now with surging possessiveness. Her hands moved over his body with the same tantalizing heat, and finding his manhood, she stroked with slow, taunting moves until he groaned aloud.

There was a need to hold this volcanic experience, to cling to it for as long as possible.

Now he pressed her back on the rug and held her writhing body while his lips found places so sensitive she nearly screamed. His fingers, gently seeking, found her wet, hot center and began a movement meant to drive her to the brink of insanity.

He drove her beyond her control, guiding her to release before he began again the delicious agony of lifting her to the summit.

With control far beyond what he believed he possessed, he slowly lifted her again and again until she sobbed raggedly and he knew her body was caught in a force beyond reality.

Only then did he let himself find the sheer pleasure of

immersing his throbbing shaft in the heated depths of her. He raised himself on his elbows to watch the glorious vision of the firelight dancing across her passion-filled features.

Her eyes were closed, her lower lips caught between her teeth to keep her cries of ecstasy from bursting forth. Her hair fanned about her as her head rolled from side to side.

He moved slowly at first, glorying in the feel of her moist depths closing around him. But he could not bear the wild, ecstatic pleasure for long. His driving thrusts increased in force and her body arched rhythmically to meet each demanding surge.

To Kairee it felt as if the awesome, stupendous thrust of life itself was breaking time down into momentous seconds, rapid seconds that were each a lifetime; as if separate lives were converging, blending into oneness. No part of her was free of his touch. Her hands spread out against the heavy muscle of his back, sliding lower, holding him closer, caressing him in a way that left him unable to stop until the climax of their lovemaking sent them both gasping for breath and lying in each other's arms, unable to speak or move.

Kairee allowed nothing but Damion to reach her. She knew this blessed numbness was only temporary. She knew the time would come when she would have to sort out her emotions, sort out hope from truth, error from pain. But not yet. Now it was enough just to sense vulnerability beneath this man's surface.

She could feel his eyes against her skin. His dark gaze lingered over her lips, the grace of her neck, and the soft tendrils of her hair lacing across her breasts.

She felt her breath grow short in a combination of surprise and sensual response.

He bent his head to kiss the hollow at the base of her throat, feeling her pulse beat under his lips. His exploring hands moved gently across her skin and he

204

heard her soft sigh. He lifted his head and again looked down into her half-closed eyes.

"Kairee, the night has just begun. The truth, now, is anyone else expected?"

"No," she whispered, helpless before his seeking gaze.

"Then give me tonight. Let's fight no battles tonight. Maybe tomorrow we can find some answers, some way to mend this situation. But for tonight . . . let's just let it be for us."

For an intense and vibrant moment their eyes held and she knew she wanted this night as much as he did.

"If there are never any tomorrows," she whispered, "we'll have this."

She held her arms up to him and clasped him passionately to her soft, yielding body when he came to her. The desire that had always existed between them took over and she was ready for him instantly. Her body arched fiercely against his, achingly impatient for the renewal of his touch.

She is the only one who has the power to defeat me, he thought suddenly. Of all the women I've known, she could be my downfall, my fatal weakness, but I'm incapable of resisting her any longer. At this moment, she is mine.

Never before, when they had made love, had she called out to him aloud, sobbing her passion and her need as she did now. This woman above all others, this wild, bold, sensual creature who gave herself to him with such complete abandon, had created an insatiable need within him, and he knew that from this night on he would never be able to blot her from his senses.

Damion leaned against the rough-hewn post that held up the roof of the porch. Kairee stood in the circle of his embracing arms, her back to him and her head resting against his shoulder. They watched the sun rim the horizon and send brilliant beams through the early morning sky. Like fine instruments, they were atuned to each other's breathing, each other's heartbeats. They had tried in a kind of frenzied desperation to hold back the dawn.

Kairee closed her eyes, subtly aware of some great need in him that had yet to understand, a deep, pulsing thing that tugged at her soul. She felt the edges of their closeness dissolving.

"I'm frightened," she whispered, almost to herself.

She had echoed his own fear, but he could not allow it to grow any bigger than it already was. He had to struggle, for today he felt as if his sense of the realistic had been altered and his instincts were as unstable as King Arthur's had been when he had wandered into the charmed circle of Morgan Le Fay.

"I'll promise one thing, Kairee. I'll try to hold this thing at bay until your father is on his feet. Maybe, if we can buy some time, we can do something."

"Do what?"

He turned her around, his face serious now. "There's an answer to this, Kairee. Come to the Circle S. Marry me. If that doesn't stop the battle—"

"And what if it doesn't?" she demanded. "I change sides, is that it? I forget everything except what I want and walk away to live in comfort at the Circle S?"

"You make being my wife sound terrible."

"You look at me, Damion, and tell me two things honestly. Do you really believe my coming with you would stop your father? And do you honestly believe I would be a traitor to my own family?"

"I can't say what would stop my father. I told you once before, he's not all wrong, Kairee, and he's not to blame for this." He motioned toward the open door to the house. "And why would you be a traitor because you chose to marry, and marry well, I might add. For

God's sake, Kairee, I'm offering you the Circle S one day. A hundred, no, a thousand times more than what you have now or ever will have with this flea-bitten outfit."

"You'll always defend him, won't you, Damion?" she said softly. "Even when you doubt yourself. Even when you're not sure he wasn't responsible for this."

"And I won't condemn him until I know. I told you the shot might have been meant for me, so someone here could be as guilty as hell."

Kairee looked at Damion in thoughtful silence for a few moments, realizing they had skirted the center of the conflict. All they had together was this passionate desire for each other, but that would not prove enough for either of them. Damion was still caught firmly in his father's web, believing the Circle S would be the greatest gift he could offer her.

He had not spoken of love. Of course, she thought, he was finding the easiest way out of a situation without sacrificing what he held most dear, the Circle S.

Instead of anger, she felt a strange sadness. Something had long ago dammed up his ability to commit to love. Was it because it had never been given?"

"Damion, I can't—"

He pulled her close to him, one hand holding her body to his and the other tangling in her hair to pull her cheek against his chest. "Don't say anything, Kairee. We're going to have the same old battle and I don't want anything to damage what's between us. Give us a little time to be together, to try."

She closed her eyes and put her arms about his waist.

"We both have to understand, Damion," she said softly, "that no matter how much we want to end this, we are not the ones in control. It's . . . it's as if we're puppets on a stage. We may have our own desires, but someone else—fate . . . your father . . . mine—pull the

207

strings. This is all beyond our control. There are too many things to fight."

"You're wrong, Kairee," he objected. "I'll run my own life. It will be what I want it to be. . . . All that has been missing has been you." He said the words, but somewhere deep inside a small, insistent voice proclaimed his cry of independence a lie. He ignored the voice. "It would be so much easier if your father knew he was in over his head here, that it would end all the conflict if he just found some land on the other side of the pass."

"How simple. The battle's over, the Sabers win as usual, and according to their will everything falls into place. All except the people who get hurt."

"More would get hurt if this went on. Besides, I'm trying to keep blood from flowing."

"There are other kinds of hurt."

"What?"

"What about my father's pride? What about my brother and his family's future? What about what I might want?"

"I don't understand your hardheadedness, Kairee."

"Why is it just stubbornness when it's our reasoning, and logic when it's yours? I think you really need to understand something, Damion. We are not going to leave here. I think that up until now you still felt we would. Just so there won't be any more mistakes like that, I'll tell you that my father's pride has been damaged enough in the past. My brother has struggled for a future too long, and I . . ."

"What about you?"

"I have a lot of dreams too."

"That never included me." He laughed softly, as if this were a revelation that had not occurred to him until now.

"I could never come to you like a grateful little

beggar. I could not come to you knowing my father had to pay for whatever I got. Why can't your father give us all a chance to stand on our feet, to prove we are no threat to the Circle S?"

Damion digested her words in silence while Kairee moved away from him. He watched her walk a few feet to the porch rail and look out over her home. In startled awareness he remembered how often he had done nearly the same thing, looking out over the Circle S with a pride that had been a lump in his throat and a surge of possessiveness that had made the blood flow more rapidly through his veins.

He did not want to say the words that leapt to his mind and stirred his confusion even more. His world had been stirred beyond control now. He knew one battle would follow another. He had fought Britt, he had fought his father, he had fought Kairee's father, and, up until now, he had fought Kairee.

He was very much aware that his tenuous peace with her was so fragile it could be broken with mere words. Whether his father would bend or not, he meant to have Kairee.

If worse came to worse and his father succeeded in driving the Kennedys to a new range, he would have Kairee. If he had to lie, cheat, or steal, he would have Kairee. Whatever else he did in the next days, the most important thing would be to mold Kairee's passion into something strong enough to make her cling to him when the moment for decision came. He had no illusions that his father would forget that the Kennedys sat on a small corner of the range he coveted.

"Kairee?"

"What?"

"You went with Britt to see his mother, didn't you?"

She looked at him, searching for a reason for this sudden change of subject. "Yes, I did. Southwind is a lovely woman. I enjoyed talking to her very much."

"Did they offer to help you?"

"Who?" she questioned as she turned her face in profile to him to escape the intensity of his size.

"Lone Wolf . . . Southwind . . . Britt's people."

"Your father and you are Britt's people too. Maybe," she added softly, "you should go there and talk to them. If I'm not mistaken, what is now the Circle S was their land to begin with."

"My brother and I aren't exactly close enough to encourage family visits," he said with a mirthless chuckle.

"Maybe you don't understand your brother as he seems not to understand you. Think about it, Damion. Maybe, if you're not afraid of what you might hear, a visit with Southwind could answer a lot of questions."

"What's between Britt and me is something you don't understand."

"Maybe not. But you might find it's not the Circle S that stands between the two of you."

"What has Britt told you?" he demanded.

"About you and him? Nothing. He's as close-mouthed as you are." She smiled to ease the sting of her words. "Besides, even if he had told me anything, I would not intrude on what should exist only between you. Damion, why don't you go to Southwind? Look for some answers. I have a feeling that what you find out might not only give you back a brother . . . it might change your life."

Damion started to speak, to demand that she explain, but at that moment Stephen called her name in a weak voice.

Without a word, she turned to enter the house and closed the door behind her, leaving him more confused than ever before.

Chapter 16

Stephen was struggling to sit up in bed when Kairee came in. He was sweating profusely and his face was gray with strain.

"Pa!" Kairee cried as she ran to the bed and put both hands on his shoulders to force him gently back onto the bed. "What do you think you're doing? Don't even try to sit up yet."

"I heard you talking on the porch. Is Gregg here? How did he come home so quickly?... What's wrong, Kairee?"

"It's not Gregg, Pa," Kairee said softly.

Damion had followed Kairee and now appeared in the doorway. Stephen's eyes widened and he lay silently looking at Damion. Then he turned his head to look at Kairee, who still held his hand.

"He helped me, Pa. He took care of you until I got home. Do you remember telling me what happened?"

"Vaguely," Stephen said.

"Do you remember anything about what happened at all?" Damion said.

"We were talking . . . him and me . . . someone shot me."

Damion breathed a deep sigh. It made him feel much

better to hear Stephen say *someone* had shot him, not Damion.

"I just wanted to make doubly sure," Damion replied, his eyes holding Kairee's, "that you knew it wasn't me that was responsible."

"Have I been out all this time? Since last night?"

"Give or take a few minutes when you came around a bit," Damion said.

"You've stayed here?"

"Kairee needed help."

"I can do fine, now, Damion," Kairee said, uncomfortable with the conversation. "I'm grateful for your help."

If she expected Damion to leave so easily she had made a mistake. He smiled. "I told you last night I'd stay until someone returns to help you. There's wood to chop and barn chores to do that your pa can't do."

"You don't need to bother," Kairee urged with a frown drawing her mouth tight.

But Damion only smiled irritatingly. "It's no bother. The Circle *S* can run without me for a day or so. It's done without Britt more often than that and still kept rolling."

Kairee pressed her lips together against an angry retort that most likely would have made her very astute father more than suspicious. She sat down on the edge of the bed.

"Are you hungry, Pa? I could make some soup."

"I could eat a mite," Stephen said, but his attention was again on Damion. Stephen had seen a fleeting look in Damion's eyes and he wanted to observe him further, for it was an emotion he recognized, and one he least expected.

Kairee turned her head to look up at Damion, who seemed to fill the room with his broad shoulders and white smile.

As if he were caught in some force he could not deny,

212

Damion's eyes met Kairee's, met and held with a gaze that came as close to a physical caress as was humanly possible. She could feel the warmth like the touch of his hands and her cheeks flushed and her lips parted slightly as if she meant to protest yet had no cause for resistance.

It was just a moment in time, yet Stephen too felt the force of it. He remembered Damion's request to let Kairee marry him. A chill of fear touched him. This was just the kind of thing that would be a match to light a powder keg. He kept his fear to himself, realizing he had the advantage over Damion. Damion might want Kairee, but Kairee was so very close to her family that she would do nothing to hurt them.

"If you'll get me a little something to eat, Kairee, I'd like to talk to Damion for a spell."

Kairee stood up, but she did not want to leave the two alone. She knew the strength of these two men and she was afraid of a confrontation that would spark words she did not want spoken.

Damion smiled. He knew exactly what Kairee was thinking. But he wanted to stay the day, or maybe two, that it might take for the men to return. He also wanted to talk to Stephen.

Reluctantly Kairee left, deliberately leaving the door open. She had not gone many feet before she heard it swing shut. She was more than annoyed at this but could not rage back into the room without looking ridiculous. She went about the preparation of a meal, trying to keep her mind off what might be transpiring behind the closed door.

There was a prolonged silence in the room for several minutes after Kairee left. Damion was having a surprising time with his emotions, for he had realized he actually felt Kairee's absence.

Stephen was watching him closely. The last words they had spoken before the shot were returning to Stephen; in fact, the entire conversation was beginning to grow clearer.

"You said you'd find a way," Stephen began, "but don't think you're going to play on Kairee's sympathies and tell her how much safer her family'd be away from here . . . just in case something like this should happen again."

"I hadn't thought of that." Damion smiled. "But it's not a bad idea—if I thought it would work, which I don't. Kairee doesn't scare easily."

Stephen chuckled, and Damion's chuckle joined him.

"I'd kind of like you, boy, if you weren't a Saber. But you are and I don't think it's something you can forget easily."

"I've tried to explain that to Kairee."

"None of this is doing any of us any good."

"What's it going to take to reach you?" Damion asked. "This range has been used by us since I was a boy. If we made you a fair offer, bought this land—"

"Boy," Stephen said quietly, "didn't your pa ever teach you that there're some things in this world you just can't buy?"

Damion was silenced effectively. Could he admit to the fact that the only thing his father had taught, and taught with an iron hand, was that the Circle *S* came first and what you couldn't buy, you took.

"Damion, I think it would be a good thing if your pa and I had another meeting. We can try to get it straight that this ranch belongs to me and my kids. There isn't much I can leave them except this. It was my brother's; that makes it mine. I don't need any charity from any man."

"You don't understand—"

"No! No, it's you who doesn't understand. We're not

214

thieves; we're not squatters sitting on someone else's land. For the first time I think the Sabers had better see the truth."

"There's only one thing that's the truth. You can't survive a winter here. You're newcomers. You don't know how. And nobody else in this valley will help you."

"Scared of the Circle *S?*"

"Could be . . . or they're just smart enough to see you can't do anything but lose. Do you want to take your whole family down with you?"

"I'll put it to my family. We'll talk about it. But when you go home you set up a meeting for when I can get out of this bed."

"It will be a good three or four weeks, maybe more."

"No matter," Stephen said quietly. "I'm not going anywhere."

"All right," Damion replied, "I'll get you two together. But there isn't much to be hoped for from it."

"At least we'll clear the air."

Damion sighed. He had made no more headway than if he had been talking to a wall.

He remained silent again, his thoughts on Kairee and the gulf that seemed to be widening between them.

Maybe a meeting would help in some way . . . maybe, but he doubted it.

The door opened and Kairee came in with a tray of food in her hands. Damion's strong arm lifted Stephen gently and braced the pillows behind him.

While Kairee fed her father, Damion returned to the porch. He stood with his shoulder against the post and looked about him.

Used to a well-run and productive ranch, Damion saw the Kennedy homestead as a disaster. The hastily erected bunkhouse and barn were nearly laughable, he thought. The house was very little better, yet they were tenacious in their grasp on it.

But beyond the barn, beyond the bunkhouse, lay a beauty that could take the breath from a man. It held him until he felt Kairee's presence beside him.

He turned and found a beauty that touched him more deeply than nature could ever hope to do.

"He's asleep again," she said.

"He needs as much rest as he can get."

"Damion?"

"What?"

"He said he was going to meet your father again, when he's well enough."

"I'm going to try to arrange it, but I'm not too confident about what will come of it."

"At least it's a step."

"Kairee . . ."

"Let me hope, Damion."

He went to her and gently took her into his arms. He held her for a few minutes without words, while he searched for the right ones. But it was Kairee who spoke first.

"Won't it make matters worse if you stay here for a day or so? Your father will be expecting you. Won't he be angry?"

"I've been out on the range two, three days at a time, sometimes even weeks. I'm not going to be missed that much. Besides"—he chuckled—"I don't know of too many things that could make matters worse."

A shiver of apprehension whispered through Kairee when she thought of the fence Gregg intended to build. She was going to do her best to keep Gregg from starting the fence before the meeting between her father and Elliot Saber.

If they could talk, could reach some level of agreement, there would be no need for the fence at all.

She had to keep the fence a secret for as long as possible.

"And what is he going to say when he finds out you

216

helped us?"

"Kairee, for Christ's sake, I'm not tied to my father's strings. He doesn't have that much to say about where I go and what I do." Damion said the words, but he was not quite sure his father did not think of him as an extension of his own arm. The thought annoyed Damion more than he thought it should.

Kairee started to speak again, but the sound of horses approaching drew their attention.

Smokey and Rusty rode up to the porch. Kairee smiled and Damion scowled. Why, he thought, couldn't they have kept busy for a day or two longer? What existed between him and Kairee was too fragile to be left alone. Too much time to allow her to think and she could easily change her mind.

"Miss Kairee?" Smokey spoke to Kairee, but his eyes were on Damion with a wary look. Both men had their hands resting lightly, but noticeably, on the guns that hung low on their hips.

"Smokey, Pa's been shot."

"Shot!" Smokey snapped. His gun hand quivered as if he would have loved to have drawn his gun. Damion leaned against the porch rail again, casually, his arms folded across his chest, and looking as if the threat of Smokey and Rusty meant little or nothing.

"We don't know who did it, Smokey, but Pa is awake and doing well . . . and he said it wasn't Damion."

"Then who was it?" Rusty demanded.

"We don't know," Kairee replied.

"I was here with him when he was shot," Damion added.

"And 'cause you were there, we're supposed to believe it wasn't someone from the Circle *S* put a bullet in him." Smokey spoke as if the words Damion had said were laughable.

"Nobody from the Circle *S* needs to bushwhack anybody," Damion said firmly. "We don't need to."

"Cocky, ain't he?" Rusty remarked with cold amusement. "Maybe we ought to send him home with a bullet in him. Sort of like a calling card, or a warning."

"No Rusty," Kairee said, "we don't need to do such a thing either. Damion is leaving, and we don't need any more problems until Pa's on his feet."

Damion could still read the temptation in both Smokey's and Rusty's eyes, but he retained his half smile and casual, relaxed posture as if nothing bothered him. They would never know the tension that strung him as taut as a bowstring. He was in an extremely dangerous position and he knew it. One false move and two guns could end his part of the conflict here and now.

Kairee understood the danger as well as he did and sought a way out of it.

"Smokey, Rusty, I think you both had best come in and talk to Pa. As I said"—she turned to face Damion—"Damion is leaving now."

His eyes held hers and for a moment she was almost terrified by a look of rebellion that told her he did not favor having it look like he was running away.

"Please, Damion," she said in a half whisper.

There was little else he could do unless he wanted to force a gun battle here and he could not afford that.

"All right, Kairee," he said gently, "I'm leaving. But expect me back in three or four weeks, as soon as your father's well enough. Make sure of one thing, Kairee"—his voice held the same promise as his eyes—"this is far from over and I don't intend to end it like this."

He walked down the steps and toward the barn, where he had stabled his horse. He turned once to glance back at Kairee, but she was no longer there.

Damion rode slowly, his mind tangled in a confusion of questions with no logical answers. Who had shot

218

Stephen and why? Had someone been shooting at him? Why? Would his father agree to a meeting? And the most important question of all: could he get past all the barriers that led to Kairee?

He began to think of what Kairee had said about Britt and Southwind. What did Kairee actually believe Southwind could say to him that would make a difference in anything?

It was only when Damion began to consider the many sides to the problem that he realized there could possibly be another side that had been left unexplored. Was there a third party interested in what was happening between the Kennedys and the Sabers? Interested enough to attempt murder and place the blame so the conflagration became explosive? But who? There was no one who stood to profit.

He pushed this thought to the back of his mind and replaced it with visions of Kairee . . . extraordinary Kairee. What a tangle their lives had become.

The problems that stood between him and Kairee were so momentous that he could have laughed if he had not been so shaken by the near impossibility of it all.

Damion arrived home by mid-afternoon. He walked into the ranch house intent on a good, strong drink to help wipe away the cobwebs in his mind and help him decide what he could say to his father that would make him restrain from doing anything to damage the Kennedys and agree to meet with Stephen.

Even if he did agree to do that, there was the little matter of the time it would take to get Stephen on his feet. If Elliot could not be persuaded to wait that long, then the problem would be unsolvable.

Damion left his horse to be cared for, a thing he seldom did. No cattleman existed who did not respect the value of his horse, and under other circumstances, though he was the owner's son, Damion would have cared for his own animal.

He walked into the cool quiet of the house. He expected to find his father away, for Elliot was still a man who kept his finger on the pulse of his empire. That was why, when he walked into his father's office to find a drink, he was more than shocked to find Elliot seated behind his desk.

For a minute Damion stood immobile, his surprise, clear on his face, preventing speech. Then he crossed to the table where the brandy decanter and glasses sat.

"Kind of surprising to see you home this time of day," Damion said. "Something wrong?"

"Nothing serious," Elliot said as he rose from his desk and walked across the room to accept a glass of brandy from Damion. "Where've you been?" Elliot questioned.

Damion took a large drink of his brandy, walked to a leather chair, and sat down before he replied.

"I rode over to the Kennedys' yesterday."

"Yesterday?"

"Yes . . . yesterday. I wanted to talk to Stephen Kennedy."

Elliot watched Damion closely, feeling there was much more Damion wanted to say.

"There was a little problem. That's why I spent the night."

"The little problem wouldn't have a name, would she?" Elliot asked. The last thing he wanted was Kairee Kennedy entangled in his family. The thought of looking into her gray eyes for the balance of his life was to his mind an impossibility. She could stir something in him that he would rather not face.

"The problem wasn't with Kairee; it was with her father. While I was there someone shot him."

Elliot chuckled softly, but the chuckle died when he saw the look in Damion's eyes.

"Sorry." Elliot grinned and shrugged. "I just didn't

think you'd make a mistake like that."

"Mistake?"

"Trying to get rid of them. You don't shoot a man unless you have someone to say you weren't there when it happened. None of us even knew where you were. You could have had a lot of trouble."

"You really believe that I . . ." Damion was shaken by the thought. But worse was the fact that if Damion had killed a man, Elliot would have shrugged it off—as long as it had been for the cause of the Circle S. "I didn't shoot him. Someone else did. You don't know anything about it, do you?" Damion added softly.

Elliot realized his mistake. Damn the boy's sensitivity! Elenor, as far as he was concerned, had cursed his son with a fatal flaw. He would have to continue to try to cut him free of it. It was a weakness, this consideration of someone who was trying to rob them, and Elliot found it hard to justify weakness.

"No! I didn't have anything to do with it, but I'd sure as hell pat the man on the back who did, if I knew him. What the hell's the matter with you? Someone took a shot at him. Maybe he'll be smart and get out of here."

Damion contained his anger. This was no time to argue with his father.

"I spent the night there making sure he was all right. This morning, before I left, we had a little talk."

"How cozy," Elliot said with bitter coldness.

"In three or four weeks he should be on his feet again."

"Too bad."

"Pa, for Christ's sake!"

"What do you want me to do, bleed for the bastard who plans on stealing from me?"

"I told you I talked to him. I don't think these people have stealing in mind. I think they just want to live in peace."

"What's all this leading up to, Damion?"

221

"I want them left alone until he's on his feet."

"I don't think that's the end of what you want."

Damion and Elliot stood a short distance apart, their eyes locked.

"I want to arrange a meeting between him and you. I want you two to talk."

"You want a hell of a lot, boy, for a man who doesn't own the Circle *S* . . . yet."

The open threat that he might never have the Circle *S* nearly shattered Damion, but he clung tenaciously to the hope that Elliot and Stephen could change everything if he could just get them together.

"No, I don't own it. But I've given it my life too. So I don't think asking you for one favor is too much. I'm asking you to talk to him, that's all."

Elliot eyed Damion shrewdly. He knew his son well. It would fit into his plan nicely to have Damion owe him. It would be a good debt to call in later, when it would be useful.

"All right. I'll talk with him. When?"

Damion was surprised. Then he replied quickly. "In about a month. In the meantime, I don't want them to have any problems."

"I haven't caused them any, yet."

"One month, Pa."

"All right. One month." Elliot set his empty glass down and walked to the door, where he turned to look at Damion again. "In that month you stay put and see to the Circle *S.*"

"Agreed."

Elliot left and Damion returned to the decanter to pour another drink. One month away from Kairee was not too much to ask if it would bring peace.

In that month, he had just decided, he would make another visit. He would do what Kairee had suggested. He would go see what answers Southwind might have to offer about the puzzle that was Elliot Saber.

Chapter 17

The two-week trip to Buffalo had been exciting for Cassie, rewarding for Lucy, and more than a little interesting for Gregg.

The wagon was loaded with something no one on the range in Taggert Valley had ever seen before. In fact Gregg had never seen the type of material he was bringing back either.

He had been amazed at it when he had gone to the store to examine it. With tentative fingers he had reached to touch, only to be pricked by the sharp barb. The wire was sturdy and the random barbs quite capable of keeping cattle contained in one area.

"That's the best there is, boy," the storekeeper had proclaimed. "You ranchin' near here?"

"Down on the Powder River," Gregg replied.

"Powder River." The man's brow had furrowed. "You ain't anywheres near the Saber range, are ya?"

"Neighbors," Gregg said shortly.

The man's eyes widened in disbelief. "You ain't tellin' me you want to fence Saber range. Boy, you sure like to live dangerous, don't you?"

Gregg's eyes narrowed and his voice grew cold. "I'm not fencing Saber range. I'm fencing my own."

"You take some prime advice, boy. Don't run up a fence across Saber range. You'll have a war quicker than spit. I heard about old man Saber and those two roosters of his. He ain't one to take to it. No, sir, he ain't one to take to it."

"Mr. Taylor, give me a price on the wire and let me worry about where I string it."

Taylor's mouth had closed on any further remarks, but his eyes and the negative shake of his head spoke volumes.

Gregg had never repeated the storekeeper's words to Lucy, and he kept the worry to himself during the ride back, unaware that Lucy had sensed the problem but did not want to add to it.

Now the wagon, with a heavy cover over the rolls of wire, moved slowly toward the Kennedy ranch.

Gregg had been giving the matter of stringing the wire a great deal of thought. He had finally made a decision. For now he would store the wire in the barn. He would try again to make some kind of peace with the Sabers.

They had camped along the way and now all three were relieved to see the house in the distance. Despite its still distressing condition, it looked good to all three, who were anxious for a comfortable bed and food prepared over more than an open camp fire.

Kairee had her father seated in a comfortably padded rocking chair by the fireplace. He had had almost two weeks to recuperate. Now that the allotted time had passed, both expected to see some sign of Gregg soon.

Several times that day she had gone to the porch to check the horizon. Now she was pleased to see the dot in the distance moving toward her.

224

She went back into the house and Stephen read her pleased face.

"Gregg and Lucy coming?"

"They're just visible on the horizon. I've time to brew some coffee and heat up the stew in case they're hungry."

"Good, 'cause I'm getting kind of hungry from smelling that stew all morning."

Kairee laughed as she began the preparations.

By the time she set the table for the evening meal she could hear the wagon drawing to a stop before the house.

In moments an excited Cassie burst through the door and threw herself into Kairee's open arms.

She was followed by Lucy carrying several packages.

"Gregg said he'll be in as soon as he takes care of the horses." Lucy hugged Kairee and then bent to kiss Stephen's cheek.

"Did you have a nice trip, Cassie?" Stephen questioned.

"Oh, Grandpa!" Cassie exclaimed excitedly as she began a long description of her discoveries in the city.

Lucy layed the packages aside, her smile fading as she began to look more closely at her family. Stephen was wan and looked extremely weak. Besides that, she could see the white bandage beneath the open neck of his shirt. She turned her surprised eyes to Kairee and was again shaken by the look on Kairee's face and the expression in her eyes. Haunted was the first word that came to mind. Frightened was the next.

"Kairee, what happened?" Lucy asked quietly.

"Yes." Gregg's voice came from the doorway where he had been making similar observations. "What has happened, Kairee?"

"Everything's all right now," Kairee said with almost desperate enthusiasm.

225

"I can see you're all right now," Gregg said firmly. He went to Kairee and took hold of her shoulders, forcing her to look at him.

"I want to know what happened."

"Don't, Gregg," Stephen said. "Kairee has had a hard enough time. I was shot."

"Shot! Who did it? A Saber?" Gregg snarled.

"Now come over here and sit down and let me explain what happened," Stephen insisted. "Don't go jumpin' to conclusions. I don't think it was a Saber."

Gregg came to sit down next to his father. "What makes you say that, Pa? Who else would do us any harm?"

"Damion Saber was here when I was shot," Stephen began. "But he wasn't the one who shot me, and he would have been a damn fool to have had me shot while he was at my door."

Gregg had been watching his father intently, but Lucy had watched Kairee. She had seen her face go ashen and now she wavered on her feet as if she had received a blow.

Stephen went on to explain all that had happened with Gregg sitting grim faced before him.

Lucy went to Kairee and without speaking put her arm about Kairee's shoulder.

Kairee turned to look at Lucy and it was only in that moment that Lucy sensed something was drastically wrong with Kairee that had more to do with Damion Saber than the shooting.

Kairee straightened and smiled her acknowledgment of Lucy's consideration.

"I've made some stew, and there's fresh bread and coffee. I'm sure you all are hungry."

"I'm hungry," Cassie said quickly.

"Then help me put everything on the table and we can eat." Kairee spoke but kept her eyes from meeting

226

Lucy's again. She may have fooled all the others, but she knew there was no way to hide the truth from Lucy.

After they had eaten, Kairee and Lucy, with some help from a still chattering Cassie, cleaned up the dishes.

Everyone kept the conversation light until Cassie was safely tucked into bed. It was only then that Gregg made his decision.

"I'm stringing that wire, Pa," he stated firmly. "I was thinking about holding off, trying to make peace. But this is too much. Once that wire is strung, there will be no doubt that this is our land and we'll tolerate no intruders. I'm not going to let this kind of thing pass without doing something about it. All these men understand is strength."

"What strength, Gregg?" Stephen asked. "Think of what they have to back them up. We'll think about the wire for a few days."

"Give it two weeks," Kairee said quickly.

"Two weeks?" Gregg turned to her. "Why?"

"Damion is setting up a meeting between Pa and his father in two more weeks. If we can talk, get past this problem, then maybe we'll end the trouble."

"Damion?" Gregg repeated, his astute gaze taking in Kairee completely for the first time since his arrival. "So . . . it's Damion Saber we have to wait for?"

"I didn't say that, Gregg," Kairee insisted in a soft but urgent voice. "But it's worth a try, isn't it? What can two weeks mean . . . just fourteen days?"

"Kairee, are you all right?"

"I'm fine, Gregg, really, I'm fine. I just don't want any more of this trouble."

Gregg and Lucy exchanged glances and Lucy gave a quick negative shake of her head. Gregg dropped the subject until he and Lucy could talk. He stood up and stretched. "Well, it was a rough trip and I'm tired. We can talk about this tomorrow when we're all feeling better."

Everyone agreed to this with a strange kind of relief, as if the problem could be wiped from their thoughts if they did not speak of it.

Gregg helped his father to bed, then wished Kairee good night with a kiss and an embrace.

Kairee was left alone in the main room of the house before a fire that was slowly dying.

She had never felt as she did now. A strange nauseating weakness swept over her and she sagged to the floor before the fire. She buried her face in her hands, suddenly unable to restrain her tears. Combined with the emptiness she felt was a longing for something she could not name. She allowed the tears, burying her face in her pillow, and she wept until the sleep of exhaustion finally claimed her.

The two final weeks of truce was not to last to its end. Three days after his arrival home, Gregg brought word that ten head of their cattle were gone. With a herd the size of theirs, ten head was an unacceptable loss.

Gregg was angry enough that words of caution from Stephen and all that Kairee could say went unheeded.

The same day he ordered Smokey, Rusty, and the two hands to begin cutting the poles that would be used for the fence posts.

It took them another three days to finish enough posts to fence in several miles of the border of their land. Gregg rode with them as they dug the holes and braced the posts. Then they began to string the wire from pole to pole.

It was a hot and tedious job, and to cowboys unaccustomed to being on their feet or even out of their saddles for any length of time, it was exhausting.

Smokey and Rusty and Gregg were in the process of stringing a length of wire and nailing it to the posts. The barbs occasionally found their marks and brought mumbled curses and complaints.

Amid this annoying confusion, they did not hear the approaching horse until the rider was close.

Gregg's attention was caught first and he stood motionless, watching Jim Sinclair ride toward him. Whatever secret it might have been, Gregg knew now it would only be a short time until Elliot Saber knew of the wire.

Jim drew his horse to a halt, gazing in disbelief at the long row of poles with the three strands of wire between each. This was something he had never seen before. The idea of being fenced in took him so totally by surprise that he remained speechless for several minutes.

Gregg signaled Smokey and Rusty to remain silent, then he walked close to Jim's horse. One hand supporting the shovel he held and the other hooked in his belt very near his gun, Gregg looked up at Jim.

"Morning." Gregg spoke with no sound of insecurity in his voice.

"This your idea?" Jim snapped, ignoring the greeting.

"Just marking the boundaries of my land."

"Boy, are you crazy? The range out here has been open since before either of us were born. What the hell do you think you're doing?"

"I lost ten head," Gregg said. "Could be they just roamed off. But I can't afford any more losses, and I can't wait until spring roundup to try to get 'em back. I'm just going to make sure they don't *wander* away again."

"It appears to me you don't know anything about the snow or the blizzards out here. Cattle got to be free to move with the wind. You keep this fence up and they'll pile up against it like a wall. You'll lose every head you got. Besides that, there ain't nobody would be fencing grass or water out here."

"Well, it's fenced now," Gregg said, his voice becoming firmer. "My father was shot a few weeks ago. I don't suppose anybody on the Saber range knows anything about that, but I intend to see that Elliot Saber gets the message loud and clear. This is my range and he can keep his cows, and his hired guns, on his side of the fence."

"You're asking for more trouble than you can imagine. Elliot is not going to sit still for this. You so anxious to push a fight?"

"Somebody on Saber land should have thought of that before he shot my father."

"Let me give you a piece of advice. Take that fence down before it starts something you can't finish. There's going to be hell to pay if wind of this gets back to Elliot. Be smart and take that fence down."

"Sorry. The fence stays. So does the warning. I'm not interfering with Elliot Saber. Tell him not to interfere with me and there won't be any problem."

Jim stared at Gregg with a puzzled frown. He could not quite believe what he was seeing or hearing. It was like a flea threatening a dog. He was sure Elliot would not take too long to step on him.

"I don't want trouble. I just want to be left alone. It seems the Sabers just can't do that. They keep thinking everyone else is just walking in their shadows. The law says this land is mine, so I'm putting a fence around what belongs to me. All Elliot Saber has to do is stay away from my range and maybe I'll try to forget that it had to have been his order that set someone out to kill my father."

Jim's face was stark in his utter disbelief. Not only

was Gregg slapping Elliot in the face with this strange-looking wire fence, he was also accusing him of an attempted murder. Jim had known Elliot too long. He had too much pride and courage to hire a man to kill for him. He would have challenged his enemy himself—and he would have killed him, not just tried.

"I'll tell Elliot what you said. But you'd better be ready to eat that fence."

Jim spurred his horse and rode away. Smokey and Rusty exchanged looks but remained silent while Gregg stood immobile, watching Jim until he disappeared.

Then he turned to face the two. "All right, boys," he said quietly. "We've got a lot of fence to string so we'd better get busy."

Damion had known Britt was in his mother's village and had not wanted to visit Southwind at the same time. Though unsure of what he wanted to ask, he was certain he did not want Britt there to share what answers he might get.

But Britt showed no sign of returning and too much time had passed for Damion to wait any longer. He wanted to know just what it was that Kairee had had in mind when she had urged him to speak to Southwind.

It had been almost three weeks and he had not broken his word to his father. He had worked like a demon from sunup to sundown. But even the strenuous labor could not wipe Kairee from his mind.

Now he made his decision. Britt's presence or no, he would ride to the village and talk to Southwind. It would be the first time he had talked to her since he was sixteen.

He had always remembered her as a very quiet and gentle person, and he remembered when she left. He had not understood anything except Britt's soundless grief. When she had gone, he had tried to reach out to Britt, but like a young, wounded bear cub Britt had struck out at the outstretched hand, and Damion, still too young himself to understand such pain, had withdrawn it.

He packed his saddlebags and left the Circle *S* unobtrusively. Unless he was faced with it, he did not want his father to know where he was going. He felt a twinge of guilt, but he needed some answers and was determined to discover exactly what Southwind had told Kairee.

He rode away from the ranch less than an hour before Jim approached from another direction.

Jim found Elliot in his study working on the ranch's books, a labor he was not fond of and one that left him with a short temper.

Jim rapped once and walked in. Elliot looked up and his look of annoyance changed to one of surprise, then interest.

"What's wrong, Jim? You look like hell warmed over."

"Elliot, that Kennedy boy, he's stringing a fence— some kind of wire fence—between his land and the Circle *S*."

Elliot looked at Jim in complete surprise. This was something that had not happened on the open range during either man's lifetime.

"He's doing what?"

"It's wire, with sharp spikes on it. I tell you I've never seen anything like it before. He's planted poles all along our border and he's stringing wire as calm as you please."

Jim removed his hat and sat down across from

Elliot. He began at the beginning, when he had gotten his first word of the fence and had ridden over to see for himself. He explained to Elliot all that had been said between him and Gregg Kennedy.

He watched Elliot's eyes grow cold and firm, his jaw clench in anger.

"You told him there've never been fences out here before? That a man grazes his cattle on open range?"

"I did, but he claims the law says the land is his and he's got a right to fence it if he wants to."

"He's fencing off some good water holes I need too."

"He says," Jim added, "that he's got to protect his family from us. He's blaming the shooting of his pa on us. Looks like he means to stand by what he says."

"Jim, do you have any idea who did do the shooting?"

"Nope. Wasn't any of our boys. Nobody here would lift a gun to a man unless you ordered it, and even if they did it wouldn't be bushwhacking."

"None of this makes sense. I don't want any more shooting, but I want that fence down and I want it down now. Take as many of the boys as you need and cut it loose. Mind you," he added as Jim rose, "I don't want anyone hurt bad . . . but I'm not against your roughing them up a bit just to give 'em a little lesson about stringing any more fence."

Jim nodded. "What about Damion?"

"He should go along. Might give him a better idea of what we're up against. Might not make him so softhearted if he sees these people are like a slow poison that's going to eat up the range until we all lose out."

"I'll see if I can find him."

"Whether you do or not, you get out to that fence and get it down."

Jim left, but after half an hour he had found no trace of Damion or a clue to where he might have gone. He

233

gave up on the search and headed out to confront Gregg and the strange new threat of wire fence.

When Jim and the three men he had brought along reached the fence, it was late in the afternoon. Having strung what wire and poles they had brought with them, Gregg, Smokey, and Rusty had gone back to the ranch.

It took some doing, but amid curses as the wire sprang back to nip each man, they laboriously cut and destroyed all the work that had taken the three men from dawn to late afternoon to do.

As the next two weeks passed, Gregg and his men stubbornly restrung the fence and tried to patrol the barrier to protect it, though they had to split up to cover its entire length. This separation led to a confrontation between Rusty and the hands from the Circle *S,* and Gregg and Smokey found him beaten and rolled painfully in a length of the barbed wire.

Damion was unaware of the conflict as he rode to Southwind's village and he had no way of knowing that Britt had left his mother's home a day or so before to hunt in the foothills with his uncle.

It was early evening when Damion arrived at his destination. Southwind knew of his presence, for word had been brought to her long before Damion's arrival that the brother of her son was riding to the village.

Southwind knew why he was coming. It was something she had known would happen one day. She was also sure it had been Kairee Kennedy who had brought him to her.

Chapter 18

Kairee sat back against the trunk of the tree and closed her eyes, sighing deeply. She had ridden away from the house before dawn because she had to be alone.

To face herself with what she now knew to be the truth was difficult enough, but to face her family, those who loved her, was almost too much. Yet she knew it would be impossible to retain her secret for long.

It had been weeks since she had seen Damion, weeks of watching small problems turn into big ones, of watching the tension between the Kennedys and the Sabers grow until it was a seething violence ready to explode.

The most crushing thing to her was the knowledge that she could possibly be the cause of the explosion.

Desperately she searched for some way to bring an end to it all, but there was none. She had known now for almost two weeks, two weeks of being wretchedly ill in the morning and denying what her body said in every way possible. Yet nature had soon made it evident that her worst fears were so. She was carrying Damion Saber's child.

She couldn't tell him! She wouldn't tell him! Her

mind conjured up visions of what could happen if she did.

Her father and brother would want to kill Damion. Elliot Saber would be accusing her of trying to trap the Sabers into giving up the fight, or worse, of trying to acquire the wealth of the Sabers through deceit. There would be unhappiness, distrust, and the complete destruction of any hope for reconciliation between the two families.

She drew up her knees, folded her arms across them, and rested her forehead on her folded arms.

She had to tell someone. Her first thought was Lucy, then strangely Southwind's face wavered before her. Could she trust Britt's mother . . . Elliot's wife? Both were women, and maybe a woman was the only one who could help her find a solution to this potential disaster.

She had cried too many tears and now was the time to dry them and regain her composure. Whether anyone stood with her or not, she would do what had to be done. She would bear her child. But it would be hers and hers alone. It would never be a Saber.

She rose and mounted her horse, hoping when she arrived at the house both Gregg and her father would have set about their day's work and she would be free to talk to Lucy. And after she spoke to Lucy, no matter what Lucy decided to do or say, she would ride to see Southwind. If the battle of the Kennedys and Sabers was to continue, she would at least take her child from the center of it. No matter what, she would see the child was safe, from both families.

When she arrived, there seemed to be no one in the house but Lucy, but both women were under the impression that Cassie had gone outside to play. It was not so.

Cassie had found her way to her parents' bedroom

and was seated on the floor by the bed playing with a rag doll her father had made her.

Despite the closeness of her family, Cassie was often a lonely child. This was why the words she overheard fell on a fertile imagination. She had not meant to listen and was prepared to come out of the bedroom, when the magic word, "baby," brought her to a halt. She grew mesmerized by a conversation that sent a tingle of delighted excitement through her.

Kairee and Lucy sat across the rough wooden table from each other. Lucy, her heart filled with compassion, had reached across the table to cover Kairee's hand with hers.

"Oh, Kairee," Lucy said, her first thought for Kairee's welfare, "what can I say or do to help you?"

"Nothing, Lucy, except to stay the friend you have always been. Pa and Gregg will be hurt and angry with me. Lucy . . . I won't let this baby be a pawn between us and the Sabers."

"Of course you mustn't. That would be terrible. But, Kairee, I know how much Gregg loves you. He'll get over the shock quickly. So will Pa. You'll see. We'll make it work out."

"I'm only afraid . . ."

"Of what?"

"Of Damion . . . of Elliot Saber."

"Don't be. Surely that man is not so heartless he would take his greedy spite out on a helpless child. And Damion . . . do you love him, Kairee?"

"It . . . it is so difficult to explain, Lucy. It was almost as if something drew us together. I wanted him, but is that love? I don't know the answer. I only know I can't let the Sabers have my child and I can't tell Damion."

"Why not?"

"I do not want him to marry me because I'm carrying

237

his child. I could never live with him without knowing if he truly wanted me or was forced into something he could not control. Please understand, Lucy, you must never let word get out. Not yet, not until I can find some answers of my own. I don't think I could bear to face Damion and see a trapped look in his eyes. I don't think I could face his father either and hear his scorn."

"Oh, Kairee, I wish there were something I could do to help you, to make this easier."

"You do, Lucy. You're the only one I can talk to. Just that is a big help."

"What are you going to do now?"

"For now, for a few days, I will just try to think, to form some plans. I think I will go talk to Southwind."

"What do you think you will accomplish there?"

"Southwind is the only one who has successfully walked away from the Sabers. Perhaps she can show me how to find the courage to face them."

"You have all the courage you need, Kairee. You always have had it."

"Well, right now I'm not so sure of that."

"When will you go to see Southwind?"

"In a week or so. It takes most of the day to get there and I would have to spend the night. I could find my way there in the daylight, but I don't think I could find my way after dark. I'll need a reason to be gone."

"We'll think of something."

"I hate to ask you to lie for me."

"Stop that, Kairee. I'd lie for you or do anything necessary to make this situation easier for you."

"You don't condemn me?"

"Condemn you? Why should I? You shouldn't have to face the consequences of this alone. If anyone needs condemning, it most certainly isn't you."

"I'm frightened, Lucy, frightened that if I don't find a way to handle this it's going to cause something really terrible to happen."

"We'll find a way. Just remember, Kairee, your father, Gregg, Cassie, and me . . . we love you."

"I know." Kairee smiled. "I know." She rose. "I think I'm going to take a walk. I want to think this out."

Lucy watched Kairee leave, then returned to her work, still unaware that the door to the bedroom was half open and that a wide-eyed Cassie had heard everything.

Cassie returned to her play, and like a child, she accepted what she now knew without shock and stored it in her mind.

The idea of having another child in the family pleased her. She would be the oldest, the leader. She would eventually have someone to lavish all her love on. The situation that might surround that fact went unnoticed by Cassie. In the purity of the child's mind, the fact was accepted with love, and the love she had for Kairee was enough to cope with all things.

Britt lazed by the fire being fed by his uncle, Lone Wolf. In Lone Wolf's presence Britt was always secure. Lone Wolf demanded nothing from Britt other than that he be his own man. He asked no questions and had a way of listening that reached deep within Britt. With Lone Wolf, Britt could say words that left him vulnerable, knowing the words would remain with Lone Wolf and never be spoken of again.

They had been hunting for almost two weeks, and Britt would never know that his uncle had prolonged the trip purposely because he felt Britt had feelings so dammed up inside him that he needed some solitude to set them free.

"So," Lone Wolf said as he broke dried branches into small pieces to place on the fire, "tell me of this woman who makes your mind forget which end of your gun kills the prey." He smiled as he spoke and Britt laughed in response.

"You know me too well, Uncle. Does anything ever get past you?"

"When it comes to my nephew, no. You are the son I never had. What is in your heart is important to me."

Lone Wolf had married once. His wife had died giving birth to their stillborn son. He had kept their memory sacred and had made the decision never to marry again. Now he placed his affections on the son of his sister, the man he had always hoped his son would be.

There were times when he hated what Elliot Saber had done to Britt, but he could not intrude between father and son. The best he could do was to provide Britt with an understanding heart, a heart Britt knew would always be open to him.

"I want to bring Kairee here again one day, Uncle. I mean, to stay for awhile."

"You want her for your woman?"

"You sound surprised."

Lone Wolf chuckled softly. "My nephew has moved like the honeybee, from flower to flower. It surprises me that he wants to stay with one flower for longer than a taste."

"There's nothing between Kairee and me yet, but . . ."

"But you would like something to be."

"She's a very special . . . very different woman than the others I have known."

"Ah." Lone Wolf smiled teasingly. "She has all the wondrous qualities all other females lack. Tell me, Nephew, what is it that makes her different from all the others you could have had." Lone Wolf's eyes grew innocent. "What is it?"

"Damned if I know." Britt chuckled. "But whatever it is, Kairee has more than her share. She has a lot of courage for one woman. In many ways she reminds me of my mother. She has the same kind of pride . . . of . . ." He shrugged. "I don't know."

"Don't be surprised. No man has ever been able to explain what makes one man love one woman."

"I told you how the situation was between the Circle *S* and the Kennedys. I had to get away from it for awhile. But when I return, I'm going to ask Kairee to come here with me again. If I can't save her family from what's going to happen, at least I can make it easier for her to come here. I can give her a place to come to should anything go wrong."

"Your father fights many battles," Lone Wolf said softly.

Britt's eyes narrowed as he watched his uncle. It was the first time in his life Britt had heard Lone Wolf make any statement that touched on his feelings about Elliot.

"You knew of those battles even before I was born," Britt said cautiously. "Why have you never told me any stories of the past? Given me any reasons for what is happening now?"

"It is not my place. Nothing is ever black or white, my nephew. I would not have you develop eyes that see only one color. You must learn to find your own reasons. Your father is my blood brother. Sometimes he is black and sometimes he is white, but always he is my brother."

Britt sighed. He had never gotten any reasons from Lone Wolf and he doubted if he ever would. As Lone Wolf said, he would have to find the truth for himself.

"Now"—Lone Wolf laughed to break the tension—"we have been here many days. Have you gotten all your thoughts gathered in your mind or would you 'hunt' many days more?"

Britt laughed. "You mean, am I ready to go back and start doing something about my thoughts? Yes, my all-seeing uncle, let's go back so I can say good-bye to my mother and get on with my life and my work."

Lone Wolf nodded with a smile. "We will break camp in the morning. Sleep well, Nephew."

Lone Wolf slept well, but Britt did not. He just could not shake the feeling that some great change was about to take place in his life, a change he might not like but was helpless to stop.

The next morning Lone Wolf observed that Britt was unusually quiet, but he did not interrupt his thoughts as they made preparations to return to the village.

Damion was well aware that he had been seen long before he arrived in the village, but no one approached him or made any effort to stop him. He knew also that he had been identified and that Southwind would have word of his impending arrival.

He had not been to Lone Wolf's village since he was very young. He remembered Southwind with the memory of a young, romantic boy. She had been so beautiful then. He wondered if the years had changed her.

As was the custom, he would present himself to the male head of the family first, but he found when he went to Lone Wolf's lodge that Lone Wolf had gone into the foothills to hunt.

No one would say a word about who had accompanied Lone Wolf into the foothills—no man spoke to others about their leader's business—but Damion knew without being told that Britt had accompanied his uncle.

A buzz of curiosity spread through the village and

Damion could feel inquisitive eyes on him as he made his way to Southwind's lodge.

He stood before the dwelling, unsure of his reasons for being here. What could Southwind say to him that would affect what existed between him and Kairee? In fact, he began to wonder, what had she said to Kairee to make her believe it could be so?

He put his thoughts aside and called out to Southwind. He was almost startled at the abrupt drawing aside of the rawhide doorway and even more surprised to see Southwind before him, a Southwind who looked as if she had not aged a day since he had last seen her.

"Welcome, Damion," she said in a velvet voice. "I have been expecting you."

"I imagine word of my arrival preceded me." He smiled. "I imagine even the wind knows of my need to speak with you."

She laughed. "The word of the arrival of Elliot Saber's son is like the wind."

"This particular son only?"

"The other son does not need the wind to bring word. He is part of this village."

"My coming is a surprise?"

"No, I have been expecting you for a long time. I have had the feeling that she would help guide your feet here."

"Kairee," Damion stated.

"Kairee. She is the reason you have come, is she not?"

"I guess you might say that. I don't really know why I'm here."

"Because you have begun to ask some questions about your life, and answers have been denied you. Because you are unsure if the years have been what you thought they were, and because you seek a way to

243

go, by looking back where you have been."

"Can I come in and talk to you, Southwind?" he asked gently.

She stepped back and nodded her acquiescence. Damion walked into the lodge and she let the rawhide curtain close them inside.

Their preparations completed, Lone Wolf and Britt moved toward their horses to begin their journey back to the village. Britt mounted slowly, and with expert control he kept his huge stallion immobile.

"Something troubles you, Britt?"

"Just decisions, Lone Wolf. I don't think I'm going back to the village. Tell my mother I will come to see her soon."

"What are you going to do?"

"I am going to return home. I am going to think and maybe I will try a little harder."

"So at least you see one truth."

"That I've never really tried hard enough? Maybe you are right. It has been a long, long time since I tried to understand my father or my brother."

"Yes, your brother. You are much more alike than you know."

"Damion and I?" Britt laughed. "For once, Uncle, you are truly wrong, but at least I can try to bridge the chasm between us. Who knows, one day we just might be able to live in the same house again without wanting to shoot each other."

"Don't let . . . things get in your way."

"You mean the Circle S?"

"It means more to you than you realize. One day you could be forced to make choices that might even surprise you."

"Choices? Like what?"

Lone Wolf shrugged, his smile widened, and his eyes sparked mischief. "Me ignorant savage. What do you want me to do, wax philosophical for you?"

"You run around like a savage spouting parables like an Indian messiah, then you have the nerve to fall back on your *savage* background to keep from answering questions. One of these days, my dear uncle, I intend to pin you down to explanations. Your solemn pronouncements for me to look inside and search for my own answers are getting to sound like words from the old Prophets."

Lone Wolf laughed outright and clapped his nephew on the shoulder, causing Britt to grin in total submission to a fact that he and Lone Wolf both knew quite well: it was unlikely Britt would ever be able to pin him down, either physically or mentally.

"Then we part here, Little Nephew. I hope to see you soon."

"Don't worry." Britt chuckled. "I need you much more than you will ever need me. I'd be surprised if you didn't forget me if I were gone too long."

Lone Wolf's eyes became serious and his smile faded. What he said next were words from his heart.

"Nephew, should you not return, part of the heart of our village would be gone. In your mother's heart and mine you could not be replaced and your loss would be felt for all the years we lived. Never speak such words again. Never think them. You are loved."

He urged his horse forward before a very surprised Britt could utter a response.

Later, when Britt thought of the words and the warm happiness they had brought, he also thought of what he would give if he could hear his father speak the same words just once.

He rode toward the Kennedy ranch, not knowing why he could not control the urge to see Kairee again or the need to find some reason for the premonition of danger that washed through him. It would be nightfall before he reached their ranch, so he decided to camp on Kennedy land and talk to them the following morning.

When he rolled in his blanket to sleep, he still had no idea what he was going to say to Kairee to convince her to come to the village with him. But he would find a way, he decided with grim determination. He would find a way.

The sun was only a hazy red rim on the horizon when Britt awoke. He rose and made a new fire, still trying to put his ideas into words.

He had camped along the banks of a shallow, swift-running stream that was not far from the ranch, and he was surprised that he had not been spotted by someone before this, surprised and worried. If this was all the protection Kairee was getting, how easy it would be for anyone to come and go, doing God knew what damage.

Now he had gathered up his blankets and rolled them to tie behind his saddle. He was just preparing to go get his horse, which was tethered nearby, when the sound of someone approaching came to his sharp, alert ears.

He moved beneath a tree, then smiled as he saw Cassie coming toward the stream.

She seemed preoccupied with the footprints she was making in the dusty path and the rag doll with which she was keeping up a steady stream of conversation.

Britt did not want to frighten her so he began to whistle and move about. He saw her stop and tilt her head to the side in an attitude of listening. Then he groaned inwardly in disbelief at her innocent trust as she began to walk again in his direction.

"Damn," he muttered, "just like Kairee. This one has

246

never been taught to be afraid of anything."

Now Cassie could see him and she smiled as she came toward him. His first urge was to frighten her silly, then he discarded that idea. Frightening children was not part of his makeup. But he sure as hell intended to frighten her family.

"Good morning," he said when she was close enough.

"'Morning," she responded. "I remember you. Your name is Mr. Saber."

"Well, it might be Mr. Saber to most people, but it's Britt to you. You're Cassie, right?"

"Yes."

"What are you doing so far from the house all alone, Cassie?"

"Jus' takin' a walk. Me and Miranda like to go for walks."

"I take it that's Miranda?" He smiled as he pointed at the well-worn doll she hugged to her like a live baby.

"Yes, she's Miranda. My daddy made her for me for Christmas. Where are you going?"

"To your house."

"Oh."

"Do you want a ride back?"

"Uh huh."

"Well, come on while I get my things together and get old Conquistador saddled and I'll take you."

"Con . . . Conq . . . what's that?"

"My horse. He's a very noble fellow, so I had to give him a grand name."

"Oh."

Cassie walked with him and settled herself beneath a tree while he began to saddle Conquistador.

Britt wanted to hear her talk of her family, unaware of how shaken he would be by what she was about to reveal.

Chapter 19

Britt slung the blanket over the horse's back, then bent to lift the saddle, setting it in place. He lifted the stirrup to lay over the saddle, reached beneath the horse for the cinch, and began to tighten the saddle into place.

Cassie sat beneath the tree watching every move and confirming her original decision. She liked Britt.

When he turned to look at her, she smiled brightly. He walked to her and sat down beside her.

"I guess Miranda's your best friend," he said.

"Nope." She giggled softly. "She's my next to bestus friend."

"Oh, I see. What about your folks? I guess they're first."

She made a soft sound of childish exasperation. "Mommies and daddies are different than just friends . . . grandpas too."

"Well"—he was amused, but he controlled the smile that tugged at his mouth—"I kinda thought there'd be room for me somewhere."

She thought about this as if it were a very serious matter. Then she looked up at him again.

"I s'pose you could be third."

Now he was forced to laugh aloud. "Then I'll make you a bet I know who's first."

"Betcha." She smiled.

"Aunt Kairee," he offered.

"Yep . . . Aunt Kairee's real special."

"She is that, little one," Britt said meditatively. He turned to look at her again. "I'll bet you get kind of lonely sometimes. When Aunt Kairee's busy, maybe?"

She nodded her head and lifted the doll from her lap to hold it a little closer. Then, as if a pleasant thought had just occurred to her, she smiled at him. "I'm five already."

"You're practically a grown-up young lady. Maybe one of these days you'll have a little brother or sister to play with."

"I could help take care of it," she replied.

"I'll just bet you could. Well, come on, Cassie. Let's get you back home."

She bounced to her feet as he rose, and she walked beside him toward his horse.

"I jus' bet Aunt Kairee will let me."

"Let you what?"

"Help her."

"Help her what?" Britt said, suddenly lost in the shift of conversation.

Cassie stopped and put one hand on her hip, a sure sign of total exasperation. "Help her take care of her baby when she gets it. Mama would let me and I betcha Aunt Kairee will too."

Britt stopped suddenly and turned to look at Cassie. Something leapt into his eyes that startled Cassie and she stepped back from him with a puzzled look on her face.

Britt felt her words explode within him and a flood of disbelief filled him. Only then did he realize he was frightening Cassie.

It took great effort to force his stiffened body to relax and to control his face. He could feel his hands shaking and he clenched them as he knelt before Cassie.

"Cassie, what . . . what makes you think Kairee is getting a baby?"

"I was just playin'," she said defensively. "I didn't mean to listen."

"Your Aunt Kairee told someone this?"

"Uh huh. She told Mommy."

Britt had to gulp back the constriction in his throat.

"Kairee and your mother were talking . . . What . . . what did she say?"

Britt knew. And somewhere deep inside some part of him writhed in agony at the bloodletting blow. But he had to hear it. He had to make certain the terrible thing in his mind was true.

"Aunt Kairee was crying, but Mommy said it was all right. I think Aunt Kairee felt better. If Mommy says it's all right, then I guess Aunt Kairee can get her baby if she wants to."

"Good God," Britt breathed as a heavy black rage rolled through him. Damion! Damn him! He suddenly felt murderous. Fighting her, fighting for the Circle *S*, and at the same time deliberately destroying Kairee's life. At that moment he would have been more than pleased to have his hands around Damion's throat.

"Cassie"—he tried to keep the rage under control—"did your mommy and Aunt Kairee make this a secret?"

"Yes . . . but I didn't." Again she was defensive.

"Well"—he smiled, but the bitter fury was tearing at him—"suppose we just keep this a little secret between us. You won't have to tell anyone you told me, either. What do you say . . . between friends?"

Again she was sunny smiles, relieved that she had done no damage, that the secret would be kept.

"All right."

He held out his hand formally and she put hers in his. "Now, remember Cassie, this is a solemn promise. Unless your Aunt Kairee tells someone, you and I keep it a secret."

She agreed.

"Come on, let's get you home," he said grimly. "I have a little matter to take care of."

He mounted Conquistador, then reached down to lift Cassie up before him. Cassie was quite pleased, mounted on the immense stallion with Britt holding her securely. She paid little attention to the fact that Britt was suddenly very silent.

Britt was not quite sure what he would say, or could say, to Kairee when he brought Cassie home. At this moment his very dangerous thoughts were on his half brother.

They approached the house, and just as Britt slid Cassie to the ground, Lucy walked out on the porch.

"Good morning, Mr. Saber."

"Britt . . . please." He tried to smile, but his usual effervescence was gone. "Is Kairee here? I'd like to talk to her."

Lucy was taken by surprise, but she tried to regain her equilibrium. Yet Britt was more aware now than he might have been an hour or so before.

"I'm sorry, she isn't."

"Where has she gone?"

"Well . . . ah . . . she's gone to visit some of the neighbors. I don't know which first, so I can't really tell you exactly where she is."

Britt knew she was lying but had other ideas that took precedence over everything. He had to vent his anger before he exploded with it.

"Tell her I'll be back in a day or so. I've got to talk to her. It's very important."

"Mr. Saber," Lucy said, obviously not wanting to use his first name, "there're enough problems between us now. I don't think you had better come back. My father-in-law is still confined to his bed recovering from being shot. I might cause you no harm, but I'm sure my husband and his men would not be so lenient.

It would save a lot of problems if you would just . . . just not come back."

"You tell Kairee," Britt said firmly, "that I will be back. That I have to talk to her . . . and that I will, no matter what happens. You tell her," he repeated. Then he spurred his horse and rode away.

Lucy watched until he disappeared, knowing he would be true to his word and come back. She prayed silently it would not be the final spark that caused an explosion no one would be able to survive.

Britt rode toward the Circle S, his thoughts in violent turmoil. He had his mind set on three things he intended to do. One was to take his stand in the battle between the Sabers and the Kennedys, the second was to do as much bodily damage to Damion as was physically possible to do, and the last was to face Kairee and do his best to convince her to marry him.

Damion sat comfortably on a blanket across a small, low-burning fire from Southwind. It surprised him that all the thoughts over which he had had control, all the questions he had prepared, seemed to have fled in the face of her wide, dark eyes.

He suddenly felt like a boy again, insecure and searching for someone to ease the insecurity.

"Can I give you something to eat or drink, Damion?"

"No, I'm not hungry . . . at least not for food."

"What is it you hunger for?"

He laughed shortly. "If I knew the answer to that, I most likely wouldn't be here. You spoke of Kairee as if you knew her well."

"It does not take long to know a person when that person refuses to hide herself."

"Britt brought Kairee to you?"

"Yes."

Southwind did not miss the muscle that twitched in

Damion's jaw or the way his hands clenched in a fist without his knowledge.

She felt the bitterness and wished again she could break down the wall that stood between her son and his half brother. But the wall was Elliot, and she knew that the wall had been reinforced by the arrival of Kairee.

"I see. Does Britt usually bring his conquests to you?"

"That was spoken like an angry child who has been refused his way," she replied, her voice chilled. "Britt spoke nothing of his intentions toward Kairee, but if it will ease your heart, I will tell you that Kairee is not a woman to give any part of herself without care."

She watched a flame leap into his eyes and at that moment Southwind knew beyond doubt both the depth of Damion's emotions toward Kairee and that Kairee and Damion had already shared much.

"I'm sorry. I guess I didn't mean to make it sound like that. Kairee has as much right to come here as I have. Maybe more."

She gave a half smile of amusement. "That you have stayed away so long, I'm sure was not your choice but your father's. You knew, didn't you, that he would not approve of your coming here even as he disapproved of Britt's coming. Britt is my son, so there was little he could do, but he soon convinced you—maybe not in words—that his love would be lessened if you did. It was the most effective way to keep a sixteen-year-old boy under his control."

"I'm a grown man now, Southwind."

"That does not change the needs that grow with the size of the person. Do you think because you are large, because you are a man, that you do not require love?" She bent toward him. "Do you think that love is a taking thing and not a giving one?"

Again she sat erect, her dark eyes penetrating him, forcing him to see that not only had he never been told of another's love, he had never told anyone of his. His mind whipped to Kairee again. In all the moments they had shared, had he ever once said he loved her? He had taken . . . and taken . . . and taken.

She watched the minute cracks in his iron defense and was pleased. The cracking might hurt, but if it removed the armor and freed him, she would be happy.

"Damion, I would tell you a story," she said softly.

"A bedtime story for a child who would be a man?" he questioned.

"Perhaps. I think you are much like your father in one way. When you give your love, it is total and complete, and you find it very difficult to handle the loss of it. Your father gave his love so completely once . . . and he has never been able to do so again."

"My mother?"

"No. This story began long before he met and married your mother. It is the story of why your mother died, and why, to regain myself, I had to leave."

Damion was more than surprised. "I didn't know there was a woman before my mother."

"The woman before your mother was the only woman your father truly loved. Her name was Emma Martin."

Damion looked at her sharply. Where had he heard the name . . . His father! He had been mumbling the name when he was drunk.

"I see you have heard the name."

"Only once." He explained where he had heard it. "What did Emma look like?"

"I don't know. I know he has a picture in the family Bible by his bed, but he forbade me to look at it, and at the time I loved him enough to abide by his wishes."

"Tell me the rest of this story, Southwind," Damion requested gently, for he realized now that Southwind spoke from the pain of a love that had been left desolately alone to die of neglect.

Southwind told the entire story and Damion sat in silence and listened. For the first time in all his years, he grasped some small understanding of his father. He felt pity first, but he knew that emotion would never be accepted by Elliot.

"So you see that you are not alone, Damion, and I hope both you and Britt can see that the battle between you is a deliberate wrong, yet somehow understandable."

"You still love him."

"It is surprising to hear the same words for the second time."

"From Britt?"

"No, from Kairee. At least her woman's heart understood. Yes, I still love him. I have from the first and I always shall. But it was for the best that I leave."

"Britt and I . . . we find it hard, maybe even impossible, to reach out to each other."

"You were close as little boys. You always the older, guiding, demanding brother."

"Demanding?" Damion repeated meditatively.

"Perhaps . . . sometimes," she said softly, "a little too demanding for the benefit of Elliot and the Circle S and not enough for what you should have been sharing."

Damion tried to think back over the years and slowly pieces began to fall into place. Sure that he could win his father's love by being what Elliot wanted him to be, Damion, in turn, became hard and unyielding toward his brother.

"God," he muttered. "No wonder he struck back at me so often. I was smothering him as badly as I was being smothered."

"Grief, pain, misunderstanding often seek company. If you had to mold yourself into something, I guess your young boy's heart felt justified at the time that it was only right Britt should fit that mold also. When he didn't, or couldn't, you just couldn't understand. It formed a gulf that was—and is—unnecessary."

"And now it's too late to do anything about it."

"You are alive; Britt is alive. Why is it too late?"

"Because," Damion said quietly, "we are both . . . in love . . . with the same woman—the one woman my father will never accept."

"There must be a beginning, Damion. Make peace with your brother. Begin somewhere to make a new start. Learn to care for each other. Kairee is not a weak woman, and you and Britt both must learn to live with her choice."

"You're not asking for much," he remarked with a wry laugh.

"I am asking for nothing," she replied gently. "It was you who came with questions. What you choose to do with the answers, after all, is your decision."

Damion sighed and for a long time he was quiet, staring into the fire, his mind on the past. Southwind remained quiet also, allowing him to walk whatever path he had found and prepared to answer any more questions that might plague him.

But Damion was gathering his forces. He required no more answers. Piece by piece he was forging his plans.

He would return home. His first step would be to talk to his father, and at least try to make him understand that there had to be an end to this war. He would make his father see that he loved the Circle S and that he would defend it. But he was no longer going to make it the center of his life.

Then would come the hardest part. He would have to find a way to breach the wall that stood between him and his father, then the one between him and Britt. Only then could he go to Kairee openhanded and try to make her see he was capable of loving.

He felt the harsh touch of shame at the way he had made something less of what could have existed between him and Kairee. But Damion was growing and he had no intention of letting the situation between them disintegrate.

If worse came to worse, he now knew the extent to which he would go. He would give up the Circle S, take Kairee, if she would agree, and find a place of his own. He would find a way to nurture this budding ability to love into something worthwhile.

Southwind watched him rise, and it seemed to her he had shed a heavy load. She smiled at the new look of resolve in his eyes.

She stood up beside him and he smiled as he reached to lay his hand on her shoulder.

"I wish I had come here when I was sixteen instead of now, or that you had remained at the Circle S. I believe I would have been a better man. And I'd like to think my mother was somewhat like you."

"Your mother was a gentle, lovely woman. Her only flaw was her sensitive nature. But she loved your father too, Damion. You were conceived in her love, and I believe she gifted you with a natural sensitivity to others. Otherwise, my dear stepson," she assured him with a smile, "you would never have come here at all."

He bent to kiss her cheek and she walked with him to the entrance.

Southwind watched Damion ride away, hoping the words she had said would somehow bring him and Britt together. Her eyes grew sad with the thought that this might be the last chance Elliot would have to redeem his sons. If he lost them both now. . . . The pain for him twisted within her. Perhaps she would go to him and try to lessen the pain. Perhaps . . .

Damion rode slowly. So many old turmoils, old battles, seemed so pointless now. He could see that he and Britt had been used as buffers against each other while the only victor had been the Circle S.

He wanted to hate his father, but he could not. All he could feel was a deep sympathy, because in the end it was Elliot who would be the loser.

He wondered if it would be possible now for Britt to understand and accept any overtures he made. Well, they had time. And he meant to give the best effort of his life to repairing the damage done between them.

When he arrived at the Circle S, he found only Margurite and Maria.

He wanted to talk to Britt and Elliot before he went to Kairee. But another thought entered his mind while he waited for their return.

He crossed the empty house and walked to his father's room. He had not been invited to this room even as a child. When he stepped inside he closed the door and stood still for a few minutes feeling like an intruder.

The room was Elliot, austere in its furnishings and functional for a man like his father, who was devoted to only one goal.

With slow and deliberate steps Damion walked across the room and around the end of the bed. He stood looking down at a large family Bible. Hesitant again, he fought a strange tingle of unrest that moved through him. He had no right here and no right to open the Bible that lay before him.

But he reached a hand that actually shook with the effort and began to turn the pages. In the center he saw what appeared to be several pictures. He lifted them and gazed intently at the first.

He knew beyond doubt that this first picture he looked at was his own mother. He had never been shown this, had never known there was a picture of his mother in existence. Again he battled the anger that rose like a hard lump in his breast.

She was tall, slim, and very beautiful. He looked into

his own eyes and felt his kinship with this woman who had been a victim of such heartbreak.

Damion thought of Kairee, and the vision of her was so pronounced in his mind that when he looked at the second picture he was so startled that he nearly dropped it.

The wide gray eyes were Kairee! The smile was Kairee! He turned the picture over and the name "Emma" was written across the back in his father's broad scrawl.

He turned it again to gaze once more in wonder at the girl named Emma who had changed the lives of so many.

He would have given anything to know the story of what had happened between Emma and Elliot that had turned his father into the hard, driven man he was.

Maybe someday he would be able to ask him. But not now. Now he had to do what he could to cement their lives back together.

He replaced the pictures in the Bible and closed it. It was difficult to believe that two women could look as much alike as Kairee and Emma. Then he realized that not only had Kairee resurrected an old memory, but it was because of this that Elliot could not bear her close proximity. One thing would one day be necessary if he were ever to heal the wounds. Kairee and Elliot would have to be brought together again.

Damion was returning to the main room when he heard a horse approaching. He walked out on the porch and in the distance he identified the rider quickly.

Britt. And he was pushing his horse at top speed. Damion watched, profoundly puzzled, as Britt drew closer. This was not like Britt, to push a horse so hard, and he would not do so unless there were some sort of emergency.

Chapter 20

Damion walked down the porch steps as Britt drew his horse to a halt. For a few minutes Britt and Damion looked at each other. Damion was startled at first by the seething fury he could read in his brother's eyes. He had no idea what Britt could be angry about now, but whatever it was, he intended to soothe the ruffled feathers and start trying to build a bridge between them.

Britt watched Damion walk slowly toward him and all the frustrations from all the anger-filled years bubbled to the surface like an erupting volcano. Damion—tall, handsome, self-assured, and the master of the Circle *S*. At this moment Britt actually hated his brother.

"Britt . . ." Damion began, but the last thing Britt wanted to hear was more recriminations and more demands for the Circle *S*.

"You damn bastard," Britt grated raggedly. "Always on top, aren't you, Damion? No matter what you have to do or who you have to hurt to get there."

"What the hell's got you all riled up now? Whatever it is, come on in and have a drink and we'll talk about it. There can't be anything that big."

"Jesus, you arrogant son of a bitch. You can just walk away from anything, can't you?"

"I don't have any idea what the hell you're talking about."

"I'd like to shoot you for what you've done. But I think I'll do better. I think it's time someone taught you what it's like to get stomped on."

He was walking closer to Damion as he spoke and Damion could not miss the murderous glow in his eyes. He put out a hand, more in surprise than anything else, to ward Britt off. But Britt swung with all the force he had. His fist connected with Damion's jaw with a sharp, resounding crack that sent Damion sprawling backward in the dirt.

For a moment he lay propped up on his elbows, looking at Britt in total shock.

Britt stood over him, his lips pulled back from his teeth in an animal grin and his fists doubled.

Damion's temper flared. He rolled to the side and scrambled to his feet, only to throw himself full force against Britt, sending them both tumbling to the ground.

They rolled, each gripping the other and seeking an advantage, but because they were similar in muscle strength and size, it was like a struggle between Titans, each straining against an equal force.

Dust roiled about them and the soft thuds of fists and answering grunts amid ragged panting were the only sounds.

The horse Britt had ridden skittered away nervously as the two heaving bodies rolled beneath its hooves. But the two men, caught up in their wild and now uncontrolled fury, ignored this dangerous threat.

A brutally hard fist found a vulnerable lip and Britt ignored the salty taste of blood as his rage continued unabated.

An eye began to close, promising a swollen, multi-colored bruise the next day. But Damion only felt a moment's numbness as his anger glared through blurred red vision.

Years of bitterness were released in uncontrolled violence as the two pummeled each other. Their breathing came in rough gasps now and they pushed away from each other to leap to their feet and face each other again.

Their clothes were dirty and torn and the dust in which they had rolled clung to their hair and skin and combined with sweat to roll in grimy rivulets down their faces.

Both were beyond words now, confronting each other in a culmination of all the pent-up antagonism of years.

It was at this moment that Elliot and Jim rode into the center of the battle. At first they reined in their horses in total surprise.

"What the hell are those two goin' at each other for?" Elliot muttered. But Jim remained silent. He had always known that one day he would see the physical battle that was only the outward sign of the battle he had seen raging for years.

As Britt and Damion leapt for each other again, Elliot and Jim spurred their horses forward. They dismounted quickly and ran to the thrashing bodies, but they saw it would not be easy to separate the two. The brothers were strong, and the rage they felt was too great now and too violent for them to hear any words Jim or Elliot might use.

It took extreme physical force to drag Damion from atop Britt, where he had finally found an advantage and was trying to beat Britt's face into an unrecognizable mess. He had succeeded in landing only a couple of well-placed blows when the combined force of Jim and Elliot dragged him off.

Once they were separated, Britt leapt to his feet. Only Jim's quick move to get between them prevented Britt from leaping on Damion again.

262

Jim threw both arms about Britt, pinning his arms to his sides, and held his thrashing body with all the strength he had.

Elliot had to do much the same as Jim. Still Damion and Britt struggled toward each other.

"Whoa," Elliot snarled. "What the hell's got into you two. Now"—he grunted as Damion struggled—"you settle down or I'll use my gun butt on your thick head. I want to know what started the ruckus."

"Britt," Jim coaxed, "calm down. Quit! Tell us what started this."

"He jumped me for no reason," Damion snapped, his anger still a bright red glow.

"No reason! Sure Damion, that's you, all right. Nobody or nothing means anything unless it's the Circle *S,* even if it's helpless people too filled with trust to see what a selfish bastard you really are."

"I told you before I don't know what you're talking about," Damion insisted coldly.

"You know what I'm talking about, all right. Boy, you plan well. If you can't get at the Bar *K* one way, you sure found another."

"Boy," Elliot said, "I don't know if Damion knows what you're talking about, but I don't. I want some answers and I want them right now."

But Britt was unprepared to throw Kairee's name in the dirt. He grew sullenly silent, but the white-hot anger still lingered in the depths of his eyes.

"You gonna answer me?" Elliot demanded.

"You want my answer, Pa," Britt said softly, "you ask your *son.*" He relaxed his body. "Let me go, Jim."

"No more," Jim threatened nervously.

"No . . . no more . . . not now, anyway," Britt answered.

Jim let Britt go slowly, prepared for anything. But Britt made no move toward Damion. He just gazed at him with eyes that had become twin chips of ice.

263

"I used to think you were something real special . . . I used to think you and the Circle S were about the best. Now"—he gave a twisted smile and blinked through the sweat and the sting of tears he would never have acknowledged—"I don't think you're worth spit. In fact, I don't think I can stand living near you. I'm going to see her . . . then I'm going to the village. You have what you wanted all along, Damion, the Circle S. I hope you find out it was worth it."

He walked to his horse, mounted, and rode away. Both Jim and Elliot were puzzled, but Damion was stricken with bitter regret that he had lost whatever chance he might have had to reach Britt, and he did not even know the reason. And he had heard, with a thudding heart, the word "her." Instinctively he knew their battle had had something to do with Kairee.

"All right, Damion," Elliot said, "what started this?"

"I don't know."

"Don't know, or won't tell me?"

"I don't know. But I sure as hell am going to find out." He shrugged his father's hand from his shoulder and walked toward the house. He meant to clean himself up, then ride to Kairee's house to try to find some answers to a multitude of questions. He had known about Britt's temper, but he had never seen Britt as angry as he had been a few minutes before. It was hatred, and that truly scared him. He had to know what Britt thought he had done and why it had produced such a violent reaction.

Jim and Elliot stared after Damion's retreating form with puzzled frowns on their faces.

"What do you think it was, Jim?" Elliot questioned. "I've seen them mad before, but never like this."

"It's been a long time brewing," Jim answered quietly.

"I don't understand either of them," Elliot stated roughly.

Jim turned to look at his old friend and shook his head slightly, drawing his lips together in a firm line. "Maybe," he said softly, "that's the whole trouble."

"What do you mean by that?"

"You been so busy makin' 'em both into duplicates of Elliot Saber, you never let 'em grow into their own kind of men. I guess, Elliot, you really don't understand. But if it's not already too late, maybe you ought to think about it."

Jim walked away, leaving an even more puzzled Elliot staring after him. Elliot instinctively sensed that Britt had been the instigator of the battle, for he knew Damion kept a stronger control over his emotions than Britt. He had to put a stop to Britt's wilder tendencies and he knew where to start. Britt visited the village too often, was fed too many stories. He meant to put a stop to it. With determined steps, he walked to his horse.

Britt had ridden to the river only a few miles from the Circle *S*. He dismounted and unsaddled his horse, hobbling it so it would not wander far.

He did not know how he looked, but he knew how he felt and that was pretty bad. Then he looked at his reflection in the water. His lip was cut and swollen and still bleeding. One eye was rapidly closing and turning an ugly shade of blue-black. There were several random bruises and cuts. "You look like hell," he muttered to himself, then he chuckled without humor. The worst blow had been to his ego when he had realized Damion was about to beat him to a pulp. Still, he knew he would do the same thing again.

He stripped off his clothes and walked into the water until it circled his waist. It was frigid, but he needed it to soothe both the inner aches and the exterior wounds. He dove beneath the surface and felt the bruises on his face smarting with the sting of the cold water.

His ablutions eased all but the seething emotions that churned within him.

He lay naked on the grassy bank for a long time, until the sun, warm after the water's chill, soothed his raw nerves.

He watched the golden orb slowly dip below the horizon. He realized it would take him a long time to reach the Bar *K*, and when he did arrive it would be very late at night.

Words were a bitter taste in his mouth. He knew he could not wake the entire Kennedy family to tell them he knew Kairee was pregnant and he wanted to marry her.

He could not simply throw the fact of her pregnancy in her face and hit her with the knowledge that he knew his brother was the father of her unborn child. He also knew Cassie might be hurt also by what she might feel was treachery. She had trusted him with a secret and he had to find a way to keep Cassie, and the rest of Kairee's family, from being hurt any more than they already had been.

He knew this almost irreparable situation, combined with the tensions that had been building since the Kennedys' arrival, could mark the beginning of a tragedy. One way or the other, he had to try to do something about it.

Words tumbled through his mind to be examined, then discarded. He soon realized he would have to wait until he faced Kairee, for he had found no words that worked. He also wondered what the Kennedys were going to think about the condition he was in.

"Some way to propose to a lady," he muttered. "I hope I get a chance to get close enough to talk to her."

He tried to think of what he would do if Kairee accepted him. They could live in his mother's village, or they could go away and find a place of their own, somewhere where none of the past could reach out to touch them.

He sighed deeply, refusing to let himself think of surrendering all he had hoped for, had loved, for so long. Could he ignore the possibility that Elliot might accept him one day and look on him as the son Britt had always wanted to be to his father.

But he realized he had to face the fact that the Circle S had never been meant for him. He wondered if Elliot's love had ever been meant for him. The seeds of resentment had been planted deeply and he could not help regretting what might have been.

It was too late to ride to Kairee's now and he was caught in the lethargy of bitterness, so he made the decision to make camp and ride to the Bar K in the morning.

After a long while the chill of the night finally forced him to roll in his blankets and seek a dream-filled sleep.

Damion removed his clothes, poured some water into the bowl, and lathered his hands. Then he washed his face gingerly, wincing as the soapy water stung.

He was doing his best to keep all questions from his mind. He had to talk to Kairee. He had to find out what had happened the last time she had seen Britt that had shaken his anger to the explosive point. He could not remember a time in their lives that he had ever seen Britt so murderously angry.

Damion tried to keep Southwind's words in mind, but in the face of his defensive anger, it was a very difficult thing to do.

He took clean clothes from his drawers and dressed, yet despite the clothes, he knew he must look like a battered gladiator.

He walked to a mirror as he buttoned his shirt and frowned at the condition of his face. "God, what a mess!" he said aloud. "Looks like you ran into a grizzly bear and came out second."

He shrugged. No matter how bad he looked, he had to talk to Kairee. He could find a way around whatever questions she might ask. At least he hoped he could.

Finished dressing, he strode to the door. He walked across the area between the house and the barn and went inside. Damion had started toward the stall in which he kept his horse when Jim's voice came from the shadows.

"Damion."

Damion spun around. "Jim?" he questioned. Then Jim moved from the shadows of the large, semi-dark barn.

"Where are you riding to?"

"Does it make a difference?" Damion asked defiantly.

"Does if you're going after your brother."

"Why would I do that?"

"Maybe to finish up what he started."

"How do you know Britt started it?"

"You forget I've known you and Britt since you were born."

"I'm not going after Britt."

"Then where are you going?"

"That's none of your damn business," Damion replied. He had never been really angry with Jim before, but this was a vulnerable moment when his bruised emotions were too sensitive to touch.

"Damion, why don't you cool down a while, boy, and let's have us a little talk."

"What do we have to talk about? If you want to ask questions about the fight, you'd better find Britt and ask him. I told you and Pa the truth. I don't have one single idea about why Britt hauled off like that. There's a lot of things brewing in his mind, but he sure as hell doesn't tell me about them."

"You ever tell him about the things going on in

your mind?"

"Why should I? He's not interested."

"Well, maybe you might find you're walkin' the same path, only in different directions."

"To tell the truth, Jim"—Damion sighed—"I think we're both beyond trying to talk it out. Whatever it is, it's too big a mountain for either of us to get over."

"Listen, boy, I've been the best friend your pa has ever had. We go back a long way. Up to now I always felt how he raised his sons was none of my business. I always hoped someday you two would make peace with each other and the Circle S would benefit."

"And now you see the truth."

"No, now I see that some of the truth should have been put into words a long time ago. When I saw you two beating the hell out of each other, I realized this has to come to a head somewhere."

"You're not the only one," Damion said.

"What?"

"I rode up to see Southwind. It seems she has the same idea, only"—Damion shrugged—"she doesn't have any more idea about how to stop it than any of the rest of us."

"Southwind," Jim repeated softly, his introspective gaze seeing more than Damion knew.

"She was a beauty. I wish to God she had stayed."

"So she got driven off . . . like me, Britt, everybody who couldn't stand as tall as he did. What does he want, Jim? What is it that drives him like—"

"Stay with him, boy," Jim said quietly. "It's going to take all the backbone you've got. But the Circle S is worth it."

"The Circle S," Damion mused. "It's been the whole of his life. It's meant more than Southwind . . . my mother . . . Britt . . . me. Tell me, Jim," Damion asked softly, "did he drive my mother until she died?"

"I guess your mother was too . . . too gentle. She

loved your pa . . . Damion, she loved him, and in his own way he loved her too. But out here . . . out here the sweet, gentle kind like she was . . . well, it was either leave him and survive, or stay. She just didn't have the strength for either."

"But that's not the whole story, is it, Jim? There's a whole lot more that happened long before."

Jim watched Damion for what felt like interminable minutes, but Damion remained silent, waiting.

"Just what do you think you know about the *whole* story?"

"I have a feeling this story is hooked up with Kairee and her family. They were no real threat to Pa or the Circle *S*, yet he tried to drive them off. At first I thought it was because of the Circle *S*, but now I don't."

"Why?"

"There's a Bible by Pa's bed. I was in his room the other day and I looked in it."

"And found?"

"Pictures. Pictures of the woman I knew was my mother . . . and another woman. Beautiful, with gray eyes and blond hair. A woman who looks enough like Kairee Kennedy to be her twin sister. Now I wonder if you'll be telling me there's nothing more to know."

"No, I'm not going to tell you that. But it's a long story, and I really don't have any right to tell it to you. I've kept my mouth shut for nearly thirty years. But I don't have the stomach to see you and Britt destroy each other. After what I've seen today, I think it's time."

"Then tell me, Jim, for Christ's sake tell me and put an end to all the tearing apart and the bitterness."

"I expect your pa will throw me off the Circle *S* after this." Jim grimaced. "But I just have the feeling it's time . . . yessir, it's time."

"Shall we go back in and have a drink while you talk?"

"It's going to take more than a drink. By the time I get through, I think I'll need a bottle or two."

"Come on, I'll join you. Right now I'm in the mood to get totally drunk." Damion laughed. He clapped Jim on the shoulder and they left the barn to walk toward the house.

Elliot Saber rode like a man possessed, his body erect in the saddle, his mind oblivious to all around him.

He had not walked into the village of Lone Wolf for over twenty years, nor had he seen Southwind since the day she had looked into his eyes and told him she was going home. He remembered her words as if they had been spoken only yesterday.

"I return to my brother's village. I return only because there is not enough love in your heart to hold me here. One day I pray you will find a way to love someone or something. At least your sons, Elliot . . . love your sons."

Now she had interfered between him and the son that belonged to him. This time he must make her understand that she could not stand between him and what he intended to achieve.

She had filled Britt with enough nonsense, and God only knew if she had found a way to Damion and had spoken to him of things he never should have known.

He wondered how many of his secrets she had imparted to his sons. His sons . . .

He had built the Circle S with his bare hands and he meant for it to be held by a Saber for generations.

One day Damion and Britt would have sons of their own and they would belong to the Circle S as all the rest of the Sabers would. He would see to it, no matter what the cost.

Chapter 21

Elliot had stopped to rest his horse for an hour or so, and now he mounted and was on his way again. He had not forgotten the trail that led from the Circle S to Lone Wolf's village, despite the years that had passed since he had ridden it.

For a short while he allowed himself the pleasure of old memories. Then he determinedly set his mind on the reason he was headed for the village.

He would not allow Southwind and her misguided sense of justice to ruin all he had planned.

The Circle S would one day cover more miles than any other ranch in the territory. The Saber men would breed a dynasty that would hold its power for generation after generation.

Had it not been his dream, his and Emma's? They would have sons and grandsons, she had said, and they would rule an empire.

It had been Emma's dream, and he had refused to let it die as he had refused to let Emma die.

Damn the gray-eyed woman who had nearly shattered it all. He would find a way to get Kairee Kennedy out of the valley as soon as he returned. But first he had to make it clear to Lone Wolf and

Southwind that his sons were to be forbidden the village again.

Thoughts of Southwind stirred more unwelcome memories. He could not forget how they had met.

Lone Wolf had been hunting and had found him doing the same. At first Elliot had been cold, even belligerent, for the memory of Emma's death was ever fresh in his mind. But logic told him that Lone Wolf had had no hand in her death. He had been from a completely different tribe.

They had become friends. Then Lone Wolf had taken him home and he had met Southwind. She had been beautiful, sleek and tawny, with long legs, a beautiful body, and hair like ebony silk. It had not been hard to face the fact that he wanted her.

He had coveted her land above all, and he had told himself that Southwind was only an excess reward when he had convinced her and Lone Wolf that he wanted to marry her.

The first few years had been wonderful, the birth of Britt marking the pinnacle of their happiness in each other. Then suddenly something seemed to go wrong, though he had not been able to face the truth at first. It had taken a loving and gentle Southwind a long time to realize that somewhere, somehow, Elliot had lost the ability to love anything or anyone but his one obsession, the Circle S.

He had not stopped her from leaving, for his stiff pride would not allow it. But he had kept his sons, knowing Southwind could not prevent this, and it gave him small satisfaction to use this power as a kind of punishment for her choosing to go.

Uncomfortable with his thoughts, he pushed them aside and concentrated on the trail ahead. It was after dusk when he topped the hill and viewed the Indian dwellings below him. He rode into the now quiet village and made his way unerringly to Southwind's lodge.

He was surprised at the virulent emotion that swirled within him. He tried to ignore the possibility that he was shaken by the thought of seeing Southwind again.

He stood before her lodge for several minutes, then called her name.

"Southwind . . . I would speak with you."

Southwind had sensed with some deep, throbbing premonition that once she had spoken with Damion it would not be long before Elliot came. She believed Elliot had learned of Damion's visit, and she was prepared to acknowledge what she had said to Damion.

She went to the entrance, and it seemed to Elliot that she had simply appeared out of the mist of the setting sun. They stood inches from each other and for a moment time seemed to whirl backward.

"It has been a long time, Elliot," Southwind said softly. "You look well," she added.

She had loved this man, had desired to be part of his life forever. It was hard to look at him and not remember the sweeter times.

He was still virile and handsome, and once again she felt the strength he always seemed to exude. It was a potent force, and Southwind cautioned herself to tread carefully. Elliot was a danger to anyone who loved him.

"I've come to talk to you, Southwind."

"Come in," she replied softly and stepped aside to let him pass. He hesitated only a moment, then walked past her. "It has been a long journey. Can I get you something?"

"No. All I want from you are assurances."

"Assurances? What kinds of assurances do you require of me?"

"Britt—I don't want him coming here anymore.

274

Your brother fills him with . . . ideas."

Southwind had been prepared for this. She had wondered how long it would be before Britt's natural sense of justice would raise too many questions. Still she sensed there was more to Elliot's demands than what he was saying.

"Britt is not a child to cling to his mother's skirts. I cannot, and do not, tell him where he can and cannot go."

"But you welcome him when he comes."

"Of course I do," she said quietly. "Despite what you feel, he is my son also."

"You left him to me."

"No! No, Elliot I did not leave him for you. I merely changed where I would live. Britt is my son. He will be welcome in this lodge, or the lodge of my brother, whenever he chooses to come."

"Damnit, Southwind, why do you poison my sons' minds against me?"

"Your . . . sons?"

She watched guilt war with anger and waited to see which would win. Anger seemed the temporary victor.

"Sons! Yes, damn it, sons! Do you think I haven't got enough imagination to know that when my sons raise a hand to each other in violence the cause must come from here?"

"You are still blinded by your own ambitions, aren't you? If there is a violence, it's bred in that imagination of yours; it is fed by your own desires and your demands." Southwind wanted to shatter his inability to see the truth, but she had faced this situation before and knew the futility of her attempt. "Elliot, what has happened between Damion and Britt?"

"Britt jumped Damion. They tried to beat the hell out of each other. I know damn well Britt got fired up over something that started here."

"Are you sure the battle started with Britt?"

"Damion's never lied, and Britt didn't take the time to deny it. He . . ." Elliot's eyes narrowed as he looked at her intently. His brows drew together in a dark frown. "What makes you think . . . Southwind, has Damion been here?"

She did not answer for several moments, but her mind spun rapidly, summoning forth Damion's words: "My brother and I are in love with the same woman, one my father could never accept. . . ." Would Damion have . . . no, she could not accept the thought. But what—

"Southwind!"

Her attention was drawn back quickly to the distrust glowing in his eyes.

"You know much more than you are saying. I don't want my sons to destroy what I have worked so hard to build!"

For the first time in their relationship Southwind allowed her anger to spring to the surface.

"Your empire! Your ranch, your sons! By the gods, Elliot, you cannot own everything within your reach!"

"Damion came here, didn't he? Didn't he?" Elliot reached out and gripped her shoulders to pull her close to him. "What did you say to him to bring this on? What lies did you tell him?"

"I had no lies to tell him. He sought the truth and the truth is what he received."

"Whose truth, yours?" Elliot demanded.

"No," Southwind replied softly, "yours. Your son sought to understand his father better. Why do you feel a threat in the truth?"

He could not find a reply that would answer the question. He pushed her away from him.

"I'm going back to the Circle *S*. Neither of my sons will forsake his duty to me. When I tell them that it must be a choice between the Circle S and their puny battle with each other, they will choose the Circle S. And I will forbid them ever . . . *ever* to set foot in this village again."

"I don't think so, Elliot. I am afraid your sons, both of them, have learned something you cannot seem to find the capacity to do."

"What's that?"

"To love."

"Love," Elliot repeated softly. "So that's it. Kairee Kennedy. Do you think I'm going to let one woman spoil everything, because they've got their hot blood up over some . . . some scheming little tramp. Well, I won't. There are ways to rid the valley of the . . . interruption she has created."

"I would advise you to be careful about what steps you take, Elliot. I would warn you that if you are not careful you are going to lose both your sons."

"You'd like that, wouldn't you? Some kind of revenge, I suppose."

"Why would I want revenge on you, Elliot? I chose to leave; you did not drive me away. I have retained the love of my son and, I hope, I have acquired the friendship of yours. You have the Circle S and you are more than welcome to keep it."

"Don't worry, I'll keep it. And I promise you that I'll keep them too. The Kennedys will be gone from this valley and the Circle S will still be strong, and Damion will run it!" His anger was so strong he did not realize what he said.

"Damion will run it," Southwind repeated slowly. A thought that had not occurred to her before made her recoil from Elliot. "And Britt," she said, forcing her voice to steadiness, "is Britt to be nothing? And you wonder why your sons battle. Is this what you have shown Britt all his life? Is this what you have shown

Damion in your subtle little ways? Oh Elliot, I feel so sorry for you. In trying to keep them, you have driven them away."

"I don't need you to feel sorry for me. I have all I need, and I know how to protect it—from you, from the Kennedys, or from anyone else who's stupid enough to get in my way."

He turned from her and started for the door.

"Elliot."

"What?"

"I . . . want you to know something."

"What?"

"The day will come when you will need someone, when you will taste the pain and fear of being alone. When that day comes, and you have learned . . . if you choose to send for me, I will come."

Their gazes held for a long time and for one instant she felt sure she had seen a vulnerable look, then his eyes closed her out.

She would not know that an emotion had ripped through him like an uncontrolled forest fire. He had, in his way, loved her and wanted her, and he found it hard to deny the loneliness he had felt since she had gone. He could not, would not, tell her that he had not touched another woman since she had gone.

The question pulsed within him. Would she come if he asked her?

"Come back to the Circle S now."

"Why?"

"Because it is your place. And you can help me convince both Damion and Britt that they belong beside me."

"I see," Southwind said. It was not the answer she had longed to hear. She walked to Elliot and put a hand on his arm. "I'm sorry, Elliot, I cannot come now. You will know when to send for me." That she felt close to tears was something she would never let him know.

"I thought not. Good-bye, Southwind."

"Good-bye, Elliot. Remember what I said. You will know when to send for me."

"I doubt it. You'll see. Damion and Britt will both come to their senses. They will see that the Circle *S* and what I want for them is more important than anything else."

"I can only pray that isn't so," she whispered.

Without another word Elliot left. Southwind continued to stand in the center of the lodge. Tears she could no longer contain flowed warm and unheeded down her cheeks. She crossed her arms and hugged her body to control its shaking.

There was a great fear in her heart that Elliot would have more bitterness and pain to bear in the future than he could possibly imagine. She only prayed it would not be shared by his sons.

Only a few minutes after she heard Elliot ride away, the buckskin door was pushed aside and Lone Wolf entered. He saw the tears in her shadowed eyes and his lips tightened.

"My heart is filled with rage, Sister. If you say the word, I will go to him and try to make him listen."

"No, my brother. It is a useless thing. The words—he does not want to hear. When a man does not hear with his heart, then he is dead."

"And my nephew? I would not see him hurt more."

"My son . . . Elliot's son . . . Lone Wolf they are . . . they battle each other."

"They have been doing so for a long time."

"Not like this. This time they have raised their hands to each other."

"I cannot believe Britt would do that. Always they have been able to laugh and to survive."

"But now . . . now there is a woman."

"A woman? Britt has chosen a woman?" Lone Wolf was smiling now. But the smile faded when he did not see it returned.

"Yes, he has chosen a woman, the same woman his brother has chosen."

"The same . . . I had thought my nephew had trouble inside, but I did not think it would be this. His father is angry?"

"Yes, angry that Britt would even consider anything before the Circle *S.*"

"If you would only allow me to go to him and tell him. . . ."

"Tell him what, brother?"

"That he is a fool. That he has been dying for a long time and cannot even see the cure for his illness."

Southwind sighed and turned to walk to a pallet near the fire. She sat upon it.

"I would not see you weep, Sister," Lone Wolf said quietly.

"I do not weep for myself, Brother."

"For Britt? For Damion?"

"No, I weep for Elliot. It must be so very lonely to have nothing but a dream."

"I worry for my nephew. He is headstrong and brave. If there is a woman he wants, he will fight for her."

"But to fight his brother," she said quietly. "To fight his brother can lead to some terrible tragedy."

"Southwind, let me go speak with him. At least let me advise him to keep his passions under control."

"I do not know if that is wise. He is no longer a boy."

"I know that. But he can make a very bad mistake that will be more costly than he knows."

"I am afraid, my brother," Southwind said in a low whisper, "that my son is now a man who must make his own mistakes and pay his own price. Unless he comes to us, we cannot tell him who he must love or hate. We must trust in the fact that Britt and Damion once loved each other, and that the love is strong enough to keep them both from harm."

"I hope you are right, my sister," Lone Wolf said quietly. "If you are not—"

"If I am not"—her whisper was almost soundless—"then we all will suffer, and a brother will face a brother in a battle caused by their father. Leave me, my brother. I would shed no more tears before you."

Lone Wolf stood looking down at her, amazed again at the depth of her love. She had remained Elliot Saber's woman despite all he was and all he had done.

It angered him that Elliot had used her love so carelessly, but she had forced a promise from him long ago that he would not interfere. He had tried to hold to that promise even with Britt, whom he would have enticed long ago to stay with them and leave the conflict at the Circle *S*.

Silently Lone Wolf turned to leave. He had learned over the years that it did very little good to argue with Southwind.

Southwind sat deep in thought, wondering if there was anything she could do to prevent what she saw coming. Elliot Saber did not make threats lightly, and she feared the charismatic power he and the Circle *S* seemed to have over Britt and Damion.

Many alternatives fought for supremacy in her mind, and it was long after the village slept that she formulated a plan. She rose and began to put a few things in a bundle. Leaving her lodge, she walked across the silent village to saddle her horse. She would speak again with Kairee Kennedy. The least she could do would be to caution Kairee. Dealing with Elliot Saber was not for the weak or the unprepared.

She rode away from the village without knowing that a concerned and sleepless Lone Wolf sat within his lodge and worried about her and the undeniable love she carried.

*　　*　　*

Elliot had ridden away from the village with his mind caught in a tempest. Being with Southwind had renewed the strong desire for her he had never been able to destroy, despite all his attempts.

She was still beautiful, still wise, and yet so foolish, he thought. He still could not believe she had simply walked away from him and all he could offer her and had chosen to live in her brother's village alone. He had never been able to understand what more she could possibly have wanted.

"It's her choice," he muttered, "but she sure as hell is not going to be allowed to poison my sons against me." He would control what Britt and Damion did as he always had. This was just a hot-blooded infatuation with a trouble-making woman and he was going to see to it that it came to a stop—now.

It was late and he knew by the time he reached the Circle S it would be near morning. But he promised himself to waste no time in gathering his men and making another visit to the Bar K. This time he would make his threat more pointed.

The Kennedys had caused him a problem from the moment of their arrival. Now they were turning brother against brother, and because of the future of the Circle S, he could not tolerate their influence any longer.

Sure of the cause of his problems, Elliot grew more firm about his decision. He would offer again to buy the Bar K. If that did not work, he would demand that they leave, threaten, and, if necessary, he would carry out his threats. One way or the other he would rid himself of the problem that stood between his sons. He never gave a thought to the possibility that any of the problems between Britt and Damion might be brought to a halt by him.

Chapter 22

The moon was high, brightening the area and making the trip to Southwind's village easier. Kairee had slipped out of the house undetected. She had ridden for some time trying to sort her thoughts. Then, to rest her horse, she dismounted and walked for awhile, leading her horse behind her.

With the reins of her horse in one hand, Kairee walked slowly along the creek bank. She was completely immersed in her thoughts.

Her life and the lives of her entire family had become so tangled in just a few months. They had come here with such high hopes for a good future, only to have those hopes destroyed by greed and deceit.

She thought of her father, still looking upon this land as an opportunity, and of Gregg and Lucy, still willing to stand and fight for their future.

But try as she might, she could not shake the urge to run away, far away. She had never been frightened in her life, but she was now.

Trying to be honest with herself, Kairee was coming to the conclusion that there was no way she could remain here. She wanted to stand with her family and fight. But now she had another life to consider.

Thoughts of the child she carried brought her mind reluctantly to Damion.

She tried to view her emotions as clearly as she could, seeking an answer. But though her mind struggled violently, her body whispered its desire to belong to him.

Yet to belong to Damion meant surrendering all she loved, all she was, to the Circle S. Could she raise her child as Damion had been raised, with no one but her to care if he ever learned to love or share? Could she watch him become the cold and exacting kind of person the Circle S and Elliot demanded, with only one thought, one goal, one thing for which to live: the Saber dynasty?

Alone with her thoughts, she could freely admit that what she felt for Damion was a unique emotion she was powerless to control. She loved him, and she could fight that idea for the balance of her life and lose. She loved him, but she could never stay with him. Nor could she ever tell him of the child she carried. She would not sacrifice it to the Circle S and Elliot Saber's dream.

It was a terrible secret to keep, for she felt a man had a right to know of his children. But she could not tell him. The price would be more than she could pay.

Damion had not loved her; he had only wanted her. And the wanting had been a magic web in which she had become irretrievably entangled.

The fact that he did not love her was difficult to face, but the knowledge that she was so vulnerable to his touch, that if he reached for her again she would surrender, was almost unbearable.

There was only one way to give her family the freedom to fight and that was to remove the weakest links, she and her child. With them as a weapon, Elliot Saber and Damion would make her family bow to their wishes. She could not allow that to happen.

She gave a low, muffled moan when she realized that she would give anything to share the same magic with Damion one more time before leaving, to know the feel of his hands against her flesh and to taste the passion his kiss could build in her.

She would learn to forget him. She would learn to live life with the memory of his passion to sustain her and the child that was the product of that passion.

She knew there were ways to destroy the life that stirred within her, and almost defensively she placed her hand over her belly in a protective gesture. If she could never have Damion, at least she would have this. It would have to be enough. But how she ached just to see him once again, to hold him one more time, to gather a memory she could grasp when the days were dark and lonely.

She sighed deeply, trying to make one more decision. She had left a note for Lucy, revealing that she was going to see Southwind and would explain when she got home. She knew telling her father and Gregg would be the most difficult thing she had ever done. Kairee was certain they would insist on hearing her plans for the future before allowing her to leave.

It would be best, she realized, to visit Southwind first. At least she would be able to confide in Southwind and ask questions about Damion. At the village she would find respite from the conflict, time to catch her breath and make decisions for herself and her child's future.

She turned to mount her horse. As she did, she saw a rider coming toward her and she realized he must have been watching her for quite some time. She was quick to recognize a man she knew so well. It would do her no good to run, and running was against her nature anyway.

She stood immobile and watched him ride closer. Damion.

Damion had poured two glasses of whiskey and had handed one to Jim. He was quick to observe that Jim's nerves were stretched taut. He understood this, for even he, the son of Elliot Saber, would not want to be talking behind Elliot's back about secrets his father wished kept.

"So, Jim," Damion urged gently. He watched Jim toss down the drink in one gulp, took the glass, and refilled it.

"The girl who looks like Kairee Kennedy, she's Emma Martin. Her and your pa came out here together. They'd been planning on getting married for near a year. Your pa . . . he loved her. He loved her so deep that he just couldn't handle what happened."

"Just what did happen?" Damion asked quietly.

Jim sighed and began the story. Damion was silent and immobile the entire time Jim talked. He even ignored the drink he held in his hand.

". . . so something inside him broke and froze. He just couldn't seem to let another human being close to him again. It was like he was afraid, afraid if he let himself love someone again and lost 'im, it would kill him."

"And he put his love the only place he could be assured it wouldn't hurt him, in something that wasn't alive and couldn't leave—the Circle S," Damion reflected solemnly.

"If only you could have seen him work to build this place. He grubbed and went hungry. He gave it everything. When he brought your ma here and you were born, I thought, Hallelujah! He's found someone to share his dream with. Now he can let go of Emma

286

and let her rest in peace. But he couldn't . . . and your ma knew it."

"And it killed her," Damion replied softly.

"She was sweet and gentle, and she loved your pa completely. It wasn't the ranch that killed her; it was knowing her love wasn't enough."

"And Kairee looks so much like Emma that Pa just can't face her."

"When I saw her, I couldn't believe it. It was like Emma come back to life."

"God, if he had only talked to me and Britt. Why couldn't he see that we loved him too?"

"'Course you love him, Damion," Jim said gently, "which puts you right in the middle. How you gonna turn your back on him and everything he's built, knowing he's built it for you? Once you were born, Damion, he had a whole new life. He put the Circle *S*, the thing he loved most in the world, in your hands. Are you going to throw it back in his face? You do and you'll kill him sure as hell."

"Kill him!"

"Same thing. You'll make everything be for nothing."

"You're asking too much, Jim."

"I ain't asking nothing."

"I've worked for the Circle *S* like a horse. I've given it my life up until now. But I want Kairee Kennedy. I want to do what my father has never done. I want to tell the woman I want to share my life with that I want her. He lost everything just because he couldn't love again. Well, I'm not about to do that."

"Damion . . . tell me why you and Britt were fighting."

"I told you the truth before. I just don't know, but I'll tell you it has something to do with Kairee. He said he was going to see her."

"Damion, for God's sake, can't you see what the Kennedys are doing? They're playing you and your brother against each other. What better way to keep you off them and tear down the strength of the Circle S than to have you two fighting each other."

"Then you think Britt and Kairee . . ." Damion was shaken by words that seemed to fit the puzzle, that seemed to be true. "I don't believe it," he declared, but conviction was lacking in his voice. He had said nearly the same words to Southwind, that he and his brother were both in love with the same woman.

Maybe they were, but was it love on Kairee's part or was it some kind of game she was playing for her family's benefit?

Faced with unwelcome emotions that tore at him, he knew he had to find out for certain. The only one who could answer him was Kairee.

He set down his glass and started for the door.

"Where are you going?" Jim called after him.

At the door Damion turned and smiled a stiff-lipped smile that had little humor in it. "Don't worry, Jim. I'm not going to tangle with Britt again, at least not until I see Kairee and get some answers to a whole lot of questions."

It was growing late, but Damion's mind was so engrossed by his need to see Kairee that he did not stop to consider that the family would be long asleep by the time he arrived. When he finally dismounted before the darkened house, the realization came to him, but he was too stubborn to retrace his steps without talking to Kairee. He walked up on the porch and knocked, waited, knocked again, then again.

Inside the house, the sound of the knocking reached within the clouds of Lucy's sleep. She stirred, sat up, and listened, only to hear the knock repeated.

At first she considered waking Gregg. Because of all

288

that had happened, she was slightly afraid. But then she realized that someone who intended harm would hardly knock.

She slipped from the bed without disturbing an exhausted Gregg and left their room. In the parlor she lit a lamp and carried it to the door with her. Opening the door only a crack, she held the lamp up to see who stood on the porch.

"Mr. Saber," she whispered in surprise.

"Mrs. Kennedy . . . Lucy, I have to see Kairee. I know it's very late, but this is important."

"Important to whom?" Lucy questioned coldly.

"To both of us, I hope. I wouldn't have come here at this hour if it weren't."

"I'm afraid you'll have to come back tomorrow. Kairee's asleep, and I don't think she wants to talk to you."

"Why don't you let her tell me that."

"Really, Mr. Saber, I—"

"I know," he said gently. "You love her and you want to protect her. I don't want to hurt her either, Lucy. I just want to talk to her."

Lucy was frightened. Had Damion somehow learned about the baby? Her mind told her it was illogical, but the intense look in his blue eyes told her he was not about to back away until he had spoken to Kairee.

If he managed to wake her husband or her father-in-law, there would be a larger problem to face. With her present, at least Kairee could face him without being afraid.

"Come in," she whispered, "but for heaven's sake be quiet."

When he was inside, she closed the door and walked past him to place the lamp on the table. Then she turned to face him again.

In the pale gold light from the lamp Damion seemed an immense force, his large form towering over her. He stood with a sense of confidence and the intense look of a hunting beast.

She was stunned momentarily by the look of him. She considered his tall, broad-shouldered frame and wondered if there were a place in the world far enough away or so well hidden that Kairee could escape him if he knew she carried his child. Such a feat seemed nearly impossible.

"I want you to understand something very clearly," she stated.

"And what might that be?" Damion half smiled at the firmness of this woman he could have lifted with one hand.

"I intend to stay right here. You are not going to say or do anything to upset Kairee or I shall have you run off this ranch."

He chuckled softly but bowed slightly toward her.

"Kairee doesn't need protection from me, but if you feel the need to protect her, by all means stay."

She held his gaze several seconds more, sure that he was laughing at her.

"I'll get Kairee."

He watched her walk across the room to open another door and step inside.

Inside the room, which was brightened by moonlight, it took only a moment for Lucy to ascertain that Kairee was not in her bed and that there was a piece of paper pinned to her pillow.

The room did not provide enough light for her to be able to read the note, so she snatched it up and almost ran to the next room.

Damion had been leaning against the fireplace, but he immediately stood erect when Lucy returned. He could read the concern in her expression.

"What's wrong?"

"Kairee . . . she's not there."

"What do you mean she's not there? Where could she be?"

"I . . . don't know. She was there when we went to bed." Lucy held the note before her. "She must have planned to go. She left this."

Damion snatched the note from her hand without apology. Lucy watched his face as he read, saw the drawing together of his brows, and noted that his hand shook slightly.

She began to wonder just what this particular Saber was feeling, and whether or not she might have misjudged him.

Shaken first by the fact that Kairee was gone, Damion read the note rapidly:

Dear Lucy,

Don't be alarmed at finding me gone. You know that the decisions I have to make are quite difficult and I need time. I am going to South-wind's village. I will stay with her for a few days and try to make some sense of what has happened and decide what I must do.

Please tell no one—*no one*—where I am. I need to be alone.

I love you all.

Kairee

Questions crowded Damion's mind. What decision was she talking about? Was she deciding which of the Saber men she would take, or which of the Saber men she could make the bigger fool of. What problem plagued her . . . and . . . My God! his rational mind exploded. This country was much too dangerous for her to be wandering about alone.

291

Could she even find her way to Southwind's village by herself? What if one of the rustlers who had plagued the Circle *S* were to find her? Worse yet, could she be hurt already, alone and needing someone? "Does she know where she's going?" Damion demanded of a startled Lucy.

"If . . . if she's been someplace . . . well, Kairee always remembers."

"When did you see her last?"

"About ten o'clock."

"Ten." He looked at the clock on the mantel. "It's past eleven now. She can't have gotten far. I'll find her."

"Mr. Saber . . . Damion," Lucy began, "maybe you should let her go, leave her alone to solve her problems."

"I can't do that."

"Why? She doesn't need you. All you can do is cause her problems." Lucy's voice rose in anger. "Haven't you done enough to her already? Haven't you made her cry enough over—"

"Over what?"

"Nothing . . . I . . . mean all of you. Just let her go, Damion. Leave her alone. Believe me when I say you can't do anything now but hurt her more than she has been already."

Damion's eyes narrowed and he gripped Lucy's shoulders. "There's a hell of a lot more to this than you're telling me. Now I'm going after her for a lot of reasons, the least of which is that it's dangerous out there for her. I don't know what this is all about, but I'm going to find out."

"No," Lucy whispered, "you're making a mistake."

"One of a million," he grated, "but at least I'll answer for them. I have to have answers and Kairee is the only one who has them."

"Answers to what?"

"That's between Kairee and me."

"Damion," Lucy said in a subdued voice, and he was surprised to see tears glistening in her eyes. "If you don't let this go, if you continue like you are, you might get hurt too. We love Kairee, and we'll stand beside her no matter what happens. And remember this: we'll defend her against anything . . . or anyone."

Damion's eyes held hers for a long time, but he knew he would get no answers to anything from her. Without another word, he strode to the door and in an instant it had closed behind him. Lucy sank down slowly in a chair and prayed silently that Damion would not catch up with Kairee before she got to the village.

Damion rode a trail he knew as well as his own hand. He urged his horse to a gallop, knowing Kairee would have to rest her horse somewhere along the way.

He was shaken by the certainty that something unknown hovered between him and Kairee, and he was afraid that the something might be Britt.

A deep fury rose in him, fury that the situation was out of his control. He could not believe what he was doing. He could find no reason for the things Lucy had told him. Protect Kairee . . . defend Kairee . . . stand beside Kairee. All the words had the same meaning and told him nothing except that Kairee was running away from something she could not face. He had to discover what it was that frightened her to such a degree.

He still believed he knew Kairee better than anyone thought he did, and he was certain she would not run unless the problem were so monumental she could do nothing else.

He faced the fact that he was bitterly jealous of Britt and more than a little afraid Kairee was about to choose between them, though he was not yet ready to admit such feelings to anyone else.

His heart had begun to hammer rapidly. He had ridden fast enough and far enough to have found her by now.

All the things that could have happened to her twisted through his mind and he became so caught up in his fears that he almost missed seeing her. If the moonlight had not been so bright he would have ridden past the bank of the creek where she walked.

He saw her look up at his approach and stand frozen as he rode closer. He stopped his horse several feet away and dismounted. Then he walked toward her.

He saw her half in shadow and half in moonlight and her beauty reached for him and drew him to her. He realized the brutal truth. He would never stop wanting Kairee, even if her choice was Britt.

Chapter 23

Damion walked to within inches of Kairee and stopped. For a few moments they looked at each other.

"What are you doing here?" she questioned.

"I've been following you."

"Why?"

"I told you I would be back, Kairee. I told you there was a lot of unfinished business between us. I guess this is as good a place as any for us to talk."

"No, Damion, not now, not tonight, please. I . . . I must—"

"Must what, Kairee, run away?"

"No, Damion, I am not running away. I am only seeking the best way out of all of this, a way that will hurt fewer people."

"Why are you going to Southwind's village?"

"I'm not sure. Maybe it is because she is so kind, so understanding. I need someone like that and maybe it's because she knows the Saber men so well. Maybe," she added quietly, "it's because she might have some answers."

"I read the note you left Lucy."

"It was not meant for you to read."

"Lucy is not to blame." He tried to smile. "She could

hardly fight me for it, could she?"

"Damion . . ."

"She said a lot of things, Kairee, and your note left a lot unfinished. Why does she feel she has to defend you, stand by you? There is so much you are not telling me, Kairee, so much that I feel I should know."

"I have no answers for you now, Damion. I need time to think."

"Kairee, are you going to Southwind because . . . because of Britt?"

"Britt? I don't understand."

"Are you in love with Britt, Kairee?"

"You can ask me this?"

"I have to know."

The association of Britt and the moon's glow catching his face and reflecting the bruises drew a startled sound of surprise from her.

"What happened?"

"I'm afraid Britt and I had a rather violent argument. I have a feeling it was over you."

"He said that he—"

"No, he said nothing. But he left to ride over to see you."

He reached out a hand and rested it lightly on her shoulder. "Kairee, what's between you and Britt?"

It was the worst question he could have asked, for it created visions of Damion and Britt fighting over her, then over the child she carried. Would Damion accuse her of having an affair with his brother because she had surrendered so easily to him? Pride would never let her plead for understanding. What if he found it impossible to believe that the child was his?

"Britt and I," she said softly, "are friends."

"Nothing more?"

"Stop this! Do you think I must answer to you, Damion? I am not a possession of the Sabers' . . . I do

296

not belong to you."

He reached to take hold of her shoulders and pull her close to him. She tried to pull away, but his hands held her in an iron grip and she felt herself relentlessly drawn to him.

"There is something you're not telling me," he grated, "something I should know."

"Damion, don't . . . let go of me."

He released her shoulders as if surprised at his own violence.

"I'm sorry. Kairee, we have to talk. You must tell me why you left, why you seem so . . ."

"So what?"

"Different." He was puzzled as he gazed into eyes that seemed shielded from him. "There is no need to go to Southwind, Kairee. It would be better if you came to the Circle S with me."

"That is the last thing I would do."

"Why? You would be safe there. There are so many things I've discovered since I saw you last. I want to tell you about them. We can put an end to all our problems now."

Not one word of love, she reminded herself bitterly. Not one word of gentle understanding or consideration. Just the welfare of the Circle S, and—she thought now of his words—a suspicion that she might have been to his brother what she had been to him. The thought was a sword that cut deep.

"Don't you see, Damion, we were ill-fated from the start. We were never meant to be. You are Damion Saber, a man dedicated completely to one thing, the Circle S. I am a Kennedy, a woman your father cannot seem to tolerate. Whatever was between us must be put to rest."

"Can you do that, Kairee, just like that? Can you push me and what we shared out of your mind like it

297

never existed? I can't," he added softly, "and I don't think you can either. I've wanted you, Kairee, as I have never wanted any other woman in my life."

"Want," she whispered bitterly. "And that is enough for you," she added as she turned away from him.

He came up behind her and gripped her shoulders, pulling her back against him. His breath was warm against her cheek and she could feel the current that flowed through her, putting the lie to her denial.

"Will you tell me what we shared was a lie, Kairee? Will you tell me you didn't want me as I wanted you?"

She could not deny it aloud, for she knew he spoke the truth. Yet she could not hope for anything more from him than passion, for she believed the only love inside him belonged to something else.

It was then that she made her decision. She would go to Southwind and tell her everything. She wanted her to know of the child. Then she would leave Wyoming and go where Damion would never be able to reach her.

She would leave, but she could not do so without taking one more sweet memory with her. Slowly she turned in his arms.

"No, Damion, I cannot deny what you say. I cannot lie and say I did not share your passion. I cannot even say that I do not want you now, for that would be the greatest lie of all."

She watched a smile touch his face and knew he believed himself the conqueror. He had succeeded in making her face the only thing that existed between them—raw, hungry desire.

He cupped her face between his hands and lifted her mouth to his. The kiss was gentle, tentative, then he lifted his head to look into her eyes.

"Don't go to Southwind tonight, Kairee. Stay here with me."

298

She nodded and heard his soft laugh as his arms came about her, and she was crushed to him as again his mouth possessed hers, this time in a release of pent-up desire.

"I do want you, Damion," she whispered. "God help me, I want your arms around me and I want to feel your touch. It would be insanity to say otherwise."

He saw tears glistening in her eyes and was again shaken by the vague knowledge that she needed something more. But he had given her everything, he reflected, without realizing that one word would have bridged the chasm that lay between them.

"You have the command of my will and I can't fight you," she admitted, and he lost his ability to think.

His mouth moved on hers again, slowly savoring its sweetness, until he heard her soft moan, felt her lips part and her body move against him.

Now the kiss deepened as passion rose and his tongue invaded the soft flesh of her mouth and found hers seeking as urgently as his. His hands slid down the curve of her back to caress her buttocks and draw her tight against him.

When the kiss ended, both were dizzy, intoxicated by the heat of it. She stepped back from him and they gazed at each other for a moment.

Then his mind cleared and he moved away from her to the horses, unsaddled and unbridled them, and hobbled them nearby. Then he took a blanket from behind his saddle and tossed it over his shoulder. He walked back to her and she extended her hand and smiled as he approached.

They walked together until they found a softer, grassier spot on the bank, then he turned to her and without a word she reached for the buttons on her blouse. But he went to her and took her hands to stop her.

At her questioning look, he smiled. "I want to do that. I've dreamed about it for a long time."

She let her hands fall and stood still while he slowly removed her clothes. When they had been put aside, he removed his. They faced each other again and he took a moment to pull the pins from her hair and toss them away, letting the silken tresses tumble to her shoulders.

He reached to slide both hands into it and drew her to him again. Their bodies touched with a blinding heat that molded them to each other.

She put her hands on his waist and closed her eyes while he savored the warmth of her parted lips. She shivered as if caught in a violent tempest, but her being was filled with a liquid warmth that emanated from the pit of her belly and spread through her like a turbulent molten river. She felt weak and swayed in his arms. His lips moved slowly from hers and he brushed light kisses on her closed eyes, her cheeks, and bent to run his warm mouth down the length of her throat to seek the rapidly beating pulse. Then his lips returned to hers to nibble and play, parting them in fierce, hungry kisses that left her breathless.

A soft moan escaped her and she slid her arms around his neck, seeking now with an intensity that matched his.

The swirling need within them burst like an exploding sun and swept them away to unfathomable heights.

He drew her down to the blanket with him and absorbed the beauty of her body, slim and white in the moonlight, her blond hair spread across the dark blanket.

He lay beside her braced on one elbow, and as he looked into her beautiful face, he momentarily felt puzzled and uncertain, yet the beauty that had always fired him ignited the heat in his loins.

The moon's glow made her shimmer like incandescent gold and he bent to touch her lips again while his hand caressed the softness of her breast, then slid gently down the curve of her waist to rest for a heartbeat on the flat belly. It continued down her hip to smooth the flesh of her thighs, slowly separating them to let his fingers play gently against the moist flesh.

Her eyes were half closed as passion sent streaks of fire skimming through her body.

He nibbled at the soft curve of her shoulder and moved to seek even softer places, catching a nipple with his lips and sucking gently. Then he lowered his head to kiss the firm flesh of her waist and the inviting curve of her abdomen.

She gasped now and gripped his shoulders to prevent what she sensed he was about to do. He looked up at her and saw her eyes glistening gray in the moonlight.

Gently he disengaged her hands from him and placed them at her sides. Then he moved to his knees and slid his hands up the inner flesh of her thighs, and with gentle force they parted.

Again the heat of his lips was against the softness of her skin. They nibbled and skimmed her flesh, seeking the source of her now brilliant white need.

She pulsed with the beat of desire and his tongue found that pulse and explored deeper, deeper, and he grew more intoxicated upon hearing her whimpers of pleasure as she writhed beneath him.

Kairee was lost in a delirium of rapture and she wanted to feel him within her as badly as he wanted to be there. But he would not end it, not yet.

"Damion, please . . . please," she groaned.

"Not yet, love," he gasped. "Not yet."

Again his mouth and hands began to torment her body until her whimpers turned to moans and she tossed her head from side to side, unable to summon rational thought or control her desperate need.

Her body was sheened with perspiration and her moans had turned to a fierce animal cry. Her slender body thrashed in ecstasy so violent it was almost agony.

She was more vibrantly alive than she had ever been before and she felt as if her very soul was spiraling upward, upward.

Driven by a hunger beyond reason now, he rose above her and Kairee could not suppress the cry that escaped her lips as he entered her.

His body was iron hard and he moved with a slow, rhythmic control that drove her to the brink of insanity. Her body writhed beneath him, and she called his name without hearing as her slim legs curved about him. Her hands gripped his sides in spasmodic passion.

She felt the swelling start in the depths of her, growing, pulsing, and she could hear his ragged gasps mingling with her cries as he thrust harder and harder, lifting them higher and higher until they were blinded by the brilliance of the peak. They could only cling together, gasping and breathless, as a pool of liquid fire engulfed them and tumbled them into its swirling oblivion.

They held each other for a long while before speech was possible. He rolled his weight from her but kept her bound to him. They lay side by side, looking into each other's eyes.

Her eyes were warm and limpid as she looked at him, revealing more than she could put into words.

He reached to brush the perspiration from her brow, then again tangled his hands in her hair to draw her lips to his. His mouth moved on hers gently and she lay in the shelter of his strong arms wishing that the night could be stretched into eternity.

His strength seemed to surround her and again she

was made aware of the futility of her wish. He could command her body, but this was all he ever meant to give her. The balance left between them would have to be her giving. And while she knew she could give herself to him and live for just this miracle alone, she would not give her child, not to a man who could not or would not love.

Damion's eyes memorized her face and he smiled, thinking he had overcome all that stood between them. He was aware also of some vital differences in her. Her eyes seemed softer, her skin glowed with a pearly luster, and her lips seemed even more inviting than they had when he had first tasted them. They were subtle changes, but they enhanced the mystery about her, a mystery he hoped to have a lifetime to unravel.

"You are so beautiful, Kairee," he whispered as he brushed his fingers lightly against her cheek, "and I wonder if there will ever be a night like this again."

She gazed at him and tears formed like silver pools in her eyes.

"It is special . . . this night," she replied. "I wish it could go on and on. I wish the sun would never rise again."

"Nonsense. When we get back to the Circle S, we have a whole new life to start."

"It's . . . it's not that simple, Damion."

"Why not? We don't have to let anyone or anything intrude on our lives if we don't want to. Look, Kairee, we can make the Circle S grow into something bigger than anyone could dream. With you I could build it into . . . God knows what."

"And what about everyone else?" she questioned softly.

"Everyone else?" He chuckled. "My father will have to get accustomed to your being there. Maybe it's the best medicine he could have, too."

"I don't understand."

"You don't need to right this minute. We'll have a long time to explain a lot of things to a lot of people."

"Damion, the Circle S belongs to your father. I don't want to live there."

"Don't make your mind up so fast. You've never seen it really. It's—"

"I know what it is."

"Now I don't understand."

"It's home for your father, your brother, and for you."

"And it will be home for you too."

"For me, for you, and all the future Sabers. And . . . and what of Britt?" She lowered her voice to an almost inarticulate whisper.

Damion remained silent for a minute, doing his best to contain the touch of jealousy that still had the power to shake him.

"Does it concern you so much . . . what Britt thinks?" he questioned.

"What concerns me is what the future holds. That's why I cannot go back to the Circle S with you, not now. It's why I'm going on to Southwind's village in the morning. I must have time to think, Damion."

He had tightened his arms about her, sensing the extent of her resistance.

"Please, Damion, try to understand. There are so many other things to consider before we selfishly seek our own desires."

"What is it, Kairee? There's something . . . I don't know. Is it that you don't want to come with me, or . . . or is it that something, or someone else, stands between us? Kairee, for God's sake, one step will settle all this. All we have to do is make it clear to everyone that you will be a Saber from now on."

She could have wept from the combined forces that

tore her apart. She could not just "become" a Saber. She could not simply marry a man because he wanted her. And she would not bring a child into the Saber fold knowing there would be no love. She envisioned living with Elliot Saber and his hate, imagined sharing the same house with two men like Britt and Damion, who could not even reach each other, much less an outsider, and her decision was made. She would not waver. But knowing Damion was hardly a man to be denied what he wanted, she renewed her vow that the child would be hers and hers alone.

"I must have time, Damion. You must understand."

"I'm not going to let you go."

"I'm only asking for time. Is that so much to ask?"

"It is when it's time we could be together, and time we're wasting."

"Then," she said softly, "let's not waste tonight."

If he was surprised at her overwhelming response, he was soon too lost in it to question her any further.

There would be tomorrow, he thought, tomorrow to bring her to her senses, to make her see that she belonged with him at the Circle *S*.

Her hands tangled in his hair and drew his head down to hers, and when their lips met again, thoughts of anything else but the magic of this night were forgotten.

Damion awoke first and until the sun brightened the sky he lay quiet, not able to understand his own urgency to hold Kairee or the even worse feeling that she was slipping away.

But he was determined not to allow Britt or his father to stand like dark shadows between him and Kairee. At no time did he realize that it would have taken so little to put an end to the misunderstandings that lingered in

Kairee's mind and had created a wall all his strength could not combat, a wall it would have taken only a word to destroy.

Reluctantly, Kairee came awake and her eyes revealed her determination. She moved from his arms and they dressed in silence. Then he turned to her.

"Kairee . . ."

"Let's not talk about it anymore, Damion," she said softly. "I am going to see Southwind for a few days."

"What is it you think she has for you?"

"I want nothing from her, just . . ." She was helplessly silent.

"All right, Kairee, I'll take you the rest of the way. But I won't be kept waiting for too long. Do you understand that, Kairee?"

Again he was Damion Saber, announcing what he wanted and expecting the demand to be understood.

Kairee was about to speak, when Damion's attention was drawn to the distance. She turned and followed his gaze. A rider was approaching.

"Who is it?" Kairee questioned.

"It looks like Southwind," Damion said. "Rather convenient. Did she know you were coming?"

"No, but if she agrees, I will ride back with her."

Damion's eyes snapped to hers and he wanted to protest, but the look in her eyes both surprised and silenced him.

In a few minutes Southwind dismounted, and leading her horse the last few feet, she walked toward them.

Chapter 24

Britt sat up slowly, stretched, and rose. The sun was barely touching the horizon, so he was secure in the knowledge that he had plenty of time to get to the Kennedy ranch before they began the day's work.

He resigned himself to not eating any breakfast, though he would have enjoyed some hot coffee or—he grinned to himself—a good swig of brandy.

He returned to the river bank to wash and rinse the taste of sleep from his mouth. Then he saddled his horse and rode toward the Kennedy ranch, forming words in his head that he thought might reach both Kairee's mind and her heart.

Lucy had awakened long before dawn, her mind aswirl with all the problems that had faced them since their arrival. She knew that both Stephen and Gregg were still enthused, despite the troubles that had plagued them. And she could still recall her own excitement when she had first learned that Gregg was to have the ranch he had so long dreamed of having. But she was frightened now, for herself, for Cassie, and for Kairee, who was being torn by many forces: her love for her family, the child she would bear, and the Saber men.

She brought water to a boil on the stove and began the wash early so she would have time to spend with Cassie. Certain that Cassie would miss Kairee sorely, she began thinking of ways to keep her child's mind off Kairee's absence. By the time the sun was up, she was in the yard of the ranch hanging clothes on the line to dry.

Her mind occupied, she did not hear Britt approach. He dismounted, tied the horse to the rail before the house, and walked toward her.

She bent to take a piece of clothing from the basket, when his shadow fell across it, causing her to gasp in surprise.

"Oh! Mr. Saber!"

"I intend to call you Lucy"—Britt grinned—"so unless you want to make me feel very unwelcome, please call me Britt."

Lucy's eyes narrowed. She had had quite enough of the Sabers' threat, and the last thing she wanted was for Britt, Kairee, and Damion to cross paths at the same moment.

"What is it you want, Mr. Saber?"

Britt tried to keep his smile intact, but the chill in her voice was enough to deflate him somewhat.

"Lucy . . . uh . . . Mrs. Kennedy"—he grinned again —"I'm not here to cause any problems. I just want to talk to Kairee. Believe me, it's important."

"She isn't here," Lucy said quickly.

"Isn't here?" he repeated blankly. "Where is she?"

"I don't believe that is any of your concern, Mr. Saber. In fact, I think it is of no concern to any of the Sabers what any of us do."

"I know things have not been easy, but—"

"Easy?" Lucy laughed harshly. "Our fences cut, our men attacked, our cattle run off, and all kinds of threats. Surely that's an understatement."

"Circle S cattle have been run off too," he protested gently.

"Yes, and we're blamed immediately."

"That's not true," he answered. "Now Lucy . . . Mrs. Kennedy, if you'll just listen—"

"Don't patronize me, Mr. Saber," she interrupted gently. "It's true and you know it."

Britt sighed. "I wish you'd believe that I'd like nothing better than to put an end to all of this."

"Then leave us alone," she said quietly.

"That's not going to do it," he replied.

"Just what will it take to be left in peace?"

"Tell me where Kairee is. Let me talk to her. A lot depends on it."

Lucy observed him closely, wondering just what Britt Saber knew. One look at his face had already told her he had been in a fight with someone. Was it Damion? How much did Britt know, and how much should she tell him?

She decided quickly that she would leave the telling to Kairee whenever she decided to do it. Until then, she would remain silent.

"I'm afraid," she said softly as her eyes held his, "I don't know where she is at this moment."

"But you expect her back soon?"

"I don't know."

"She's visiting one of the other ranches?"

"Yes."

"Whose?"

"I'm not sure. She just said she'd be back in a day or two."

"A day or two," Britt repeated, exasperated now. Getting information from a woman intent on saying nothing was nearly impossible, he decided.

Before Britt could mount a serious attack on Lucy's

defenses, the door to the house opened and Gregg walked out. He stopped at the edge of the porch and looked down in surprise to see Britt Saber with Lucy.

Britt walked toward him and he waited, suspicious.

"Good morning," Britt began.

"Morning," Gregg responded warily. "Can we do something for you, Mr. Saber? Or are you just trying to see if enough damage has been done to run us off?"

"Look, I didn't come for trouble."

"Then what are you doing here? Doesn't the great Saber ranch have enough work that needs to be done?"

"I want to talk to Kairee."

"What about?"

Lucy was frightened of the answer Britt might give. But Britt remained in control.

"I don't see how that's anybody's business except mine and Kairee's."

Gregg walked down the steps and Lucy moved rapidly to his side. Her first thought was to get between Gregg and Britt.

She reached Gregg's side and he turned his head to look into her eyes with a half grin that told her he knew exactly what she had in mind.

"I think it would be best if you left, Mr. Saber. If Kairee wants to talk to you—and I doubt that very much—then I'll ride over with her." Gregg's voice was firm and he had the look of a man intending to support his words.

"There aren't that many places to visit out here," Britt replied. "It might take less time if you tell me where she is, but either way I intend to find her."

Lucy was reasonably certain that Southwind's village was the last place he would think to look, so she volunteered no information. She also knew Gregg was just as puzzled as Britt, though her husband would keep his silence until Britt had gone. Then there would have to be answers for Gregg and that would prove difficult. She had never found it easy to lie to Gregg.

"Mr. Saber," Lucy said, hoping to end now what might build into a confrontation. "Let me tell Kairee you were here when she comes back. I feel she might be more inclined to talk to you after . . . I mean when she gets back. If she does, I'll send a message with Rusty or Smokey."

Britt held her eyes, knowing there was much more to uncover but that he was not going to learn more from Kairee's family unless Kairee gave the word.

For some reason they felt they were defending her, but from what? Why would a few words between Kairee and him be considered a threat? He began to wonder if he could gain some positive results if he extended a hand to the Kennedys and tried to build some kind of bridge between them.

"All right"—Britt smiled his most disarming smile— "but it was a long ride here and I missed breakfast. How about extending a neighbor a cup of coffee? I'll be on my way right after, I promise."

Both Lucy and Gregg were suspicious, but they could not find a reason to refuse him.

"Come on in. There's still hot coffee on the stove," Gregg said.

"If you don't mind, I'd like to care for my horse first."

"There's water down by the barn," Gregg told him, nodding in that direction.

Gregg and Lucy watched Britt walk to his horse, untie the reins, and lead him toward the barn.

"Lucy, where is Kairee?"

"She . . . she just went riding, Gregg. She has a lot to think about and she just wanted to be alone."

She was not sure Gregg accepted her answer, for his eyes held hers a long time. She would never know that

Gregg had not believed her, but had felt that if Lucy had chosen to lie to him, she must have had a good reason. He would let her tell him in her own time. Kairee and Lucy had been too close for too long for him to pressure her now.

"What does he want with her?"

"I don't know, but"—she looked up at Gregg with a firm expression on her face—"I think Kairee has a right to make her own decisions without pressure from the Sabers. Or from us," she added in a whisper.

There were many questions on Gregg's lips, but he refrained from asking them as Britt strode toward them. He and Lucy would be alone later and he could put his questions to her and get more definitive answers.

When Britt joined them, the three walked into the house together.

Southwind had been greeted by Damion and Kairee with smiles, but it had taken her only moments to sense the almost tangible force that seemed to flow between them.

When told that Kairee had been on her way to the village, Southwind was pleased, until she saw the shadowed look in Damion's eyes.

There was much wrong between these two, she realized, but perhaps if she spoke to Kairee alone again she would be able to extend some words of help. At the moment she could see that Kairee's nerves were drawn taut and she felt the best thing might be to separate Kairee and Damion for awhile, at least until she could talk to Kairee.

When Damion went to retrieve the two horses and saddle them, Southwind found the opportunity.

"Kairee, I was on my way to your home to speak

with you."

"And I was on my way to you. Southwind, can I come stay with you for a day or so? There is so much I want to tell you. I need your advice . . . and I need your help to prevent a bad situation from becoming a disaster."

"You are always welcome in my lodge. If I can help prevent what I know is happening, then I will do whatever I can."

"Southwind . . . I . . ." Kairee's eyes fled to Damion's broad-shouldered form.

"You want to be alone, to think and to plan . . . and maybe just to catch your breath." Southwind smiled.

"Yes," Kairee breathed gratefully.

Damion walked toward them, leading the two horses behind him. His eyes were on the two women, and Kairee, as always, was conscious of the sky blue intensity of them in his deeply tanned face.

When he was near enough, he handed the reins of Kairee's horse to her.

"Damion, it is not far to my village now," Southwind said, "and Kairee and I have foolish women things to speak of. We would not take you from your work any longer and subject you to the chatter of women. My brother has told me often of his impatience with such things." Southwind laughed.

Damion was not fooled for a minute, but this only enhanced his curiosity about the purpose of Kairee's ride. Still he could not be less than considerate. He smiled only because he knew Southwind was aware of this too.

"You're sure you'll be all right?" His words were for Southwind, but his eyes never left Kairee, for again he was struck by some subtle difference in her.

"We'll both be fine. Within hours we will be in sight of my brother's scouts. From then on we will not

313

be unattended."

Damion did not want to leave them. It was clearly visible in his eyes as he waited for one word from her, one slim reason to stay. Despite the fact that she yearned to feel the strength of Damion's arms about her, Kairee remained silent. She needed to say things to Southwind that she could not share with Damion.

Though he realized Kairee might be running from him, Damion could do little about it except remind her that he had no intention of allowing what had passed between them to end.

"When do you plan to come home, Kairee?" he questioned quietly, and Kairee was not certain he did not mean the Circle *S* and him when he referred to "home."

"In two days."

"I'll come for you."

"Damion, I—"

"I'll come for you. In two days." He said the words with firm authority that would tolerate nothing less than total acquiescence.

She could only sigh and nod. Damion mounted his horse and sat for a moment looking down at her, fighting the urge to sweep her into his arms and ride so far away that nothing could interfere, then make love to her until he reached that elusive Kairee who danced behind her eyes.

"Two days," he said firmly. Then he turned his horse and rode toward the Circle *S*.

Kairee closed her eyes for a moment and swayed under the combined forces of relief and despair. Southwind was by her side and reached to touch her arm.

"Are you all right?"

"Yes, yes, I'm fine. Please let's go before Damion decides to change his mind."

314

She mounted and Southwind followed and they rode toward the village.

When they arrived at the village, the sun was already on the descent. They had traveled without stopping long enough to eat and now both women were tired and hungry.

Southwind led Kairee to her lodge quickly and within an hour they were seated before a crisply burning fire finishing a meal Southwind had made after refusing Kairee's assistance.

"You look very tired, Kairee," Southwind observed. "There are shadows beneath your eyes and your skin is very white. Are you well?" The concern in her voice choked Kairee for a few minutes, and tears she could not control, or, for that matter, understand, welled up in her eyes.

"I am tired," Kairee admitted. Southwind's eyes clung to Kairee's face for a long time, her brow furrowed in a frown. Then those perceptive eyes skimmed down Kairee's body to her hands, which now clutched each other in her lap.

A strange, intuitive feeling shook her, a feeling she could not identify. "Would you like to rest a while? I must go to assure my brother that I am safe and well." Southwind smiled encouragingly. "He still tends to believe I am the little girl he used to watch over when we were children."

"I really would like to lie down for awhile."

"Good. Then find your comfort in my bed and I shall return before long."

Southwind stood and walked to the entrance. There she stopped and watched Kairee lie down on her bed and gratefully stretch out and close her eyes. She shook off the same feeling that had plagued her before. When

Kairee chose to tell her her purpose in coming here, she would listen. Until then, Southwind would give her the peace of mind of knowing nothing was demanded of her.

Southwind left the lodge and walked across a wide clearing to reach her brother's lodge. She stepped inside only to find the lodge empty, but as she turned to leave, the sound of hoofbeats stopping before the door told her her brother was back. It also told her he was impatient. The door flap was pushed aside and Lone Wolf entered.

His face was clouded with both worry and anger. She tried to smile, but Lone Wolf was beyond pleasantries by now.

"Why did you not tell me you were leaving the village?" he demanded.

"I am sorry, Lone Wolf," she replied, undaunted by his scowling face. "I had intended only to go to speak again with Kairee, but I met her and Damion, on her way here."

"Here? They are here?"

"No, Kairee sleeps in my lodge. Damion has returned to his home."

"It was her purpose to come here again? Why?"

"I have no answer for that question yet. She rests and soon we will talk. I feel something terrible is brewing and she can provide the reasons."

"I am surprised Damion left the two of you to travel alone."

"So was he." Southwind laughed softly. "I am afraid he had little choice. Kairee wished to speak to me alone, so I convinced him to let us continue ourselves."

"Convinced him?"

"He went reluctantly," Southwind admitted.

"Southwind?"

"Yes?"

"This woman lights a fire that might burn many people in its flames. Maybe you should advise her to return to her own land and forget the trouble that smolders here. She can only be hurt."

"I have a strange feeling, my brother," Southwind said softly, "that Kairee has already been branded by a flame she cannot put out."

"I don't understand."

"It is not for me to give answers until she speaks with me and chooses to tell me what is in her heart. I will wait."

Lone Wolf sighed, knowing there would be no more answers from Southwind this night.

Southwind let Kairee sleep for over three hours before she returned to her lodge. As she stepped inside, Kairee was just sitting up and rubbing the sleep from her eyes.

"You feel more rested now?" Southwind inquired.

"Yes, thank you, Southwind."

"I have brought some cool water from the stream and some more food."

Kairee reached for the water and drank greedily. Then she accepted the food, realizing she was hungry.

"I have such a ravenous appetite lately." She laughed. Southwind watched her closely, knowing the truth but waiting for Kairee to put words to it.

Slowly she sat down across the low-burning fire from Kairee. Dark brown eyes met gray ones and Kairee was the first to turn away.

"Kairee, I shall listen with my heart if there are words you wish to speak to me," Southwind said softly.

"Oh, Southwind, I am so frightened," Kairee whispered miserably.

"You are with child?" Southwind questioned.

"Yes, I am. You knew?"

"You need not tell me if you choose not to, but I feel

317

the father must be Damion. Maybe part of the reason I knew was the way he looked at you. Does he know? . . . Does Britt know?"

"Neither of them know; I've been tearing myself apart, imagining what might happen, knowing Elliot Saber and Damion. They would force my child to walk as they have walked. I want more for my child than the loveless, cold world in which Damion and Britt have lived their lives. Do you think I could stay there, one day have more children and see them battle each other as Britt and Damion have done? I could not bear it."

"And my son loves you too."

"That can only make things worse. What might happen between Britt and Damion would only make Elliot Saber hate me more than he already does."

"You must not allow Elliot to force your decision," Southwind said firmly. "Look at me, Kairee."

Kairee looked into Southwind's calm face. "Do you love Damion?"

"Yes, I do. Enough that I cannot destroy him . . . I cannot come between him and what he truly wants—the Circle *S* and his father."

"Listen to me. Damion came here not long ago. I have listened to him and I think I know his heart." She went on to explain the conversation between herself and Damion. "Can you not see, Kairee, that he is just learning to love. He is just learning that his life has been empty until now. He is like a boy who has been wandering in the dark so long that the light has blinded him for awhile. Don't make a mistake, Kairee. If you love him, go to him and tell him so. Teach him what love really is. Tell him of his child."

"And what of Britt and Elliot?"

"Do you love Britt?"

"As a brother."

"Then Britt must know and understand the truth

also. He must be told so that he can go on with his life. As far as Elliot is concerned, you must not let him destroy your life, Damion's, or your child's in his greed. The truth, Kairee, will be a force that might set everyone free."

"And . . . and if we are wrong about Damion?"

"We are not."

"But if we are?"

"Then Damion is lost."

"Southwind, I will never let him have my child. I will run for the rest of my life before I do that."

"If you find that I am wrong about Damion, then I will help you vanish so he will never find a trace of you again. But, Kairee, I'm not. You will see. Damion carries an untapped source of love, the strength of which he doesn't even know yet."

"I will try, Southwind. I will go to him and tell him the truth. I pray, for my child's sake, that you are right."

Chapter 25

Damion rode back to the Circle *S* plagued by the thought that he should have remained with Kairee. He should have discovered the reason for the uncertainty within him.

He could not shake the feeling that there was something Kairee wanted, or wanted to say to him, that would change many things.

Question after question filled his mind. Why would Kairee go to Southwind when she had a family to support her? Why would she not listen to reason and allow him to take her out of the conflict?

He had to give her the two days she wanted. But he intended to be there when the two days were over. He would give her what time she felt she needed, then he would make certain that her resistance was brought to an end.

Thoughts of Kairee led to thoughts of his father. What he owed his father would be well repaid, for he would bring Kairee home and begin a new generation of Sabers.

It would also put an end to the problem of the Kennedys. He would see to it that they had all the support they needed to build their place. He would make it clear to his father that the Kennedys were not to be driven away.

The idea of going home and explaining the situation to his father was not very appealing to Damion, but he knew it had to be faced.

That Elliot would resist, perhaps violently, was a foregone conclusion. But this time Damion meant to stand his ground.

He also knew he had to do something to repair the damage that had been done between him and Britt. He had no idea how to do that, but he vowed it would be done.

That Britt was in love with Kairee was another fact too certain to deny. But he could not let Kairee be the wedge that stood between them.

Once he and Kairee were married, Britt would understand the finality of it and come to his senses. Then the bridge, nearly destroyed, could be repaired.

Thoughts of Britt again brought his mind to Kairee. Try as he might, he could not completely exorcise the vision of Kairee and Britt together. His heart and his common sense said it could not be so, but the deeply planted seed of jealousy was a hard one to destroy and it was still lodged in his subconscious mind.

There were too many strings to be tied and he felt he had to regain control over himself first before he tried to tie them all. He did his best to push everything to the back of his mind so that when he was ready he could deal with one problem at a time.

Before he reached the ranch, he came across several Circle S riders who were moving a small group of cattle to a place where they would rendezvous with another group. Then the cattle would be moved toward the main herd.

The three riders hailed him as he approached. Hard work had been the release Damion had often sought to

321

keep his mind from problems. He was sure he could never get Kairee from his mind, but he could resist thinking about his other problems for the moment. He made the decision quickly as he drew close to them.

"You boys need another hand?"

"These cows are as skittish as a new bride," one of them complained with a wry grin.

"We could sure as hell use another hand."

"I'll ride with you," Damion stated firmly.

They did not find his offer unusual and made no remarks as he fell in with them.

Damion decided he would spend the next day and a half working as hard as he could. Perhaps, he reflected, this way he could find some sleep at night, and the two days before he could go for Kairee would pass more quickly.

Lucy watched in utter fascination as Britt used every ounce of friendliness and charm he could summon as a weapon against Gregg's suspicions.

They had sat at the table and Lucy had poured some coffee and had placed a plate of gingerbread cake before them.

"This gingerbread cake is the best I've ever eaten," Britt said with a boyish grin as he reached for a second piece.

Gregg sipped his coffee thoughtfully. Then he spoke in a voice that was devoid of any harshness.

"I don't believe, Mr. Saber, that you came here to sample Lucy's gingerbread cake, although"—he smiled slightly—"I'll be the first to agree with you it's the best in the territory."

"No, I didn't come here for cake. I came here to find and talk to Kairee."

"What about?"

Britt chuckled. "You can ask me that? Seems to me there're a lot of problems to talk about."

"The best cure for the problems would be for you to go back and tell your father not to cross over boundaries again. To leave our cattle and our fences alone. All the trouble would be over then," Gregg said confidently.

"You think so?" Britt replied. "Then who's going to tell you what a damn fool thing you've done, fencing land that has never been fenced. Who's going to tell you to leave our cattle alone. We've lost quite a few head in the past few months."

"You accusing me of rustling?" Gregg demanded.

"I'm not accusing you of anything," Britt said mildly. "Any more than you're accusing me."

"Seems to me," Lucy said, trying to keep calm, "you're accusing each other of things . . . and nobody knows who is really responsible."

Both men looked at each other, then at Lucy.

"What are you getting at?" Britt asked.

"I don't really know. I mean, I'm not sure. It just seems to me that somebody wants us to do it—fight, I mean. If we keep on fighting, well, we won't be watching anybody else."

Britt and Gregg exchanged glances again.

"That could be true if there were somebody else," Britt offered, "but who else is there?"

"I don't know," Lucy said helplessly. "But Mr. Saber," she added softly, "it isn't us. I swear, it isn't us."

Britt looked at Lucy for several moments. He did not have a logical reason, but he began to search for one. For the first time he began to look in other directions.

"Maybe," he said thoughtfully, "we ought to talk about a few things. Maybe see if there're some pieces of this puzzle that just might fit together."

"We'd have to find someone who could be making a

profit out of our squabble," Gregg offered. "There must be someone who has a grudge against the Circle *S* besides us."

"Somebody who has something to gain if we keep fighting. But most of the neighbors around here have been our friends for years. If they were going to rustle our cattle, why wouldn't they have started a long time ago? Before . . ."

"Before we came," Gregg finished. "You mean you never lost any before we came?"

"There're always some losses," Britt admitted, "but we've always blamed it on"—he shrugged—"just the natural course of things. Your building that fence didn't help."

"You thought we were rustling your cattle. We felt we needed protection. The Circle *S* got a little touchy when we came looking for strays. We built the fence for two reasons: to keep the Sabers out and to keep our cattle in."

"But to build fences out here is unheard of."

"Better a fence than to send someone after strays and have 'im get shot."

"We'd only shoot someone found rustling," Britt replied, his temper beginning to stir.

"We have to count on your discriminating before someone pulls a gun?" Gregg laughed harshly. "We've come close a couple of times. The next time someone might get killed. Then what? You say I'm sorry and we forget the whole thing?"

"I'm telling you we don't shoot people without good reason," Britt said.

"Then you tell me just how my father got shot," Gregg answered, his own temper becoming frayed.

Lucy could see the same problem beginning to mount: two strong men, both thinking they were right, with volatile tempers ready to explode.

"You men are still rehashing old problems without trying to find any solutions." Lucy spoke firmly, drawing their attention to her. "You're doing just what those rustlers would want you to do. You're fighting each other again."

"Looking for someone else is like searching for a shadow in a dark room," Britt protested.

"As long as you think that way, you'll never look any further, and that's just what the rustlers want," Lucy replied.

"Well, where do you suggest we look?" Britt asked.

"I'd like to suggest," Lucy said softly, "that we attempt to look together. We might frighten someone drastically if we began to help each other instead of fighting each other."

Before Gregg could speak again, voices were heard coming from outside. The clumping of booted feet crossing the porch heralded the arrival of Smokey and Rusty to talk to Gregg before the day's work began.

Lucy walked across the room to open the door for them and both wore broad smiles until they saw Britt. Then the smiles faded. Neither man felt himself in a position to ask questions about someone Gregg had obviously invited into his home, but the rigidness of their bodies and the questions in their eyes spoke for themselves.

"Morning boys." Britt grinned amiably.

"Mornin'," both muttered.

"Breakfast is ready," Lucy said quickly. "Sit down and I'll get some coffee. Mr. Saber," she said, helpless to do less than invite him to join them, "would you like more coffee . . . or . . . some breakfast?"

Britt laughed. "More coffee sounds good to me."

Smokey and Rusty sat down opposite him, still trying to control their surprise. Gregg smiled as Lucy began fussing with the food, trying to keep her mind from the confusion she saw in everyone's eyes.

At that moment Lucy's bedroom door opened and Cassie appeared in her nightgown, sleepy eyed and dragging the same rag doll.

Her eyes widened along with her smile when she caught sight of Britt. Without hesitation, and in an attitude of complete trust, she started toward him.

Lucy was not nearly as startled as Gregg was, yet Gregg remained silent while Cassie went to Britt's side.

He chuckled and reached down to lift Cassie onto his lap.

"Good morning, little one," Britt said gently.

She tipped her face up to smile at him and Lucy was more than certain that in that moment Gregg, Rusty, and Smokey began to consider believing Britt.

To everyone's surprise Britt remained at the Kennedy ranch for the balance of the day, riding with Rusty and Smokey and doing as much work as either of the two hands. They were silent and wary, but Britt made no effort to win them to him. He would let time take care of that.

That he stayed because he still hoped to talk with Kairee was something Lucy knew, and when they sat around the supper table, she was well aware of Britt's questioning gaze.

When the evening meal was over Gregg and Britt sat before the fireplace to talk. Lucy suggested that Stephen might like to join them and the two men helped Gregg's father to a chair beside the fire. Britt purposely kept the conversation light and the time passed quickly.

Finally Stephen was returned to his bed and Lucy excused herself and found sanctuary in her room. Gregg could do no less than invite Britt to stay the night and was surprised when Britt agreed. He went to bed still wondering, and Britt sat before the fireplace wondering also. He was wondering where Kairee was spending the night.

He found it hard to sleep because of the anger that twisted within him and the blossoming jealousy that had to be restrained by stubborn control.

He forced these thoughts aside by bringing Kairee to mind. He held her there, in the center of his thoughts, and summoned a vision of how it could be if she were to agree to marry him.

Their marriage would thwart all his father's and his brother's plans, he knew, and that thought brought him a moment of grim amusement. He held his vision until he drifted into a restless and dream-filled sleep.

The next day, breakfast with the family and Rusty and Smokey was a quiet, reserved meal. They still could not quite accept the Saber in their midst.

Britt could sense their disquiet and knew he had to leave. Still he lingered a while longer, hoping Kairee would return.

It was midday when he surrendered to the facts that Kairee would not be coming home soon, that no one was going to tell him where she was, and that his welcome was still thin and very shaky. It was time for him to return to the Circle S.

With a worried frown, Gregg watched Britt leave. He turned when Lucy walked to his side, her eyes following the broad-shouldered man who rode away so reluctantly.

"Why did he stay so long, Lucy?" Gregg asked quietly. "What is really going on between Kairee and the Sabers?"

"Gregg . . . please have patience until Kairee gets

back. I cannot say things that are Kairee's to say."

"I don't want Kairee hurt, Lucy."

"She'll be better protected if she's free to tell you the truth herself. She'll most likely be home tonight. Gregg, please, wait until then."

Aware that there was something terribly wrong, Gregg had an abundance of questions on his lips, but the pleading look in Lucy's hazel eyes pushed the inquiries inside.

"All right, I'll wait until Kairee gets back. But then I want some questions answered. Whatever is going on, it could cause more trouble than we've already got."

"Maybe you're right, Gregg, but we have to let Kairee manage her own life."

"I know the Sabers are a constant threat to our ranch, and I can handle that. What I need to know is, are they a threat to Kairee. If they are, we'll have to do something about it." His gray eyes held hers as he spoke softly. "Are they, Lucy?"

"I don't know yet, Gregg," Lucy replied quietly. "I just don't know yet."

Damion was in a state of near exhaustion when he opened the front door of the ranch house and walked inside. He was also in desperate need of a strong drink, so he did not go to his room immediately but into the wide, spacious parlor.

He went directly to the decanter of brandy and poured a liberal amount into a glass. He had just raised the glass to his lips when the door swung open. Britt was several steps inside before he realized Damion was there and momentarily halted.

For several minutes they stood in painful silence, looking at each other. Finally it was Britt who spoke in bitter amusement.

"You look like hell."

"You don't look much better yourself." Damion tried to smile. "Britt, it's time we had a talk."

"Do we really have much to talk about, Damion? Seems to me we lost that somewhere a long time ago."

"We have something very important to talk about."

"Such as?"

"Such as, what the hell the fight was really about."

"You really don't know, do you?" Britt spat in a surge of new anger.

"I thought you might enlighten me," Damion replied, his own frayed nerves growing taut.

"Damion, I don't think it would do any good. You're so blinded by Pa and the Circle *S,* I don't believe much else could make a difference."

"There you go making judgments for me again. Why don't you just spit out what's bothering you."

Britt walked to the table and poured a drink for himself. He gulped it down and poured another before he turned to look at Damion again, whose puzzled gaze had never left him.

Britt remained silent, wondering if Damion were as uncertain as he looked. He could never remember a time in Damion's life he had ever looked so strained.

"Britt?"

"What?"

"This fight, was it over Kairee? Is that where you went?"

"Well," Britt said softly, "you're suddenly more astute than I imagined. Did you finally get around to giving Kairee a second thought?"

Jealousies held in brutal control strained at their leashes. The blue of Damion's eyes glittered in icy crystals. Britt's eyes narrowed as he absorbed Damion's cold look.

"What's between you and Kairee, Britt?" Damion

329

questioned softly.

"Damn you, Damion," Britt answered, his teeth clenching in renewed anger, "you have the guts to ask me a thing like that? I knew you were hard, brother, but I never dreamed you were the kind of man to use a sweet woman like Kairee, then just walk away."

Damion's anger was growing to match Britt's and he took a step closer. "Stop talking in riddles. Whatever you think, I didn't use Kairee."

"No?" Britt snapped. "Of course not. You didn't even give it that much thought, did you?"

Now Damion, physically tired and mentally strained, lost what fragile control he had.

"Give what thought, damnit?"

"Christ, Damion, do you go around planting your seed in every woman you meet?" Britt was shouting now. "Don't you care about where your kids breed or the woman who is unlucky enough to be used?"

Damion felt as if someone had struck him a mortal blow. For a minute his breath caught in his chest and he felt a painful constriction.

"Kairee is . . ."

"Pregnant, as if you didn't know," Britt sneered.

"How do you know?" Damion demanded.

"That's none of your business. It's enough that I know. It's also enough that I know you never meant to do a thing about it. Your vengeance is kind of rough, isn't it, Damion? Did you tell her you loved her? Did she tell you she loved you?"

"Britt," Damion said in a smothered voice, "have you been with Kairee?"

Britt's face froze in a mask of fury. "I wouldn't honor a question like that with an answer. But at least I have an answer to my question. You couldn't love Kairee and ask a question like that. If you don't love her, don't stand in my way, because I love her and I'm going to take her as far away from you as I can get."

"The baby is mine."

"You don't deserve it or Kairee."

"But it's still mine." Damion's voice turned cold.

"Let me console you, Damion. I'll try to love it, which is more than you can do. I just don't believe you ever bothered to leave room in your heart for a little thing like love. I've done without it for too many years, so I've got a lot to spend, and I intend to spend it away from you and the Circle S. Stay out of my way, Damion. Stay the hell out of my way or I won't hesitate to push you out."

He slammed down his glass on the table and walked out while Damion stood in numbed silence.

Kairee had known two nights ago and had never told him. Could she hate him that much? Words she had spoken tumbled about in his mind until the confusion made his head thud painfully. She had gone to Southwind with the knowledge of his child. Had she ever meant to tell him?

He had to know the answers, and he had to look into Kairee's eyes when she told him. Grimly he swallowed the last of his drink, put his glass on the table, and walked out of the house.

Chapter 26

Elliot was tired when he walked up the steps to the ranch house, and he felt a definite urge for a strong drink.

In the large front room he took a bottle of whiskey from a cabinet, along with a glass. These he carried to a chair and sat down, extending his long legs before him.

He poured the glass nearly half full, set the bottle close by, and took a sip of the whiskey. Then he sat back in the chair and gave himself over to thoughts of how he was going to rid himself of the Kennedys forever. He knew he could not allow Kairee to destroy his world and therefore whatever he did would have to be quick, thorough, and very final.

He was so deeply engrossed in his thoughts that he did not hear the door open. Jim stood in the doorway several minutes watching Elliot. He knew the signs before him meant problems. He had seen them entirely too often. Elliot was contemplating trouble for someone and he was more than sure that trouble was going to be aimed at the Kennedys.

"Elliot?" Jim spoke softly at first and when Elliot did not answer he realized he had not even heard him. He spoke louder. "Elliot."

Elliot turned toward him with a deep frown, as if he could not understand the interference with his thoughts. When he saw Jim, he smiled. "Come on in and have a drink, Jim. We've got some planning to do."

They had planned many things together in this room over a bottle, but this time Jim was shaken by a premonitory fear.

He walked to the cabinet and took a glass and returned to Elliot's side. He poured a drink and sat in a chair opposite Elliot.

"So, Elliot, what's on your mind?"

"We been losing any more head, Jim?"

"I'm expecting some of the boys to report today."

"But you've got your finger on things. I'm pretty sure you have an educated guess."

Jim was uncomfortable, not because there were so many losses, but because he knew the blame would surely be placed on the Kennedys. He wasn't too certain they were guilty, yet he wasn't certain they weren't, either. He hated to point a finger without proof.

"I think we're running short every day. But there can be a lot of reasons."

"Sure," Elliot said angrily, "and the main reason is because I got soft enough to let those Kennedys move in and get settled. I should have run them off a long time ago, before they got a good hold."

"I wouldn't say they got a good hold," Jim responded with a short, rough laugh. "They've got nothin', barely a roof over their heads, and they're scrapin' just to get by. You leave 'em be, and one good winter will put 'em out of commission."

"I don't think we have that much time," Elliot said in a brittle tone.

"I don't understand you. We're as secure here as the mountains are. All we have to do is wait 'em out."

"I can't do that."

"Why not?"

"Because they're more of a threat than you know."

"You mean the fight."

"You saw Britt and Damion tearing into each other. The Kennedys seem to have found some truth in the old adage, 'Divide and conquer.'"

"They're kind of hot-blooded, but they're young. If you hold on, this will pass."

"I don't see it your way. Kairee Kennedy is playing my two sons against each other. She's a clever little girl. Either way she thinks she'll come out on top. Well, I'm not about to let her split the Circle *S* with promises she doesn't intend to keep."

"You don't know her, Elliot. You don't know if she's just an innocent—"

"Innocent! Come on, Jim. She has a pretty good idea what she's doing. She's a threat I can't afford. I'm going to drive her and her family out of this valley, and I'm going to do it as soon as possible."

"Elliot . . . are you sure you're being completely honest about what's eating at you?"

"What are you talking about?"

"Elliot, for Christ's sake. I've been with you since you first planned on coming out here. Do you think I don't have a long memory too?"

"What does your memory have to do with this?" Elliot demanded, but his eyes turned from Jim and he reached for the bottle to pour another drink.

"Elliot . . . I got a good look at the Kennedy girl," Jim said softly. "Don't you think I saw what you saw? Don't you think I know how you hurt? But . . ."

"But what?"

"But what you're doing . . . is almost unnatural."

"You're talking. Go ahead and say your piece."

"Elliot, you've carried this thing too long. It's eaten

334

you alive for so long you just can't let go. But it's time . . . it's long past time."

"Time . . ." Elliot muttered.

"Time to let her go, Elliot," Jim said gently. "I've watched you do a lot of things I never approved of. I watched you use your sons, one against the other, just to build your own private dream. But this girl is innocent. She can't be blamed for looking like a dream you can't get rid of. Damnit, Elliot, let Emma rest in peace! Let her go! She would have hated what you're doing and the way you've been using your sons. Emma was a gentle, sweet, loving woman. She would never have stood for what you're thinking."

"There were no problems 'til that Kennedy woman came along!" Elliot thundered.

"There was a problem. There's been one since the day Emma died. You've been so blinded by your dream, you just couldn't see it."

"She's the one turning my sons against me and the Circle S—for her own reasons. If the Sabers fall, then the land would be theirs for the taking."

"I never thought you were a damn fool until this minute. Nobody could turn your sons from you but you, and you've been doing a damn good job of it for years. If Britt and Damion have reached the end of what they can take, if they're beginning to fight back, it was you who pushed 'em to it. Open your eyes, for God's sake, and see what you're doing. You're going to end up being a lonely old man with nothing but these four walls to keep you company. You're driving your sons away, Elliot, and I can't stand here and watch it anymore." He turned to walk away, rage and pain temporarily blinding him. He reached the door and looked back at Elliot's storm-filled eyes.

"Elliot, it's hard leaving a friend who's been beside you over thirty years. I'm goin' up to the hills to stay at the old line shack so I can think about what I'm gonna do with myself. I wish you'd just take a minute to think about what's happening. I'd hate to see boys who love you like Britt and Damion do be pushed away because you're so blind. I'd hate to see them at each other when you could make peace if you wanted to."

"You never said any of these things before. All these years have you been thinking them?"

"I have, but I was sure the day would come when you'd be man enough and strong enough to put Emma to rest and try to keep your two sons. You've got the whole world to lose, or a whole world to gain. I reckon the choice is up to you."

Jim turned and walked out, not even bothering to close the door behind him. Elliot stood looking at it for a long time, then he turned and reached for the bottle of whiskey.

Jim wondered, as he walked across the area between the house and the stable, if it would be the last time he would be doing so as the right arm of Elliot Saber. They had been together from the beginning and the thought left a bitter taste in his mouth.

Elliot had been the best friend Jim had ever had, and Jim had tried to reason with himself that it was not his place to condemn Elliot over his relationship with his sons. But now he had reached his limit. Seeing Britt and Damion battling each other had torn away his veil of indifference. He could no longer stand by while Elliot sowed seeds of discontent between two men who should have been the best of friends. And he was sure now that Britt and Damion could have been if Elliot had not made it impossible.

He had never been a hungry or ambitious man. He had been content to remain with Elliot to build what he knew had been his friend's lifelong dream. But he could not watch Elliot's self-destruction any longer.

He also would never consider betraying Elliot or his sons, so there was no way he could go to the Kennedys and change anything.

"I'm like a damn old grizzly looking for a cave to hibernate in for the winter. Reckon I'll just find me a place and lay low so's I can think for a spell. Maybe I'm just too close to the fire."

He entered the stable and picked up his saddle and bridle along with saddlebags in which he would carry enough to sustain him for several days. From there he went to the stall in which he kept his horse.

He uttered a bitter laugh when he realized that if he made the leaving final he would be going with the same amount of possessions with which he had arrived. "Only I'll be carrying the excess baggage of a whole lot of memories. I kinda think that's going to be a heavy load."

Slowly he saddled his horse, then led the animal from the stall. He was about to fill his saddlebags with supplies, when the door opened and Britt came in leading his own horse. Both Britt and the horse looked as if they had been punished by endurance riding.

"Where ya been, boy? That horse looks near finished."

"I'll rub him down and cool him. I guess I pushed him pretty hard," Britt answered.

"Looks like you kinda pushed yourself a mite too."

"Yes . . . I guess."

"Britt?"

"Yes?"

"I'm leaving for a spell," Jim said quietly.

Jim had been so much a part of Britt's growing years that his reaction was the same as if Elliot had told him he was leaving.

"Leaving? I don't understand. Where are you going?"

337

"At this point I don't reckon I know. Just away from the Circle *S* for a spell."

Britt looked at Jim through narrowed eyes. It took him no time to realize that something drastic had happened.

"You and Pa have a falling out, Jim?"

"Sort of. It's best we just get a little space between us for awhile. We both have some thinking to do."

"Jim?"

"Yeah?"

"What's happening to us?" Britt asked quietly, almost as if it were a thought over which he had lost control. "What's happening to Pa? I know he's always been hard, but I just have a feeling something's driving him that I should know about."

"Maybe you're right, son," Jim said gently, "but I don't rightly guess it's my place to say. Britt, go talk to your pa. I know it hasn't always been easy, but then life hasn't always been easy for him, either."

"You think it will do any good, Jim? Pa and I . . . well, I guess I'll just never be the son he expected. Maybe it might be best if I left the Circle *S* to Damion. Maybe that would make them both happy."

"Right now," Jim said in mild anger, "I don't think your pa has any idea what happiness is. But if I were you, I'd try. I'd hate to see this family scattered when maybe some words would help. Besides, you belong here, boy, and no matter if you believe it or not, you and your pa would both be hurtin' if you went."

"I wish I believed that," Britt said quietly. "I'll try, Jim . . . I'll try. I'd like to talk to you . . . Where are you going?"

"For now I guess the old line shack on the north ridge. Your pa and I used it to live in while we built the main house."

"It's funny, Jim."

"What?"

"That you helped Pa build everything he has and you've never taken anything for yourself."

"Well, I never was one for gathering things. I'm not tied down by 'em. The only thing that's been good in all this is you two boys. I guess that's why it will kind of tear me up some if you and Damion can't keep this place and this family together. You might not think it now, but you two have something in common. Like it or not, you both take pride in being Sabers. So, fight for it, but watch who you fight . . . and whose reasons you fight for. Maybe, just maybe, you might be the one to hold it together."

"Don't put too much hope in that. I have to say some things to Pa that just might make this kettle boil over. I'd . . . I'd like to ride up and talk again if you don't mind."

"I'd be pleased." Jim held out his hand to Britt, who took it in a strong grip. Britt walked into the house and Jim watched until he had entered. Then he returned to his preparations for the trip.

Britt turned toward the house, reluctant to walk the distance and face what he knew would happen when he told his father his plans.

With a heavy sigh he walked toward the house. If his father did not accept what he was about to do, it would mean cutting himself away from all he had ever known and loved. Despite the problems, the Circle S and his father had been his life, and leaving them would be difficult. Yet he knew the situation would be nearly impossible if Kairee and Damion were living beneath the same roof.

He could not understand what Damion had done. It was so unlike Damion to use someone, then walk away. Perhaps there was more of Elliot in Damion than Britt realized.

He walked up the steps, across the porch, and into the house. When he entered the front room he saw that Elliot sat in morose silence, while in his hands he held a glass containing the remains of a whiskey. His elbows rested on his knees and he seemed to be caught up in deep introspection.

"Pa?"

Elliot looked up, his eyes still clouded with old memories.

"Britt . . . good, I'm glad you're here. We have a lot of planning to do."

"Planning?" Britt questioned cautiously.

"Sit down, boy. Have a drink. I'm going to settle this Kennedy affair once and for all. I sent one of the men to round up everybody. If the Kennedys don't leave this valley peaceably, I'm going to drive them out."

Britt's hand shook as he reached for the drink he now needed.

"Pa, we've got to talk about this."

"That's what I've been doing. I talk, Damion talks, you talk, and the Kennedys go about their business. Even Jim gives me an argument. Pretty soon the Kennedys will be eating away at our land. I wonder if all the rest of you are blind except me."

"No, Pa," Britt began, "I think the only person who is blind is you."

Elliot swung his head abruptly to glare at Britt.

"So both my sons turn on me at the same time."

"I'm not turning on you. I'm trying to bring an end to all this."

"There's only one way to do that."

"I . . . I can't do that."

Again Elliot's eyes narrowed. He gulped down the last of his drink and set aside the empty glass before he spoke.

"And just why can't you?"

"Because"—Britt sucked in his breath—"because

I'm going to ask Kairee Kennedy to marry me."

"Marry! No son of mine is going to marry into that family. If they can't get us one way, they'll get us another! What's she been doing, whoring for you, heating you up to the altar?"

Britt had tried to retain his hold on his emotions, but the slur on Kairee and the blame again being placed on him was too much.

"Don't be calling Kairee such names. It was we who were guilty this time. It was your precious Damion who seduced a sweet girl who trusted him, then walked away laughing. Well, maybe that's all right with you as long as you have the Circle S and Damion to ramrod it. Then the world's right. Well, I'm going to ask her to marry me. Then we'll leave and you and Damion can have everything. That should make just about everybody happy."

Elliot was gazing intently at Britt, hearing only the words he wanted to hear. "Kairee Kennedy is pregnant?" he asked gruffly.

"Yes. Does that please you, Pa? Your son Damion is quite the stud, and he's also a bastard. It's the first time in our whole lives that I can honestly say I'm ashamed of being a Saber. I'm ashamed of Damion for being less of a man than I thought he was and I'm ashamed of us all for the way we've dealt with people who should have been our friends if we had let them."

"You can't leave the Circle S just like that. You love it too."

"Yes, I do . . . but I have to make some choices here and I can't turn my back on what needs to be done."

"You marrying her because you want to protect her? She can't get one son so she gets the other?"

"You don't understand a thing I'm saying, do you, Pa?" Britt asked gently.

"I understand that baby's a Saber. It's as much your brother's as it is hers. We have all the control of the

341

Kennedys we need."

Britt gazed at Elliot now in total shock.

"You can't mean that."

"The hell I can't."

"You can't take take the baby, for Christ's sake! What kind of men have you turned us into? I won't be part of a thing like that. Pa, for God's sake, think about what you're saying."

"That baby is a Saber."

"Another pawn like me and Damion?"

"That's crazy. You're my sons."

"Are we, Pa? Have you ever really looked at us as sons, as brothers, or have we been pieces to manipulate in whatever game it was you were playing? Have you ever once, just once, told me or Damion that you cared about us? Hell no, it's always been the Circle *S!* The Circle *S!* It's been drummed into me since I was a boy. The Circle *S* and your damn dreams. Well, you keep the Circle *S.* It means more to you than I ever did. But I'm going to warn you. I won't let you do to Kairee what you've done to all the other women in your life. Before I do that I'll leave the Circle *S* and you'll never see me or your grandchild again. This time you'd better make the right decisions because all the other decisions in your life have been mistakes."

Elliot was about to respond when the sound of hoofbeats marked the arrival of many riders.

In the barn Jim had packed the last of his things and was getting ready to mount and ride away when he heard the riders.

He dropped the reins of his horse and walked toward the barn door to swing it open. At the same moment he shouted for Elliot and Britt.

He was just preparing to enter the yard when he saw Britt and his father open the door of the house and step out on the porch.

342

Chapter 27

Kairee was slowly drawn awake when she heard Southwind moving about preparing a breakfast for the two of them.

They had talked a great deal in the two days she had been there, and for long hours into the night. For the first time in many days, Kairee felt relaxed and confident that she could face her problems.

She had decided upon the course she would follow. She was going to tell the truth, first to her family, then to Damion and his family. She would also explain to all of them that she intended to stand firm in her decisions. The child was hers and Damion's and he would have to choose what he wanted: the Circle S or her and his unborn child.

But whatever he decided, she could face her life herself. She was no longer afraid.

She waited with Southwind while her horse was saddled and brought to her.

"You have made all your decisions?" Southwind questioned.

"Yes." Kairee smiled. "I'm grateful to you, Southwind."

"To me? Why? I have done nothing."

"Nothing but given me a quiet place to think and some honest advice to think about."

"What have you decided to do?"

"I will go home and tell my family my . . . situation. Then I will go to Damion and tell him."

"But you will not belong to the Circle *S?*"

"No. I will not demand anything from Damion. I just believe he has a right to know of the child."

"You must be careful."

"Of Damion?"

"No, of Elliot."

"Do you truly believe he will try to do something about this? Southwind, it's beyond his power. What can he possibly do?"

"You forget, Kairee, that a father . . . can take his child when and where he chooses."

"Damion wouldn't—"

"I'm sure Damion loves you, Kairee, but a man can manage to do a great deal of harm when he's been hurt. He might think of the child as a way to hold you."

"You've been through all this, haven't you, Southwind?"

"I left Britt with Elliot because I did not have the power in the eyes of the whites to fight him . . . and I could not bring more difficulty to my people than they had already faced. My only salvation was the fact that even from boyhood Britt wanted to know of me and of his . . . other family. I'm sure it did not please Elliot, but he couldn't stop it."

"I cannot bear the thought of my child being tugged between two people as Britt must have been."

"You will tell Damion that you love him?"

"I . . . I don't know. I'm not sure. If I do, would he use it as another weapon to get what he wants? I love him . . . yet I'm afraid. His father has the hold of years over him."

344

"And you have the hold of your love and your child."

"Is that enough, Southwind?" Kairee whispered half to herself.

"I believe it is. I believe that without even knowing it, Damion has always belonged to himself. Maybe that's why he had so much trouble giving Elliot all he demanded."

"I hope it's enough. I guess there is only one way to find out and that is to face the problem. Thank you again, Southwind."

"Come back, Kairee," Southwind invited sincerely.

"I will, my dear friend, I will."

When her horse was brought to her, Kairee mounted. She was surprised to find a smiling Lone Wolf at her side.

"Lone Wolf?"

"I could not face the anger of my sister if something were to happen to you."

"I am perfectly safe alone." Kairee laughed.

"But I would ride with you to assure both myself"—he raised an amused eyebrow at Southwind—"and others that you arrive safely."

"It is useless to argue with him, Kairee," Southwind declared with a laugh. "He will have his way no matter what you say."

Kairee surrendered to Lone Wolf, bade Southwind a last good-bye, and rode beside Lone Wolf as Southwind stood and watched them go. She wanted to believe everything was going to work out well for Kairee and Damion, but she had a cold feeling of dread that worse was yet to come.

Lone Wolf and Kairee rode for a long time without exchanging words. He watched Kairee carefully but did not break the silence, letting her decide whether to speak or to continue to keep her thoughts to herself.

After a few hours of travel, they dismounted to rest the horses. Kairee found a comfortable seat near a tree and Lone Wolf dropped to the ground beside her.

"Lone Wolf?"

"Yes?"

"You have been Elliot Saber's friend for a long time?"

"We were very close friends for a long while, but that was many years ago."

"Before Britt was born?"

"My nephew," Lone Wolf said quietly, "is the only link between Elliot and us now."

"You were against the marriage?"

"It was difficult for me to understand the fact that my sister loved a man whose heart was set on the land and not on her. She loves him still. I believe she still would join him if he needed her."

"She would." Kairee smiled. "She loves him and Britt is the link between them that can never be broken."

"Being the link does not always make Britt happy."

"No, I suppose it doesn't. It must be very hard for Britt to be torn between his mother and his father."

"It has not been so hard now that he is a man. Britt is not weak. In fact he is much stronger than Elliot would give him credit for. Elliot is blind to many things."

"Lone Wolf, would . . . would you have thought it better if Britt had stayed with his mother always?"

Lone Wolf thought for awhile. "No, Southwind's choice was right. In letting her son go, she held him closer. Can you understand that?"

"Yes, I think so."

"Kairee . . . do you love my nephew?"

"Why do you ask that?"

Lone Wolf chuckled. "Because I think it is you who

346

has held his mind for the past weeks."

"I . . . I'm not in love with Britt Saber, Lone Wolf."

Lone Wolf turned to look into her eyes. "So," he said gently, "it is his brother, Damion."

She nodded. "I don't want to hurt Britt."

"Britt is no boy. He would not want you to come to him without love. You are afraid to be the thing that causes a lasting break between them."

"Yes."

"I will tell you what I told my sister long ago. You must follow your heart, but you must walk with the truth."

"That"—she sighed deeply—"is what I'm going home to do."

Kairee rose and Lone Wolf followed. They mounted and continued their ride.

After several hours, the sun began to dip toward the horizon and long shadows indicated the arrival of early evening. Lone Wolf was about to call a halt when he and Kairee caught sight of the same object at the same time.

They had just crested a hill and looked down to see a small group of men moving about a crisply burning fire.

The nature of their activity was obvious to both. They were branding cattle.

"Do you know who they are, Lone Wolf?"

"They're on Saber land, so I imagine Elliot is again enlarging his herds."

"Shall we ride down and see?"

"Why not?" Lone Wolf smiled.

The men about the fire were not aware of their approach until they were quite close.

"Boss!" one said when he caught sight of them.

"What?"

"Riders comin'."

347

"Damn! Do you recognize 'em?"

"I think it's that Kennedy girl, and the other is that Indian friend of the Sabers', Lone Wolf."

"I told you we should have worked faster. The last thing we need is those two getting wise to what we're doing."

"We'll have to kill them."

"What? How dumb can you be? Kill one of those two and you've got more trouble than you've ever seen before."

"Well, what are we gonna do?"

"Just be quiet and leave this to me."

"Hello." Kairee smiled. "Are you from the Circle *S?*"

"No, ma'am, we belong to the Barber place. You're Kairee Kennedy, aren't you?"

"Yes."

"Well, we're just the other side of Talbot's place."

"You're well out of your way," Lone Wolf observed.

"Yeah, well, we chased these strays all the way here. Now we have to slap a brand on 'em and ease 'em home."

The man's nervousness was not obvious to Kairee, but Lone Wolf had noted it immediately.

"You hold the cattle far from your fire," Lone Wolf commented. "And there are a lot . . . for strays."

"We been wrastlin' strays for five days to get this bunch. We'd like to get 'em branded before we settle down for the night."

While they spoke, Lone Wolf and Kairee made the mistake of letting one of the men slip into the shadows and work his way behind them.

Lone Wolf did not believe what he had been told, and he realized they had ridden into a serpents' nest. What worried him was how he was going to get Kairee away safely.

"We are passing by on our way to Kairee's home," he

348

said. "You are busy and the day is growing short. We will be on our way so you can continue with your work."

Lone Wolf did not know if his words and actions hid his tension. The leader's eyes narrowed and he seemed to be watching Lone Wolf more closely than was necessary.

Lone Wolf pulled gently on his reins and slowly began to back his horse away. Kairee looked at him in surprise but followed his lead.

But knowledge of the danger of the situation came too late to Kairee. She grew motionless, as did Lone Wolf, when a rough voice spoke from behind them.

"I wouldn't make no quick moves if I was you two. Just set easy and keep your hands where I can see 'em."

Lone Wolf turned his head and cursed himself silently for not being quick enough. Now his mind spun. He had to get Kairee away from this unsavory group before they could do her any harm. He turned back to look again into Kairee's eyes.

"Lone Wolf?"

"Rustlers," Lone Wolf said bluntly. "If we were to ride into that group of cattle, I'm sure we'd find some from every ranch around here, including yours."

"You're a wise Injun," the man said with a cruel laugh.

"And those are running irons in that fire," Kairee added. "You're the ones responsible for all the rustling around here."

"And you're a smart girl, too."

"You've been stealing Circle *S* cattle and letting us take the blame for it!"

"Better you than us, little girl. Only you wasn't so smart this time. Now we gotta take you to the boss and see what he wants us to do with you."

"You'll never get away with this."

349

"Just who's going to stop us?"

"The Circle *S*," Kairee said confidently. "Damion Saber will eventually catch up with you and you'll wish you'd never seen this territory."

Lone Wolf looked at Kairee with a half smile on his face. He was afraid for her but still proud of her courage. He also knew, at this moment, where Kairee's heart lay and that her acknowledgment of her love for Damion had been the truth.

"Get down off those horses."

Lone Wolf slid to the ground and went to Kairee's side to pretend to help her. "Kairee," he whispered, "be very careful and do not anger them so they will do something foolish. There is always a chance we can escape if we are watchful."

She nodded and dismounted. She could feel every man's eyes on her and her taut nerves made her tremble.

They were led to the fire where their hands were bound before them. Lone Wolf quelled Kairee's resistance with a glance, and when the men had forced them to sit side by side near the fire, he bent close.

"It is better that our hands are tied before us instead of behind. With them bound so, at least we can ride and guide our own horses. Take heart, little one. All is not lost."

"Why are they keeping us here?" she whispered.

"My guess is that they are waiting for someone, probably their leader."

"The man behind all this," Kairee spat angrily. "The one who has caused so much trouble between us and the Sabers."

"How easy to camouflage what he does by putting the blame on someone else."

"Damn him! I hope they catch him and hang him."

"That will not help us right now. Be alert. If an

opportunity comes, I want you to take it."

"And leave you behind? . . . No!"

"Don't be foolishly courageous. One of us free is better than both of us dead. Now don't argue with me. Promise me if you see a chance, you'll take it. Promise me," he demanded.

"All right, all right," she replied. Still he looked at her suspiciously, reasonably sure she would not run unless he could.

They watched in silence as the men went about the task of breaking camp. There had been six. Now three rode in the direction of the cattle, and soon they were herding the animals away. The other three gathered the cooling irons and began to pack their equipment.

All was done in silence, for voices carried in the crisp air. It was obvious they were quite experienced in what they were doing, for there were no wasted movements or sounds.

When the three men joined Kairee and Lone Wolf, the only thing left to do to break camp was to extinguish the fire.

"We wait for the man who gives you orders to do what you are doing, stealing from men who work hard for what they have," Lone Wolf observed.

"I told you you was a smart Injun, but you're also goin' to be a very dead one if you don't shut up."

"You will not shoot me, I think." Lone Wolf smiled.

"You sure of that?"

"I think the sound would carry far and your boss would be quite angry if you were careless enough to do so."

"You're very clever. But I wouldn't mind knocking you on the head with my gun butt. That would keep you quiet for a spell."

Kairee's mind was racing, searching frantically for some means of escape, but time moved slowly by and the rustlers never relaxed their guard.

The sun was barely a red streak on the horizon when a rider broke from a nearby stand of trees and moved toward them.

To Kairee he looked vaguely familiar, but the brim of his hat was low, shadowing his face, and the collar of his jacket was turned up to break the very crisp wind that had risen.

From the reactions of the three rustlers, both Lone Wolf and Kairee were more than certain this was the man behind all the problems.

Lone Wolf had stiffened to alertness as all eyes remained focused on the rider.

No one was more surprised than Kairee when he walked to the fire and removed his hat. The firelight was reflected in the silver-white of his hair and the same friendly smile touched his face, only this time Kairee knew it was a chameleon's smile and that the man not only was less than what he appeared, he was deadly.

"Mitchell Talbot," Kairee breathed in disbelief.

"I'm sure you're quite surprised, Kairee," he said with a chuckle. "I'm sorry you were so foolish as to interfere in my business. Now you force me to do something I'd really rather not do."

"No, of course you wouldn't," Kairee sneered.

Talbot smiled and motioned to the leader of the rustlers to join him as he moved away from the group.

"What kind of fool are you?" Talbot snarled in a rough whisper. "This was the last thing we needed. We were trying to keep from being uncovered, not open a door for them."

"They ran across us by accident. What was we supposed to do? We coulda killed 'em first off, but we waited to see what you wanted to do."

"You sure as hell left me a lot of decisions. She'll be missed before long. Take her up to the shack and keep her until I come. And Bradley," Talbot said coldly, "don't let any kind of harm come to her. You understand me? Any kind of harm, or you'll never live to see another day after that."

"Okay . . . okay. What about the Indian?"

"He's a problem too. If we kill him we'll have a bunch of young bucks on our back. But I don't want them together. Take him to the cave. And Bradley, use your head. Tie his hands behind him. Do you know what he can manage to do with his hands in front of him if he gets a horse?"

It was obvious that Bradley had not thought of this, so he remained silent as they returned to the group.

"Tucker, you and Case take the Indian to the cave. Tie his hands in back of him and keep an eye on him."

"I'm not leaving here without Kairee," Lone Wolf insisted. "You harm her and this territory won't be big enough to hold you. She is the woman of Damion Saber."

Two men took hold of Lone Wolf, released his hands, drew them behind him, and bound them securely again.

Lone Wolf tried to hold Kairee's eyes with his to give her courage, for now she was beginning to realize they had no intention of setting either of them free.

Kairee was more frightened than she had ever been in her life as she watched them force Lone Wolf to mount his horse.

"Kairee, don't give up hope. Before long all of your family, Damion, my people, will be looking for us. There's no way for them to get away."

She was frightened, but her fear was quickly turning into anger. She wheeled on Talbot.

"You can't do this! You can't get away with it. Damion will find you . . . he'll kill you!"

"I don't think so, sweet Kairee," Talbot said calmly.

"You see, it's a long, long story. I came here to destroy Elliot Saber. I thought to do it slowly and see him wriggle while he died, but it's been too slow a process." She looked at him questioningly. "We will get away with it, Kairee love, because all the other men I command—all sixteen of them—are on the way to the Circle S. They are going to kill all the Sabers and burn the Circle S to the ground. What he built for a lifetime, I'm going to destroy in one night."

Lone Wolf made a forceful attempt to reach Talbot.

"Don't push me into doing something you are definitely going to regret," Talbot warned Lone Wolf. "Get him out of here!"

"Why? . . . Why?" she whispered, horrified.

"That's something you don't need to worry about. By morning it will all be over. Then . . . maybe we'll let you go."

She knew he was lying. She knew by this time the next night she would most likely be dead. But Damion . . . Damion would be dead too, and the Circle S nothing but ashes.

She could not bear the thought. She would never have the opportunity to tell Damion that she loved him. "Lone Wolf?" Kairee cried as Talbot's men jerked the reins of Lone Wolf's horse and drew it after them. Kairee stood silently and watched them disappear. "You are insane," Kairee cried.

"Maybe. But then maybe I have more reason than you think."

"What reason could justify murder?"

"There is no time to explain to you." He nodded toward the rustler who gripped her arm, and the man dragged her toward her horse.

He forced her up on it and while Talbot watched Kairee closely, he tied her hands to the pommel of the saddle, mounted, took the reins of Kairee's horse, and rode away.

They traveled half the night and Kairee eventually lost track of where they were. She was exhausted and her body had begun to ache from the enforced riding by the time they reached the line shack.

The rustler untied her hands and pulled her down from her horse. He half dragged her to the door of the cabin and thrust her before him into the interior.

The shack consisted of two rooms. The man dragged her to an inside door, opened it, and pushed her inside. There were no other doors to the room, just one small window. It appeared that the shack had been hastily thrust together, for pale beams of moonlight piercing the cracks in the pine logs made the room a gray-black space filled with dark shadows.

Kairee made her way around, trying to identify whatever furniture there was. She finally found a cot and sank down upon it.

Her mind was in turmoil. She could not face the fact that if Talbot's words were true, at this minute Damion, his family, and his home were being destroyed. She would have given her life to have been able to save his and to feel his arms about her once more.

Chapter 28

Damion rode at a steady pace, so engrossed in his thoughts that he gave no heed to the time or distance. He had to reach Kairee. He had to find the truth, to hear her say it.

It horrified him that Kairee had run from him and that she still had no idea of the depth of his love for her.

He had to get to Southwind's village as soon as he could and face Kairee with the truth of his love. One way or the other, he had to make her understand that he wanted her and their child more than he had ever wanted anything else, and that included the Circle *S*.

Thunderous truths poured over him like scalding water, burning the shield he had worn all his life and revealing his sensitive core to his own eyes.

Seeking the warmth of love, he had reached in every direction except the one that could provide what he truly needed.

What held him in profound misery now was the terrible thought that Kairee might never forgive him, that she would take herself from his life and with her take every chance for self-redemption he might have.

He thought of his unborn child and knew he could never hurt Kairee more by using the child as a force to keep her.

Such an idea led him to thoughts of his father. Somehow he sensed what Elliot's reaction would be, but he would never allow it.

Britt had been so certain that the child Kairee carried was Damion's. Now the truth struck Damion with a force powerful enough to injure further his already bloodied heart. Britt was sure because he had never touched Kairee, though Damion's jealousy had surfaced enough to wound Kairee and the brother whom, despite their differences, Damion still loved deeply.

Like a tottering house of cards, one thought crashed upon the other and the truth of his entire life was forced upon Damion in a kaleidoscope of images. He realized how he and Britt had been maneuvered, manipulated, used to fulfill a goal that offered them nothing but the dubious privilege of worshiping continually at the feet of Elliot and his dream—a dream that was no longer his, Damion reflected, and no longer Britt's, either.

He felt a pang of sympathy for his father, for he would never taste what Damion intended to possess if he could only convince Kairee what a fool he had been and how he intended to change. Though his sympathy did not mask the fact of Elliot's guilt, it eased Damion's anger enough to make him able to bear it.

His horse was lathered and breathing heavily and he realized he would have to rest it for awhile if he wanted to reach the village without losing the horse and having to continue on foot.

He halted and dismounted. Taking the reins of the horse, he walked him slowly for a time, wanting to rest him and still cover some ground.

Soon they reached a stream, and both Damion and the horse drank deeply. Then Damion sat beneath a tree and gave the horse an extra few moments to regain its strength.

It was getting extremely cold and as he gazed at the piles of heavy gray clouds forming overhead, he wondered if there might not be snow before morning.

When the horse was again capable of being ridden, he remounted and set the same, steady, mile-eating pace.

It was beginning to grow dark, but he had no intention of stopping for the night. He would keep moving, restoring his horse occasionally but pushing on. His urgent need to get to Kairee was a force he could not deny. It drove him on.

The evening shadows grew into darkness, but Damion knew this land like he knew his own hand.

The moon turned gold and hung low in a midnight sky. Heavy clouds eclipsed it occasionally, giving his path moments of light followed by periods of heavy blackness, and still he pushed forward.

Accustomed as Damion was to the saddle, still he began to feel the strain, as did his horse, and he was forced to stop and rest more often.

The moon began to drop beyond the mountains and the first gray streaks of daylight rimmed the horizon when he approached Southwind's village.

He made little sound, yet he knew he was being observed and recognized by many dark eyes. The hidden sentries were allowing him to ride in, but he knew if he had not been recognized, he would not have made it so far.

He dismounted before Southwind's lodge, disregarding custom in his urgent need to see and hold Kairee again.

"Southwind, it's me, Damion Saber. I need to speak to you and to Kairee," he called out. When silence met him, he called out again and yet a third time before the flap was pushed open and a very surprised Southwind stepped out.

She had been sound asleep and had thought Damion's call was part of her dreams. By the time she struggled awake and reached for her dress, he was already calling out the third time.

She could not understand why Damion had returned, for he should have long since overtaken Lone Wolf and Kairee on their journey home. A tug of unexplainable fear made her brow furrow and she stepped out of her lodge to face Damion.

Her first observation was that both man and horse were near exhaustion.

"Southwind, is Kairee still asleep? It's urgent that I talk to her."

"Asleep? No, Damion, Kairee is no longer here."

For a moment it seemed he had not understood her. In truth, he did not believe what he was hearing.

"Not here . . . I . . . she has to be."

"She was here, Damion, but she returned home yesterday."

"Damn!" Damion muttered.

"But I don't understand. You should have crossed their path."

"Their?" Damion questioned, his mind on where Britt might be. His jealousy had eased, but still he worried that Kairee might make a choice before he could tell her how he felt. He was frightened that his declaration might not make a difference to her anymore.

"Lone Wolf rode with her to make sure she got home safely. He does not miss much and it surprises me he did not spot you."

"Southwind, could I have a fresh horse?"

"You look like you need to rest as well."

"I don't have time. It's urgent that I reach Kairee now."

"Why, Damion?" Southwind questioned softly.

Damion looked into her deep brown eyes and discovered a new truth. God, had Kairee told everyone but him? Was she that afraid of him?"

"You know why, don't you?"

"Maybe I know Kairee's reason for what she is doing. I don't know your reasons yet."

"Kairee is pregnant with my child." It was a statement, not a question. "I have to reach her, Southwind."

"You say 'my child' as if it belongs to you alone."

"No, it does not belong to me alone. It belongs to Kairee and me. I don't want to do anything but share it with her . . . share the rest of my life with her."

"You know what this could cost you? I don't believe your father would understand your sacrifice."

"I'm not asking him to understand it. I want to have Kairee and our child. If he'll accept that, we can all make a good life together. If he can't, then I'll have Kairee and our child, and he'll lose because the Circle S will never give him what we could."

Southwind sighed audibly with relief. "What of Britt?"

"Britt and I have been pitted against each other too long. I'll make my peace with him if it takes the rest of our lives. I know he is in love with Kairee, but I don't intend to give her up. We'll just have to face one battle at a time. With any kind of luck, Pa will come to his senses and see that he could have everything if he just reached for it."

"I have hoped for that for years, but I think it will take a great deal for him to see it. I will see that you get a fresh horse."

"Thank you."

Damion waited, trying to control his impatience. He could not seem to ignore the overwhelming feeling that he must get to Kairee soon. It was like a vibrant current calling him to hurry.

Southwind awakened a warrior and asked that he find Damion a horse. The animal was brought to Damion and he prepared to leave again, hoping he could catch up with them where they camped for the night. It would be difficult, since he would have to pick up their trail in the darkness, but he faced the task with grim determination.

Lone Wolf sat in stoic silence as he watched the two men who had imprisoned him in the small cave. His hands were still bound securely and the men had taken what weapons they could see, though to Lone Wolf's amusement they had overlooked the small knife he carried in his high leather moccasins. If he could free his hands, he would make good use of it.

The men built a very small smokeless fire in order to keep their whereabouts a secret. They were both tired after their day of work, and Lone Wolf knew the best time to strike would be when their defenses were low. He waited patiently for his opportunity.

He worried about Kairee and wondered how long it would take before someone at her home or in his village questioned their absence.

The men had made some coffee, a drink Lone Wolf loathed and one he considered an example of white ignorance. But with the coffee an opportunity presented itself, and he could hardly let it pass.

"The blood no longer flows to my arms and I thirst for some of your coffee. There are two of you and one of me, so escape is impossible. Can I not share your coffee?"

"Look, Injun, just stay over there and be quiet before I put you out of your misery."

"Your boss did not say that you were to kill me. He

might be angry if your neglect should cause my death. It might not fit into his plans."

The rustlers exchanged doubtful looks. They had only been told to hold him in the cave. Uncertainty reigned for a few moments, then one spoke to the other.

"Stay by the cave mouth and keep your gun on him. If he makes one false move, plug him between the eyes and we'll worry about what the boss says later."

The second man nodded, pleased that someone else had made the decision. He walked to the cave mouth and sat with his back braced against the wall. Then he drew his gun and rested his hand in his lap with the gun pointing at Lone Wolf.

The first man moved toward Lone Wolf tentatively, as if he were still uncertain. Lone Wolf tried to look relaxed and somewhat helpless.

Sliding a knife from his belt, the rustler made Lone Wolf turn, then he sliced through the bonds to release him.

Lone Wolf's arms ached and he knew they would be useless for a short while until the circulation returned. There would be no chance at all for him to survive if he did not have the full use of his strength.

He rubbed his hands together briskly, then crossed his arms to allow the blood to flow back into them.

The man who released him went back to the fire, poured coffee into a tin cup, then brought it back to Lone Wolf, keeping as much distance between them as he could. Even though the Indian seemed incapacitated, the rustler had a great deal of respect for Lone Wolf's size and the muscular look of his body.

Lone Wolf could feel the tingle of life beginning to flow back into his arms and hands, but he remained seated, his knees bent and his hands cupping the coffee cup to use its warmth for further stimulation.

While he waited, Lone Wolf speculated on what he would do if he were fortunate enough to achieve his freedom. He would have to make decisions then, and he found, when he examined all paths, none of the alternatives offered much hope of success.

He sat relaxed, his eyes half closed, lulling his two guards into carelessness.

The one who had untied him sat now with his back against the wall, warmth and exhaustion battling his awareness. But the one who sat closest to the entrance was brushed by the crisp wind, which kept sleep away. There was no doubt in Lone Wolf's mind that he would have to dispose of him first if he were going to have any chance of escape.

Slowly he set the cup aside, then he again began to massage his legs, letting his hands roam up and down as if the sitting position was making him cramped and uncomfortable.

He would have one chance only and if he failed, there would never be an opportunity to try again. He would be dead and of no use to anyone.

His hand slid slowly down his leg. Then he struck. The knife seemed to leap into his hand and out in the same movement. In a matter of seconds, the guard was looking at the hilt of the knife protruding from his chest with eyes already glazed by death.

Lone Wolf breathed a sigh of relief as he sagged forward without summoning the strength to fire the gun.

He looked quickly at the other man, who was nearly asleep. He would have to pass him to get to the cave entrance.

He rose slowly, keeping his eyes on the remaining rustler. Then step by step, with agonizing slowness, he made his way toward the mouth of the cave.

He was very nearly there—a few more steps—then, despite his caution, a dry twig snapped beneath his foot.

He did not take the time to look back to see if the man had awakened. It would have cost him time he could not spare.

He leapt for the cave mouth at the same moment the gun in the rustler's hand barked.

He could feel a stab of white hot pain in his back, but he leapt through the entrance and into the night, stumbling and falling and fighting the darkness that sought to claim him.

He gathered all the strength he had and ran for the unsaddled horses. Throwing himself across the back of one, he slapped the rumps of the other horses, sending them skittering away and making it impossible for anyone to follow.

He bent forward, holding the horse's neck, unable to guide him and fighting with all his strength to hang on.

The horse ran blindly for quite some time, the scent of blood and the strange position of his rider alarming him. Lone Wolf no longer had control of the horse, or himself.

After awhile the horse slowed, first from run to trot, then to walk, and finally he stopped. Lone Wolf, unable to retain his hold, slid slowly to the ground, unconscious.

Damion had been forced to move at a snail's pace, trying to keep his eyes on the trail before him. It was a vague trail and more than once he had had to double back to pick it up again. He would have given a great deal to have had Britt with him.

Finally he came across the deserted camp and alarm filled him when he realized that Kairee and Lone Wolf had obviously crossed paths with a group of people who had made camp there.

Then all the signs melded and he saw that three groups and a single rider had left the area at about the same time. It was obvious to him that Kairee and Lone Wolf had been separated. His fear grew as he speculated on the reasons why.

Pieces of the puzzle began to form and presented more questions. Had they run into rustlers? Where were they going, and which trail should he follow?

He examined the signs again carefully and made his choice. Then he prayed silently that the choice he was making was the right one.

Damion had ridden less than an hour when he reined in his horse suddenly. In the shadows was a horse calmly grazing and nearby he saw a form lying on the ground.

His heart began to thud and for a moment he could not move. Could it be Kairee?

Her name escaped his lips in near panic. Then with grim determination he moved forward. After a few moments he knew who lay in the dirt, Lone Wolf. And if Lone Wolf were dead, as he suspected he might be, then where was Kairee?

He dismounted, knelt beside Lone Wolf, and laid his hand on his chest, searching for a sign of life. Even though he drew his hand back wet with blood, he was relieved to feel a steady heartbeat.

He gathered some dry branches and made a small fire. By its light he would attempt to discover just how badly Lone Wolf was wounded.

He saw that the bullet had entered his lower back, ricocheted off a rib, most likely cracking it, and then had exited. Damion was almost elated to find that the wound was not as severe as he had thought.

He cleaned it and bound it and covered Lone Wolf with his blanket. Then he brought his canteen and forced some water between Lone Wolf's lips.

Lone Wolf choked, stirred, groaned, and opened his eyes. It took him several minutes to focus his eyes and identify the dark form that bent over him.

"Damion," he gasped.

"Where is Kairee, Lone Wolf?" Damion questioned.

"They have taken her."

"Taken her where? Who has taken her?"

"I don't know for sure. He said—"

"He . . . who is he?" Damion insisted.

"Mitchell Talbot."

"Talbot!"

"Yes . . . please. It is hard for me and I have much to say. Just listen."

"All right. Go on."

Lone Wolf used all the strength he had to explain to Damion all that had transpired. Damion remained quiet only by extreme effort when he was told where Kairee had been taken. But he could not contain a cry of rage and frustration when he found that he would have to choose between searching for and rescuing Kairee and trying to make it back to the Circle S before the rustlers destroyed it and his family.

He knew there would only be time to reach one.

Kairee was alone and defenseless, and her faith, as Lone Wolf had said, was in him.

He knew his father's strength and Britt's, and he prayed they would be able to defend the Circle S.

Then he realized the ultimate truth: that the Circle S could be lost to him and he would survive. But he could not lose Kairee.

Britt and Elliot, he reasoned, would have the sense to retreat should the attack prove more than they could handle.

"Lone Wolf, if I leave water and food, will you be all right for awhile? If I get through to Kairee safely, I'll send someone for you."

"Who?" Lone Wolf tried to laugh. "If you do not succeed, there will be no one. Besides, Southwind will send someone. She is a clever woman and expects me back in a day or two. Build up the fire and leave me. I'll be all right. Go and find her, Damion. She is alone and very frightened."

"Don't worry," Damion replied angrily. "I'll find the bastards, and when I do, they'll wish a million times over they had never seen Mitchell Talbot or reached out to take what's mine."

Damion rose and rebuilt the fire, then placed more wood nearby. He was ready to go.

"Is she yours, Damion?" Lone Wolf asked softly.

Damion smiled. "You bet your life, Lone Wolf," he said with growing confidence. "You bet your life."

Lone Wolf smiled as Damion mounted and started toward the line shack, the location of which he knew well.

Chapter 29

Damion wasted no time as he covered the distance to the line shack. He was aware that the building had long been deserted, almost forgotten, but he knew where it was and he took the most direct route. He intended to give the man who held her the biggest shock of what he promised himself would be a very short life.

As he headed for Kairee, his thoughts turned to his father and Britt. He wished he could have physically torn himself in two as he was mentally doing. But that would have been impossible. He was convinced he had made the right choice, for without Kairee and his child, life would be a very empty existence.

He struggled to control the wild fury that burned inside him and to set his mind on a plan that would allow him to get Kairee free.

When he knew he was almost within hearing distance of the shack, he stopped, tied his horse so it could not stray, and began to move quietly toward the ramshackle structure.

Mitchell Talbot had solidified his plans for the destruction of the Circle *S* and Elliot Saber. Now he found his mind drifting again and again to Kairee Kennedy.

She would be the only survivor, for with the discovery of the evidence he would plant at the destroyed Circle *S,* the Kennedys would most certainly be blamed.

It would not be long after that that the ranchers in the area, incensed at such brutality, would take the matter of the Kennedys into their own hands and drive away what Kennedys were left after the men of the family had been punished for the crimes committed.

But Kairee Kennedy . . . she intrigued him. She had been a beautiful shock when he had first met her. And even as he had just seen her, wide eyed and frightened, she was still a captivating creature. The more he thought of her, the more he was stirred by the desire to taste such beauty.

Feeling that everything was under his control, he started back to the shack where Kairee was being held. Once rid of the only guard, he would take the time to enjoy Kairee before ridding himself of the damning evidence.

Kairee had given in to her exhaustion and had lain across the cot, only to drift into a sleep filled with tormenting dreams. Though her body found rest, her mind turned her fear and helplessness into the stuff of nightmares.

She had no idea how long she slept, but she came awake with a startled jump when something heavy dropped in the next room. Once again she was made aware that she was a prisoner, and that this might be the last night of her life.

She laid her hand flat against her belly and closed her eyes. "Damion," she whispered softly, "how I wanted you to know . . . to see and hold your child. I love you."

Her eyes filled with tears and she knew she was succumbing to self-pity, but for one minute she allowed herself the luxury. Then she gathered her strength and pushed pity aside to make way for an even stronger emotion: self-preservation, coupled with her instinctive maternal need to protect her child.

She rose from the cot and went to the door to press her ear against it and listen for sounds from the other room. She heard nothing.

Reaching a trembling hand to the door handle, she tried to turn it noiselessly. To her surprise, it moved easily and she realized the door was not locked.

She opened it a crack and tried to see into the room. It was lit by one oil lamp and she saw that her captor was seated at the table with his back to her and his hand on a half-full bottle of whiskey.

He did not appear drunk to her, but she was afraid that if he was, Talbot's orders not to harm her might mean very little to him. He could always say she had tried to escape.

Her eyes were becoming accustomed to the pale light filtering into her room and she began to search around for some kind of weapon to use. It took a great deal of time, most of it spent on her hands and knees, to find the piece of rough wood that lay on the floor beneath the rickety cot.

She gripped it firmly in her hand, and with her pulses pounding, she tiptoed to the door again. Catching her lower lip between her teeth, she reached for the door handle.

Damion moved cautiously when the small shack came into view. Kairee was there, but how many guarded her? There was a small clearing before the shack, which, he felt, would be dangerous to try to cross until he knew how many men were inside. He swung around in a wide circle and moved again toward the cabin, this time coming from a direction that had the small protection of underbrush and trees.

When he reached the side of the weather-beaten shack, he placed his hands on the rough wood and used it to steady himself as he silently moved step by step toward the front and peered around the corner.

The small porch was only a few inches from the ground and the roof over it was supported by young trees skinned and braced at random intervals. Slowly, fearing the porch might not support his weight or that it might make a multitude of noises as he made his way across it, Damion stepped up on it with one foot, then very gently put his weight on it. No sound. Good, he thought. Now, if he could be as lucky until he got to the door, it would be fine.

"Damn," he muttered to himself, seeing a small window between him and the door. He would have to get past that unobserved.

He had examined the shack well enough to know there was no back entrance. Without a sound, he drew his gun from its holster, readying it in case he drew the attention of whoever was inside.

The wind had picked up in intensity and now crystalline flakes, half snow, half rain, whipped against his face. The way the temperature was dropping, even if he were able to free Kairee, there might not be enough time to get to safety before the snow came.

It could be a sudden thing. He knew this from experience. In just a few short hours they might find themselves in the midst of a blizzard that could dump many inches of snow and make traveling temporarily impossible.

That no sound at all came from within multiplied his worries. Either there was only one guard and he had no one to talk to, or . . . He did not want to think of other possibilities.

Laboriously and with tension that made him sweat, he moved slowly, one step at a time, placing his weight carefully, then waiting for the telltale sound that would draw attention to him. When he came to the window, he paused, then cautiously tried to look inside, but years of accumulated dirt made it impossible. He would have to count on blind luck.

Inside the shack, Kairee had eased the inner door open and was standing within a few feet of the guard, who did not as yet suspect her presence. The last thing he expected was for Kairee to fight back. He had a rifle leaning against the edge of the table and his gun lying close to the bottle of whiskey.

Kairee held the piece of wood in her hand. She had to strike hard and fast, for there would be no second chance.

She took a step toward him and paused, her heart in her mouth, as he stirred into a more comfortable position and reached again for the bottle to pour another drink.

Another step . . . a third. She was within four feet of him, too far to strike but close enough to be terrified that he might hear her controlled breathing. She could have sworn her heart was pounding loud enough for him to detect it.

She took a fourth step and all her fears were realized as the guard stood and took a step away from the table, then turned to look directly into her terror-stricken features.

For a moment he was as startled as she. Then with an oath he reached for the gun and pointed it at her. A leering grin on his face, he chuckled.

"What's the matter, pretty thing? You can't sleep? Wal, that's all right. I could do with a little company. Might have an interesting time, just you and me."

Kairee tried to swallow the lump of fear in her throat. She lifted her chin in defiance and the light of battle shone in her eyes. He might win, but she would defend herself to the death. She would rather be dead than surrender to a man like him.

"You'll have to kill me first," she snapped.

"Wal, I expect that's what the boss has in mind to do . . . in time. But there's no sense letting a pretty thing like you go to waste. Shame to see you killed without having a taste or two."

He took a step closer to her and she raised the piece of wood like a club.

"Now you don't expect me to be scared of that little bitty piece of rotten wood, do you?"

He took another step toward her and Kairee swung with every ounce of strength she had.

The wood was as rotten as he had said it was. The blow caught him on the arm he raised in self-protection and splintered.

The force of the blow numbed Kairee's fingers and she dropped the remnants of the makeshift club. She turned to make a dash for the door, but he caught her as she passed him. He held her struggling body about the waist from behind so that all her attempts to strike or kick him were ineffectual.

At that moment Damion kicked open the door and plunged inside.

"Damion!" Kairee cried in joyous relief.

Her relief was short-lived, for the rustler swung up his gun and touched the barrel to Kairee's head.

"Don't take one more step, Saber, or she dies."

"Don't be a damn fool," Damion said coldly. "You kill her and you're a dead man."

"I don't think you're gonna do it," the man sneered. "Now get out of my way."

"Not a chance. Let her go."

"Saber, you're pushin' somethin' that's gonna cost you your life."

Damion was holding Kairee's eyes, giving her strength with his calm gaze, trying to make her understand that he would not let her be hurt again. He smiled.

"Don't be afraid, Kairee. He's not fool enough to kill you. He knows there's no place far enough away to run to after that."

"Don't be too sure," the rustler snarled.

"Let me tell you something, my friend," Damion said in a controlled voice. "You've got some mighty slim chances. If you shoot her first, I'll get you sure as hell. If you try for me first, you'd better make it dead center or I'll get you anyway. You'd be a whole lot smarter if you let her go."

"Yeah, then you plug me anyway."

"I'll let you clear out of here . . . if you let her go. You can ride away clean."

Something flickered in the man's eyes and Damion knew the hesitation was a good sign. He pushed it.

"You can be out of this territory in a couple of days and no one will ever know. All you have to do is let her go."

Kairee was trembling and her eyes were frozen on Damion, as if he were all she could see.

"Come on," Damion coaxed. "Don't be a fool. Do you want to die for someone else's gain. Do you suppose for one minute Talbot cares if you live or die? You're expendable and Talbot knows it. He knew someone might get killed in all this, and he wouldn't care for a minute if it turned out to be you. Think about it, friend," Damion said softly. "Stay and die . . . or let her go and ride out of here with your life."

The rustler began to sweat. He was straining to hold Kairee close, but the effort was telling on him as her taut body resisted his hold.

"All right," the rustler grated. "I never had a mind to be mixed up in killin' anybody anyhow. You keep clear."

Damion nodded. He would agree to just about anything to get Kairee free of him. Her face was pale and her body was visibly shaking. He was afraid she might collapse, and then the rustler might be forced into a shoot-out.

The rustler edged toward the door, drawing Kairee with him. Damion watched closely. Any sign of a trick and he would be forced to jump him just to keep Kairee from getting hurt. If he had to take the bullet, he would to keep it from her.

Kairee and her captor were close to the door, which still stood half open after Damion's entrance. He backed the rest of the way, dragging Kairee with him. The glint in Damion's eyes should have warned him that Damion had no intention of letting him leave the shack with Kairee.

"You step out that door and try to take her with you and you'll be a dead man. I've shot at smaller targets than you, my friend." Damion's smile was deadly and the rustler understood that beyond a doubt.

"Look," he muttered, "I never wanted to kill nobody. I only went into this because Talbot said it would be easy money while he played you all against each other. You swear you won't use that gun"—he motioned to the gun in Damion's hand—"and you won't come after me, and I'll let her go."

"You know me and my family," Damion stated. "Our word is good. You have my word I won't stop you. Just let Kairee go."

The rustler was almost through the half-open door. With a rough shove he pushed Kairee toward Damion.

She would have stumbled and fallen if Damion had not reached out to catch her.

He gathered her up in his arms, hearing her sob of relief and almost overwhelmed with the joy of having her safe once more.

The rustler had taken this moment to slip across the porch and down the steps. Neither Damion nor Kairee cared that he was escaping. It was enough that they could cling to each other and feel the security of each other's arms.

Damion rocked her in his embrace, holding her until her fear passed, until he sensed she had regained control of herself. Then he tipped up her chin to look into the depths of her gray eyes.

"How . . . how did you find me?" she whispered raggedly.

"I came to the village after you."

"For what reason, Damion?"

"I could put my reasons into a million words and excuses, Kairee. But the only words that are important are these: I love you, Kairee. I love you—more than anything else in the world. And I want you to forgive me for being so damned stupid and not seeing what I almost lost."

"Damion . . . is it enough for you or—"

"If you're talking about making choices, Kairee, let me tell you that I finally made the choice I should have been smart enough to make a long time ago. There's just you and I, Kairee, and whatever you want to do, wherever you want to go, I'll be with you."

"And the Circle *S* . . . your family?"

"The Circle *S* is Britt's. It should have been Britt's from the start. Pa will have to see that and realize the truth. I love them both . . . I love the Circle *S*, but not like I love and need you, Kairee."

He kept to himself his knowledge of the child she carried. He wanted her to tell him; otherwise she might believe it had been the reason he had come for her. He needed her to understand first that it was she he wanted.

The tears that clung to her lashes and the glow in her smiling eyes were reassuring, yet he wanted her to trust him with the truth now, the truth that would free them both and confirm their trust in each other.

"You've been through a lot," Damion stated gently. "You have to rest here awhile, then I'll take you home."

He led her to a chair and she sat down, then he knelt before her and took her hands in his.

"Kairee, I know this has been hard on you and I wish I could change all that's happened, but I can't. I can only say that I'll try to make a difference in both our lives . . . if you want to try with me."

Kairee withdrew both her hands from his, then lifted them to cup around his face, feeling the rough stubble of his beard as she noted the strain in his crystal blue eyes.

"Damion," she uttered softly, "I want to share the rest of my life with you. I think I have loved you since the moment I first saw you. I think I can understand how hard it has been for you too. With love we can start again. I was afraid Damion, but not for me. I . . . I'm carrying our child, and I didn't want it to be just an object for the Sabers and the Kennedys to fight over."

He was shaken with relief. "You needn't worry about that." He smiled. "Our baby, Kairee, will be enough to build a whole lifetime around. When we get you back home, we'll make our decisions—together."

Kairee bent her head to kiss him, telling him there were no doubts standing between them now.

Damion stood and drew her up into the circle of his arms to seal their future with a deeper kiss.

Neither heard the shot that put an end to the life of the escaping rustler. Neither of them noted the sudden intensification of the storm or the sharp, biting wind that accompanied it. And neither of them suspected they were about to have an unwelcome visitor.

"I'm sorry you've had to go through all this, Kairee. But I'll make it up to you. We'll settle the problem between our families by marrying and—"

"But that's not the only problem. You know how your father feels about me. Our marriage would only make matters worse."

"I know the reasons for a lot of my father's problems and in time we'll work everything out. You've just got to trust me, Kairee, that this time I'll try to do what's best for all of us and not just for myself. Do you trust me, Kairee?" he questioned gently. "Would you put yourself and our child into my care? I swear I'll be careful of both."

"Oh yes, Damion, I trust you. . . . I love you."

"How touching," came a cold, sneering voice from the door. "Too bad the sentiments will be wasted."

Kairee gasped in shock and Damion cursed as they turned to see Mitchell Talbot framed in the doorway, a white sheet of falling snow behind him.

The gun in his hand was level and steady and his confident smile was enough to underscore the impossibility of their situation. Mitchell Talbot was not an ignorant guard they could easily rid themselves of.

"I had come to collect you, my dear Kairee." Talbot laughed. "But I'm afraid you'd now be excess baggage I can't afford. Traveling in a storm like the one brewing outside will be hard enough for one, and I have other things to do. I must say it is convenient to find you close together. It will be easier to dispose of both of you at the same time. How nice that you will have a lot of time to declare your undying love. It will be a long time before anyone finds you. But I'm afraid it will be too late by then."

"What are you talking about?" Kairee demanded. "You can't just shoot us, for God's sake. Don't you

378

think there will be a lot of people asking questions?"

"Kairee," Damion said gently, "he doesn't intend to shoot us."

"Very clever." Talbot grinned.

"Look behind him, Kairee," Damion said.

There was a thick sheet of heavily falling snow.

"When I leave I take your horses with me. It will be impossible for you to leave on foot and live . . . It will be just as impossible to stay here."

"Why, Talbot?" Damion demanded. "Just tell me why?"

"To destroy your father and his dreams, dreams that destroyed lives."

"Then what Lone Wolf told me is true? You've sent men to attack the Circle S?"

Kairee looked up at Damion in shock, understanding what his coming for her had meant when he had already known his ranch and family were in danger.

"They attacked the ranch this afternoon," Talbot admitted. "By the time I get back, we will be able to put the blame where it belongs." He chuckled. "On the Kennedys."

"You won't get away with it." Damion's face was pale and his expression grim. "If you've harmed my family, I'll find you, and when I do, I'll kill you."

"I don't think you'll be around to do much about it," Talbot said casually. "You won't be able to walk out of here, and now there is no one to come and find you, so . . ." He smiled and backed out, pulling the door shut.

In moments they could hear the sound of many hoofbeats as Talbot rode away, and they knew he had taken their horses with him.

Damion ran to the door and threw it open, only to be confronted by a wall of blustering, blowing snow carried on a fierce, bone-chilling wind.

He turned to face Kairee and slowly closed the door.

379

Chapter 30

The hands of the Circle *S* had been spread thin across the range. There were only three men in the bunkhouse and two of them had been ill and could not ride.

Britt and Elliot ran out onto the porch when Jim shouted. The three realized almost at once that the group of men riding toward them were intent on some form of destruction.

Heavy gray clouds covered the sun and the hazy half shadows foretold bad weather.

"They mean business," Britt shouted as Jim ran toward him.

"Who the hell are they?" Elliot demanded.

"I don't know," Jim answered, "but rustlers would be my bet. Maybe they had a way of knowing we were shorthanded here and they've come to cripple us."

"Get inside the house," Britt said firmly. "We can hold 'em off for awhile anyway. Maybe we'll be lucky and they'll just want to talk."

"The way they're coming, they don't want to talk," Jim said.

At that moment Britt made the decision final for them all. He grabbed his father's shoulders with one hand and forced a very angry Elliot to move with him

"Let's get in the house," he insisted. "We need shelter and we need guns."

They ran up the steps and into the house almost at the same time the riders entered the open area before the house and stopped.

"Saber!" the leader of the group shouted. "If you're not a coward, you'll come out here and face your betters. The Kennedys think it's time you paid for what you've been doing to them."

"Kennedys!" Elliot snarled and started for the door. Britt reached out and grabbed his arm before he could tear the door open.

"Pa, wait. They're lying."

"Lying? Why? How do you know?"

"I've been with the Kennedys for the past few days. I know them and the men who ride for them. None of those men out there belong to the Kennedy ranch."

"Saber!" the voice called derisively. "You a coward, Saber?"

Elliot shook Britt's hand from his arm and ran to the door as Britt tried to catch up with him and stop him before he could go outside. But he could not reach him in time to prevent him from pulling the door open.

Elliot stood in the open doorway for a moment, then, his face like a granite statue, grim and filled with fury, he stepped out on the porch.

Britt, afraid more for his father than for himself, walked out to stand beside him. Jim followed and stood next to Elliot.

Elliot was a man whose very presence commanded respect, and his attitude of strength and self-assurance made the men grow momentarily silent. He had faced so many threats in his life that now he seemed invulnerable, and the men paused in quiet awe. Elliot Saber was a man who stood tall, and in that moment

Britt was proud of him and his love for his father flooded him like a warm river.

He was Elliot Saber's son, whether Elliot truly loved him or not. He was Elliot Saber's son, and he was proud of it.

"You're on my land," Elliot said coldly. "Get off."

The leader of the group laughed, though he had become slightly nervous in the face of a man who seemed unafraid of twenty men with guns.

"Too late, Saber. We're gonna burn you out. The Kennedys are tired of your being king around here."

"You're a bunch of damn liars," Britt said. "You don't have any connection to the Kennedys at all. I know every one of them. I don't know who you work for, but you'd better forget trying to blame whatever you're going to do on them. Why don't you just clear out of here before you start some trouble you can't stop. The Circle *S* is too big and we're a lot of men. We'll wipe you out."

"Get off my land," Elliot growled, "or by Christ I'll see every one of you hanged for rustlers."

It was the worst possible thing Elliot could have said, and Britt knew it.

He felt sudden dread as he watched the men facing them unite with purpose. He knew they had no intention of leaving any of them alive.

Strangely his fear was not for himself but for Elliot, who was still so blind he could not let go of his dream even to save his life.

What happened next occurred so fast that later they would not even remember what had set it in motion.

It was a sudden move on Elliot's part, seen by one of the men and misconstrued as a threatening reach for his gun.

He shouted a warning. The leader went for his gun. Britt saw only that he meant to shoot Elliot—his father. He had to protect him.

The leader's gun cleared its holster at the same moment Britt threw himself between the bullet and his father's heart. The bullet caught Britt in the back, slamming him into Elliot's arms. In the confusion that followed, Jim and Elliot dragged Britt inside and slammed the door shut.

Slowly Elliot let Britt slide gently down to the floor. Then he knelt beside him.

Looking down into Britt's pale face, Elliot was shattered by the force of the love he felt for him and the knowledge that if he was dead it was because of him.

Jim knelt beside him and Elliot looked up. He could have groaned out his pain when he saw the same truth in Jim's eyes. Britt had taken the bullet meant for his father.

"Britt . . . son," Elliot choked out. He had never felt such emptiness, so much pain.

Jim bent to press his ear against Britt's chest, then he straightened and looked again into Elliot's eyes.

"He's barely alive . . . I don't know if he'll make it."

Elliot closed his eyes and for a long, heartrending moment he wanted to scream out his helpless rage at the sudden knowledge that he was losing Britt and had never once reached out to him.

The riders outside were shouting now and firing random shots that ricocheted off the walls and splintered glass in the windows.

They were prepared to ignore this harassment and protect themselves, but their hearts sank with the next shouted words.

"Burn 'em out! Burn the cowards out!"

Torches that had been carried along for this purpose were lit and tossed through the windows. In moments the curtains caught fire and the room began to fill with smoke

"Elliot, we've got to get out of here! We've got to get Britt out of here!"

"I've killed my own son," Elliot groaned in wild agony.

"Damn it, man, we've got to get him out!"

"I wanted it all for them . . . They didn't understand."

"You didn't understand, Elliot," Jim said, angry now. "All they wanted was you." He had to say something to get Elliot to move. "Are you going to let him lie here and die? If we don't get him out, we'll all burn. We can make it out to the patio . . . Good God!"

"What?"

"Maria and Margurite. They must still be in the kitchen. They're probably terrified too. We've all got to get out of here. Elliot, get up and help me!"

Elliot bent to lift Britt in his arms. "I'll carry him," he said in a deadened voice. "Go see to the women."

Jim found Maria and Margurite cowering in a corner of the kitchen, frightened of the gunfire and just beginning to smell the smoke from the fire. He gripped both women by their wrists and hauled them forcefully from the corner amid their terrified screams.

The smoke was rolling through the house now, and Jim heard Elliot coughing as he carried Britt to the side door that led to the walled patio. They would be safe from the fire there and able to defend themselves temporarily, at least until someone could see the smoke and come to help. The most important thing now was to try to keep Britt alive, for Jim could plainly see in Elliot's eyes the guilt that was tearing at him.

Bending low, Jim raced to the bedroom and grabbed blankets, then he ran to find heavy coats. They would need protection from the weather that was rapidly going from bad to worse. It was beginning to snow lightly.

The men before the house were shouting, shooting, and milling about, caught up in a stimulating orgy of blood lust, and Jim began to worry about being trapped with no way to fight back.

Elliot seemed to be stunned, and Jim knew he was overwhelmed by grief that was intensified by his tremendous guilt.

In the corner of the patio wall he knelt beside Britt and Elliot and the two very shaken women. He passed out the coats and the blankets, then bent to wrap Britt.

"Elliot, let go of him," Jim had to command, but Elliot refused. Instead, he grabbed a blanket, and forgetting himself, he wrapped Britt gently and held him cradled in his arms in a way he had never done when Britt had been a child. Jim was afraid it might be too late to repair the damage, either to Britt, or to Elliot.

The rustlers, satisfied to see the house in flames and thinking they had killed Britt, began to retreat before the heat of the fire. It seemed impossible to them that anyone could have gotten away from the burning house, but even if someone had, it seemed unlikely he could survive the cold and snow long enough to be rescued.

After awhile they rode away.

Lone Wolf had lain by the fire for some time. But his knowledgeable eyes had seen the gathering clouds and he knew what was to come.

He also knew that despite pain or loss of strength he had to do something, for being caught helpless in the coming storm was suicide.

Damion had made sure his horse was tethered nearby, and he was determined to reach it.

Gritting his teeth against the pain that burned through him, he turned first to his side, then to his stomach. He lay still for a moment, catching his breath, then he drew himself to his knees.

He had to gasp for breath as the white-hot shots of pain streaked through him. He had to fight unconsciousness and for a moment he thought he might lose. Then he struggled to his feet and one step after another he moved toward his horse.

When he reached the animal, he was faced with the effort it would take to mount, let alone ride the distance to the village.

He gripped his saddle and with every ounce of strength he had left he pulled himself up into it. He bent forward in the saddle, praying to all the gods he knew that he would be able to retain his hold long enough to get back to the village. The horse was skittish from the scent of blood, but Lone Wolf nudged him forward, hoping the same scent would not draw other animals.

Gregg paced the porch, a worried frown on his face as he watched what appeared to be a heavy gray cloud. The clouds had been heavy all afternoon, and though he knew from experience they indicated bad weather, somehow this one cloud seemed different.

He watched it while his thoughts returned to what really drew his nerves taut. From what Lucy had told him, Kairee should be coming home. He just hoped she would be riding ahead of the weather.

For the hundredth time in the past few hours, he cursed Kairee's hardheadedness. His worry was slowly turning to fear in the face of mental visions that had her lost on the trail and caught in the midst of the coming blizzard. He saw her falling, unable to get up . . . dying.

He muttered another curse just as Lucy came out onto the porch.

"I don't understand why she had to pick up and run like that," he muttered. "I sure as hell hope she has sense enough to stay in the village until this storm is over."

"I'm sure they wouldn't let her go, Gregg. They have a keen sense for the weather."

"Lucy, I think it's time you told me just what's going on. Kairee is not the kind of girl to run away from anything. What's wrong?"

Lucy had been thinking about that from the moment Kairee had gone and Damion had gone after her. It was going to be impossible to keep the truth from Gregg, and, she felt, he had a right to know in case things went even more wrong between Kairee and Damion.

She was about to answer him when her attention was drawn to the growing black cloud on the horizon.

"That's such a strange-looking cloud, Gregg. It . . . it almost looks like black smoke . . . as if something very large were burning."

"The only thing over that way is the Circle *S*."

"Do you suppose something is wrong over there?"

"We could hope so," Gregg said bitterly.

"Gregg, that's terrible."

"I know." He laughed shortly. "I'm sorry. It's just that they've given everyone in the territory so much trouble. If they lost a barn or bunkhouse, it might serve as justice."

"But, that cloud . . . it's so immense. Gregg, you don't suppose the house is on fire?" She was alarmed now. "Suppose it is and they find a way to put the blame on us!"

"Maybe I should ride over and see," he said thoughtfully. "I couldn't beat the storm back, but if there's trouble, I could help them, then bunk there for the night."

"Not alone," Lucy said firmly. "Take Smokey and

Rusty with you. I don't want them to be able to cause you any trouble just for being neighborly."

"All right, my worrier, I'll go down to the barn and get Rusty and Smokey. We should be back by day after tomorrow. Will you, Pa, and Cassie be all right?"

"We'll be fine."

"I'll put in more wood so you won't have to fetch it if the snow gets deep."

"We'll be fine, Gregg. Don't worry."

Gregg smiled, kissed her, and started toward the barn. Within its shadowy depths, he found Smokey mending a halter.

"Smokey, where's Rusty?"

"Out along the south fence. It was cut the other day and he's repairing it. Why? Some trouble?"

"Come out and take a look. I've never seen smoke like this. I have a feeling the Circle S is burning."

Smokey rose to his feet quickly and threw the halter aside. He strode to the door and in the yard he turned his gaze toward the horizon.

"Sure as hell looks like smoke, all right. Whatever is burning must be some blaze or we wouldn't see it at this distance."

"I'm riding over to see." Gregg grinned. "And my worrying wife doesn't want me to face the Sabers alone. Maybe she's right."

"Well, we have to pass pretty near Rusty on our way. Wait 'til I get saddled and we'll collect him and go have a look."

"I'm going to lay in some wood for Lucy in case that storm hits us. It looks like it's heading this way. How about saddling for me, too?"

"Sure thing," Smokey replied and quickly set about preparing both horses.

Gregg carried several armfuls of cut wood into the house, then stacked a great deal more on the front porch.

"You're sure you'll be all right?" he questioned Lucy.

"I'm going to be fine. You just make sure you are too. If it's not the Circle S, don't linger until they find some way to cause trouble."

"I'll be good, Mama," Gregg promised with a grin. "Don't worry and don't let Cassie stray. If that storm's as bad as it looks, it's going to be rough."

Lucy nodded her agreement and Gregg pulled her into his arms for a fierce hug and a deep, heated kiss.

"Hurry back."

His eyes were warm as they held hers. "It would take a hell of a lot more than the Sabers to keep me. Not with the promise that kiss gave me." He laughed huskily as he hugged her again. "I'll be back as soon as I can. It's probably nothing anyway, and I'll find my behind kicked for trespassing on Saber land."

"Just don't push any trouble."

Smokey arrived with their horses and Gregg mounted. Lucy stood on the porch and watched until their forms disappeared.

She walked back into the house slowly, trying to ignore the tingle of doubt that tugged at her thoughts.

Jim had formed several blankets into a tent in the corner of the patio. His major concern was to do what he could to keep Britt alive.

He had gone to the small well in the patio for some water and had washed the wound carefully. There was no doubt in his mind that Britt was in extremely bad condition. He could not even give odds for his chances of making it.

Elliot had been silent since Britt had been shot, but he had worked feverishly to get the tent up, to strip off Britt's shirt, and to prepare, as Jim was doing, to remove the bullet. It was Britt's only chance for life.

Jim also saw that Elliot was going through mental

hell, knowing that if Britt died he had died for Elliot, to protect his life.

Visions of Britt's growing days plunged Elliot into a deep morass of dark recriminations.

He wanted to say to Britt now all the things he had resisted saying to him all his life. He felt a greater sense of loss and emptiness than he had at any time since Emma's death. He realized the truth of his wasted life, and the truth was almost too painful to bear.

He had cheated his sons to pay a debt to the dead. When he looked into Jim's eyes, he understood that there was a possibility he would never have the chance to redeem himself in Britt's life, for Britt might not have his life much longer.

They had a small fire burning and Jim produced his knife. He held it in the fire, intending to make the removal of the bullet as sterile a procedure as possible.

"I'll have to tie him down somehow," Jim said.

"I'll hold him," Elliot stated firmly.

"Elliot . . ."

"I'll hold him!" Elliot's voice was rock hard.

Gently Elliot braced himself against the rough wall and eased Britt across him to get a firm hold on him.

He gripped Britt so that even if his body jerked in pain it could not move too much.

"Get it out, Jim."

Without a change in his expression, Elliot watched Jim cut into Britt's back in search of the bullet. He could feel Britt's body shudder in spasms of pain, yet he held him firmly. Each surge of pain was his own. Each groan from Britt's dry lips was echoed in Elliot's soul.

For the first time in nearly thirty years Elliot Saber prayed.

Chapter 31

The horse continued to move at a steady gait despite the poor visibility and the accumulating snow that was making the trail slippery.

Lone Wolf guided the animal by sheer will. If he relinquished control, the horse would drift and both of them would be lost, for the horse had no way of knowing the destination.

Still the snow had become a thick blanket by the time he saw the welcome sight of the village. He could feel a fresh trickle of warm blood running down his leg and he was dizzy from the effort it had taken to remain on horseback. He heard the horses of the guards following him and he signaled them to leave him be as he came to Southwind's lodge.

When he drew the horse to a halt, he was in front of her dwelling. He half slid and half fell from the horse, leaving the reins trailing on the ground. He bent to enter his sister's lodge.

Southwind had been seated cross-legged before a fire, mending a dress and letting her thoughts roam, as they often did when she was alone, to Elliot and the way it might have been for them.

She allowed these dreams as a balm for her loneliness.

That she could have chosen a man from her village long ago and might have found a fuller and happier life was something she knew well. But Elliot and Britt had possession of her heart and she could never, in all honesty, have given the empty shell to another man.

She sighed. If Elliot could one day see the loneliness that spread before him like a dark ocean . . . if only he would send for her, ask her to be with him, she knew she would be eager to go. But, as she had told him, it would have to be for the right reason. And that reason could not be the selfish one that had driven Elliot from the day she had met him.

She thought of Damion and Kairee and hoped they would find a way to be together. She wondered if Elliot could face what he would consider desertion on Damion's part. And Britt . . . Her thoughts wandered. Britt would be hurt by Kairee's choice. But he was a man of strength who would find his way. Maybe he would come to her for awhile and enjoy a carefree time before he took up the reins of the Circle *S*.

She smiled to herself. She had never enjoyed the immense ranch in which Elliot had taken such pride. Despite its size, she had always felt confined and almost imprisoned within its walls.

She recalled that when she had first met Elliot he had been a lonely man with an even lonelier son. She also remembered the depth of her sorrow when she had left.

She heard a scraping noise at her door and wondered if a stray animal was searching for a source of warmth and protection from the sharp wind she could hear blowing outside.

Her alarm rose and she had just reached for a sharp-bladed knife to defend herself when the door moved, then swung open.

She gasped in surprise when a snow-covered Lone Wolf stumbled inside and nearly collapsed.

He dropped to his knees, choked for air, his body heaving in strain. What was worse was the huge red stain she saw on his coat, a stain that was obviously blood.

"Lone Wolf!" She leapt to his side and put her arm about him to help him recline on her fur-covered pallet. "What has happened? Why are you hurt? How bad . . . Lone Wolf, where is Kairee?"

He laughed breathlessly. "I do not have the strength for a million questions, woman. Be silent while I tell you what has happened."

Between ragged gasps he told her all that had happened since he and Kairee had left the village.

"I thought I would have to come here for help, then go after her myself, but Damion has already gone. There was only one guard with her, and I am sure Damion has gotten her to safety by now."

"But Elliot . . . Britt! The Circle *S!*"

"There is nothing that can be done until the storm is over. I will send men then. Britt and Elliot are together. They can defend the ranch. With a storm like this, the attackers could not stay long. Southwind, there is nothing we can do now but wait. No man can travel in this storm and survive."

"It's hard to do nothing when my son's life and so many other lives are in danger. Why would Mitchell Talbot do this thing? He has lived in the valley for so long and shown no interest in the cattle."

"No obvious interest. His horse ranch was a good shield. Yet I suspect from things he said that there is much more. He has a deep hatred for Elliot Saber. He has accused him of killing someone."

"I'm frightened, Lone Wolf," Southwind said softly.

"I know, Sister. We will move as soon as the day breaks and the snow ceases. Until then, there is no choice. We must wait."

"I will see to your wound. Lone Wolf, you cannot ride with such a wound. You must remain here."

Lone Wolf's face was grim. "I will look into Mitchell Talbot's eyes again and see if he has the courage to face a man . . . if the Saber men do not get to him first."

Southwind was silent, worried that perhaps the three Saber eagles might never fly again.

Damion closed the door in the face of the rising storm and turned to confront a wide-eyed Kairee.

"One thing is more than certain, Kairee. We have to sit out the storm here."

"And what then, Damion? We have no horses and no one knows where we are." Her face was pale and her body tense. He knew she was on the verge of panic.

He could understand her courage being shaken. She had been through a great deal. He went to her and took her into his arms.

"Don't be frightened, Kairee. We're together and we will survive. We will take one thing at a time. But"—he tipped up her chin to smile encouragingly into her eyes—"we're together, Kairee, and it's going to take a hell of a lot more than this storm to take you away from me again." He bent to kiss her trembling lips gently and his hand brushed the still-flat plane of her belly. "We have something very important to live for, don't we?"

She put her arms about his waist and rested her head against the breadth of his chest. His arms encircled her to draw her against him and she sighed, absorbing his strength and the welcome feeling of security he imparted.

He knew that Kairee was still shaken, so as he held her, he silently examined the position they were in.

There was a potbellied stove in the center of the room, two small cots, and some blankets, for which he was extremely grateful.

He held Kairee away from him, saying, "I want you to sit on that cot and wrap a blanket around you."

"What are you going to do?"

"I want to see if someone was smart enough to stack any wood around here. If I'm lucky we'll find some; if not I'll have to go out and get some. We've got to have a fire even if we don't have anything to eat."

"You can't go out there!"

"Kairee, make sense. We'll freeze in here without a fire. Now just curl up and stay as warm as you can until I see if I can get this stove a little hotter."

The fire, built by the rustler, had burned very low, and a cold chill had already begun to spread through the cabin.

What Damion had not told Kairee was that the storm could last a day, or a week.

She sat on one of the cots, pulling a blanket about her.

"Good girl." Damion bent to kiss her again, then went to the door. He was wearing a heavy jacket and he pulled his hat low over his eyes, but still he was unprepared for the bite of the wind and the sting of the blowing crystals of snow.

He walked around the side of the shack and was more than relieved to find a small stack of wood already chopped. Obviously someone had planned on using, or had been using, the cabin.

He gathered up enough wood to make a large armful and returned to the porch, grateful for even the small amount of warmth that met him when he opened the door.

He stacked the damp wood in a corner to dry, selected a few fairly dry pieces, and took them to the stove. Opening the small door, he fed the wood into it piece by piece until the fire burned crisply. He could feel the heat beginning to permeate the shack.

Satisfied there was enough wood to burn for awhile, he dragged the second cot near. Taking one of the blankets, he went to the one window and lifted the blanket, catching it on the rough wood of the window's frame, to protect them from the wintry draft that poured through. Then he returned to check the fire.

Kairee watched him, aware that his mere presence and the firm confidence with which he moved did so much to ease her fears.

She watched the play of yellow flame across his face as he knelt to examine the fire. It brought dazzling reflections to his sky blue eyes. His concentration allowed her to study again the strength of his face. Her love for him suddenly seemed to expand into a brilliant glow within her, almost overwhelming her with its power.

Sure now that there was little else he could do at the moment for their protection, Damion turned his attention to Kairee.

"Come over here closer to the fire and sit on this cot with me, Kairee," he invited as he sat down. Kairee rose and went to sit beside him.

Wrapped both in the blanket and the strong arms that held her close, Kairee realized she would be willing to spend the rest of her life in such a small, comfortable place if Damion's love surrounded her.

The world outside ceased to exist and they sat for awhile in a companionable silence. Resting against him, Kairee was confident there was nothing now that could shatter what they had finally found.

"Oh, Damion," she said softly, "if only it could always be like this . . . If it could have been like this at the beginning."

"Would you be happy here, with me, Kairee?"

She turned to look up into his eyes. "Don't you know

that it's all I've ever really wished for, Damion? I . . . I just believed that the things we wanted were so very far apart we could never meet on common ground."

"Kairee . . . were you ever going to tell me about our child?"

She could hear the touch of hurt in his voice. "Don't believe that, Damion! It's not true! When I left Southwind's village, I was going to tell you. I felt you had every right to know."

"And after you told me?"

"I had so many things prepared in my mind when I left the village. Now, I'm so unsure. I guess I meant to force you to make choices. I suppose that was just as wrong as anything else that has happened between us."

"Whatever else has happened, right or wrong, the fact that we love each other is the only important thing. That, and knowing we're responsible for a life that is helpless and will need us both. Kairee, you and the baby come first. Remember that. You don't have to force choices. I made them long before I found you. I faced the real truth: that if I lost you I would have lost a great part of myself I would never have been able to find again."

"But," she whispered softly as tears blurred her vision, "the choices will cost you so much."

"No, love." He smiled into her eyes. "We will stay and build and have our family and we will make the valley, the world, and my father understand that nothing is more important than that."

"Your father hates me, and after this he will hate me even more."

"Wrong again." Damion chuckled. "And if you'll kiss me and let me hold you a little closer, I'll tell you a very long story."

Obediently she moved closer and lifted her lips to his.

Their mouths blended in a deep, satisfying kiss that wiped all thought of stories from Damion's mind. He lifted her to lie across his lap and his hands explored most thoroughly while their lips lingered.

"Now," she whispered in satisfaction, "tell me."

"Tell you what, that I love you?"

"Tell me a story."

"I can think of more interesting ways to find sleep than bedtime stories," he teased.

"Damion"—she laughed softly—"if you don't put your mind on serious things . . ."

"But I am serious," he replied as he tightened his arms about her. "Love, you have no idea how serious I am at this moment."

"Damion!" she threatened.

"All right, stories . . . first."

She smiled and her eyes warmed with her more than willing response as she drew his head to hers for another heated kiss that urged him to relate the tale quickly.

He told her the entire story that had begun so many years before, and he watched her eyes fill first with pity, then with sorrow. He saw her surprise and held her more tightly as he described Emma and her strange resemblance to her.

"Kairee, it was like looking at you when I saw the picture. Can you imagine the shock when my father first saw you? It must have been so overpowering that it destroyed his judgment. Part of the problem is that he's been running away from facing you and the ghosts of the past."

"Will he ever be able to look at me without the pain of remembrance?" she asked, disappointment heavy in her voice.

"In time, sweet, with all the love we intend to share with him. Besides, we have the best cure in the world, the thing that could bind us all together again." He caressed her belly.

"Not as a weapon, Damion."

"No, never as a weapon. As a tie—to hold us all together, to help us build a life in which we can all find happiness. He needs a little happiness too, and maybe we're the only ones who can show him where he can find it."

"And the Circle *S?*"

"Britt can run it as well . . . maybe even better than I can. Besides, after all this, I think my father and Britt will be able to . . . well, to make some changes in their lives."

"Britt . . ." Kairee said softly.

Damion paused for a moment and Kairee lifted her eyes to him.

"He's in love with you. That's no secret, Kairee. He tried to pound my head in when he thought I had hurt you."

"So that's why you were so bruised. I . . . hurt me? Why would Britt feel you had hurt me?"

Caught in a dilemma and not wanting any lies to exist between them, Damion held her close and told her.

"It seems someone told him about the child. He wanted to kill me and I don't blame him. But at the time I didn't know what he was so mad about."

"How did he know?"

"I don't know. I do know he was coming to see you."

"Why?"

"To ask you to marry him," Damion answered quietly. "Even though he knew. Even then he wanted to solve a problem he wasn't sure I would solve. Seems whatever respect he had for me died a very ignoble death. Whatever his intentions, Kairee," Damion said firmly, "I wouldn't give you up . . . not to anyone for any reason. You and the child you carry are part of me, a part I can't afford to lose or I'd be lost myself."

"I never meant to hurt Britt so."

"Neither did I, and I've hurt him much worse than you ever could. I've been doing it for years. I'd give my soul to be able to reach out to Britt and be . . . brothers again."

"If he'll let us," Kairee said softly, "we will both reach out."

Damion looked into her eyes silently, then smiled. "I do love you, Kairee, so very much. We will both reach. We've got a lot of rebuilding to do . . . together."

"Yes," she whispered as his lips found hers again.

The room was still chilly despite the fire, so Damion rose from the bed to put more wood in the stove. He would have to remain awake through the night to make certain the fire did not go out. He looked skeptically at the stack of wood and assessed the balance that remained outside. He concluded that he might have to go in search of more if he meant to keep them from freezing.

Huddled in blankets, Kairee lay on the cot and watched him. When he returned to the cot, he lay beside her, keeping her between the fire and him and placing himself between her and the shack's persistent drafts.

Kairee giggled softly as his hands came across barrier after barrier of heavy clothing, but the laughter turned to pleased sounds as his nimble fingers slipped beneath the shirt he had tugged free of her breeches and warmed her skin with gentle caresses. The belt she wore was quickly stripped and tossed aside, the buttons loosened on the snug breeches, and he slid his hand inside to seek the softness of her belly, her thighs, then the furry warmth between.

"Cold?" he questioned hopefully.

"I'm rapidly becoming warmer," she replied with a husky laugh.

Slowly, teasingly, his fingers massaged, stirring her to move against his hand. He slid his other hand from beneath her and moved to caress her breasts. She turned her head so their lips met and for a heart-stopping moment she enjoyed the sensual pleasure his large hands elicited with each probing touch. But these ministrations were not enough to quench the fire that was building.

She turned in his arms and reached for the buttons of his shirt to loosen them. Then she sought the heavy belt buckle and with a few quick tugs removed that barrier from her questing hands.

While she sought the warmth she knew lay beneath the barrier of his clothes, he was doing his best to ease her breeches down over her hips. Once successful, she heard his murmur of pleasure as the softness of her body pressed to his.

Neither felt the chill of the room now as he drew the blanket over them. Piece by piece, the clothing was pushed aside until flesh lay against flesh.

There was a fiery urgency in them now as they sought to fill this need, this wild hunger, that seemed more powerful than ever before.

There was a newness to their lovemaking that was the seal to their promise of forever, and both were awed to silence as their passion gained momentum.

His open mouth took hers in a kiss so deep it seemed to draw the very breath from her body and she blazed with the urgency to feel him deep within her, to feel the strength that seemed to flow from his body to hers.

She could not contain a cry of rapture when he lifted her hips to meet his first deep thrust, and she could hear his answering groan of intense pleasure as their bodies joined and began to move in matched rhythms.

She was his and he was hers, totally, and beyond anyone's ability to deny. It would be so for as long as they lived, for they gave all to each other in a momentous climax that left them unable to do more than gasp for breath and hold each other.

When Kairee finally slept the sleep of exhaustion, Damion rose to put more wood in the fire. Placing more blankets on Kairee, he dressed silently and went outside to carry in the balance of the wood, praying it would last at least through the night.

When he returned to the bed, Kairee nestled against him with a contented sigh. Damion remained awake. It was imperative that he did not sleep. If the fire went out, they might die of the cold before they could be found.

The remaining hours of the night brought Damion the opportunity for deep thought. Unanswered questions filled his mind.

Had Lone Wolf gotten back to the village? Damion believed he should have been able to do so after some rest, and probably before the storm struck.

But the most terrifying question of all was, had his father and brother survived? And if they had, when the storms were all over, could they build a future again? There was so much yet to face. He drew Kairee close to him and held her, knowing she and his child were his lifeline. Whatever else they had to overcome, they would do so together.

Through the long hours of the night, another of the Saber eagles prayed.

Chapter 32

Mitchell Talbot beat the severest part of the storm on the ride back to his ranch. He was pleased to see that the riders he had sent to destroy the Circle *S* had returned. If all his plans were working, he would have succeeded in doing what he had come to Wyoming to do five years before. He would have destroyed all the Sabers and the Circle *S*.

It had been his ultimate goal for so long that he began to wonder if he would feel the loss of his hatred like a dark void when it was over.

He dismounted and led his horse to the barn and left it in the care of one of his hands. Then with shoulders hunched to fend off the growing wind, he walked to the ranch house and opened the door.

Several men sat before a crisply burning fire and they turned to look at him as he closed the door against the rising storm and smiled.

"Well?" he questioned.

The leader rose and his grim, tight-lipped smile half answered Talbot's question. "We've wiped them out."

"We shot the boy," another added.

"Boy? You mean Britt, or someone else?"

"The Indian kid."

"Britt."

"Yeah. He's dead. We set fire to the whole thing. The old man and the rest of the family burned with it. Anyone who might have gotten out of that blaze alive has no protection from the storm. One way or the other, they're dead men. As far as chances go, there ain't any. The Circle *S* is gone."

"You've done a good job and you've earned your money," Talbot stated in satisfaction. He went to the next room and returned with a heavy wooden box, which he handed to the leader.

"Everything I promised is here, and you can take whatever might be left of the Circle *S* herds that you can run off. When the storm is over, I want you to get started on the next phase of my plan. Stir up the entire territory. Fill 'em with rumors and stories. I want them to lay the blame on the Kennedys. They'll never suspect me, a man who has no interest in cattle. I'll soon buy the Kennedy and Saber land for next to nothing. In the long run I want every trace of Elliot Saber and what he tried to build wiped from the face of the earth."

The leader took the box and motioned for the others to follow him. They would sleep in the bunkhouse tonight and be gone as soon as the storm ceased. Talbot had no way of knowing that not one man among them would have wanted to share his house for the night. Unsure of his sanity, but more than sure of his cold brutality, they chose to be as far away from him as possible.

Talbot watched the door close behind them, then he went to a cupboard and took several things from it: a bottle of whiskey, a glass, and a small black book. These he carried with him to a chair beside the fire. He sat comfortably, poured himself half a glass of whiskey, and set the bottle aside. He took a deep drink, then placed the glass next to the bottle. Finally he picked up the thin black book and opened it. Within lay two pictures, one of a lovely, gray-eyed, golden-haired woman, Emma Martin. The other showed a smiling young man with golden hair and blue eyes, a man, who had been known to no one in the valley but Elliot Saber and him. And, he reflected bitterly, a woman who had died a long time before.

He looked at the picture of the young man and his eyes grew cold and hard. His expression was grim as he reached again for the glass of whiskey and drank deeply.

"I told you, Richard," he said softly, "that I would make him pay in full, didn't I? Well, he has paid. He is dead and his sons with him. There will never be another Saber to walk this land. All he has built I have destroyed. I only wish there had been a way he could have known. But it will have to be enough that they are dead and their house destroyed. I have made very sure by leaving his son to die in that shack that no Saber lives."

There was madness in his blue eyes and the hand that reached again for the glass was trembling with barely contained passion.

He continued to gaze at the photographs for a long time, time enough to finish the bottle of whiskey. After awhile he slept, the pictures still in his lap and his face twisted with dreams that had assailed him for over thirty years.

Gregg, Rusty, and Smokey barely made it to the Circle S land before the fury of the storm hit.

"She's blowing up a big one," Smokey stated as he studied the darkening sky.

But Gregg's eyes were still on the spirals of what he knew was smoke just over the hill.

Whatever might have been forming in their imaginations, none of the three were prepared for the blackened, smoldering ruins that met their eyes.

"Holy God," Rusty breathed. "The whole place is gone."

"What the hell could have happened?" Smokey mumbled meditatively.

"Something more to blame on the Kennedys, I suppose," Gregg replied. Then they looked at each other in shock at the realization of how much truth there could be in his statement.

Gregg's face was grim and pale. "If they're all dead, we're sure as hell going to have a hard time explaining. They carry a lot of weight in this territory. This could just about put an end to us."

"Maybe somebody got away," Rusty suggested hopefully.

"Where would they go in this? Somebody was sure careful to pick just the right time," Smokey answered. "Even if anyone managed to escape from the house, the barn's burned too. I'll bet all the stock is either run off or dead. Somebody wanted to make real sure."

"Let's go on down," Gregg said. "Maybe we might find somebody alive. We have to, or nobody in this territory will believe us. Besides, we might not be able to make it back home in this. There's a wall down there—must be the back patio wall. We can make camp and maybe sit out the storm."

They nodded, for they were as reluctant as Gregg to try to make it back home in what was rapidly growing into a severe bout of weather.

They nudged their horses forward and rode down the hill toward the remains of the Circle *S*. Only as they drew closer did they realize there was a makeshift shelter near the wall, and they saw that not only was a fire burning, but people were moving about as well.

Elliot and Jim had melted snow and had boiled it for drinking water. They had also melted snow for cool compresses, for his fever was mounting by the moment.

Jim watched Elliot closely. He had not spoken much since Britt had been shot. He sat beside his son now and to Jim's surprise he was holding Britt's hand, as if he could force his own strength into him.

Elliot seemed to be lost in deep thought so Jim said little to disturb him. He kept his eye on Britt, who had not regained consciousness and who, he was reasonably sure, was losing ground.

Elliot's mind had taken him wandering in the darkest valley through which he had ever walked. He had found his own private hell where the thundering truths of his guilt held him.

In deep despair he prayed that Britt might live so he could tell him all the things he knew he should have told him a long time ago. He knew one thing for certain: Southwind had been right, and he needed her. He made himself promises, as all desperate men did, that he would rectify all the mistakes, that he would love his sons as he should have, and that he would ask Southwind to be his wife once more. All this he vowed, almost as if it were a bribe to the Angel of Death for the life of his son.

Elliot held on to Britt, afraid that if he let him go his life would drain away. He was totally oblivious to all else when Jim became aware that riders were approaching.

Jim's first concern was that the attackers had returned to finish the job they had started. He took his gun from its holster and aimed it at the shadowed, snow-covered form that was moving toward him followed by two others. He was ready to pull the trigger at the first aggressive action when Gregg called out.

"Hello! Hello!" Gregg called through the now-rising wind. "I'm Gregg Kennedy from the Bar *K*. Are you all right?"

Jim sighed in relief. "We're over here. Come on over."

The three men appeared as vague forms that slowly materialized out of the swirling snow. Cautiously they came close enough to be identified.

Gregg knelt near the fire, as did Smokey and Rusty. "Who's inside the lean-to?"

"Elliot and his boy . . . Britt. Britt was shot by the men who did this." Jim waved his hand at the destruction about them.

"Who was it? Did you recognize them?"

"No," Jim replied. "They said they were men sent by you and your family."

"That's a damn lie!" Gregg protested. "You didn't believe them?"

"Me and Elliot did for awhile. It was Britt who called their lie. He swore he knew you too well and you wouldn't be party to this."

"He was right. This was none of our doing. I'd like to thank Britt for the confidence."

"So would I," Jim said softly, "but I'm not sure we'll ever be able to. He took a bullet meant for his father . . . Elliot hasn't been . . . right since the boy got shot."

"Christ," Smokey muttered.

"Damn bastards," Rusty snarled.

"I'd like to talk to Elliot," Gregg said.

"Go on in, but don't be too surprised. He's . . . well, he's had a blow I'm not sure he's strong enough to survive."

Gregg stood and walked to the corner of the lean-to, then he bent and went inside.

Elliot did not acknowledge Gregg's presence, and by the light of the fire Gregg could see that his face was a ghastly white. It also took Gregg very little time to realize that Britt's condition was grave. He began to wonder if Jim were not right and Britt was dying.

"Mr. Saber?" Gregg questioned softly. For several moments Elliot did not move, then slowly he dragged his eyes from Britt and raised them to Gregg. Gregg was shaken by the amount of pain he saw reflected there. He had said so many times that Elliot Saber deserved whatever he got, but he found now that sympathy choked him and the thought spun through his mind that no man should have to suffer the anguish he saw in Elliot's eyes.

He knelt beside Britt and looked down into his pale face. Britt's breathing was slow and ragged, and Gregg could almost smell Elliot's fear.

"Mr. Saber, none of us are responsible for this. Britt . . . well, he was becoming sort of a friend of ours. He spent time with us, ate at our table. We wouldn't have done this, please believe me."

"No need to say it again," Elliot grated. "Britt said the same thing. But . . . if he dies, it doesn't matter who's to blame for anything else. I'm to blame for this."

"From what I hear, it was you they meant to kill."

"It was . . . it was me they should have killed."

"I never thought I'd see Elliot Saber so defeated that he let one of his own pay a price without fighting back."

Elliot's head snapped up and he narrowed his eyes at Gregg.

"I've made too many mistakes. This one I'll have to pay for, for the rest of my life. I don't need your pushin', boy. It's over."

"Maybe that's *just* what you need. Someone has decided to wipe you out and put the blame on us. Now maybe you're going to put up with that. But I sure as hell am not, and I'll tell you, Mr. Saber, if it were you lying there, Britt wouldn't stop until he got some answers."

Elliot's anger was growing and that was exactly what Gregg wanted. He continued. "It sure might be hard on whoever is responsible if we made peace . . . joined forces."

Elliot's interest had begun to grow. "You have something in mind?"

"Not exactly," Gregg admitted. "The only thing is, if we do get together, somebody is going to get upset, maybe upset enough to play his hand wrong. When he does, at least we'll know who's behind this. Seems to me," Gregg added softly, "somebody ought to pay for this."

"There's a lot you don't know about placing blame."

"Maybe you ought to tell me. Could be it just might make your mind easier. With this storm, we can't move. When it's over, you can come to my place. Lucy can help Britt, maybe better than anybody else around."

If Elliot was surprised at the offer, he made no sign. He stared at Britt as if the power of sheer will could awaken him. But Britt did not stir.

With a ragged sigh, Elliot returned his gaze to Gregg. "Maybe," he said softly. "Maybe."

Gregg waited in silence, then Elliot began to speak. As the storm raged about them, he spoke of the bitter storm that raged within.

It was near dawn when the storm's fury began to abate. The snow stopped falling, though it already lay over two feet deep on the ground. The wind was still crisp and sharp, but the power behind it was steadily growing weaker.

Britt remained still, and now, after hours of talking, Elliot was silent too. Gregg felt more sympathy for the man who was awake and feeling the greater pain than for the one who was mercifully unconscious.

"So Britt and Damion are both in love with Kairee," Gregg said softly. "No wonder she's been so troubled lately. I wish she had told me about the child. Surely she knew I would have supported her, that it wouldn't have mattered as long as we didn't lose her."

"You are right," Elliot said in a half whisper. "It is

time this was brought to a halt. For awhile I was angry at her, then at Britt and Damion. Now I know it was I who drove them. I want an end to it."

"I think it's time we tried to move. We can make a litter to carry Britt."

"The trip might kill him," Elliot protested.

"Yes, it might, but staying here would make it a certainty. At least we've got to try."

Elliot took a deep breath, then nodded.

Jim agreed that waiting any longer in the cold might kill Britt faster than the wound.

The five men made an Indian-style litter and placed Britt on it, covering him carefully.

Jim and Elliot rode and Maria and Margurite were doubled on one horse while Gregg, Smokey, and Rusty walked alongside the litter. It would be a long, tedious trip, and they were not aware that as they made their way toward the Bar *K* the wind was wiping away their trail almost as rapidly as they made it.

They moved slowly toward the Kennedy ranch. The going was hard for those who walked, and after awhile Jim and Elliot insisted on changing places and walking, letting the walkers ride for awhile. After that, the changes were made often so that one man would not face the danger of dropping from exhaustion.

Elliot kept close watch on Britt, but there seemed to be no change. His only consolation was that his son seemed no worse than when they had started.

The hours of travel seemed endless to the men and women who were now wet, cold, and extremely tired. They were a grimly silent group as each one drew on the reserves of strength he or she had and prayed in silence for the one who lay quiet.

Stephen poured a cup of coffee and eased himself down into the rocking chair before the fire. It did not

411

take Cassie long to find her favorite place at his feet, hoping he would be in the mood to tell a story.

But Stephen's attention was on Lucy, who seemed uncommonly nervous. He had watched her move from chore to chore without finishing one. "Lucy." Stephen spoke gently, then he realized Lucy had not heard. She had gone to the window for the sixth time in the past half hour, obviously searching through the still-swirling snow. "Lucy," he repeated, raising his voice.

Lucy spun from the window as if she suddenly realized what she was doing.

"Yes, Pa? Can I get you something?"

"No, Lucy girl," he replied. "You can come over here and sit by me and tell me what's bothering you."

"There's nothing bothering me. I just don't like it when Gregg is out in weather like this."

Cassie watched wide-eyed, knowing as well as her grandfather did that her mother was telling a deliberate lie. This was something that shocked Cassie speechless.

"Lucy."

"What?"

"Come over here."

Reluctantly Lucy walked to his side. Stephen reached to take her hand. "Girl, there hasn't ever been a day we couldn't have the truth between us. We've been family a long time. You're as much my daughter as Kairee. Now you come and tell me what's hurting you."

Lucy knew he was right, and she hated keeping secrets from him, believing he had a right to know. She sighed deeply and knelt beside him.

"Okay, Pa. I'll tell you the truth. But you have to promise to listen clear through before you say anything."

"All right," he agreed.

Lucy cast a reluctant look at Cassie, then returned her eyes to Stephen. She began to speak.

412

True to his word, Stephen remained silent, but his face was pale and the hand that held Lucy's clutched it spasmodically.

"Kairee . . . sweet Kairee. Why did you think you had to be afraid?" he said half to himself. "Don't you know we love you girl? . . . we love you."

"Pa," Lucy said tearfully, "she didn't run from you. Kairee is the strong woman you raised her to be. She knew her own mind, but she had to make choices. She only needed time to think. She'll be safe with Southwind."

"I hope she comes home soon so we can tell her that everything's all right, that we're all she needs and we'll stand between her and anything in the world that tries to hurt her—and that includes any of the Sabers."

"She'll be home as soon as this storm is over, Pa. You know she'd be smart enough to stay with Southwind until the weather changed. She'll be fine."

"Sure she will . . . sure she will," Stephen agreed. He looked intently at Lucy. "Now suppose you tell me what it was took Gregg and the boys off in this weather?"

"Do you know everything, Pa?" Lucy laughed.

"Being a grandpa"—he winked at Cassie, whose brow had furrowed in worry—"it's my job. So come on, out with the rest of it."

"There was a fire at the Saber ranch."

"How do you know?"

"We saw the smoke."

"And Gregg went to see." Stephen chuckled. "I'll bet you had nothing to do with that."

"Pa, it's how enemies stay enemies. If there was a fire, they might blame us. If we go to help . . . well, maybe we can create a little understanding. It could be a first step, Pa."

Stephen looked into her eyes for some time before he smiled and laid his hand gently against her cheek.

413

"Every day of my life I'm a little more thankful that my son had the good sense to take you as a wife. You've been nothing but good for this family, Lucy girl, and I'm mighty pleased you chose to come with us."

"Thanks, Pa," she whispered, smiling through happy tears.

"Gregg's been gone most of the night and now the day is near over. When do you think he'll be back?"

"The weather's been calming most of the day. I wouldn't be surprised if he came soon."

Almost as if her words had been prophetic, a shout came from outside and Cassie leapt to her feet and ran to the door with Lucy close behind.

"It's Pa and the men!" Cassie cried.

"It is Gregg, Pa," Lucy said, "but he's got a lot of others with him. I think we're getting a return visit from some of the Sabers. At least Elliot Saber. They all look exhausted."

She went out to help and was surprised at the point of tears when she saw Britt being carried gently on a litter.

Gregg took Lucy into his arms for the warmth of a welcome kiss, while Elliot stepped into the house slowly, as if still unsure of his welcome.

"Lucy, Britt's been shot," Gregg explained quickly. "See what you can do. I'll take care of Elliot."

Lucy nodded, following Smokey, Rusty, and Jim as they carried him into her bedroom, then she closed the door behind her.

Gregg and Elliot stood for several minutes in silence, watching Stephen as he rose slowly from his chair. Gregg breathed a sigh of relief as Stephen smiled and extended his hand to Elliot.

"Welcome to my home, Elliot Saber. Come in and rest. It is long past time that you and I talked."

Chapter 33

Southwind stepped outside her lodge to gaze in awe at the splendor nature had created with the storm. There was a blanket of snow over two feet deep and thick piles of snow hung on tree branches, which bent gracefully under the weight. The brilliant blue sky and a heatless sun made the snow sparkle in untouched sheets of purest white.

The beauty was overwhelming, but her thoughts quickly turned to her brother, then to Kairee and Damion, who were trapped in a cabin somewhere in the frigid wilderness.

She knew that despite his wound Lone Wolf was most likely up and planning the rescue of his friends.

She walked the distance from her lodge to his and stepped inside without calling out.

Her suspicions were proved correct, for she found him sitting before his fire. She understood the kind of effort he must have put forth merely to rise from his bed.

He smiled at her across the room, sensing her displeasure. She pressed her lips together and shook her head in disbelief.

"You are not well enough to ride."

"I am all right."

"You are most stubborn."

"Somewhat like the rest of my family," he retorted with a grin.

"Do not evade the issue. You cannot ride. I will send men to rescue them."

Lone Wolf stood slowly and went to her. "He saved me, Southwind. When he could have ridden on to find his woman, he stopped to bind my wound and build a fire. He saved me. Whether you approve or not, my sister, I will repay such a debt. Have horses brought. Food and furs also . . . and pray they are all right when I arrive."

"I will go with you."

"No, you will remain here."

"Lone Wolf!"

"Southwind, I am chief here. You will remain," he said forcefully, then his voice gentled. "Trust me. I just have a feeling it is better that you do."

"Do you think they are dead?" she whispered.

"It is a possibility."

"Elliot could not bear the loss of his son."

"I know. It is better that you remain here. Do you understand, Southwind?"

"Yes . . . I will stay."

Lone Wolf nodded, and Southwind left to see to obtaining the horses and equipment Lone Wolf had requested.

Less than an hour later, Lone Wolf and two warriors departed, leading two extra horses and packhorses behind them. Lone Wolf also ordered three warriors to ride to the Circle S to discover what had occurred there.

Southwind stood outside her lodge and watched them until they were lost from sight.

Lone Wolf knew the trail well. There was not a

section of the land about him he had not traveled. But the journey began slowly because of the depth of the snow, and they were forced to move at a pace that frustrated him.

They followed each other in single file, each trying to widen the path for the packhorses bringing up the rear.

They made their way slowly toward the cabin and the two who had been trapped there through the violence of the storm. Lone Wolf hoped he would find them both safe.

Damion had put wood on the fire throughout the night, moving quietly, then returning to the cot to hold Kairee near as he attempted to dispel recurring visions of what might have happened to his family.

The house could have been a fortress, he told himself. They had enough arms to defend it from an army had they been forced to remain behind its walls.

But would they? Or would his father, with his immense pride, meet his enemies on their terms?

The possibilities created nightmares that kept him from sleep and only the softness of the woman in his arms occasionally distracted him from such terrifying thoughts.

Before dawn he had used the last of the wood he had carried inside. He rose slowly and began to dress. Then he went out to gather what remained of the pile at the side of the shack. He hoped it would last until morning. But even then he knew he would have to find a source of more if he meant to keep them alive, and he was grimly determined to do just that.

When he returned with the wood, he was nearly frozen. He leaned against the door with all his weight to close it against the force of the storm.

Kairee had missed his warmth almost at once. She

had sat up, drawing the blankets about her.

Their eyes met when he entered and she was shaken with relief. He read it in her face.

He dropped the wood and came to her, throwing aside his coat and sitting on the bed to remove his boots. Then he slid beneath the blankets and gathered her warmth close to him.

"Good God, it's cold out there."

"Damion . . . that is a very small amount of wood." Her eyes held his. "There is no more out there, is there? It's all gone."

"Don't panic, Kairee. This might last until the storm is over. Then I can scout out some more."

"Damion . . . we're going to die here, aren't we?"

"No, Kairee! We're not going to die. We'll be all right. Just don't be frightened, love." He held her close and kissed her fiercely. "We'll survive . . . believe that. I've no intention of dying or of letting you and my baby die. Now"—he laughed, trying to force her to smile— "suppose you warm me up a little. If I have to go for wood, I have to be warm before I go."

She tried to smile for his benefit, but terror filled her heart. She had found so much only to face losing it all. She clung to him and they made a desperate kind of love that soothed her into a troubled sleep again. Still he remained awake, searching his mind for some way to save her.

When dawn came, he was so weary that just keeping his eyes open was an effort.

But he slowly became aware that the howling storm had died and there was utter silence outside.

He rose and went to the door and opened it to view the white, majestic scene before him.

Kairee rose silently from the bed and came to stand beside him.

"So beautiful . . . and so deadly," she murmured.

"Kairee," he said, turning to her with a smile, "if it stays calm, I can fashion a kind of snowshoe. We can make our way back. It will be hard going, but we can try."

"Do you think we could make it?"

"I do. But first we'll wait to make sure the storm has passed."

"How long?"

"Today and tonight. In the morning we'll give it a try."

"All right."

"We've got to keep warm while I try to put together some snowshoes and make some extra coats out of those blankets."

"How?"

"Cut a hole for the neck and put them over us. They'll be a little more protection at least."

He looked down into her frightened eyes. Then he cupped her face in his hands and kissed her gently.

"I love you, Kairee. We've got a whole future ahead of us. Have faith and we'll get out of here . . . together."

"I have faith," she said softly, "and I love you too, Damion Saber."

He laughed softly and kissed her. Then they shut the door and returned to the fire to solidify their plans to escape their frozen prison.

There was an expectant yet nerve-shattering silence in the Kennedy home. Britt remained unconscious, his eyes closed and his breathing shallow.

Lucy had worked for two hours to clean the wound and soothe his feverish body.

Elliot stood on the porch with Gregg and Stephen, but unlike the Kennedy men, he did not stare in awe at the unsurpassable beauty around him. Elliot's eyes looked beyond the horizon.

"Elliot," Stephen said quietly, "if there is any way in God's heaven to save your boy, Lucy will find it. She's nursed us through a lot of terrible things."

Elliot nodded in response, but still Gregg and Stephen knew his mind was elsewhere.

"We'd like to help if we can," Stephen offered.

Elliot turned to him. "Stephen, I need someone who can travel in this."

"Travel?" Stephen asked in surprise.

"Travel where?" Gregg questioned.

"To Lone Wolf's village."

"Why?"

"It is most important that a message be delivered to Britt's mother."

"I see," Stephen replied. "It would be very difficult to travel in this and I'd have to say two men should go in case they run across a problem. No man should be out there alone."

"I agree," Elliot said. "I would go without asking another man if it were not for Britt. If he . . . dies"—his mind found it hard to cope with the thought of death— "then I should be here. But his mother should be here too."

"I'll go," Gregg offered. Stephen wanted to protest, but the look on Gregg's face stopped his words. "They're both tired, but I'll ask either Rusty or Smokey to go with me."

He turned away as if to indicate his words were final and he would not listen to any contradiction of them. Stephen watched him go to the bunkhouse, and pride mixed with worry in his eyes.

"You've got a good boy there," Elliot said quietly.

"Yes." Stephen's eyes held Elliot's. "I think we are both very lucky men."

420

"I found out how fortunate I was too late to keep it all from being destroyed."

"The Circle *S*," Stephen replied, thinking the ranch was still where Elliot's heart lay.

"Hell no. Britt and Damion. I've been a damn fool for so many years. Now, I guess it's time to pay for it. I don't know if Damion is alive or dead, if he was caught somewhere in this storm to die alone. I don't know if Britt will live or die. And I realize now that the only woman who could make my cold house a home won't even look at me again."

"Have you asked her to?" Stephen replied quietly.

Puzzled, Elliot looked at him for a moment. Then he recalled Southwind's last words: he would know when he needed her and she would come.

"No," he answered, smiling slightly. "But I intend to."

"Elliot, Damion just might have weathered this storm somewhere. Kairee is in the Indian village. She and Southwind have become very good friends. Damion might even be there. Either way, I truly feel your sons are as strong as you, maybe even stronger. We've got to have a little faith that the good Lord sees it that way too."

"Maybe you're right," Elliot agreed.

Gregg returned with Smokey and Rusty, who were more than willing to make the trip, despite their tired bodies.

"We'll be back as soon as we possibly can, Pa," Gregg said.

"You take care, son," Stephen said firmly.

Elliot felt a twinge of real envy when he saw the unspoken affection between Gregg and Stephen. He wondered if he had lost all chances of seeing that look of warm devotion in the eyes of his sons. How many opportunities like this had he missed? How many times had they reached out for him only to confront a man whose back was always turned. The bitter pain tore at him, for he knew that despite his desire to be forgiven and to try to mend the past, he might not have the chance.

"Gregg," Elliot called as the three men mounted the horses Rusty had brought to the porch steps.

"Yes, Mr. Saber."

"Tell Southwind . . ." He paused, then he smiled. "Tell her I know the time is here and for the first time I understand. Tell her about Britt, but tell her I need her . . . maybe more than her son does, for my wound needs healing too. Can you remember that?"

Rusty and Smokey smiled as Gregg repeated the message exactly. Then the three turned and rode away.

The last of the wood was burning in the stove and Kairee sat close to it. Damion had been gone for over an hour to find more. He had told her they would need enough for the balance of the day while he tried to make some form of snowshoe for the trip back to her home.

She had no idea how he intended to do this, but she smiled to herself as she realized she had complete confidence in his ability to accomplish whatever he set out to do.

The door swung open and Damion filled it, carrying a huge bundle of tree branches he had found. His breath was a white mist and he was covered with snow. She rose to go to him.

"Is it snowing again?" she questioned fearfully, knowing that if another storm had begun, they were lost.

"No." He laughed. "I was damn fool enough to walk beneath a tree. I just got a pile of snow dumped on me."

He was shrugging off his coat as he spoke. She watched him and smiled to herself, wondering what she would have done without him in her life. She realized what a great, empty place he would have left. It was as if they had spent so many years together they had become part of each other.

"Are you hungry?" He grinned.

"Starved. Don't tell me you just happened across some food out there. It would be like you, Damion."

"I've trapped with my brother and Lone Wolf enough times up here to be able to snare a rabbit or two." He drew a skinned and gutted rabbit from the pocket of his coat. "It's kind of scrawny and there's no salt, but you can roast it on top of the stove. At least we won't be so hungry."

Kairee took the rabbit gratefully. With melted snow water, she washed it, then she placed it on top of the stove, tearing it into small pieces as she did so.

While it cooked, Damion broke the branches into smaller pieces that would fit into the stove. He fed some to the fire and placed the balance in the corner to dry out.

He felt Kairee watching him and looked up to smile into her eyes, forcing a confidence he did not feel. He was shaken by the sudden desire to crush her in his arms. He was well aware of the courage she had. She had not complained once but instead had insisted she would rather be anywhere with him than safe without him. At moments such as this, the magnitude of her love for him, a love he had almost let slip through his fingers, swelled within him and choked away any words he could have uttered.

How could he tell her how grateful he was for her love, how it warmed him and filled him as nothing had ever done before? How could he tell her that his life had been so empty until he had found her? Damion Saber, a man with everything at his fingertips, had never tasted love, and now he could not imagine surviving without it.

It still made him sweat to think of how close he had come to losing Kairee. It stiffened his resolve to get her to safety, no matter what it took—only he was still uncertain of just how he was going to do it.

Lone Wolf and his men, knowing the trail as well as they did, found the traveling much easier than most would have. Yet Lone Wolf could not shake the worry from his mind over what he might find at the cabin. He was certain Damion was a resourceful man, but still he knew it would be difficult for anyone to survive in these conditions.

He pushed himself to the limit and his men followed his example without a word, sensing an urgency in their leader that made speech unnecessary.

The sun continued to climb, but its brilliance was deceiving, for it did nothing to dispel the cold.

The two warriors watched Lone Wolf to see if he intended to stop for a midday meal, but there was no sign their chief intended any such thing. His chiseled features remained stoically inexpressive, yet the intensity of his concentration told his companions that time was of utmost importance now.

Well used to traveling a hard trail with little food or rest, they bent themselves to the effort and, if anything, acquired more speed.

Still it was late afternoon when the cabin came into view in the distance. A thin spiral of gray-white smoke was a sight that made Lone Wolf's pulses beat rapidly. To create fire they must be alive. The thought brought with it relief that made him realize how tense he had become. Without a spoken word, he signaled his men to follow, kicked his horse into motion, and rode toward the cabin.

Within the cabin Damion and Kairee sat side by side on the cot near the stove, wrapped in blankets and chewing on pieces of overfried rabbit. To them it tasted better than any meal they had ever had.

In this impossible situation they were still caught up only in each other. They talked of themselves and their future, ignoring the fact that they might not have one.

Determined to shut her fears away for the moment, Kairee gave herself up to family memories. And Damion, who had very few such memories, listened and promised himself that his own family would have such shared experiences to remember.

"I remember"—Kairee laughed—"speaking of this excellently prepared rabbit, the first time I cooked a meal for Pa and Gregg. Mother had always done the cooking, but I was thirteen and I thought, since I had watched her from babyhood, that I knew all there was to know about cooking. Well, I promptly burned everything. But what was so funny was Pa. He sat at the table and made a fuss over each bite, as if it were the best meal he'd ever eaten. Gregg choked down as much as he could stand, then almost begged Pa to let him leave the table. I think he knew he was going to be sick and he didn't want to hurt my feelings.

"Anyway, Pa, very seriously, told Mother to make sure she put all the leftovers away very carefully in case he wanted a snack later. Well, Mother did it, but I'm quite certain I wasn't in bed five minutes before they threw it out."

Damion laughed, seeing Kairee young and sweet, seeing her grow, seeing her family as she did, and building in his mind the kind of home he would have.

"Kairee, this shack, it's on Lone Wolf's land."

"Is it? I thought it was your land."

"No, we just use the shack when we're too far from home to get back or we're looking for strays. Anyway, I thought I'd talk to Lone Wolf about buying some of it from him."

"Some of it?" Kairee questioned.

"I thought it would be nice to build a house here, where the cabin is now. In the spring or summer, even in fall, it's beautiful. It would be a great place to live, to raise a family. It's about dead center between your family . . . and mine. What do you think?"

Her eyes sparkled into his, knowing instinctively what he had not said.

"I think," she said softly, "that this place will always be very special. And I'd like nothing more than to live here with you. You . . . you're so sure we'll . . ."

"I'm sure, Kairee. I've found something so very special that I'm not going to lose it. We'll get out of here." He took another bite of rabbit. "We'll have to." He chuckled. "I don't think I have the strength to live on this kind of food for long."

"Ungrateful wretch!" She giggled. "I place a feast before you and all you can do is complain."

The glow in his laughing blue eyes was decidedly wicked as he dropped the piece of rabbit and reached to pull her into his arms. "I never hesitate to grasp any treats that are thrown my way, and I'd be decidedly grateful for anything you might have to offer." He heard her answering laugh with pleasure and as her arms were thrown about his neck, their lips met in a kiss warm with promise.

But suddenly Damion held her a little away from him and seemed to be listening intently.

"What is it?" Kairee questioned.

"I'm not sure." He rose. "Stay right here. I'll take a

426

look and see. It might be some kind of animal."

He said the words, but he was more than certain the animal noise he had heard had been made by the two-legged kind.

Without a gun, he had no way to defend them and this thought plagued him as he went to the door and opened it.

The heavily clothed riders were almost unrecognizable. Kairee came to his side and they watched the riders grow closer.

"Damion?" Kairee whispered.

"It looks like—" Then he broke into a smile and turned to grab her up into his arms, laughing and kissing her. "It's Lone Wolf! He brought horses and food and safety! Kairee, we're safe!"

She joined in his laughter and clung to him as he spun her around, kissing her again and again. Then they stood close and watched as the riders approached.

At some distance Lone Wolf saw them in the doorway and raised his arm to wave. He had never been so pleased to see anyone in his life.

When the riders stopped near the cabin, Kairee ran to Lone Wolf and hugged him fiercely. Lone Wolf laughed and held her with one arm while he extended a hand to Damion.

"Lone Wolf, I have to say I've never been happier to see you."

"And I you, Damion. I have brought food and furs to warm you and horses to carry you home."

"Food!" Damion grinned. "I think that's most welcome."

Damion and Kairee fell into each other's arms amid gales of laughter, and though Lone Wolf smiled politely, he was quite puzzled by their strange behavior.

Chapter 34

The world was engulfed in a brilliant white stillness and Southwind could not shake the strange feeling that something momentous was about to occur. In the face of this feeling of anticipation that had settled over her, she was helpless to accomplish anything.

The walls of her lodge seemed to close in on her. Bundling herself well in furs, she walked through the winter wonderland without being aware of its cold beauty.

She found a fallen log and sat upon it to try to force her thoughts into some kind of order. It was becoming harder all the time to keep her longing for Elliot and her son under control.

How she wanted to be part of their lives, to live with them. But she would not surrender everything to a man who would not even be able to understand the price she would have to pay.

She thought of Elliot with heavy remorse, and of Britt with painful pity.

It was a terrible thing that Elliot had never shown his sons one ounce of love, but not to have taught them to love was even worse. She thought of Damion and Kairee and was pleased that Damion, unlike his father, had learned before he lost what was precious to him. She only hoped he would have the opportunity to share his knowledge with Kairee.

For a little while she allowed tears for herself and those she loved. The worst of her tears were for Elliot and the lonely pain he would know one day when all he had left was the land he valued, land that would provide him with no sympathy or comfort in the empty future he had earned.

Southwind looked carefully into her own heart and understood that the love she had had for Elliot Saber had never died. She sighed. It was hard to live without Elliot and impossible to live with him.

Reluctantly she rose and walked back toward the village. She imagined it would be some time until Lone Wolf returned with answers. Her prayers had gone with him that he would find Damion and Kairee unharmed and that Elliot and the Circle *S* he loved were safe as well. She also wondered what steps Elliot might take when he found out that Kairee and Damion were determined to make a life together. Elliot would feel betrayed and angry, that she knew, but would he be foolish enough to push Damion and Kairee away from him forever? And what of the grandchild? Could Elliot really be so cold he would turn his back on it, or even worse, try to use it as a weapon that could destroy Damion. These thoughts frightened her, for even if Damion did not realize Elliot's power, she did. She wondered if she could find a way to protect them both.

Weary from such emotional stress, she returned to her lodge. Once inside, she stirred the fire and placed more wood on it so she could prepare a meal. She hoped that by nightfall or early morning Lone Wolf would return and she would at least know the fates of Damion and Kairee.

When Lone Wolf did not appear by the time for the

evening meal, she ate and retired to her bed early in hopes of erasing all her concerns with sleep. But she slept in sporadic patches and awoke often, having had dreams she could not understand, dreams of fire and ice, of unrecognizable faces, and deep, heartrending cries of agony.

Unable to stop the dreams and unable to cope with them in sleep, she rose in the wee hours of the morning. She curled up near the fire with a blanket about her and fed twigs to the blaze to increase the warmth.

She tried not to think at all but merely sought to secure herself in a warm womb of forgetfulness. She was failing abysmally when she heard approaching horses.

Quickly she rose to her feet, tossing her blanket aside, and ran outside. One of the young men set to guard the village was just dismounting.

"What is it? What has happened?" she asked quickly.

"Riders coming," he said breathlessly.

"Lone Wolf?"

"No, he does not ride among them."

"Then it cannot be Damion and Kairee," she said thoughtfully. "Who else would visit us in such weather? Is it Elliot Saber?"

"No, Southwind, I would know Elliot Saber by sight. These three men are strangers to me."

"Then take several men with you and lead them to the village. I will speak to them."

He nodded and in one swift motion was mounted and riding away into the first gray light of dawn.

Southwind waited impatiently. Who else in the valley would visit her village? Most of the whites kept their distance. She was more than a little curious to see them and only returned to her lodge to grab up a warm, fur-lined buckskin coat and pull it on. Then she returned to stand before her lodge to await the strangers.

Over half an hour passed before Southwind could see the dark forms of the riders in the distance. As they drew closer, she realized she did not recognize them either.

She watched the heavily bundled men closely as they walked toward her. The tallest of the three spoke first and she assumed he was the leader of the group.

As he spoke, Gregg reached to remove his hat and Southwind smiled. There was no doubt in her mind who he was.

"Are you Southwind . . . Lone Wolf's sister?"

"Yes, I am, and I believe you are brother to Kairee Kennedy."

He chuckled in surprise. "Yes, I am Gregg Kennedy. How did you know?"

"When I look into your eyes I look into hers."

"I'm glad Kairee was wise enough to stay with you here rather than try to come home alone."

"I think," Southwind said quietly, "you must come to my lodge. There is a great deal I must tell you."

"Is Kairee there? I'd like to see that she's all right."

"No, she is no longer in the village."

Gregg's face paled and his brows drew together in a frown. "What do you mean, she isn't here? She didn't leave . . . try to come home by herself? Good God, is she lost out there somewhere?"

"Gregg, come to my lodge. It is warm there and you all look very cold and tired. We can talk there."

"I want to know where Kairee is," he demanded.

"And I shall tell you. Now, come with me." She said the last words with firm authority, then turned and walked toward her lodge as if she fully expected them to follow. They did.

Once inside, she put more wood on the fire and sat down. Gregg, Smokey, and Rusty completed a circle

431

around the warm blaze.

"Now tell me about my sister." Gregg's voice was choked with worry now as he imagined Kairee lost in such a wilderness, helpless, crying. The thought was so painful he could hardly stand it.

"Your sister is alive and well. She is with Damion Saber and by now I believe Lone Wolf has had enough time to reach them."

"How do you know all this? Southwind, please tell me what you know. I can't stand this."

"All right. Listen and I will tell you."

The three remained silent while Southwind told them all that she knew from Lone Wolf and all she believed was happening now.

"Kairee can find happiness with Damion Saber. They could bring your families together if they are allowed the opportunity. I hope you try to understand."

Shaken with relief that Kairee was safe, Gregg found it hard for a few minutes to speak. Southwind waited hopefully. Then Gregg smiled.

"I'd like nothing better than for Damion and Kairee to be happy together. Hell, I'd like us all to live in peace for a change. Now you just sit back and let me tell you some things."

Surprised at the strange turn of events, Southwind remained quiet even though she smiled.

But as he spoke, as the story of her son's almost fatal wound was told, the smile faded and tears glistened in her eyes. They were followed by a soft, muffled cry of shock as Elliot Saber's message was relayed to her.

Even after Gregg stopped speaking, Southwind sat in total silence, but the tears flowed freely, washing down her cheeks in hot rivulets.

Gregg and his friends could see she was caught up in an emotion so powerful, words were of little use.

Southwind was caught in a maelstrom that swept her from ecstasy to agony in moments. Her son was lying near the door of death. She wanted to cry out her pain. She wanted to chastise herself for ever having left him to Elliot . . . Elliot. Elliot had sent for her. Elliot had told her he wanted her, needed her, words she had waited so many years to hear.

"This is what he told you to say?" she whispered.

"Word for word," Gregg said firmly. "I made it a point not to miss a word."

"You . . . you must be tired," she began.

Gregg's smile returned. "Not in this case. I know how anxious you must be to get to Britt. We wouldn't ask you to wait while we took the time to sleep. Britt needs you now. Mr. Saber needs you too. We can rest anytime. Besides, the sooner I get you home, the sooner I can go after Kairee. I have to make sure she's well."

"I'm grateful. I'll make ready at once. Please," she said as they started to rise, "at least you must eat. Do so while I get ready. We will leave soon."

They agreed. It took Southwind less than an hour to prepare herself for travel. In that time, Gregg, Smokey, and Rusty rested and ate and had their horses exchanged for fresh ones.

It was a very anxious group that left the village and rode toward the Kennedy ranch.

Lucy stood by the bed and looked with sympathy at the young man who lay so helpless before her. He moaned softly and called out, first for his father, then for Damion. He is so handsome, she thought, yet so vulnerable. She had heard the misery in the soft, moaning call.

She sighed, knowing there was little else she could do. His life was now in God's hands.

Reluctantly, she turned from the bed and walked to the door, wishing there were something more she could do to help him survive.

She reached for the handle of the door at the same moment a weak, ragged voice, husky with pain, called her name.

"Lucy."

She spun about and could have wept when she saw Britt's eyes, still glazed with the remnants of fever but open and full of recognition.

She rushed to the side of the bed.

"Britt," she cried. "I'm so glad you're . . ."

"Alive," he finished. "I'm not too sure of that yet. Where's my father?" Britt tried to rise, but he was too weak to move. "Is my father alive . . . all right?"

"Shhh, Britt, don't worry. Your father is fine. He's right here in our house."

"God," Britt whispered. He closed his eyes again and for a minute Lucy thought he had sunk back into unconsciousness. Then she saw the tears that slipped from beneath his lashes.

She went to the door and stepped into the next room where Stephen and Elliot were seated near the fire talking. When the door opened, Elliot leapt from his chair and went quickly to Lucy's side. His face was a ghastly white.

"Britt . . . is he . . ."

"He's alive . . . and he's awake, Mr. Saber. I think he needs you. He's been calling for you."

"Me . . . He's been calling for me?"

Lucy nodded, smiling through her tears. "It was the first thing he said when he woke up."

Elliot looked at her through eyes blurred by happiness the likes of which he had not felt for thirty years. "Thank you, Lucy."

"You're more than welcome," Lucy replied softly.

Elliot went into the room and Lucy reached to pull the door closed behind him.

Elliot stood just within the room and looked at his son who lay so still, his eyes closed. He began to wonder if he had lost consciousness again. He walked slowly to the side of the bed. Sensing his presence, Britt opened his eyes. They looked at each other in silence for several minutes, neither knowing what to say.

"Pa," Britt began, "you all right?"

"Thanks to you, I'm fine. You're the one who's been scaring the hell out of me the past few days."

"Damned if I can remember what happened." Britt's voice was like rough sandpaper. "I'm thirsty."

Elliot moved to a table where Lucy had set a pitcher of water and a glass. He filled the glass halfway and went to the bed. Kneeling beside it, he gently lifted Britt's head to let him drink. After he replaced the glass on the table, he returned to the bed and sat beside Britt, whose eyes had not left him from the time he had entered the room.

"So tell me how we got into the Kennedy house. In fact . . . what happened at ours."

"Britt boy, there's no more Circle *S*. They burned it to the ground."

Britt's face became even paler and he cursed softly. "I'm sorry. I guess you've lost everything. I wish . . ."

"What, Britt?" Elliot asked quietly. "What do you wish?"

"I wish I could have done something to stop it. To save the Circle *S* for you."

"For me," Elliot muttered. "You'd save the Circle *S* for me. You'd protect me from taking that bullet. For me . . . for me. Christ, Britt you just about gave your life for me."

"What is it, Pa?" Britt questioned, alarmed at Elliot's strange reaction. He had expected to be berated for making a mistake.

"It's us, Britt. It's you and me and Damion."

"I don't understand."

"Neither did I until now. I didn't understand how damn blind and stupid I've been. I didn't understand all the things I think both you and your brother have been telling me for years in so many ways."

Britt looked at Elliot in what could only be described as profound shock dissolving into total disbelief.

"Pa?" he questioned so blankly that Elliot could have laughed if he had not been so near tears.

"Britt, it doesn't matter anymore. The Circle *S* is gone . . . but I've got my sons. I have you and Damion. That's all I need. I'm just hoping you both will find it in you to forgive me for the jackass I've been. I want you to know something, son. I've sent for your mother. I want her to forgive me too. I want to start a real life again, not one built on a dead dream. I want my wife . . . and more than anything else in the world, I want my sons."

Elliot reached to lay his hand on Britt's arm. He could feel the quiver of his muscles and he could read the uncertainty in his eyes.

"So, Britt?" he asked gently, "are you going to give a very foolish old man a chance to tell his son just how much he means to him? That a part of me would have died with you? Will you let me tell you that I loved the boy even when I didn't show it and I respect the man? In fact, I'm damn proud of the man. If your mother comes, if I beg her forgiveness, do you think we could start over? We've got nothing now. Nothing but each other. But if the two of you agree, that's good enough for me."

"And Damion . . . what about Damion?"

"We don't know."

"What do you mean, you don't know?"

Elliot explained that Damion had gone off before the storm and no one knew whether or not he had been caught somewhere in it. "I think," Elliot finished, "it's going to take more than my prayers to keep him safe."

"There're a few things I'd like to know."

"About the baby." Elliot smiled.

"What about it, Pa?"

"It's Kairee and Damion's baby. If they'll let me, I'll be its grandpa. If not"—he laughed softly—"I'll fight like hell to get back into the family."

"Pa, I'm not sure I'm not dreaming all this. It's . . . well, I've had so many of what my mother calls visions lately, I'm not sure this isn't one of them."

"It's no dream, son. It's no dream. I want to do my best to wipe out the bad memories and, with your help, try to start some new ones. Ones that won't hurt anyone."

"I . . ." Britt found it hard to speak. "Pa, I . . ." He grinned. "I never thought you were a foolish old man."

Elliot chuckled and gripped Britt's arm more firmly. Both men were overcome by an explosive emotion, an emotion that shattered the walls that had stood between them for years. The dam burst and the waters of love and forgiveness washed away the past and left new and fertile ground in which the seeds of the future would sprout and grow.

"I suppose," Elliot said with false gruffness, "that you must be hungry. You've always been, since you were old enough to eat at the table."

"Well, I could eat a steak or two." Britt laughed. Elliot rose to leave. "Of course, if they want to add some potatoes and a slice or two of pie, I wouldn't be upset."

"You're getting well," Elliot replied as he walked to

the door. With his hand on the door latch, he turned again to look at Britt.

"Get well, son," he said gently. "Get out of that bed. I'll be needing your help to build a house, a small house for us to start. We'll divide up Saber range. Give back to Lone Wolf what should have been his, give to the Kennedys enough to grow on, and give to Damion and Kairee a piece to share. Then, God willing, we'll be the family the Sabers should have been from the start."

"Don't worry about me, Pa." Britt smiled. "I'm ready to start as soon as you are. A couple of good meals and I'll be ready to go."

Elliot left the room and for several minutes Britt lay with his eyes closed. He wept in a paroxysm of joyous pleasure that seemed boundless. For so many years he had wanted to hear Elliot call him "son," tell him he cared and wanted him. Now it had happened and he was afraid to open his eyes again for fear it had been a dream and he would find himself betrayed and lonely again. It was a breathlessly long time before he opened his tear-filled eyes and realized that the truth was finally his.

Despite his hunger, Lucy refused to provide Britt with anything but clear broth, and that in very small amounts until his stomach would accept more.

"Now how can I get my strength back if all I can have is soup?" Britt protested.

"You'd soon find your stomach fighting back if I gave you anything stronger. Now you be good and eat this soup, and if you keep on being good, I just might cook you something a little sturdier . . . tomorrow."

"I'll starve to death by then."

"I doubt it." Lucy smiled amiably.

Britt finished the soup, then fell into a deep,

comfortable, and healing sleep.

Lucy, Stephen, Elliot, Jim, and the two maids, Maria and Margurite, tried to remain quiet while Britt sought the rest he needed to restore his strength.

Cassie found this enforced quiet quite unacceptable until Elliot drew her up on his lap and began telling her stories. She found as much pleasure in this as Elliot did, and he began to wonder if the child Kairee carried might be a girl. He fancied the idea of having a pretty little granddaughter to dandle on his knee and enthrall with his stories.

The hours drifted by. That night most of the occupants of the Kennedy house slept lightly, but Elliot slept not at all, burdened as he was by so many unanswered questions. Was Damion still alive? Would he be as forgiving as Britt had been? And there was one question that filled his mind and heart with tremendous turmoil. Would Southwind come, and if she came to see her son, would she stay to share her life with his father? He hated the hours until he knew.

Southwind traveled with ease. She gave no thought to rest or to food. Her only concern was Britt. Her son lay near death. She had to be with him. She had to hold him in her arms again.

The three who rode with her made no mention of her firm, stubborn resolve to reach the Kennedy ranch as soon as possible. She set the pace and they accommodated themselves to it.

Gregg rode beside her and they talked as they rode, yet still she could not quite believe that Elliot Saber had changed so profoundly.

She questioned Gregg relentlessly, and he had to smile to himself when he realized that by the time he reached home she would know as much about him and his family as he did.

When they could see the house in the distance, it was very late, though pale light shone through the windows.

They stopped for a minute and Gregg knew Southwind was gathering her courage to face whatever she might find.

"Britt . . ." she whispered softly.

"He'll be alive," Gregg said firmly.

"Yes." She nodded. They spurred their horses and rode toward the house.

Inside, Stephen and Elliot sat before the fire playing a slow game of checkers. Cassie was asleep and Lucy sat sewing.

When the sound of horses came to them, all eyes turned toward Elliot, who rose slowly and took two steps toward the door.

It opened and Southwind stood in the doorway with Gregg behind her.

"You came," Elliot said.

"I could not stay away. My . . . my son . . ."

"He is recovering . . . He will live."

"Thank the gods," she whispered.

"Southwind"—Elliot's voice was soft—"there is one here who is closer to dying than Britt was. I need you to heal a wound of many years."

Their eyes met and held, then slowly Southwind extended her hand to Elliot Saber.

Chapter 35

Damion and Kairee bundled gratefully into the furs. Then they put the fire out carefully to avoid an accident. They did not want anything to happen to a place in which they had found so much of each other, a place in which all barriers had been destroyed.

Kairee was exuberant, though she had not yet learned that Damion had asked Lone Wolf to take her home.

"Why aren't you coming with us?" Lone Wolf had questioned Damion while they were making preparations for travel.

"You know why," Damion answered quietly.

"Your woman will want to be with you."

"It's best I see what happened. If all is well, I want to break the news to my father first. I wouldn't want Kairee to take any abuse and my father can be tough at times."

"She is a good woman. Your father should be made to see that she is good for you."

"I'm going to try doing just that, but at first, until he realizes I mean business, he's going to bellow like a mad bull. The Circle S is more important than any woman, and besides," he added half to himself, "Kairee brings back too many old memories. No, I've got to go to the Circle *S* first and you've got to take Kairee home."

"I don't mind," Lone Wolf replied with a grin, "as long as you tell her it is so."

"Lack of courage, Lone Wolf?" Damion laughed.

"An attack of wisdom," Lone Wolf responded.

"I'll tell her, courageous one, don't worry." Damion finished adjusting the saddle of the horse Kairee was to ride and shortened the stirrups. He walked to where Kairee was waiting on the porch. "All ready?"

"I'm not too sure," she said softly. "I rather enjoyed part of our stay here."

"What do you say we come back in the spring and start on that house?"

"Sounds fine to me."

"Kairee . . ."

"What is it, Damion?"

"I'm having Lone Wolf take you home."

"Without you, why? Where . . ."

"I've got to find out what happened."

"I'll go with you."

"No. You go with Lone Wolf." He saw the argument forming in her eyes. "Kairee, it's best this way. I have to find out what happened while I was gone, and I have to explain a lot of things to my father."

"It's going to be difficult for you?"

"No, not for me. I imagine it's going to be harder on him. Having seen the picture of Emma, I can predict he'll be upset."

"Then let me go with you. The sooner we face each other and understand each other, the better it will be for all of us."

"I think I ought to try to smooth the way a little. There's still Britt to tell."

"And that should be my place too."

"Kairee, from what I understand from Lone Wolf, the ranch was a target for Talbot. You remember his

442

threats. A whole lot might have happened there, and if they did have to fight off Talbot's men, my father will not be the most pleasant person to face. Between him and Britt . . . well, I just think it would be better if I went alone."

"And then, after you see about your family and your ranch, you're going after Talbot, aren't you?"

He wanted to deny this, again to protect her somehow, but Kairee read his face too well.

"Damion, once Talbot finds out he's failed, he'll know there's no safe place for him in this valley. He'll run and we'll be rid of him." But again she read his face and her eyes widened with renewed understanding. "You plan to go after him no matter where he goes, don't you? You don't plan to let him go, even though he can't do us any more harm. Damion," she cried, anxiety growing in her voice, "you plan to hunt him down!"

"Just like the animal he is!" Damion admitted angrily. "Kairee, he tried to kill you. Do you realize what kind of man he is? He doesn't deserve to live. Yes! I plan to hunt him down. I want to see if he can face me when I can fight back."

"But Damion, we have so much to look forward to. He will be like a cornered rat. He might kill you!"

"I'm going after him, Kairee," Damion said, his anger more controlled.

"What's more important, Damion, bringing your family back together, starting new lives . . . or tracking this man and killing him?"

"Don't fight me like this, Kairee. It's something that has to be done. Go back to your home with Lone Wolf. After I check on my father, I'll come to the Bar K."

"You'll come there first, before you go after Talbot?"

He hesitated. "Can't you try to understand? Talbot had pure murder in his heart. He's not the kind to run far. He'll look for a way to get us. This is not the kind of man you can let go, Kairee. If we want to plan a future, then we've got to make sure there's nothing in the past that's unsettled, unfinished. Believe me, Kairee, he's the kind to strike again and it would be just at the time we were happiest, or when we'd let our defenses down."

"Oh, Damion." Kairee threw herself into his arms. "I'm so afraid. If anything happened to you . . ."

"Nothing's going to happen to me, Kairee. I promise I'll be at the Bar K in a matter of hours."

"And promise me you won't let your father's anger push you into going after Talbot first."

"All right, I promise you that too. Now we'd best get moving. It's a long ride for you yet and"—he tried to smile away her fears—"I want you to take better care of yourself. You've been through too much already. My child has to be handled more carefully."

"Please hurry. I won't feel safe until you get back."

"And as soon as I do," he said softly as he bent to kiss her, "I'm sending for the preacher. I'm not going to feel safe until I get you tied to me permanently. Kairee love, don't worry. I'll be there before you know it. I did promise."

"And a Saber's word is his bond. I love you, Damion Saber. Keep that in your mind above anything else."

"I will. But I might need reminding often."

"Just you hurry back to me and I'll remind you as often as you can stand."

"Ummm, now that's a threat I'll have to examine closely."

He kissed her again, crushing her to him and savoring her soft mouth as if he had all the time in the world. Then he held her from him and his eyes warmed her with the promise that there would soon be more.

"Now go with Lone Wolf. And stop worrying."

He watched her mount and saw tears glistening in her eyes, yet he knew she would not cry. He waved as the horses moved away and he could see Kairee turn in the saddle to look back until they were out of sight. Then he mounted and rode toward the Circle S.

Elliot and Southwind had gone to Britt's room together and no one could have been more pleased than Britt was. He had not seen his parents together since he was a young boy. He did not know what event had brought them to this, but if it had been his getting shot, he now believed it had been worth it.

He reached a hand out to his mother, who smiled and took it in both of hers. Tears glistened in her eyes. "My son has been very careless with the life I gave him."

Britt laughed softly. "I promise to be more careful from now on."

She sat down on the bed beside him. "I am grateful to find you recovering so well. I owe a great debt to the Kennedys."

"We all owe a great debt to them, Mother, but I think our friendship is the reward they want."

"This they have."

"Mother . . . where is Kairee?"

"She was with me for awhile, but . . ."

"She is all right?"

"I pray so. I can only explain to you what I know and what Lone Wolf told me before he left to go to them."

"Go to them? Who is *them?*"

"Rest easy, my son, and don't be alarmed. I will explain all that I know," Southwind assured Britt, who had tried to sit up. She placed a hand against his chest to gently push him back against the pillow. "Kairee was with me. She came to speak of the troubles in her mind and the difficulties she felt they could cause. She was filled with pain that she might be the cause of more problems in your family."

"Damion came after her?" Britt asked leadenly.

"Yes, he came after her," Southwind replied. "Britt, it was right that he did so. Kairee loves Damion. She carries his child. But Kairee had already left the village before he came. She planned to come home and tell the truth to everyone."

Now alarm leapt back into Britt's eyes. "But she didn't get home! What—"

"Britt, listen! I am trying to tell you everything." Southwind went on to relate the rest of the story, how Kairee and Damion had been left trapped in the cabin, and how she hoped that at that very moment Lone Wolf was there with horses, food, and warm clothes. "Lone Wolf will bring them here," she assured him, then watched the battle on Britt's face. "Will you greet your brother and Kairee with hatred and jealousy in your heart?" she asked softly. "Or are you the man I have known you to be? It is time, Britt, to make the same peace with Damion you have made with your father. You now have the power to unite us, or destroy us, for all time. You must think of this, my son. You must think that you have everything to gain and a very great deal to lose."

"Britt," Elliot said, "no one knows better than I the foolish mistakes a man can make. I almost destroyed my whole world. I'd hate to see my son do the same thing. You cannot force someone to love you."

"I know that," Britt answered. "I suppose I've known it all along. I just didn't want to believe it. It's not going to be the easiest thing I've ever done. Damn it!" he cursed, momentarily letting his frustrated anger show. "Damion doesn't deserve . . ." He grew silent, then sighed. "I guess that doesn't make much difference, does it? She loves him." He looked at his very worried parents and finally smiled. "I'm not going to cause any trouble. Kairee has the right to her own choices." Then he chuckled. "She's entitled to her mistakes too, and my stubborn, opinionated brother might be more than

446

she bargained for. If she can tame his arrogance, they just might stand a chance of making it. Anyway, I'll be the best uncle this territory has ever seen."

Both Elliot and Southwind were relieved that at least one major problem had been solved.

At this moment there was a knock on the door and Elliot opened it to find Maria holding a tray laden with steaming food. Maria and her mother, Margurite, had proved most helpful to Lucy in the past several days, and during the last hour the three women had been hard at work preparing a hearty meal for the newest arrivals.

Both Elliot and Southwind were amazed by the transformation in Britt as Maria came forward to place the tray before him. It was easy to see that many a pretty face would be attracting Britt, just as the moth seeks the brightness of the flame.

Southwind laughed softly as they left the room, and Elliot bent near to whisper, "Our son has tremendous recuperative powers, doesn't he? I think he'll be just fine."

Southwind smiled up at him. "I think we will all be just fine."

Elliot nodded, grateful beyond words for the chance to redeem his family and his future.

The small and very crowded Kennedy ranch seemed permeated by a sense of expectancy mingled with excitement. All that was lacking was the presence of Damion, Kairee, and Lone Wolf to make the family circle complete.

Britt could finally sit up slightly with pillows propped behind him, and having Lucy and Southwind hovering over him pleased him immensely.

Their temporary contentment would have been shaken, however, had they been aware of the fact that two men had been watching the ranch house all day.

They had spotted Elliot and Jim moving about the yard, chopping wood and caring for the animals, and both men were certain that the news they carried with them as they rode away was going to cause trouble.

They covered the distance between the Kennedy ranch and the Talbot ranch as fast as they could.

Mitchell Talbot was well satisfied with the completion of the plans he had made so long ago.

He sat before a crisply burning fire, his legs crossed and a glass of warmed brandy in his hand. Contemplating the fire, he brought to mind the punishment he had meted out to Elliot Saber and his sons.

His only regret was that he could not explain to Elliot why he had been destroyed. How he would have loved to have faced Elliot and seen him when his son had died in his arms. How he would have enjoyed telling him of Damion's death too, and to have listened to Elliot's cries of agony as he died amid the flames that destroyed his home.

But it would have to be enough to know that the Saber dynasty was finished. There would be no more Sabers. He had seen to that. Now, when the furor had risen to the boiling point, he would calmly point the juggernaut of angry ranchers at the Kennedys. And when all the problems died away, he would be ready to pick up the pieces before anyone else had the opportunity to do it.

He sipped his brandy and smiled again to himself. But the smile turned to a puzzled frown when he heard horses outside and heavy boots on the porch, then a rough, insistent knocking at the door.

He set the brandy aside and rose to go to the door. When he pulled it open, he was surprised to find men he had not expected to see for some time.

"What are you doing here?" he questioned.

"We've got some news for you, news I don't think you're going to like," one stated.

"Come in and close the door. It's damn cold out there."

They entered and stood just inside the door, as if they would have preferred to be anywhere else but there.

"Well," Talbot said impatiently, "what's this news that's so important it's dragged you away from what I ordered you to do?"

The men exchanged glances, then the first man spoke again.

"Elliot Saber . . . he's still alive."

"What the . . . Alive! Damn you two, I told you I wanted him dead. What about his son?"

"We ain't seen the boy, so he must have died when we shot him. But that foreman and the old man . . . they're still alive."

"You burned the Circle *S* to nothing?"

"Yes."

"How did they survive?"

"We don't know. It was impossible to live through that blaze."

"Impossible . . . but they did. Where are they now?"

Again the men exchanged looks that indicated they were both tense and very nervous. They cleared their throats, but the same man spoke again.

"They're staying with the Kennedys."

Talbot glared at them in furious speechlessness. He struggled for the words to match his anger and disbelief.

"Kennedys!" he exploded. "How the hell did this miraculous resurrection of the supposed-to-be-dead come about? How did you idiots let him slip through your fingers?"

"We don't know. The place was an inferno when we left. Nobody could have survived that and then the storm that came after."

"Well, it's pretty obvious somebody did survive. Just as it's pretty obvious we are forced to the wall. Now we have to do something about it."

"What are we going to do?"

"First you two are going to round up a couple of the boys. Send them over to the Circle *S* and see if there's anything they can find out. We are going over to the Kennedy place and see just how we are going to correct your bit of stupidity."

They nodded, quite unwilling to push his anger any further.

Just over an hour later two men left the ranch, riding in the direction of the Circle *S*. A little later Talbot and his two unexpected visitors rode toward the Bar *K*.

Kairee was so relieved to see home that she did not hesitate to ride quickly toward it. Lone Wolf understood and did nothing to restrain her.

Near the porch she dismounted quickly and ran up the steps to throw open the door.

There was a cry of pleasure from Lucy, accompanied by those of the shocked men. Gregg ran to Kairee and caught her up in his arms, laughing. He was followed by her father, who held her close.

Everybody seemed to be laughing and talking at once, and it was some time before they could settle down to logical questions and answers.

"Kairee, you're all right?" Lucy queried.

"I'm fine, Lucy."

"You're not hurt, girl?" Stephen demanded.

"No, Pa, really, I'm fine." Her attention then was drawn to the fact that both Elliot Saber and Southwind were there.

"Kairee," Elliot asked quickly, "has Damion been with you?"

Before Kairee could answer, Lone Wolf appeared

beside her. "Damion has not been harmed. He and Kairee were trapped by the storm. Had I not been wounded, I might have gotten help to them sooner, but I don't think I could have gotten them from the cabin to here. They were safe in the cabin, at least as safe as they could have been considering the circumstances." He laughed.

"You two had best do some explaining," Stephen declared. "Wounded, trapped in a cabin—just what has been going on with you?"

"And," Southwind repeated, "where is Damion now?"

"I think I had better start from the time I left here so you'll understand," Kairee began. "First, Damion has no idea his father is here. Lone Wolf told him the Circle S was to be attacked. Damion has been so worried about you," she said to Elliot, then her eyes skimmed the room. "And his brother," she added softly. Her heart began to pound furiously. "Britt . . . where is Britt?" Her eyes fled back to Elliot and they were filled with fear. "He's not . . . ?"

"No," Elliot said, calming her fears, "he's not dead. In fact he is in Lucy's room. He has been wounded though."

"Tell me what happened."

"First, tell us, please, where Damion is," Southwind begged.

"He . . . he has gone back to the Circle S . . . to explain to his father"—her eyes held Elliot's—"about us. He was afraid," she added softly, "that seeing me before he had a chance to . . . to explain so many things might . . . might upset you."

"There is nothing left to tell us about you and Damion," Elliot told her with a smile. "I couldn't agree more with my eldest son's taste in women. It will be a pleasure to have you as part of the family, Kairee Kennedy . . . or can I say Kairee Saber one day soon?"

"I . . . I don't understand."

"Why I am welcoming you to the family?" Elliot chuckled.

"No. Why you're both here. Why Britt is here. Just what has happened?"

"The Circle S has been totally destroyed," Elliot said quietly. "Burned to the ground. Burned by the same men who shot Britt and left him for dead. Left him in my arms while they tried to burn us alive in the house. I think it was only the storm that saved us."

"Britt was—"

"Almost killed," Elliot finished.

"Where is he?"

"He's in my room, Kairee," Lucy offered.

Kairee turned to Lone Wolf. "Please stay, Lone Wolf. You and your men are in need of sleep and food. Stay for awhile."

Lone Wolf nodded his agreement and Kairee started for Lucy's room. Just before she opened the door, Elliot called to her. She turned and waited while he walked to stand close to her.

"Kairee, I think we should have a little talk before you go in to see Britt."

"Talk?" she questioned and he could see her old defenses rise.

"Not an angry talk, Kairee," he said gently.

"Just what kind of talk do you have in mind?"

"An honest one. I owe you one. I just want you to know that I couldn't be more pleased about you and Damion . . . or more sorry that it had to happen like it did. I don't know if I can really tell you why . . ."

"You don't have to. Damion already has."

"He's told you about—"

"Emma, the woman I look so much like. I'm sorry too. I know it must be hard for you."

"No, it's opened a door that had been locked for

452

years. And when you opened it for me, my two sons had their first chance to walk in."

"Your two sons?" Her voice caught. "Britt . . . is he as . . . forgiving?"

"He's got nothing to forgive. You love Damion. He understands that."

"Does he?" she asked hopefully. "The last thing I wanted was to hurt Britt."

"Everything is going to change, Kairee. When Damion gets back, we'll all talk together. We couldn't do that before. There was too much"—he shrugged—"too much heartache to be mended. But I think, my girl, that you've done a hell of a good job of mending."

"Thank you." She smiled through tears that made her eyes glow like gray crystals.

He reached a large, callused hand to rest against her cheek. "Can you kiss an old fool who's learned a lesson he'll never forget?" he asked softly.

She choked back her sobs and stood on tiptoe to kiss him. He hugged her to him for a moment, then released her.

Kairee turned back to the closed door. With a hesitant hand, she turned the knob and opened it.

Once inside, she closed the door behind her and leaned against it, her eyes sweeping across the room to lock with Britt's.

Britt gazed at her, taking the moment to capture her beauty in his mind. Then he smiled and extended his hand to her.

"Come over here and give me a kiss before you become my sister-in-law and Damion shoots me for trying."

With a soft laugh Kairee walked across the room and sat on the bed. Then she bent to kiss him.

"Now," he said softly, "just what are you planning to name my nephew?"

Chapter 36

Damion rode with determination, making slow but very steady progress. He went over and over in his mind the words he intended to say to his father. He knew that Britt was more than capable of running the Circle S well, and it was one of the first arguments he meant to use. Of course, he told himself with a smile, it certainly was not the only argument he had in his bag.

This was one time he intended to face his father down, even if he had to stand toe to toe with him for a week.

He wondered who he would have the bigger battle with, his father or Britt. He had tangled physically with Britt, for the last time. He knew Britt was in love with Kairee, but he ignored that fact now. Kairee was his and he meant to keep it that way.

"Oh well," he said aloud with a sigh, "let's just cross our bridges when we get to them."

He was not too far from the Circle S when he saw other riders approaching. They were Circle S hands and he was mildly surprised to see them this close to the ranch house. Usually the Circle S riders roamed farther out, using line shacks strategically placed for just such occasions as the storm.

He reined his horse to a halt and waited until the riders neared him.

"You boys roaming a little close to home, aren't you?" He smiled, but his smile wasn't returned. He looked into their closed faces and something within him stirred in vague apprehension.

"Damion, look . . . ah . . . something pretty bad has happened. We was just on the hunt for someone to . . . well, to see. . . ."

"What?" Damion asked quietly, almost afraid to hear the answer. "My father . . . Britt? What the hell happened?"

"We really don't rightly know, and it's hard to say it to you. Damion, you've got to come and see . . . you've got to see for yourself."

Damion's heart had begun to pound fiercely and he was as close to real fear as he had ever been. He knew something had to be drastically wrong to make these strong, forceful men so pale and somber.

Could it be that fate had only intended to give him one taste of happiness before giving him a crushing blow to match?

He kicked his horse into motion, as the rest did, and they rode together. The closer they got to the ranch, the more grim Damion became.

He might have been prepared for any kind of problem, but not the total, blackened destruction that lay before him.

His mind burned with only one thought: were his father and brother alive, or were they lying amid the smoldering ruins? He could not bear the thought.

While he still had the courage, he moved toward the huge pile of charred debris and dismounted.

The others remained in their saddles, watching him closely, as he slowly walked toward what had once been his home.

Damion walked toward the remains slowly, still unable to accept what he was seeing. He tried to keep his mind from focusing on the brutal possibility that his father and his brother were lying beneath the debris.

What could have caused such a tragedy? he wondered, his mind numbed by shock.

Just as he was about to reach the area that had been the porch, his boot struck an object he at first thought was just another part of the house. But when he looked down, the stunning realization struck him with such force that for a moment he could hardly believe it. It was an extinguished, carefully made torch. There was no doubt now. What had happened here had been done deliberately.

At the same moment his mind was grasping this thought, another struck with the same force. If it had been set deliberately, it had been done to destroy those who were inside. To make this horror more real, the name of the perpetrator leapt into his mind . . . Mitchell Talbot had incinerated his family, maybe alive! Hatred roiled within him.

Had he not heard Talbot say he meant to destroy the Sabers? He remembered the words as if Talbot were speaking them now: ". . . to destroy your father and his dreams . . . the dreams that destroyed lives."

If anyone had survived the fire, he could not have gotten far from the disaster in the storm. Damion turned to the riders.

"You've searched?"

"Everywhere. There's no sign of Jim or your . . . of either of them."

"Split up," Damion ordered roughly. "Half of you make another search. Make a big swing around the area. The rest of you help me." He turned back to the destroyed house, his expression bleak and yet determined. "We'll dig . . . we'll dig until we're sure." His voice died to a ragged whisper. "I've got to find them . . . I've got to be sure."

He began to tear at the debris with his hands, ripping at burnt wood, throwing pieces aside, each time fearing what he might find beneath, yet each time relieved to see only more rubble. As he tore at the remains, he prayed. And he remembered.

Lone Wolf had said that Talbot had sent men to attack the Circle *S*, but Damion's mind could hardly grasp the cold, merciless thing that must have occurred here.

Damion groaned softly as more of Talbot's words came to him: "There is no one now to come and find you. . . ."

"Pa . . ." he whispered softly. "Britt." The pain of such a loss cut through him like a knife. Never having had the chance to make peace with his brother or to talk again with his father, he felt the ache of guilt that much more. The weight of it nearly crushed the breath from him.

He tore at the blackened wood until his hands bled, and the men with him worked as fiercely as he did.

Finally they could do no more. The inevitable had to be faced.

He felt tears sting his eyes, tears he could no longer control. He wept unashamedly for a past he could not change and a future that would be forever altered.

Then the tears slowly dried. The hard lump of pain within him began to glow with his fierce anger. It grew and grew into a white-hot rage that filled him until his breath came in ragged gasps and his mind could grasp only one thing. Mitchell Talbot had struck at him and had nearly dealt him a mortal blow.

Now it was his time to strike back, and he would make sure he struck so hard that Talbot would be unable to harm anyone ever again.

He walked back to his horse, mounted, then turned to look at the silent men who surrounded him.

"Ride to the Kennedy place. Talbot and his men are still loose and might do the same to them. I want you to defend the place until I can get there."

457

"Where are you going, Damion?"

"I'm going to find, and kill, the black-hearte[d] bastard responsible for this. I'll come back to the Bar as soon as I can."

"Let some of us ride with you," one protested.

"No. It's likely he'll send his men against th[e] Kennedys and be coward enough to remain at hom[e] and wait to hear word about the lives he's twisted. He[']s crazy, and I'm going to corner this animal in his de[n] and rid the world of the rotten thing he is. You get t[o] the Kennedys'. If he's going to strike there, they'll nee[d] all the help they can get. There's only four men, tw[o] women, and a little girl. You boys make sure they sta[y] safe until I get there. And maybe Lone Wolf and som[e] of his men might be there too."

"All right, Damion. But at least one of us should rid[e] with you."

Damion's eyes were as cold as the frigid blu[e] Wyoming sky. "Don't worry, I have enough hate in m[e] to handle Mitchell Talbot. I'm going to give him a tast[e] of his own medicine. I'm going to wipe him and hi[s] place from the face of the earth. Now get riding."

The look on his face was enough to keep any furthe[r] protestations from their lips. In grim silence the[y] turned their horses toward the Bar K and rode awa[y.]

Damion watched until they disappeared, then he to[o] turned his face away from the destruction about him[.] Death lingered in his eyes as he rode toward Mitchel[l] Talbot's ranch.

Kairee lifted the tray of food from the table[,] intending to carry it to Britt for his dinner. There wa[s] confusion in the very crowded house, but despite he[r] constant worry about Damion's whereabouts at th[e] moment and how soon he would return, Kairee felt th[e] sense of closeness that was slowly evolving.

Elliot and Southwind found a great deal to talk about, as did Lone Wolf and Stephen. The men with Lone Wolf occupied the barn and Cassie was ecstatic about the number of people who seemed pleased to cater to her childish enthusiasm.

Britt and Kairee had had a great deal of time to talk and had stabilized their relationship on a comfortable plane of warm affection.

If Britt felt the tug of stronger emotions, only Elliot and Southwind suspected it. He was working hard at rebuilding his life and knew jealousy had no place in it.

Kairee took the tray of food to Britt's room to find him sitting up in bed and Cassie seated cross-legged at the foot. Both were laughing and Kairee could read the dawning of hero worship in Cassie's wide eyes.

"Making more conquests, Britt?" Kairee laughed. "You've already gotten Maria involved in seeing to your every comfort."

"Cassie and I are special friends, Kairee," Britt replied. "She's been able to explain Kairee Kennedy a little better too. From her point of view, I think you're a combination of Queen Victoria, Cleopatra, and Mona Lisa."

"She's a little prejudiced," Kairee retorted.

"Well, come to think of it"—he grinned—"I think you come pretty close."

"Flatterer! I can see why you've been so successful. You have so much charm it's almost sinful."

"I also have an empty stomach, woman," he declared, denying the words he wanted to say. "Are you trying to starve me?"

"Hardly," Kairee said dryly. "You eat like the proverbial horse."

"I need to regain my energy so I can dance at your wedding."

Kairee's smile faded as she set the tray before Britt. "I wish I knew where Damion was now . . . or what he's doing."

459

"Don't worry, Kairee, Damion is not going to stay away from you for too long." He chuckled evilly. "He's smart enough to know that if he doesn't claim you there're others around who would. He'll be back soon."

"You go ahead and eat. I want you to dance at my wedding, so I guess I have to get you up out of that bed first. . . . I hope you're right, Britt. I'll pray that it is so."

Britt nodded and attacked the food with his usual gusto. Kairee left him with a still-chattering Cassie and returned to the kitchen. Despite Britt's words, she found it hard to fight the smothering mood that hung over her. She had not been able to sleep since Damion had left her, nor had she eaten much. The unwelcome thought kept nagging at her that there was something very wrong.

Her mood darkened as the day progressed, and Lucy, who had sensed it from its inception and had watched it grow, felt a need to try to do something to alleviate it.

It was just dusk and the day's work was done as Lucy approached Kairee.

"Kairee, the night is so pretty. Would you like to walk with me? We could walk up to the stand of pines on the hill. Even with all the snow, it seems to have gotten warmer."

"Sounds fine." Kairee smiled. "I could use a little air. I love everyone here, but it is rather crowded.

After explaining where they were going and smiling at the words of caution from almost everyone, they took their coats from the hooks behind the door, drew on heavy boots, and left the house.

The air was crisp, but not as breathlessly cold as it had been. They walked for a few minutes in silence, hearing nothing but the crunchy squeak of packed snow beneath their feet.

Kairee inhaled deeply, closing her eyes for a second to draw in the comfort of silence.

"It's going to be a lovely night," Lucy observed. "Just look at the moon. It's full already."

"It's just about perfect."

"If only Damion were here," Lucy concluded.

"I wish he were."

"You've been so quiet and nervous, Kairee. What's wrong?"

"I don't know." Kairee laughed. "The foolish moods of a pregnant lady, I guess. I just wish Damion would come. I can't shake this feeling that something's going to happen."

"Good heavens, what more could happen? We know now who started all the trouble and we can protect ourselves. Talbot will be ruined in this valley when the other ranchers learn he's been the rustler all along."

"I know. It's just that . . . I don't know." Kairee laughed.

"Anyway, Kairee, what have you decided to name the baby?" Lucy asked brightly, trying to change the mood.

"I've thought of a lot of names, but I'd like to talk to Damion about it. We've never really had the chance to discuss the baby at all."

"Well, what names are you thinking of?"

"Elliot Stephen, if it's a boy, and Emma Elizabeth, if it's a girl."

"Kairee, Pa and Elliot would be very pleased at that, and I wouldn't be surprised if Damion was too. I'm just so sure everything is going to be fine for us all once the baby comes."

"We'll have to stay in this cabin until spring, when we can build," Kairee observed.

"Talk of crowded!" Lucy laughed. "I'll bet by spring we're all going to enjoy getting out."

"I wouldn't be surprised."

"Of course we have to have some sort of party for the wedding."

"I think we could use a party right now. As soon as Damion gets back, we'll bake some goodies and fix a big celebration meal."

Everything in Kairee's mind now hinged on the moment of Damion's return.

They had reached the shelter of the trees now and stood for a few moments, reluctant to return to the clamor of the overcrowded house.

The shadows had darkened, and the area in which they stood sheltered from the moonlight brought into relief the moon-bathed snow and the quiet house. The glow of light from the windows reflected on the white landscape, exuding a sense of welcoming warmth.

Both women were temporarily captivated by it, captivated to the extent that neither heard or sensed the dark forms that moved in behind them.

At the moment of awareness it was already too late, for rough hands closed over their mouths and hard arms gripped them in iron holds that all their struggling could not break.

Talbot and the men with him had tied their horses in the shadowy depths of the trees and had been watching the Kennedy house for some time.

Talbot had cursed angrily under his breath when his eyes had gleamed with a maddened look that shook his companions when he saw Elliot and Jim moving about.

"Damn you, bastard! You have the nine lives of a cat. Well, you may have gotten away from the fire, but this time you'll have no place to run to. This time we'll finish the job."

"You want us to go down and—"

"No, there's not enough of you."

"Shall we go round up the rest of the boys?"

"Soon, but not quite yet," Talbot said quietly, his eyes still on the house. "We'll stay here for now. They'll make a mistake, and when they do we'll be here to take advantage of it."

He did not turn to see whether or not they agreed with him but kept his eyes on the house as the shadows lengthened and light began to glow from the windows.

Exasperated and filled with a fury that made him burn as if he had a fever, Talbot watched, and saw the mistake.

The two women came out of the house and the sound of their laughter floated up on the crisp, clear night air to the man who smiled with the feral grimace of the predatory wolf.

He motioned to his men, who took the horses deeper into the trees, then returned to him. They watched the women walk closer and closer.

For a moment Talbot could not believe that it was Kairee moving toward him. Kairee Kennedy, the woman he had left with no food and no means of escape, had cheated death.

When he realized the truth of this, he also realized that Damion had to be alive too. All his plans had failed.

"How the hell did they get out?" he muttered.

"Boss—"

"Shh. Move back into the shadows. The foolish girl is walking right to us. I want them both taken. No sound! Do you understand? One noise and everybody in the house will be up here. Make it quick and quiet."

The men melted into the shadows in absolute silence. Talbot stood behind a tree in a pool of darkness, and as Kairee and Lucy approached, he heard their conversation and the demented anger in him roiled like a cauldron of witch's brew.

"Emma . . ." he heard Kairee say. Kairee and Damion were expecting a child. "Emma." The name echoed in his mind. No! No! He would not allow a child of Damion Saber's to be named Emma.

The women stood talking softly and Talbot's lips drew back back from his teeth in an animal snarl. They planned a party, a celebration.

Well, he had no intention of letting their celebration come to pass.

He made a slight motion with his hands and his men began to move stealthily toward the unsuspecting women.

It took only a moment's silent struggle and the women were dragged to face Mitchell Talbot.

Kairee recognized Talbot immediately and the hand over her mouth muffled her angry yet frightened response as she remembered his bloodthirsty and coldhearted abandonment of Damion and her in the cabin where he had hoped they would die.

Lucy watched, shaking with fear. She could read the response in Kairee's face.

"So, Kairee Kennedy"—Talbot's voice was barely controlled—"I see you have made a miraculous escape from your little . . . love nest. I take it Damion escaped with you."

Kairee's eyes flashed her defiance and she stood frigidly still. Talbot chuckled. "It does not matter. By the time he knows you are gone, it will be too late anyhow."

Talbot walked slowly to Lucy, whose eyes grew wide with her terror. He reached out and gripped her hair roughly, drawing a moaning sound from Lucy. Even more roughly, he tightened his grip and shook her slightly. Then he smiled. "I want you to take a message back to Elliot Saber and his son Damion. Tell them I've taken Kairee with me. I am going to take her to a very safe place. Then I'll send a message where they can meet me. Tell them they had better come—the two of them—or they will never see her alive again. Remind Elliot Saber that I killed his Indian son and I will kill Kairee if he does not follow my instructions. Bringing anyone else other than Damion with him would be a very serious mistake."

He walked to Kairee, gripped her arm, and withdrew his gun from its holster, placing the barrel next to her temple. Again he smiled. "Let her go," he told the man who held Lucy. "But one sound from you and she dies before your eyes. You understand me?"

Lucy nodded and she was suddenly released. For a moment she felt so weak she thought she might fall.

"Please," Lucy whispered, "let her go."

Talbot gave the gun and Kairee into the hands of one of his men. Then he walked to Lucy. Suddenly his hand shot out and struck her so hard she tumbled backward. He reached down to grip her and drag her to her feet. Blood flowed from the corner of her mouth and her nose and her eyes filled with tears. Calmly and deliberately he struck her again and let her slip to the ground.

Again he dragged her to her feet. Kairee struggled but could not get to Lucy, and the gun remained pressed to her temple.

Again Talbot struck Lucy, and again and again until she whimpered and sagged in his hold.

"Now," Talbot said softly, "take the evidence back to Elliot Saber and his son. Tell them I'll say when and where to meet me . . . alone, or Kairee will suffer at my hands much more than you have."

He thrust Lucy from him and she slipped to the ground. Then slowly she rose to her feet. Her eyes were nearly blinded by tears as she looked at Kairee. Her face was smeared with blood, but she stood resolutely, then she started back to the house as fast as she could move.

She slipped and slid going down the hill and when she reached the door of the house she threw herself against it, bursting into the room.

Everyone in the room stared at her in total shock for a moment. Then Gregg gave a cry of fury and ran to her in time to catch her in his arms as she collapsed.

Chapter 37

Damion had held his horse motionless as he sat looking down at Mitchell Talbot's ranch. His narrowed eyes did not miss the fact that no one seemed to be around at all. There was no movement near the corrals except for a few horses. There was no smoke coming from the chimney.

But Damion walked his horse toward it slowly, suspicious of the silence. Near the barn he dismounted. He slid the rifle he had taken from one of the Circle *S* riders out of the sheath on his saddle and checked to make sure it was loaded. He had also acquired a gun, and now he took it from his holster to check it.

Replacing the gun in his holster and holding the rifle in hand, he began to move slowly toward the house.

Closer and closer he moved, prepared for any kind of surprise. But still the ranch was uncommonly silent.

When he came to the porch, he stood again and listened. No sound came from the house. He walked up onto the porch and crossed it to the door. He put his hand on the door handle and tried it. It was locked.

Sure now that no one was home at all, he could not fight the sensation of danger. The hair on the back of his neck prickled and every sense he had tingled a warning. But a warning of what? There was no one around.

His anger at Talbot was still the predominant emotion that drove him. He had to find answers, and something that might give him a clue to where Talbot might be.

He inhaled in an effort to keep control of his frustrations, but he failed. With a well-aimed boot, he kicked the locked door and it slammed open.

He waited . . . no sound. Then he walked inside and pushed the door shut. Standing inside Mitchell Talbot's house, Damion was struck again by the eerie sensation of overwhelming danger.

Holding the rifle ready, he moved slowly. The house itself was not as large as the Circle *S*. It was long and low. The main room was about fifteen feet in length and boasted a huge fireplace, which was directly ahead of Damion as he entered. There was a door on each side of the room and he quickly chose one and crossed to it. He turned the handle and swung the door open to find a rather spartan bedroom. It contained only a bed with a red and white quilt and a small chest of drawers. It was a room that gave no indication of the identity of the occupant. He looked through the room carefully but found no clue as to the person who slept in it.

He left the room and walked across the main room to the other door. When he swung this door open, the same warning sensations shrieked at him.

This room was so totally different from the others that he found it hard to believe. Cautiously he walked into a room that boasted comfort. There was a large brass bed, polished to a gleaming finish. A large chest sat at its foot, with a brilliant quilt folded on it. To Damion's amazement, the floor was almost completely covered by a large oval rug.

There were oil lamps on the two dressers in the room

and bright curtains hung on the windows. The walls were papered with a small pink rose design, which Damion considered quite unique, but even more so were the framed pictures hanging on the walls and the small, delicate figurines sitting on little wooden shelves.

Then the subtle realization came to him. This was not a man's room—it was a woman's.

But Talbot had lived here alone. Everyone knew that. Then why such a feminine touch?

He moved further into the room, first to examine the pictures on the walls. They were of people he did not know, or at least it seemed so at first glance.

A small oval portrait hung over a dresser, a portrait of a woman. Damion felt a tingle of recognition, yet he did not know her. She displayed so many of Kairee's features.

He moved to the dressers and examined the drawers. All of them were empty.

He returned to the main room, but still the unnamed woman plagued him.

He walked to the large, comfortable chairs before the fireplace. Beside one was a small table, on which rested a less-than-half-full bottle of brandy and a glass that still contained some.

He would wait. Talbot could not be too far away, and now that Damion knew Kairee was safe and that his family was beyond any more damage, he had all the patience of any predatory animal waiting to kill its prey.

It was then he noticed the small black book that lay on the floor next to the chair. He laid the rifle across the small table so it would be near his hand and picked up the book.

It was only six inches in length, about five in width, and three in depth. He flipped open the front page and read the name scrolled elaborately on the first page:

Talbot Mitchell.

Again he turned a page and realized he was reading a diary. For a moment his instinct was to close it, but he realized Talbot Mitchell, or Mitchell Talbot, as he now called himself, had given up his right to privacy a long time ago.

He turned to the first written page and began to read. After a few pages, a soft sound of shock broke the silence.

He kept reading now, involved in a story he found almost unbelievable. He reached the center of the book and when he turned the page, he found two pictures lying face to face.

He separated them and this time the sound he made was sharper. He looked first into the eyes of a young man he supposed might be the Richard Mitchell about whom he had been reading. But it was the other picture that brought the shock. He looked once more into the gray eyes of Emma Martin and saw the smile of Kairee Kennedy.

Then he had another thought. He took the two pictures to the bedroom and held them near the girl whose portrait hung on the wall. Now he knew why she had drawn his attention. She looked enough like Emma and Kairee to be part of their family.

He was lost in the puzzle but felt the diary might contain more answers. He returned to the main room and set the pictures aside while he took up the diary to finish reading.

He read without movement, forgetting the brandy, or even the reason he was here as he learned of an old tragedy that was being finished many years after it had begun.

Finally he put the finished diary aside. He thought a long time about the forces that brought people together and tore them apart.

He thought of how easily Talbot could have

destroyed them all, and he thought of the years of torment that had twisted Talbot's mind and had created his demented condition. He was not quite sure how he would have handled such a thing, for he acknowledged the murderous condition he himself was in at the moment.

He stood up and walked to the door, carrying the rifle with him to prevent surprises. He realized then that the house was well chilled. Talbot had to have been gone for some time. He would come back soon.

Going back outside, he took his horse into the barn to keep it out of sight. Then he returned to the house, took up the bottle of brandy, and drank. Once again he sat back to wait.

Gregg held Lucy close while he bathed her cut lips and bruised cheeks with cool water. She struggled against his ministrations as she had since she had first returned. It had been a battle because of her condition, and the shock had taken their minds from Kairee.

"Kairee," she had gasped, but her bruised mouth had muffled the name. Now she pushed people away from her. "Don't! No! They've taken Kairee."

"Who?" Elliot and Stephen demanded in unison. "Who's taken her?"

"Talbot," Lucy sobbed. "We just walked to the trees and we were talking . . ."

"Lucy, calm down," Gregg demanded in the face of her hysteria. "Maria, get some more water." Gregg's cold fury was written in his eyes, but his face was controlled and his hands were gentle. "Let me help you," he said softly. He pulled her into his arms and held her until her sobs ceased and her trembling body regained some fragile control. Then he washed her face clean of blood. "Who did this, Lucy?"

"Mitchell Talbot. Kairee and I didn't know anyone

was there. We were just talking and the next thing we knew they had grabbed us and were dragging us back into the trees. Gregg," she cried, "he's taken Kairee away."

"Away where?"

"I don't know where!"

"He wants something, doesn't he, Lucy?" Elliot asked quietly. "What did he say to you, Lucy?"

"He . . . he wanted me to deliver a message to you . . . and your son."

"Son?"

"I don't think he knows Britt is here. I think . . . he wants to kill you and Damion."

"I know." Elliot smiled. "Tell me, child, what did he say?"

Lucy repeated word for word what Talbot had forced into her memory. Elliot did not interrupt, and when she was finished all eyes turned to Elliot.

"He wants to wipe out all the Sabers. I wish to God I knew where Damion was right now. But here or not, I wouldn't allow him to go. This man will have to face me. He's been too much of a coward to do that or he wouldn't have nipped at me piece by piece and played this little game. Well, I've finally realized who he is and what he wants, and I'm ready to make an end to all this."

"You can't go back there. He'll be waiting for you with God knows how many men," Gregg protested.

"No, Mr. Saber," Lucy pleaded, "don't go. He will kill you!"

Before Elliot could answer, the sound of approaching horses silenced everyone. It did not seem logical that it would be Talbot's men, but no one present had any idea who else it could be.

Elliot was first to the door and he smiled when he went out and saw his own men dismounting before the house.

"I'm glad to see you boys. How did you know where we were?"

The men stopped short and gazed at him in absolute shock. To them it seemed they were looking at the resurrected dead. Elliot laughed. "No, boys. They can burn a house, but I'll be damned if they can wipe out the Sabers that easily. Come on in. We have to talk and we've got some work to do."

Still awed by his presence, they followed him into the house.

"Now, how come you boys are here?"

"Damion sent us."

"Damion? Where is he?" Elliot demanded.

"Well . . . he came to the ruins of the house and was real shaken up. You see, Boss, he thought you and Britt was under all that mess. He started diggin' with his hands until he couldn't do no more. Then he went off to Talbot's place . . . to find him and to kill him."

"God, the boy thinks we're dead."

"Yeah," one of the men agreed, "and he was real shook. I ain't never seen Damion like that. He was set on murder. If he catches up with Talbot, he's going—"

"He's going to get himself killed. Does he think Talbot is going to fight fair? Lord, it's come to murder . . . and it's my fault." Elliot's voice died.

"Your fault?" Stephen questioned quietly.

Elliot turned to face Stephen and the two men regarded each other for a moment. Stephen held Elliot's eyes. "It's a long, hard story, and I have to tell it to the people hurt by it first. To Damion and Britt. I never thought it would come to this. I guess I've never given any thought to what I've done to others' lives until now . . . now, when it might be too late. Stephen, I won't let him hurt Kairee anymore. And believe me"—his voice grew soft—"I'll give my life for Damion's if I have to."

472

"You're going back to your ranch and meet him alone?"

"I have to."

"No!" Gregg said. "There has to be a better way. Talbot said he'd send a message where and when to meet him. Let's wait until it comes. If we all go wandering all over the countryside, we'll be playing into his hands. God damn it! If you think I'm going to let a bastard like that beat my wife half to death, then just stand here while you go chasing him, you're crazy. If you want to do something right for a change, Mr. Saber, why the hell don't you wait until he tells you where to go. Then we'll find a way to kill him—but I'm going too."

"And Kairee?" Elliot questioned.

"Kairee's my sister. I love her. That's why I want to know where we meet. That's why I go. That man has ruined enough lives. If it takes all of us to unite to rid ourselves of him, then we damn well better unite, because divided we fall."

Elliot and Stephen exchanged a look of understanding that was beyond what the others saw. Then Elliot turned again to Gregg.

"Take care of Lucy. We'll wait for word from him and when it comes we'll make plans on how we're going to move. Maybe Damion will come here before he finds Talbot."

Gregg nodded and turned to lift Lucy in his arms and carry her to the small cot she had slept on since Britt had come.

Lucy wept softly, clinging to Gregg as he lay beside her to comfort her.

"Oh, Gregg," she whispered, "he . . . he is so cold and unfeeling. He is so heartless. Gregg, do you think he will hurt Kairee? She was so frightened. I don't think

I'll ever forget the look in her eyes when he held that gun to her head."

"Stop it, Lucy. That does no good. We have to wait, and he knows it. He wants us to fall apart. We won't be any good to Kairee if we do that. He won't hurt her," Gregg added, hoping he sounded more confident than he felt.

"Gregg, do you think he went back to his own ranch?" Lucy asked hopefully. "We could go there! Elliot, you, and his men. . . ."

"And as soon as they see us coming, they kill Kairee. Most likely he didn't go there. He knows we'd think of that. No. We wait, as patiently and hopefully as we can . . . and we pray."

"Gregg."

"What?"

"He . . . he must know Kairee is pregnant. He must have been close enough to hear us talking. We"—she choked on her tears—"we were naming the baby."

"Stop it, Lucy. Now stop it!"

"I can't! I can't forget her face. I can't stop hearing her say she was upset and worried about when Damion would come. It was as if she knew something terrible was going to happen."

"Lucy, you can't go on like this. Cassie is right here with Maria. She's scared to death now and you're going to make it worse. Lucy, you have always had ten times more courage than any woman I've ever known. You've got to use it now. We have to show Cassie you're all right. Do you understand me, love?"

Her eyes were filled with tears and she clung to him, but he could feel her control returning.

"All right, Gregg," she whispered. "Let's go and take care of our baby."

The silence within the Talbot ranch house was so

deep it was oppressive. It allowed Damion's mind to throb with the need to see Talbot in the rifle sight.

He had sat for a long time, until his nerves had been stretched to the breaking point. Then he had risen to pace the floor.

A million reasons crossed his mind as to why Talbot had not returned home. He would feel extremely secure in thinking he had killed all the Sabers.

He stopped pacing. Maybe he had been wrong. If Talbot believed all the Sabers were dead, maybe he intended to vent his particular brand of hatred on the Kennedys next . . . on Kairee.

Of course, he thought. The reason Talbot had not returned to his ranch might very well be that he was gathering his men together to spread his vengeance to the Kennedys. And he had sent Kairee home.

He was torn. It was agony for him to think of the deaths of his father and brother, and all the good people who must have died with them; Jim, Maria, Margurite. He was so bitter he could feel it burning inside like a live coal. He needed revenge. He needed to stay and wait for Talbot. But then he thought of the danger he might have sent Kairee into and what Talbot might be able to do to the Kennedys. There would only be Gregg and Stephen to defend them, unless his men reached them in time to help.

Again he was forced to make a choice. Which came first, the brutal need to eliminate the one who had hurt him so badly and had robbed him of everything, or the need to assure himself that Kairee was safe?

He did not debate long before, with a muttered curse, he grabbed up his rifle and, almost intuitively, the small black diary and the pictures it contained.

He left the house and almost ran across the yard to the barn. In minutes he was headed toward the Kennedy ranch and, he hoped, Kairee.

Chapter 38

Kairee struggled, but her efforts were ineffectual as she was placed in front of Talbot on his saddle and felt his arm go about her waist. He chuckled, but his hold was brutal.

"Go ahead, struggle. The challenge of taming you might be as pleasant as it was with your sister-in-law. You see, no one will know if I kill you or not. They will still ride out to get you . . . and right into my path. You see, they'd like the whole world to think they're such noble, fine men. Maybe, now that I have you to myself for awhile, I'll tell you a story that might change your way of thinking."

"I don't want to hear what you've got to say and I won't believe anything you tell me."

"Oh, my sweet Kairee, I'll bet you will. I'll just bet you will."

"I can't understand such hatred. What in God's name could anyone do to provoke such a brutal response?"

"I told you so. You're already interested."

"You are unbelievable!"

"I have every right to do what I'm doing."

"A right to kill? No one has a right to kill."

"Does that include the Sabers?"

"Of course. But I know them. Damion would not kill

anyone. He is a kind and sensitive man, and Britt could never kill."

"The sins of the father are visited on the sons," Talbot responded coldly, "and on any who choose to be part of them."

"The sins of the fathers," Kairee repeated. "You believe children should be blamed for what their fathers do?"

"In this case destroying every Saber will be destroying a blot . . . a disease of humanity."

The words left Kairee speechless for a moment as the terrible truth came to her. He would draw Elliot and Damion here and kill them. Then he would turn on her, for he knew she was carrying Damion's child and he would not let another Saber live.

She closed her eyes and tried to choke back the lump of fear that nearly made her cry out. She refused to give Talbot the satisfaction of knowing her terror.

But Talbot did know, and the thought excited him.

They arrived at the ranch after dark, and Talbot relentlessly dragged Kairee with him into the cold, lightless house while the men took care of the horses.

He pushed her into a chair and she remained still only because she could not see and did not dare move about for fear of increasing Talbot's antagonism.

She heard Talbot moving about and soon the room glowed with the mellow gold light of oil lamps.

She found herself seated before a large fireplace that contained the dead ashes of a once large fire.

Talbot stood by a small table where he had lit the lamp, then turned to face her.

He was smiling, but Kairee could see his deadly cold eyes as he moved toward her. She stiffened and gripped the arms of the chair, prepared to defend herself and the unborn child she carried. No matter what Talbot had in mind, she was not going to let harm come to her child.

But Talbot's smile froze, then disintegrated. She stared at him in total amazement as his features contorted into profound shock.

He raced to the chair and before Kairee could move to defend herself, he gripped her arm and dragged her from the chair to thrust her aside.

Her startled gasp was unheard by him as he tore at the chair, then tipped it over and gazed around wildly. She was convinced the man had gone totally insane.

"What are you doing?" she cried.

"It's gone!" he gasped frantically. "It can't be gone! It can't be gone."

"What? What is gone?"

Talbot raced to the door and jerked it open. As he screamed for his men, Kairee could hear an emotion in his voice she had never heard before, and it terrified her more than anything else he had done.

Several men ran into the room with guns in their hands, at the very least expecting to find an invasion of men.

"Someone was here while we were gone. Search the area around the ranch. Find him! Find him and bring him to me!"

The men left and Talbot turned back to Kairee. His face was wild and she backed away from him.

With an effort that seemed to be superhuman, he regained his control. He began to move around the room, his eyes intently searching every shadowed place.

"What are you looking for?" Kairee whispered.

"A book . . . a small book. Do you see it anywhere?"

Kairee was too frightened to take her eyes from him. She had never seen anyone in this crazed condition before.

He motioned her toward a chair and continued his frantic search as she sat in bewildered silence.

Talbot's men returned to confirm his suspicions.

"Somebody was here. Tracks lead toward the Kennedy place. They're pretty fresh. I'd say whoever it was couldn't be gone more than an hour or so."

"Damn!" Talbot muttered. He paced back and forth for awhile, then he turned back to his men.

"Two of you ride over to the Kennedy place. Tell Elliot Saber to come here with his son. Tell them if we see more than two riders, we kill her . . . Wait! Find out who the rider is who just arrived there. I want whoever it was to come back here with them. Tell them the diary had better come with them . . . or Kairee Kennedy and the child she carries are both very, very dead."

Used to his eccentricities, his men did not question him. They turned and left and soon the sound of their horses died in the distance. Then Talbot turned to Kairee.

Damion rode as fast as his tired horse could carry him. The animal skittered to a halt in front of the ranch house and Damion slid from the saddle before it came to a complete stop.

He took the four steps in two and crossed the porch to pound on the door.

There had been an abundance of confusion and disruption in the Kennedy house and the fierce knocking was the culmination that made everyone in the house leap as if burned.

At first they exchanged glances, wondering who might be at the door other than the one carrying the message for Elliot.

Elliot was the one who rose. "I'll answer it. It has to be for me," he said softly. He walked to the door and reached for the handle.

Damion expected Lucy, Gregg, or Stephen. Elliot expected a stranger with a message. He pulled the door open and both Elliot and Damion were stricken with shock so deep neither could speak.

Their eyes filled with amazement, then an almost agonistic pleasure.

"Pa?" Damion whispered. "I don't . . . Pa . . ."

"Damion . . . son." Elliot could have wept with the flood of intense relief and pleasure that filled him with brilliant warmth.

They hovered on the brink of uncertainty for a moment longer, still unable to believe. Then Elliot stepped over the threshold and with a cry of joy they threw their arms about each other.

They embraced, knowing it was the first time in their entires lives they had done so.

For Damion, all the battles were over. He had sent Kairee to safety and now he had found out his father was safe too. The tears in his eyes were ones of fabulous joy, yet the joy would soon be replaced by another emotion.

When he could finally speak, Damion moved back from Elliot to look at him again.

"Britt . . . Pa, where's Britt?"

"He's in the other room."

"Then he's alive and well too?"

"He's alive and very well."

"God, it's over. All this damn, horrible, stinking mess is over. Where's Kairee?"

"Damion . . ."

Just the sound of his father's voice told Damion more than any words could have. "Where is she? What's happened to her?"

"Calm down and I'll explain," Elliot said.

Damion inhaled deeply, trying for control. "All right. Tell me."

Elliot drew Damion inside the house to see a group of very silent people. One look at Cassie's pale face and silent mood, another at Lucy's battered face, and something in him seemed to come to a cold stop.

"Tell me," he repeated, including everyone.

He stood immobile and silent and listened as Elliot told him how Kairee had been taken and by whom, and of the message they expected.

"So he holds Kairee and we just have to sit and wait?"

"There's not much else we can do," Elliot said.

"All right, Pa," Damion said gently. Wearily he sat down in a chair near the fire. 'Since this ugly thing was started a long, long time ago, and since it's very nearly destroyed everybody's life"—he looked at his father— "I think we should have all the truth."

"All the truth?" Stephen questioned while Elliot just stood staring at Damion. Then Elliot walked to Damion and rested a hand on his shoulder.

"You know all the truth?"

"Yes," Damion said softly, almost with regret. "I know all the truth."

Elliot stood in silence. For a moment he closed his eyes, then he opened them and tried to smile. "Then I guess your brother has a right to the story too. Shall we go in so all of us can share it?"

If Damion was surprised, he said nothing. He simply rose and walked behind Elliot to Britt's door.

Britt lay half awake and half asleep. He looked at the door when it opened and an inarticulate sound was torn from him as he identified his visitors.

"Damion."

"Britt . . . what happened to you?"

"He took a bullet meant for me. You finish your story and I'll tell you the rest of it."

Damion nodded. He sat on the edge of Britt's bed while the others crowded about. Elliot stood on the periphery of the circle. This was a story he knew much too well.

"This whole problem," Damion began, "all the things between us"—he motioned to Britt and himself—"and all of you, began long before we were even

481

born. It began back East"—he turned to look at his father—"when Pa met Emma Martin, a woman who was married and already had a little girl. They met and they fell in love, and Pa soon found out what went on between Emma and her husband. It seems he was . . . somewhat brutal. He used to abuse and mistreat her. Emma was terrified of him and wanted to protect her daughter. Pa begged her to come west with him and bring her little girl. He swore he would protect her and that Richard Mitchell—that was her husband's name —would never be able to find them. Pa promised he would take them away and build a new world for them."

There was absolute silence as Damion continued the story. "But it seems that while Pa and Emma were meeting, Richard was having them followed. When Emma came home one night, Richard went insane with jealousy. He began to beat Emma, who, after being badly beaten, finally escaped him and ran to Elliot.

"Elliot said he would go back and get the little girl— her name was Amy—and they both went back that night. But Amy was not there. Only Richard, who laughed and said Emma would never leave because he had put Amy in a safe place and she would have to go without the child if she wanted to go. Emma was terrified, but Pa was angry because he knew Emma would never leave without Amy. Pa was so mad he tried to beat the truth from Richard about where Amy was. The battle got out of hand, and in the process . . . Pa killed Richard.

"It seems they still couldn't find Amy. They didn't know that Richard's brother, Talbot—our Mitchell Talbot—had put Amy in an institution.

"Talbot sought revenge and Pa and Emma were forced to hide from him while they continued to search for Amy. It took them a long time to realize they would never find her.

482

"All this time Talbot was searching for them. It seems," Damion added quietly, "he wanted Emma as well. He, too, had been in love with his brother's wife. He had even planned to do in his brother himself. But in his shaky mental state he used Richard's death as an excuse to avenge himself on Elliot and to ensnare Emma, whom he still wanted.

"Pa and Emma decided to move west, and Talbot followed until he lost them. It took him years to discover where the wagon train had been attacked and more years to find Pa. You see, it was only because Pa had built the Circle S and had become so prosperous and well-known that Talbot was able to find him at all. And it was then that he learned that Emma was dead. He must have lost his mind completely at the same time he found us. He called himself Mitchell Talbot to keep Pa from guessing his relationship to Richard. That's where our story began. And now we have to end it. Somehow we have to save Kairee. Don't you see, Pa"— he turned to Elliot—"in his demented state, I'm damn scared he's soon going to turn Kairee . . . into Emma."

"Yes," Elliot said hoarsely. "Damion . . . how . . . how did you know . . . ?"

Damion silently reached into his pocket and withdrew the diary. He handed it to Elliot.

"Pa, in Talbot's house, there's a picture of a girl who looks like Emma. It could be Amy. She's young in the picture, maybe seventeen or so. But it may mean that Amy is alive somewhere. She at least deserves to have someone find her and tell her about her mother. I'm sure Talbot never did."

His father nodded.

"It's strange, though," Damion mused thoughtfully, then he went on to explain about the feminine room with Amy's picture.

The knowledge struck them both at the same time. In his mind Talbot had already transformed Kairee into

Emma, and only he knew what he planned for her in the room where ghosts lived.

They all realized they would have to formulate some kind of plan, but no one knew where to begin. Damion had already informed them that he had seen no one at the Talbot ranch and he had been there for hours.

"There are a lot of places he could hide her," Britt said. He knew he could not help physically and the knowledge made him even angrier.

"No," Elliot said thoughtfully. "If he's made that room into some kind of shrine, then he's got to take her there sooner or later."

"You're right," Damion said. "You expect his messengers to come before long. If and when they come, try to hold them here as long as you can."

"What are you going to do?" Elliot demanded.

"I'm going back to Talbot's ranch. If he takes Kairee there, I want to be there. She's going to need me."

"But Talbot wants you and me together, Damion," Elliot protested.

"I know, Pa, and that's a chance we have to take. Tell his messengers I went off searching for Kairee and you don't know where I am. They won't have Talbot to ask, so the decisions will have to be theirs. They might just swallow it. Stall them."

"But if worse comes to worse," Elliot said, "I'll go with them."

"Just make sure I get a good start. And if you come, come slow. Drag 'em back as long as you can."

"I'll do that," Elliot said quietly. "You find Kairee before she has to pay any of the debts I owe."

"I'll find her, Pa . . . I'll find her."

"And I'm going with you," Gregg said firmly.

Damion looked from Gregg's determined face to Lucy's bruised one. Then he nodded slowly. He knew Gregg's reasons and could not deny them, for he felt the same bitter fury, the fury of helplessness. The Sabers had always been in control and Damion found it hard now to be unable to quell the fear of failure that tugged at him.

"I'll hold them here, Damion, for as long as I can," Elliot assured him. "I'll also take a hell of a long time to get from here to there. Good luck, son. Bring Kairee home." He extended his hand to Damion, who took it in a strong grip.

It took Damion and Gregg a very short time to saddle fresh horses and start toward the Talbot ranch. They knew they would have to be especially careful now not to run into any of Talbot's men.

It was after midnight when they saw the well-lighted house in the distance. They had ridden in absolute silence, not wanting their voices to carry on the night air to alert any riders who might be near.

They exchanged quiet looks, nodded, and rode slowly toward the house.

Cautiously they came as close as they could, then dismounted and tied their horses. Now they stayed in the shadows and moved toward the lighted windows.

Elliot found that the only thing that helped control the difficulty of waiting was his new ability to talk with Britt.

In fact, it was a new experience for Britt too, and he absorbed it as a starving man would a feast.

Britt, Southwind, and Elliot lifted their almost extinct relationship to a plane that seemed miraculous to them. The rain of understanding fell on the arid ground of doubt and fear, creating new, fertile soil on which to build.

They talked, and waited, yet after awhile the talking ceased, and all that was left was the waiting.

Chapter 39

Kairee watched Talbot move toward her and she could taste the fear in her throat that rendered her silent. She had seen many things in the eyes of men, but never this look, this strange look, as if something had broken deep within the man—some irreparable thing.

Talbot stopped close to her and stood for several minutes just looking into her deep gray eyes.

"You're still very lovely, Emma," he said as he gently reached out to brush his hand over her hair.

She was terror stricken, but she knew she was battling for her life and she could not run.

"I am not Emma," she said firmly.

For a minute she saw a flicker of something wild in his eyes, then he smiled again.

"Emma, you don't need to be afraid any longer. I've taken care of Amy all these years. I've kept her locked in that place, safe . . . until you come back. But you must come back to me. You know Richard is dead." He reached out to grip her arm and pull her close to him. "But you don't need to worry. I will rid the world of Elliot Saber and his sons. I have already eliminated one. Soon it will be you and I, Emma. Come and I'll show you the room we will soon share."

There has to be some way to escape him, Kairee thought wildly as his rough hand gripped her arm firmly and he dragged her toward the bedroom.

He flung open the door and watched her face to see her reaction to a luxury she had never known.

"It's beautiful, isn't it, Emma? You'll like it here . . . with me."

"I am not Emma," Kairee said firmly. She jerked her arm from his hold and turned her back on the room.

She looked about her for a way to escape, but there was no kind of weapon in sight and he was much too strong for her. She would have to use her wits.

She turned to face Talbot, who had been watching her. She had no idea what she could say about a woman named Emma, and even less knowledge of who Richard was or how he had died. She only knew that in his mind they were connected to her.

"Why did Richard die?"

"Richard?" He seemed puzzled for a moment. "Richard was so stupid, so careless. He deserved to die. I'm sure you were pleased when Elliot killed him." His voice held a plaintive tone, like that of a pleading child. "You must understand, Emma, I have to avenge his death. But"—he smiled again—"once I've killed Elliot, you can come home with me." His eyes turned sly. "If you are good . . . really good . . . I won't have to punish you for running away with him. I may even let you see Amy."

Who is Amy? Kairee asked herself. She was getting beyond her depth in trying to comprehend the machinations of this man's tormented mind. Her terror was taking over. She had to escape.

He must have read her intention in her eyes, for he gave an almost animal snarl and leapt at the same moment she did.

He caught her arm inches before she reached the door, and the power of his grip swung her around and slammed her against him. She gave a low, muffled scream as he bound her to him in an unrelenting grip.

The eyes that now looked into hers had lost all semblance of sanity and she had time to scream once as his mouth descended to hers.

The kiss was brutal and she could taste her own blood in her mouth as he continued to savage her.

She fought wildly, but with grim determination he pulled her relentlessly toward the bedroom.

He held her in a grip of iron and when he reached the bed, he tossed her on it. She came up fighting and caught him across the cheek with all the strength she had.

She gasped as again he threw her down on the bed and this time he fell upon her. He tore at her clothes.

"Don't fight me anymore, Emma," he gasped. "You know Richard has hurt you. You know you want me as I have always wanted you."

Kairee fought desperately now and a stroke of luck freed her for a moment from his hold. She rolled from the bed and got to her feet, but Talbot stood between her and the door. The look of passion had gone and hatred filled his face.

"You want Elliot Saber, don't you? Well, you can't have him. I'm going to see that he and his only son die tonight, just as I have seen everything die that has stood between us. Everything but Amy . . . and I shall see to her too—just as soon as I see to the Sabers." His eyes narrowed and he drew a pistol from the stand near the bed and pointed it at her. "You are carrying a Saber child, aren't you?" His voice grew soft as velvet and his words made her heart pound until she could hardly breathe.

Her blouse was torn open and the soft flesh of her

easts was revealed as she tried in vain to hold the
mnants together. Slowly she backed away, and just
slowly he advanced.

There was no sound from the house as Damion and
regg crept up to the porch and moved across it. They
ad almost reached the door when a scream pierced the
ight.

"Kairee." Both men echoed their fears in the
reathing of her name. There was no time for caution
ow. They ran the rest of the way, breaking into the
oom with no care for the splintered lock. They found
o one in the main room, but Damion surmised
uickly where Kairee and Talbot might be.

Damion crossed the room in several long strides to
ush open the door of the bedroom, only to find it
mpty too. For a moment he and Gregg simply stood
nd looked at each other.

It had not been too long after Damion and Gregg
ad left that the sound of approaching riders was
eard.

"Here they come," Elliot said as he rose to walk to
he door.

The riders remained mounted as they told Elliot
heir demands.

"Damion isn't here," Elliot responded.

"You're lying, old man. He's here somewhere."

"You can search if you want. He went out a long time
go to see if he could get some help from Lone Wolf's
eople."

"Well then, it looks like you'll have to come yourself.
albot's not going to like this. No sir, I think he's gonna
e real fired up about it."

489

"What difference does it make if he kills 'em one a[t] time or separate," a second man offered. "He's going [to] kill 'em both anyhow."

"Yeah, you're right. Get ready, Saber. You're goi[ng] with us."

"I'll have to saddle my horse."

"Stay right where you are. We ain't trusting you o[ut] of our sight."

"How am I supposed to come with you, on foot[?]" Elliot asked angrily.

"Go and saddle his horse, Mack," the first rid[er] ordered.

One of the men left the group and went to the ba[rn] where, as Elliot well knew, his own men were waitin[g.] He hoped they were as alert as always. Maybe, wi[th] luck, they could lessen the number of Talbot's me[n.]

It was almost fifteen minutes before a man left t[he] barn leading Elliot's horse behind him. The leader [of] the group did not look closely or he would have se[en] that the dark, heavily dressed man was not his own. B[ut] Elliot knew. He smiled. If he didn't have Dami[on] along, at least he would have one of his own men at h[is] back. He would think of other tricks along the way [to] slow them down.

When Elliot stepped out on the porch, Lucy broug[ht] his coat and handed it to him. Then she reached up [to] kiss him and whispered quickly as she did, "Lone W[olf] and his men have slipped out the back. He said not [to] worry. He will meet you on the trail and relieve you [of] your company."

Elliot smiled and hugged her, then he walked dow[n] the steps and mounted. Lucy watched him ride awa[y] and her prayers went with him.

Damion regarded the room closely for only minut[es]

490

efore he realized that Talbot must have heard them nter and fled quickly, for the window stood open. 3regg and Damion moved simultaneously and reached he window at the same time.

Obvious evidence was before them. Clear prints vould have told any observer that Talbot and Kairee ad left by this route, but for where?

The snow was more than six inches deep and the prints upon it were clear. It took Damion and Gregg ittle time to exit by the same window and follow them.

"Where the hell could he go?" Gregg whispered.

"I don't know. It's damn cold and I wonder if that naniac dragged Kairee along without protection," Damion growled.

"If he did, he didn't take any for himself either, so I'll pet he's not going far."

"But where . . . damnit, where?"

"We follow the tracks, wherever they go. God knows vhat he has in mind."

They continued to move slowly, bending low to nake the smallest targets possible and keeping their guns ready in case they crossed Talbot's path.

Talbot had pushed Kairee toward the window with a ough, whispered demand for her silence as soon as he heard the footsteps coming across the porch. He forced her to climb from the window and followed imme- diately after to prevent her from running.

He gripped her arm and dragged her with him away from the house.

"Where are we going?" Kairee cried. "We'll die out here in the cold."

"No, my dear," he said calmly, "we won't die. Do you think those Sabers are so clever they can outwit me?" He laughed. "They think they've won, but they've lost.

In the end I'll get them . . . I'll get them. But for now have you"—again he laughed—"and where you go, m sweet, the Sabers will follow."

As they moved into the shadows of a stand of tree Kairee was surprised to see a rather large shed, an soon she could hear the nervous stomping of horse Talbot had considered every means of escape. Withi the shed he forced Kairee to saddle two horses while h pointed his gun at her and kept constant watch fc anyone who might be following.

Once the horses were ready, he motioned her into th saddle and swiftly mounted himself. Soon they wer rapidly moving away from the shed.

The sound of horses brought Damion and Gregg t an abrupt halt. They looked at each other, then withou a word both men began to run. They reached the she just as the sound of horses' hooves was dissolving in th distance.

"Damnit, he got away. Come on, Gregg, let's ge back to our horses while the tracks are fresh."

Gregg turned to follow Damion, who was alread moving back toward the house and their mounts. The were starting away from the house when the sound o new arrivals brought them to a halt.

"Who is it?" Gregg whispered.

"It could only be Talbot's men coming here with m father. They have no way of knowing what's happene here."

"Damion, if we stay to free your father, we los Kairee's trail. If we follow Kairee . . . well . . . mayb Talbot didn't give them any orders to harm you father." He paused for a moment, then added, "Wha are we going to do?"

Damion's face was grim as he turned to Gregg an

492

.ld him quickly and quietly what he planned to do.

Elliot rode as slowly as he could, knowing one of his
.wn men was bringing up the rear of the group and
.aiting for an opportunity to assist. He was also alert,
.xpecting Lone Wolf's attack at any moment.

To Elliot the minutes seemed like hours, and his
.erves were stretched to the breaking point. It had not
.ken him too long to curse himself furiously when he
.ad realized they actually were headed for Talbot's
.anch. He had been the one to resist their going there,
.inking Talbot too clever to return to his own home.
.e had not understood that Talbot had long passed the
.oint of logical, sane thinking. This thought frightened
.im more than anything else he had ever faced.

They rode on in silence until they came to a narrow
.ass between two steep hills. The thick snow had piled
.p here, forced into drifts by the storm's violent wind.
.he horses lumbered through it, bounding in rough
.umps and forcing their riders to place all their
.oncentration on remaining in the saddle.

As they reached the mouth of this narrow channel,
.one Wolf launched his attack. A bullet sang and
.truck with a solid thud, and the first of the guards fell
.rom his saddle without a sound. The one who rode
.ext to Elliot was momentarily stunned, giving Elliot
.he edge he needed. He lashed out with a heavy fist and
.nocked the man from his saddle. At the same
.noment, Elliot's man, who had remained in the rear,
.rew his gun and called to the balance of Talbot's men
.o give up. They attempted to resist, but Lone Wolf's
.ifle barked again and a bullet ricocheted close as Lone
.Wolf and his warriors seemed to materialize out of
.owhere. Talbot's men promptly raised their hands in
.urrender.

Elliot gave quick orders that Talbot's men were to be taken back to the Bar *K* and kept under guard until he could return.

"Where do we ride, Elliot?" Lone Wolf asked with a grin.

"This isn't your fight, Lone Wolf," Elliot said softly. "I gave up any right to your friendship a long time ago. I made the problems and I guess it is my job to finish it."

"I have the feeling that we are going to become brothers again soon. You will again be part of my family. That makes it my duty too. Besides, I have the courage to face men with guns, but I would not have the courage to face my sister if you were foolhardy enough to get yourself killed. I will ride with you."

Elliot chuckled and nodded his agreement. He directed his own man and Lone Wolf's warriors to keep the prisoners under close guard as they took them back. Then he and Lone Wolf turned their horses toward Talbot's ranch. They rode for quite some time in silence.

"I'm going to ask Southwind to come to me again, Lone Wolf. I'm going to build a small place and try to make a new life and get to know my sons."

"I had thought you might do so. You are late in acquiring wisdom, my brother, but it is better than never acquiring it at all."

Elliot laughed softly, but soon the laugh died as he considered the magnitude of what he had almost lost forever in search of an elusive dream.

He thought of the past years, and his sons, sons who had loved him despite his barbaric methods of raising them.

He shuddered in relief to know that Britt would remain beside him and that Damion would soon give him a grandchild, a child through which he might be

494

able to redeem himself.

"Lord, I hope Damion and Gregg find Kairee safe," he groaned.

"I too, brother," Lone Wolf breathed softly. "I too."

Gregg eased through the window and stood just inside the door, which he cracked open slightly to have a better view of the visitors he now heard moving across the porch.

He held his gun ready, for surprise was his best defense.

Elliot had stopped in front of the ranch house and he and Lone Wolf were strongly aware of the total silence. Had Damion found them, only to fall by Talbot's hand? Were Kairee and Damion alive, or . . . He could not bear to retain the thought.

Both men dismounted quickly and moved to the door as cautiously as they could. Elliot put his hand on the door handle, then, after he and Lone Wolf exchanged glances, he flung open the door and they exploded into . . . an empty room.

Gregg was, at first, shocked into immobility. Then he smiled and drew the door completely open.

"I don't know where those guards are," he said with a grin, "but I sure as hell am glad to see you two."

"Gregg"—Elliot was surprised, but pleased—"where're Damion and Kairee?"

"Talbot got away with Kairee. Damion's hot on their trail. He left me here to see if I could get the drop on the others and get you free. I guess," Gregg added, "you all must have done all right for yourselves. Where's the rest of Talbot's men?"

"They've been taken back to the Bar _K_. Lone Wolf's men and my boys will hold them until we get back. Right now it's important that we follow Damion and

495

Kairee. Talbot is insane. He means to wipe out ever Saber and that includes the child Kairee is carrying.

"Damion's not going to let that happen. It's on against one now, and Damion is mad enough to trail Talbot to the ends of the earth if he has to. The only thing we'll have to worry about is keeping Talbot alive to pay for what he's done."

"I think we ought to get moving," Lone Wolf said "and try to catch up to them as soon as possible."

"You're right. Let's go," Elliot said and turned to the door. Lone Wolf and Gregg followed.

As Elliot opened the door, he stopped in his tracks and his brows drew together in a dark frown. Lone Wolf's eyes followed his, and he too scowled and inhaled sharply.

"What's wrong?" Gregg questioned.

"Take a look," Elliot replied.

Gregg strode across the room to stand beside Elliot at the open door and gaze outside. He too felt the sudden prick of panic. He made a soft, inarticulate sound.

A thick blanket of new snow had slowly and silently begun to fall and all of them knew one thing for certain: In no time it could wipe out any trail they might have been able to follow.

Chapter 40

Kairee shivered as the frigid wind whipped the snow against her skin like sharp needles. She struggled to keep her clothes together as best she could, but she could feel the cold sapping her strength.

She also knew, with sinking heart, that the freshly falling snow would effectively wipe out any chance of anyone's following them.

The cold was slowly making her numb and she felt the paralyzing need to close her eyes and sleep.

She was startled when Talbot drew his horse to a halt, but she could not move. Talbot reached for the bundle rolled behind his saddle and removed a blanket, which he quickly wrapped around Kairee.

She felt the prick of heavy wool, but her body savored the new warmth and her mind began to function again.

If Talbot had prepared for this, he must have a destination, she told herself. She would have to remain calm and in control of her wits. There was still a life to protect and she meant to have Damion's child until her final breath.

They moved slowly but steadily, and Kairee became more certain Talbot had a well-thought-out destination in mind.

To Kairee it seemed as if they had been traveling for hours. She felt a throbbing exhaustion and did not even realize that Talbot had stopped until her horse, having been pulled along by Talbot's hold on the reins, came to a halt.

She opened heavy-lidded eyes and gazed about her. They seemed to be in the center of a wilderness caught in the swirling snow. She did not see the mouth of the cave for a long time, and then it seemed only a dim light.

Talbot dismounted and went to Kairee to drag her roughly from the saddle. At first she could hardly stand and she sagged against him. He half carried, half dragged her to the cave mouth and she felt the welcoming warmth of a fire that must have been burning for some time.

Talbot had prepared the cave for occupation but had not expected to be greeted by a fire or the man who appeared at the mouth of the cave just as Talbot and Kairee reached it. Talbot immediately recognized the man as one of those he had sent to guard Lone Wolf.

"Where's the Indian?" he demanded at once.

"He managed to get loose. He killed Tate and got away before I could get to him. But I put a bullet in him."

"Why didn't you go after him?"

"He spooked the horses and ran 'em off. I've been stuck here waitin' for the snow to clear or some of the boys to come check on me. What're you doing here with the girl? I thought you was making a deal with the Sabers."

"It's a long story. Get the girl something to eat and drink, and another blanket so she can lay down by the fire. We're safe here. The snow is wiping out any tracks, so we'll have some time to plan. When I get ready, you'll ride to the Bar *K* and to Elliot Saber with my proposition. He thinks he's won, but I still have her to bargain with and it's going to cost Elliot Saber his life and his son."

Talbot pushed Kairee ahead of him toward the heat of the fire. At first she knelt before it gratefully, absorbing the life-renewing warmth.

She ate the food brought to her and drank the tepid water only because she knew she had to gather her strength. She prayed Damion could, by some miracle, find her. But if he didn't, then she would have to fight the battle for her life and the life of Damion's child by herself. She lay on the blanket near the fire and closed her eyes, drawing strength from her memories with Damion to sustain her until she slept.

Damion followed the trail, looking up occasionally at the dark, heavily clouded sky. He cursed softly as the first flakes of snow touched his face, but his grim determination pushed him on. He would not stop until he found Kairee. He knew he could not be too far behind Talbot, but where he could be heading was a mystery to him, for he seemed to be riding directly toward the mountains and the wilderness. He knew one thing for certain: he would follow Talbot to the bowels of hell if he had to. The murderous anger within him kept driving him forward. Even after the tracks began to fade with the new snow, he kept pushing on. He would find Talbot and he would find Kairee, and if Talbot had harmed her, he would revenge himself in ways that even Talbot could not imagine.

With the exception of Britt, very few men knew the land around him as well as Damion did. As a boy and as a man he had roamed across this range often, yet the fact that he and Britt had also played here as children in the hidden caves did not yet occur to him.

He rode on, holding the vision of Kairee in his mind to keep his strength from waning. He could not let the only happiness he had ever found be torn from him.

Another hour and the snow became a white curtain that reduced his vision to just a few feet in front of him, and he noted that the tracks he followed were rapidly being obliterated. Often he rode several yards between tracks. After a few more minutes, the tracks had totally disappeared.

Damion reined his horse to a stop and looked about him. Now the choice of direction was his and his alone, for there were no tracks to lead him. Some thought nagged at his memory and he strained to grasp it.

Kairee's face wavered constantly before him and the heat of tears touched his eyes as he realized if he made the wrong choice Kairee and his child would be lost to him forever.

Gregg, Elliot, and Lone Wolf pushed forward against the driving snow. Each was silent, contemplating the terrifying possibility that they might never find Kairee or Damion in the swirling white mist.

Lone Wolf reined in his horse so abruptly that Elliot nearly ran into him.

"Lone Wolf," he said sharply, "what the hell are you doing?"

Lone Wolf turned to Elliot as he stopped beside him and smiled a grim smile.

"We need not follow their tracks anymore," Lone Wolf said.

"Sure as hell we don't. There aren't any more to follow," Elliot replied, then he looked more intently at

Lone Wolf. "What is it, Lone Wolf?"

"I know where he is going."

"You know?" Gregg asked excitedly.

"You . . . where?" Elliot added quickly.

"To the cave where his men had taken me to meet my death. I wonder if he feels secure and thinks no one else knows his destination."

"The caves," Elliot grated raggedly. "I had forgotten their existence. I wonder if Damion would remember the times I used to chase him and Britt out of them. God, we might have looked forever and never found them."

Now they could ride faster, or as fast as the horses could move in the ever-deepening snow, for no longer did they need to search for the elusive tracks. They knew exactly where they were going.

Damion made his decision, relying more on instinct than knowledge. He moved forward, still harassed by the nagging thought that he was overlooking something important.

There was no trail left, blinding snow and defeat were staring him in the face, and his desperation, like a final blow, stirred a memory long forgotten.

Where else could anyone go for safety in a snowstorm? Where else had he and his brother sat out many a rainstorm cozily nestled by a fire and dreaming up adventurous fantasies? Where else but the caves in which he and Britt had played so often!

He suddenly felt the heat of rejuvenation course through him. Talbot would never believe that he could be followed in this. He would feel safe and secure, safe to weave another web and try again to catch and destroy the Sabers. But this was one Saber who intended to find his evil nest and destroy Talbot and the dark past that had very nearly done the same to him and his entire family.

He rode now with renewed confidence. It did not matter to him if Talbot had a hundred men in the caves. He would trade his life for Kairee's if necessary. He would do whatever needed to be done. His mind was set on one path. One way or another, he meant to kill Talbot.

Kairee stirred awake and found Talbot kneeling close to her. She sat up abruptly with a soft sound of fear on her lips that she quickly quelled. She would not give him the satisfaction of knowing she was afraid.

Talbot handed her a plate of food and a tin cup of hot coffee. The last thing she felt was hungry, but she obediently took them. She would consume both to preserve her strength and to satisfy Talbot enough to keep him from resorting to force. She looked toward the cave mouth and saw that the snow was still steadily falling. The wind had ceased and the snow fell silently.

Despair tugged at her, but she fought it. She would not surrender if there was even one chance in a million.

Gazing around her, Kairee could see that the cave seemed to stretch on into infinity. She wondered just how far it did go and if there was a remote chance of escape there. At some distance she could see that it branched into several different dark extensions. Was there another way out? And did she dare take the chance?

But Talbot's eyes had followed hers. "I wouldn't try it, my dear. As far as I know, no one has ever explored these caves. You could find yourself lost in an endless darkness filled with bats and rats . . . and who knows what else."

Kairee shivered at the thought but knew she would try it before forfeiting the life of her and Damion's child.

She ate slowly and listlessly and watched Talbot closely. He stood by the mouth of the cave, one hand braced against the rough rock wall, his back to her.

She contemplated running past him before she became aware of the second man's eyes on her. She turned to him to find his heated, lascivious gaze on the torn blouse that revealed soft curves of smooth flesh beneath.

He smiled as she drew the blanket about her and turned her head away, but neither his eyes or his hungry thoughts left her. Talbot might leave him to guard her, the man thought hopefully. He would more than enjoy sharing this cave with a sweet, soft beauty like Kairee for as long as Talbot wanted him to.

He rose and walked into the darkness at the rear of the cave to relieve himself.

Neither Kairee nor Talbot was aware of a soft, muffled sound or the renewed silence that followed it.

Damion sat motionless, staring at the glow of firelight from the cave entrance through the mist of softly falling snow. He strained to remember childhood games and began to envision in his mind the web of caves he and Britt had explored.

A grim smile tugged at his lips as the door of memory, once opened, flooded him with answers. There were many ways into and out of the caves. He hoped Talbot did not know them all.

He moved away from the cave mouth in search of another he knew was not too far away.

It took some time, for his childhood memories were not quite as accurate as he had hoped. He finally found the deeper spot of blackness that indicated a cave mouth. With a silent prayer that it was the right one, he dismounted and tied his horse. Then, gun in hand, he moved to the entrance and resolutely stepped into the darkness.

He braced one hand against the wall and after bumping his head several times on low-hanging rock, he tried to keep in mind the fact that he had grown a lot since the times he had played there as a boy.

He crouched as low as he could and still move, then inched himself forward. Soon he was enveloped in total blackness, his only guide a hand on the cold rock wall.

On and on he moved in the thick blackness. The cold air from the entrance died away and still he could see no sign of light from the cave he sought. Had he taken a wrong turn? He moved on, refusing to allow himself to believe he was gradually growing lost in a maze while Kairee needed him.

The darkness was thick and oppressive, and he found it hard not to turn around and run out into the cold, clean air.

He moved forward until there was hardly a breath to take and the deep, thick blackness felt like a solid rock pressing soul and spirit to the ground. He'd been wrong! he agonized. He'd chosen the wrong path, the wrong cave! He could have cried out in his bitter disappointment. It took all the will he could muster to make the decision to go just a little further.

The cave wall suddenly seemed to curve and he followed it with his hand and carefully took a few more steps. Then he felt it, a soft, cool breeze, a breeze that came from somewhere ahead of him. He began to move with more confidence and in a few more minutes he saw a faint glimmer of light in the distance. The light made his heart leap with joy, for it was firelight, not the glow from outside. He had found them!

He remained motionless for a few moments to regain control of himself, though the sense of relief he experienced made him so weak he would have found it hard to move anyway.

His lack of movement seemed perfectly timed, for all at once a broad-shouldered form blotted out the light. Damion knew it wasn't Talbot, and as the man moved toward him, Damion remained breathlessly still. The man walked only a short distance into the darkness and Damion could hear him relieving himself. Then he turned to go back to the light. It was an opportunity Damion could not lose. He moved rapidly toward the unsuspecting man, striking swiftly and with all the strength he had. The man crumpled and Damion caught him as he fell and eased him to the ground. Then he turned toward the light, toward Talbot, and toward Kairee.

Having risen from the depths of his thoughts, Talbot moved away from the cave mouth. He turned to look at Kairee kneeling by the fire. She was gazing into it, lost in thought, and was not aware that the blanket had slipped from her and that the firelight had kissed her skin into burnished gold. Despite the present situation, her fear, and all she had been through, she looked so unbelievably vulnerable, beautiful . . . desirable.

He felt all the pent-up desire for Emma that had been leashed all these years burst through his veins like a molten river. He would deny himself no longer. He moved toward her.

Kairee gazed at the flames licking at the logs and sought sweeter memories to ease her fear. She thought of the cabin and being marooned in a white world of love. How she longed to feel the hard strength of Damion's arms again, to taste the gentle fury of his mouth on hers.

She sighed deeply, then suddenly became aware of the dark shadow that had fallen across her. She looked up and a scream formed in her throat that nearly choked away her breath. She leapt to her feet, vainly drawing her torn clothes about her like a fragile shield.

His eyes reflected the glow of the fire, but the gleam turned evil and lusting.

She began to back away and he moved relentlessly toward her. There was no one in the frozen wilderness to aid her now and she knew it. But she meant to fight him to the limit of her strength.

"Don't run from me, Emma," he whispered. "I can make all the old dreams come true. We'll go away, you and I . . . we'll be happy, I promise. Come to me, Emma love . . . come to me."

She could only shake her head slowly, negatively, as she continued to back away. Any words of resistance froze on her lips, for she realized she had nowhere to run but into the darkness, and nothing to run to but death.

Talbot sensed his triumph and he uttered a heavy, satisfied laugh. But the laugh died abruptly as a form exploded from the darkness to crash against Talbot, knocking him to the ground.

Kairee was so astounded she could not for the moment identify the man who had come to her rescue. Then the two thrashing bodies rolled near the fire.

"Damion!" Kairee gasped, unable to take her eyes from the battle raging before her.

Like two Goliaths they struggled together, each intent on the death of the other.

There was no mercy in Damion's heart and Talbot could feel his cold, calculated intent to kill. It was the first time fear had ever struck him.

They struggled fiercely, soundlessly, murderously,

506

he shadows of their straining figures danced on the
ave walls.

Suddenly Talbot pushed Damion violently away
nd reached to draw his gun.

Elliot, Gregg, and Lone Wolf approached the cave
nd could see the reflected fire glow. They were about
o dismount when a shot pierced the night. It was
ollowed by a deathly silence.

Disregarding any danger to themselves, they drew
heir guns and ran toward the cave entrance. Their
earts pounded and fear made their mouths dry.
Questions filled their minds.

All three men stopped just within the mouth of the
ave and tried to contain their relief and pleasure at
vhat they saw.

Talbot lay motionless near the fire, and there was no
loubt in any of their minds that the tragic vendetta he
iad perpetrated through so many years had finally
ound its end with his death.

Damion held Kairee in his arms and both were
oblivious to all but the grateful joy they found in their
:lose embrace.

Kairee wept as Damion kissed her feverishly, again
ind again.

"It's over, Kairee love, it's over. We can go home,"
Damion whispered as he held her face between his
iands and gazed into her tear-filled eyes.

"Yes . . . oh yes, love. I want to go home."

Epilogue

Spring gave way to a brilliant summer that boasted breathtaking beauty. The wildflowers blossomed profusely and the aspens whispered as they swayed gently in the summer breeze.

The small, four-room cabin, new home to Elliot, Saber, Southwind, and Britt, was alive with excitement, excitement over a celebration to be held at the Bar *K*.

Britt whistled lightly through his teeth as he finished dressing for the occasion. He found it hard to remember a time when he had been any happier.

He completed his preparations and left his room to join Elliot and Southwind in the parlor. He was even more pleased to find them seated close to each other, holding hands and talking softly.

"Come on, you two," he said, smiling broadly. "The party is waiting and I don't want to miss a minute."

"I don't think it's the party you're so anxious to get to," Elliot replied with a laugh. "I do believe it's a pretty little set of twins that seems to have done what no woman has ever succeeded in doing—capturing your heart completely."

"They are perfect, aren't they?" Britt grinned. "I do believe it has annoyed my brother just a bit to know his n looks like me."

"But he's named for me," Elliot challenged with a ugh.

"Well, I'll admit that young Elliot looks like you, ritt, but little Emma does look exactly like Kairee," outhwind observed.

"Good combination, don't you think?" Britt grinned evilishly. "Come on, I'm anxious to torment my rother a little more."

"Britt, try to behave today and just enjoy the party. ou give Damion a nasty time occasionally. I can't nderstand why he allows you to get away with it."

"I'll tell you in a word, Mother." Britt laughed. Love. The man's so head-over-heels about his new rife and mother of his twins, he's besotted. He's so arn happy he couldn't get mad if he tried. Now let's get oing. My niece and nephew are waiting for Uncle Britt ɔ dandle them on his knee and start telling them tories about their pa."

Elliot and Southwind could only laugh as they ɔllowed him to the wagon they would use to travel to he Bar *K*.

At the Bar *K* there was happy confusion as Lucy ustled about, preparing the house for the party. tephen, Gregg, and Cassie were so caught up in her nthusiasm they obediently yielded to all her demands nd laughter prevailed.

"Mommy," Cassie questioned for the hundredth ime, "will Aunt Kairee let me hold the babies like she lid the last time? She said I did real well."

"I'm sure she will, Cassie. She knows how much you ove them and how very careful you are. She'll be more han pleased to let you care for them a while."

"Of course you'll have to do battle with Britt first, or t least promise to share with him. He doesn't let go of

509

them when he's got his hands on them," Gregg tease

"I do hope Kairee and Damion aren't late," Steph
remarked with a chuckle, "or I do believe Britt a
Cassie will go after them."

Before anyone could speak again, there came t
sound of approaching horses. Cassie was the first to t
door. She threw it open and her face lit with pleasur

"It's *Britt* and the Sabers," she cried excitedly. S
brought laughter to everyone's lips with the speci
emphasis she placed on Britt's name, as if he were mo
like a god than an ordinary person.

Britt came in and lifted Cassie in his arms to hug h
fiercely. He did not want her to feel one moment
jealousy over his profound love for Damion ar
Kairee's children.

He set her down on his lap and held her while I
looked around.

"You mean Kairee and Damion aren't here yet?"

"No, they're not. But they ought to be along at ar
moment."

"I wonder," Britt said softly, with knowing amus
ment in his dark eyes.

The next arrivals at the Bar *K* were Lone Wolf an
several of his men. They were welcomed with the sam
enthusiasm and their inquiries concerning the wher
abouts of Kairee and Damion were answered the sam
way.

Lone Wolf caught Britt's eye across the room an
Britt winked wickedly. Lone Wolf could only laug
and silently agree that it might be some time yet befor
the loving couple arrived.

First the cabin had been repaired, then four room
had been added to make it a warm, comfortable home

It was the same shack in which Kairee and Damio
had been temporarily marooned, and it was filled no

510

with a happiness only a deep and satisfying love could supply.

Kairee bent over the two matching cradles that sat side by side and reached to touch each child.

"What a blessing you are," she whispered, "and how much I love you . . . and your handsome father."

"Well, if you love their father, maybe you should come over here and show him." Damion spoke from the bedroom doorway.

A smile lighting her face, Kairee turned to see Damion leaning against the door frame, his very appreciative gaze warm as it surveyed her.

She moved toward him to step into the circle of arms that pulled her close.

Damion smiled down into her warm gray eyes. "I swear, Kairee, you get more beautiful every day. It seems every time I look at you I want you more. Have I told you lately that I love you very much, woman?"

"A time or two," she whispered, "but I never tire of hearing it."

"Well, I love you," he murmured as he bent to touch her warm, receptive mouth with his. The kiss was deep and fulfilling and renewed the flames that always lay just below the surface and were easily ignited by a touch or a smile.

Damion held Kairee closer, profoundly thankful that he had found her in time that cold winter day and grateful for the abundant love she had given him.

"Your family and mine will be expecting us," Kairee whispered as she felt the passion within him reach to enfold her.

"They can wait a while," he murmured as he kissed her again.

"The party is for Amy's arrival and we want to be there when she gets there, don't we?"

"Speak for yourself, woman." Damion laughed. "I'd be just as happy to stay here and wait for them to come

511

visit us."

"Damion"—Kairee laughed softly—"we have to go. This is important to your father. Though the paper we found in Talbot's study finally led him to Amy, Elliot had a difficult time convincing her she should make her home out here."

"I know," Damion replied, but his arms remained tight about her and the warmth of his gaze made the core of her being melt and left her weak with the love she felt for him. "Just let me take a minute to tell you how important you are to me. You're a life I never thought I'd have, Kairee . . . and I love you more than my own life. It's important to me that you know, every day, how much you and the gift of our children have meant."

"I do, Damion. It's the thing that's created this wonderful place. I know, Damion . . . but I thank you for telling me again because I can never hear it enough. I love you too."

Their mouths blended once more in a kiss that held a world of promises they intended to keep in the new future they were building.

"And now, my beloved husband, I must dress the children so we can go. We can continue this . . . discussion later."

"That's a promise," he declared with a smile.

She watched him walk to the cradles and reach down to lift his daughter gently in his arms.

Her heart was full as she beheld his tender love. She had the world now and she meant to hold it forever. With a smile, Kairee moved to his side to lift her son. They faced each other and again he bent to touch her lips in a full and promising kiss that would sustain them until the moment they could return to their sanctuary and renew their deep commitment to a love that was as wide as the blue Wyoming sky.